The Standing Stone

on the

Moor

THE TALBOT SAGA

Allie Cresswell

Characters

Beth/Betsey and Frank Harlish Stewards of Tall Chimneys
Arthur Harlish   Their brother, an engineer
Mr George Talbot   Owner of Tall Chimneys
Mrs Jocelyn Stockbridge (formerly Willow)   His relative
Lucas Willow   Her son

Mr Oscar Eagerly   Vicar at Moorside
Mrs Eagerly,
Rose Eagerly and
Edgar Maybury   His family

Mr Algernon Golightly   Moorside tea merchant
Mrs Golightly,
Flossie and Johnny Golightly   His family

Ned Widderington   Landlord at The Plough

Peregrine Somersall   Mine owner
Mildred Somersall,
Herbert Somersall   His family

Stephen Milton   Mine Engineer
Mr Jessop   Mine Foreman

Mr and Mrs Brock   Local lawyer & his wife
Misses Felicity & Arabella MacAllister   Local spinsters
Professor Bissel   Academic
The Treddlebarrow family   Farmers
Mr Slade   Local merchant

Lord and Lady Riding,
Hon Ladies Petronella & Veraminta Landowning family

Irish Characters with pronunciations

Ruairi Connolly	Pronounced: Rory
His sister, Aoife	Pronounced: Eee-fah
His cousin, Dónall	Pronounced DOH-nal
Cillian	Pronounced: Kill-ee-an
His wife, Brónach	Pronounced Brona
His son, Conn.	Pronounced: Kon
Cormac	Pronounced Kor-mac
His wife, Caitlin	Pronounced: Kat-lin
Fionn	Pronounced: Fee-yon
Tadgh	Pronounced: Tyge (like tiger without the 'r')
Fearghal	Pronounced: Fear-gal
Mícheál	Pronounced: My-kuhl
Eistir	Pronounced Ayst-er
Elíse	Pronounced: El-is

Part One

Chapter 1

Yorkshire, June 1845

The moor was vast and largely impassible—an expanse of black bogs, impenetrable undergrowth and dense woody swathes of small tufted shrubs. Here and there were smooth green deceptive clearings but these were sucking swamps where the unwary sank up to their necks in stinking water. Trees were few and far between, very stunted, and the whole moor—though beautiful in its wildness—was also exposed and bleak. The wind was constant, either benign—just riffling the heathers—or malevolent, a howling tearing violent thing that made men mad who were exposed to it for too long.

Lacing across the moor was a network of tracks used by carters and farmers and by those on foot crossing the heath. Some were wide enough to accommodate a cart or a carriage but dangerous to traverse at night when no light, kerbstone or other guide prevented the unwary from miring his horses up to their chests in black oozing swamp. Other pathways were suitable for foot travellers only, being narrow and meandering. It could take a lifetime to learn the secret ways, and many were the drovers and shepherds who had been lost along them. Sheep possessed a peculiar intuition that kept them from sinking in the bogs as they grazed the tracks, so the grass there was short, and in summertime threaded with innumerable small, sweet-smelling flowers that hummed with bees.

Strung along the northern periphery of the moor was Moorside, a village of some twenty cottages, almost all of a low agrarian character inhabited by farmworkers. At one end of the village stood the church and the vicarage. At the other end, the schoolhouse. The Plough and Harrow, with its back to the moor, took up the middle ground, offering accommodation of a basic sort and supper of a dubious greasy nature to travellers. There was stabling for horses, although few ever occupied that ramshackle lean-to. Ned Widderington, the sharp-nosed publican with an instinct for anything nefarious, supplemented the inn's income as he could by facilitating gambling, the rustling of cattle, the storage of stolen goods and contraband. Officially, the Plough served ale and gin and hosted card games, but sometimes on Saturday nights a troupe of musicians would come and play.

Opposite to the inn was Mr Golightly's store, where dried goods— tea, tobacco, candles, kerosene, flour and sugar, salt, soap, seed, string and all manner of other useful items—were available to purchase. Also available there was gossip, which was supplied free of charge by Mrs Golightly. Mr Golightly honoured himself with the title of Tea and Wine Merchant, but it can be assumed from the general status of his clientele and the humble nature of the village that he sold more of the former than of the latter.

There had been a forge but it was now closed, the smith having taken his family to Leeds to work in the railway yard, inspiring an exodus of other workers—both men and women—to work in mills and factories. Of the twenty cottages in the village, scarce two-thirds were now occupied.

Some half-dozen farms were scattered across the pastureland that surrounded the moor on its northern and western flanks; and to the east at a distance of about two or three miles stood Brayton, a market town.

Of genteel residents, Moorside had few. The vicar, the doctor and the schoolmaster were the entirety of the premier sphere, although the Golightlys and Ned Widderington pretended to be encompassed within it. Amongst the outlying properties, a pair of ladylike spinster sisters had recently come, but they had no social ambition. There was also a lawyer with a downhearted wife, but they held themselves aloof from the village apart from the obligatory attendance at church, and that rather infrequently than otherwise. Professor Bissel, a curmudgeonly academic recently retired from some university, had made no moves towards social intercourse. A Mr Slade, rumoured to be a successful merchant, had recently commenced improvements at Clough Farm to convert it into a gentleman's country residence; but these were at an early stage, and so far Mr Slade had not been seen in the village or at church.

Another gentleman—or one who so styled himself—had recently completed the construction of an enormous property some four miles or so beyond Brayton, on the road that led to the port town of Whitby, which was twelve miles beyond. This gentleman considered his eponymously named Somersall Grange to be the only great house in the district worthy of note, but the *real* great house, Tall Chimneys, predated its new neighbour by two centuries. Long since deserted and hidden as it was in a curious wooded depression, many inhabitants of Moorside would have entirely forgotten the existence of Tall Chimneys if it were not for Frank and Beth Harlish, who resided in the gatehouse and acted as estate stewards, faithfully maintaining the grounds and buildings for a family who never came.

It behoves us to mention one other cohort of inhabitants, though temporary. This was a small band of itinerant Irish families currently encamped upon the moor. They were refugees from the potato famine that had ravaged their own country, come away—like so many thousands of their fellows—to seek work and survival on foreign soil. The majority made the perilous crossing to America, but many others had sought a living in England where mills, factories, railways and mines had an insatiable appetite for workers. These, though—the Irish on the moor— were variously unsuited to the hard physical labour, noise and frenetic nature of industry, and hoped instead to fill the roles left vacant by those who had pursued their fortunes in the towns and cities. The immigrants sheared sheep and assisted with lambing, made hay and milked cows, dug peat and shifted manure—anything at all that would pay. Sadly this work paid little, and their desperation caused some unscrupulous farmers to withhold a fair wage on the basis that the itinerants were untried or unpractised at the work or to cheat them simply from the bigoted idea that they were inherently untrustworthy because they were immigrants.

About a mile from the village was where the Irish folk had made their encampment on the moor, at a spot where the cropped turf formed a compound, roughly circular, encompassing perhaps an acre. At the centre of the space was a standing stone. This monolith was very ancient and much weathered, used in latter days as a milestone. Whatever legend was formerly inscribed upon it was long since lost; all four faces of the roughhewn obelisk were scoured by weather to blank, bland unhelpfulness. The standing stone stood about twelve feet high, visible from miles around— even when three feet of snow lay on the ground. There is no knowing why the immigrants chose this spot for their camp. The flat nature of the turf perhaps. Or the fact that, just there, several of the moor's paths and tracks intersected, allowing them quick access to the village, the market town or the farther-flung farms. There was water fairly close at hand, so it made practical sense. But there was something mystical about the place and the stone—so old, placed there by unknown hands many centuries before. To what purpose? Folklore whispered that horrible rites of sorcery and sacrifice had been conducted there, and that witches had been tied to the stone and burned. When the wind blew from the east the stone had a sort of resonance, seemed to hum and almost to vibrate, a conduit between past and present. Those who were sensitive to such things declared the place to have a concentrated energy, though what its source might be, none could say.[i]

Five or six wagons formed a rough circle around the standing stone. All but one of these were adapted farm or dray vehicles, converted into living accommodations by the addition of canvas roofs—much patched—and sleeping platforms. One, however, was a bow-topped *vardo*[ii] of Romani design and possibly even of genuine Romani origin. It was made entirely of wood and boasted a small window or two. Its roof was punctuated by a chimney from a pot-bellied stove within, but whatever else might have been its appurtenances were impossible to see as the door was always fastened shut. Makeshift tents and lean-tos provided further accommodations for the itinerants and their livestock of several sturdy but ragged horses, a handful of goats and a flock of scrawny hens. There were also three or four dogs—wary curs who often fought amongst themselves but never failed to give united tongue when any stranger approached. These congregated in the lee of a small and very rough cart which the workers used to transport themselves to their work, when work could be found.

The summer having been so far very fine and dry, the camp had sometimes quite a holiday air, with bright washing flapping from a line or laid over the low shrubs to dry, a peat fire burning like a beacon in the night and the sound of music and laughter sometimes drifting across the moor. The people were shabbily dressed, to be sure, but they were diffident and polite, and they worked hard when work was available. To some amongst the villagers they seemed exotic—rumoured to have "the sight," and one young man was "touched." One fellow did magic tricks, but whether by wizardry or just clever sleight of hand none could tell. And there was a beautiful woman with long dark hair and jet-black eyes who danced, and an old man played a harp with such poignancy that his hearers found they had tears in their eyes as though his gnarled old fingers plucked the strings of their hearts.

Amongst the village folk the Irish were "interlopers" and "ne'er-do-wells," sure to be eye-deep in reprehensible goings-on, little more than beggars and likely thieves and rogues to boot.

This, then, was Moorside and its surroundings, at the commencement of our tale.

Chapter 2

There had been no rain for a fortnight, and the lane to the gatehouse was dusty. The moor to either side of it bloomed with fairy flax, marsh marigold and willowherb, but the woman who walked wearily along the way hardly saw the pops and sprinks of colour amongst the sage-grey brush. Neither did she particularly notice the haunting call of curlew or the thrill of lapwings as they swooped and darted over the moor. She kept her eyes fixed on her feet, which were shod in sturdy boots, not much repaired, and on the little clouds of dust that rose up in crazy puffs and eddies as she walked along.

She had removed her bonnet, and the soft summer breeze had loosened her hair from its fastening. It was thick and wavy, but a rather ordinary brown in colour. Her face was likewise unremarkable—neither strikingly pretty nor unusually ugly. It was oval, with a pleasing symmetry, the complexion of such a healthy, sun-kissed hue as to suggest much time spent out of doors. The chin was pointed and determined, the mouth somewhat small though well-formed, the nose aquiline, the eyes an intelligent hazel but not large, their pale lashes thick beneath level, serious brows. Just now, as she walked, her downcast eyes had a distracted look as though focused inwardly, signalling a vibrant inner life perhaps more appealing to her than the well-known pathway or the landscape itself, which was familiar to her since infancy in all its guises and seasons.

She carried a basket over her arm but it was not heavy. A roundel of cheese and a small loaf were all it contained, and the woman being young—she was eight-and-twenty—and of hardworking, country stock, was used to much greater burdens. Yet it was clear from her somewhat bowed shoulders and worn-out gait that she was burdened; and if not by the basket, then what other than her thoughts could have incumbered her?

The gatehouse, her destination, came into view. It was a small dwelling but an ornate one, built to impress and intimidate those who would venture past it down the long drive into the hollow that contained Tall Chimneys, the manor over which the gatehouse stood sentinel. Hexagonal in shape, two storeyed, its imposing stone parapets were formed from the same dressed stone as the remainder of the building. Mullioned windows, glazed and leaded, were set too high to allow anyone to peer inside unless on horseback. But it contained only two rooms, one below and the one above that was reached by a steep and narrow stair. A lean-to provided a sort of kitchen or scullery. A little garden encompassed the house on four of its faces, incorporating burgeoning vegetable and flower beds, a hen run, a wood store, a shed and, right at the far corner where the garden was lost in the shadowy discretion of the pressing plantation, a privy. One of the two remaining faces of the building shouldered the right-hand gatepost and the other bordered the lane which, as the driveway to the house, disappeared in a precipitous slope down into the gloom of the trees.

Across the driveway stood the partner gatepost, and beyond this there ran a high drystone wall that followed the circumference of the entire combe within which the manor and the plantation were contained, a distance around of some three miles. The wall served to divide the woodland from the moor and to keep out those who would trespass on the residents of Tall Chimneys, should the gatehouse prove an insufficient deterrent. But a wall of such height and obduracy could have equally been designed as a mechanism for keeping those same residents in.

The gates themselves—ornately wrought in iron, tall and bristling with spikes at the top—were closed and padlocked.

As the woman neared the gatehouse she seemed to slough away the troubles that had dogged her steps. Her eyes regained their usual alert focus and her mouth quivered with the beginnings of a smile. She passed the basket from one hand to the other and reached over the little gate to lift its latch. A dog of indeterminate breed that lay in the sunshine on the path lifted its head and banged its tail a few times in greeting.

A man who bent over one of the vegetable beds straightened up and came to relieve her of the basket. He was so like the woman in feature and colouring that it was impossible not to identify them as brother and sister. His hair, an identical brown to hers, fell in unkempt waves across his brow and over his collar. His face was more tanned than hers and his chin was square but in all other respects they were mirror images of each other except that he stood a head or so taller.

'Frank! You are home!'

'I am,' he said. 'Did you not expect me to be here?' His voice was rusty, as though not often used, and indeed he coughed a number of times as if to clear his throat of some blockage.

'I hoped,' said his sister, 'but lately ...'

Frank reddened, and his gaze slid away from hers. 'How were the Misses MacAllister today?' He peered into the basket, seeming not dissatisfied with what he saw there. 'There are salad greens,' he said, motioning with his head to where he had been working. 'Bread and cheese and some greenery will make us a good supper, won't they Betsey? And we could boil an egg or two.' Betsey was the name by which the woman had always been known amongst her family, but at school she had been teased for it, looked down upon by 'proper' young ladies as being vulgar and disgustingly countrified. She had amended it to Beth then, but old habits held fast with Frank.

Beth sighed. 'It would, Frank, except that I am invited to the vicarage to dine this evening. Had you forgotten?'

Frank's shoulders dropped an inch or two but his face betrayed no sign of his disappointment. 'Never mind,' he said. He lifted the basket. 'This will keep. I can finish off last night's pie. What time are you expected? I'll walk you, if you like.' His gaze fixed on a place on the flagstone pathway between their feet. 'I ... I need to see Ruairi Connolly in any case,' he mumbled. 'He'll be at the Plough.' He peered again into the basket, as though its contents might have changed, thereby avoiding his sister's eye, which had darkened at his last remark.

'You were at the Plough last night, Frank,' she said with an attempt at lightness. 'Could you not have conducted your business then?'

'There was no business done at the Plough last night,' he said.

'Ah no. There was music. The Irish people played. And I suppose the young lady danced. That must have been a distraction.'

Frank felt himself flush bright crimson as the vivid and disturbing image of a beautiful girl whirling and gyrating haunted him still, as it had done all night. The great poise and fluidity of her limbs, her raven hair flowing like liquid jet, her dark eyes meeting his again and again across the packed tap room as though only the two of them were present was a sort of enchantment he could not shake off. She had surrendered her body— her very soul—to the music; he had never seen anything so breathtaking, so free, so wanton and yet at the same time so utterly pure … yes, it certainly had been a distraction.

Beth waited a few moments. It was easy to tease Frank but he sometimes took it poorly and she could see that this was one of those occasions. Taking pity, she released him. 'We won't dine until eight. Fine folks eat so late. But I am invited to sit with the ladies while the vicar conducts evensong, which is at six-thirty. I ought to go and dress. But show me the garden first. Are there any strawberries yet?'

Glad of the change of topic, Frank took Beth around the raised beds. They pulled weeds and tied in runner beans, pinched out the side shoots of tomato plants and admired their crop of first early potatoes, which promised to be prodigious.

'I can take some to the MacAllisters, and … there are other families who will be glad of them,' Beth said.

Frank nodded but didn't meet her eyes. 'Most folks can grow potatoes,' he demurred, rummaging amongst the foliage of the strawberries to see how the fruit fared.

'The MacAllister ladies can't. They came too late for planting, even if they were hale enough, which they aren't.'

'Nice patch of garden at Laurel Cottage,' Frank observed. 'The Mitchells worked it pretty well until they went to Sheffield. I don't mind going and turning it over for them.'

'I'll tell them. But they can't pay.'

Frank shrugged. 'Doesn't matter.'

'And the Irish families can't grow their own crops,' Beth said grimly, as though grasping a nettle that had sprouted up between them.

'I don't like you mixing with them,' Frank said gruffly.

'They're struggling,' Beth said. 'And you mix with them willingly enough.' She threw him an accusing look. Ruairi Connolly, whom Frank hoped to meet at the Plough, was of the Irish cohort.

'That's different.' Frank began to shoo the hens back into their coop.

The situation of the brother and sister was unusual. Their parents— a kitchen maid and a gamekeeper—had been uncomplicated, unambitious working people who were fortunate enough to gain employment and a home at the furthest-flung of one of several properties owned by the Talbots, a wealthy merchant family. Frank and Beth Harlish and their siblings would doubtless have followed their parents into service or some agrarian occupation had their well-being and education not been taken in hand by a philanthropic Talbot cousin. All four Harlish offspring had been given an education far superior to any of the other village children, equipping them for lives several tiers above their natural stations. Only Frank had not thrived at school, learning but not enjoying his lessons, yearning for no advancement beyond his native sphere. Like his father, he loved the land and the trees and to nurture the wild things. He had returned to the village and taken over his father's work on and around the Talbot estate.

Beth would have liked to follow her older sister into teaching, or even her brother Arthur into engineering. Indeed, she would have welcomed any opportunity for escape, but her father's death and her mother's increasing mental incapacity had required her to return from school to the gatehouse. Nursing and watchfulness over Sally Harlish's wayward moods, and the housekeeping duties at Tall Chimneys that Sally was supposed to do, had deprived Beth of her chance to pursue her own dreams. After her mother's death, Beth remained at the gatehouse, keeping house for Frank, caretaking Tall Chimneys and often thinking of the life she might have had.

Beth Harlish was an anomaly. She was low-born but well-educated. Her manners and speech were refined but she was comparatively poor, having only the stipend paid out by the Talbots to support her. She must work, and that work was not of any trivial kind—a house as large as Tall Chimneys did not run itself even when there was no family at home. Beth was ladylike but not a lady. Her superior accomplishments meant that the cottagers and farmers' wives who should have been her natural associates were wary of her, and yet few of the more elevated families in the district would notice her. Her conversation was good, and she could read aloud, play the pianoforte and draw quite well, but her wardrobe was sadly lacking, and of course she could by no means return any hospitality that was meted out to her.

But recently, under the auspices of the newly-arrived vicar, Mr Eagerly, openings for Beth's particular talents had begun to emerge. Now she had become a regular and useful visitor to some of those in the expanding circle of respectable neighbourhood society. From being invited to chaperone the vicar's daughter on country walks and to take tea at the vicarage there had come the request to keep occasional company with the sickly wife of the local lawyer. There, Beth had encountered the doctor, who needed someone to write up his notes. The doctor in turn recommended her services to the professor lately retired to the area with a library of books requiring to be catalogued. Today, as on several previous occasions, Beth had attended the MacAllister sisters for the purposes of genteel sewing and mending. One of them was blind, which precluded her from repairing her own underclothes, the other self-confessedly hopeless with a needle, but their purse was not sufficiently ample to allow the services of a professional seamstress. From the MacAllister sisters as from her other clients, there was always payment—often in kind—always inconspicuously proffered as an informal recognition of services discreetly rendered. Today it had been the bread and cheese.

But Beth was a naturally compassionate young woman, kind and caring, and being an oddity herself was drawn to others who for some reason did not quite fit in. She had lately become a frequent visitor to the band of itinerant Irish families encamped upon the moor from whom she neither expected nor received payment of any kind, other than their diffident friendship.

They, indeed, were the subject of her distracted musings as she had returned home along the lane.

She would take them some potatoes, no matter what Frank decreed.

Chapter 8

Two hours later, three ladies sat in the small parlour of the vicarage. The vicar's wife occupied the armchair close to the fireplace but the grate was empty, the day having been warm and fine. The stuff of her full-skirted gown was very superior bombazine, though a sober brown in colour. She had a matronly air befitting her station, but she was in fact a comparatively young woman—not more than forty-five years of age— and indeed a comparatively recent wife, being the vicar's second, his first having passed away some years previously. Mrs Eagerly's face was thin and sallow, suggesting a period in the not-too-distant past of hardship or illness, and her eyes were flinty. She sat very upright, so the last rays of daylight that filtered through the window beside her could fall upon the pages of her book. Its contents seemed to absorb her, and she took no notice of the sighs and fidgets of the younger of her two companions.

This fidgeting lady sat at the end of a sofa, unless she was up and pacing the room and peering through the window—which she frequently was—clearly anticipating an imminent occurrence. In between these restless meanderings she took up and toyed half-heartedly with some knitting—an indeterminate article of coarse brown yarn that hung stiffly from the needles. Her hair was so strikingly dark as to be almost black, and was smooth, thick and very lustrous. It was becomingly arranged in the latest fashion, with a central parting and curls prettily gathered over her ears. Her eyes were brown, large and very limpid, and her skin of a hue that declared at least one of her parents' ethnicity as exotic. Her gown was pearl grey in colour, satin, fashionably low on the shoulder, with the long, wide pagoda sleeves very much in vogue.

Beth was the third lady. She occupied a straight-backed chair towards the back of the room where a small round table held a box of silks, scissors and other notions. She stitched assiduously at a piece of embroidery. Her gown was clean and unexceptionable but boasted neither the quality nor the mode of the other women's clothes.

The younger lady approached the window for the third or fourth time and squinted her eyes to peer across the vicarage garden and down the lane towards the church.

'Evensong is interminable today,' she said in a cross voice, turning and regaining her seat on the sofa. 'I am eager for the party to begin.'

Her stepmother closed her book with resignation and placed it on a side table. 'It is not a party,' she said, smoothing skirts already perfectly straight. 'It is Sunday, so we cannot have a party. However, even on Sundays, people must eat and so we are to have a quiet, comfortable and very informal dinner for some of our friends and neighbours.' She spoke as though defending herself from some charge that had not yet been made.

'Very informal!' Rose, the girl, laughed, and flung aside her knitting, which she had taken up long enough to drop two more stitches. 'With poor Charlotte commanded to get out and wash all the best crystal and china.'

Mrs Eagerly made a vinegary face. 'We have not enough place settings in the second-best service,' she demurred.

Rose crossed the room and sat at her stepmother's feet. She was only just home from school, barely a woman, and had not quite sloughed off the habits of childhood. 'Tell me again of the guests,' she said, resting her chin on Mrs Eagerly's knee.

Mrs Eagerly composed herself as though to tell a story she had already narrated several times.

'Yourself, your papa and me,' she began.

'And Edgar,' Rose put in.

Edgar was Mrs Eagerly's only child from her first marriage, twenty-one years of age, just ordained and now employed as Mr Eagerly's curate in the parish.

'And Edgar. Then, Mr Herbert Somersall.'

'The Somersalls are but lately come to the parish,' Rose recited. 'The elder Mr Somersall owns a coal mine, but life in town does not suit his wife and so he has built her a country mansion on the other side of the

17

moor. They are very wealthy but,' and here she fixed her face with an appropriate expression of regret, 'Mrs Somersall is yet to benefit from the country air.'

'That's right.' Mrs Eagerly smothered a smile that threatened to bend her lips. 'Poor woman. She is to be pitied. Mr Somersall is rarely at home due to his business concerns and so their son, Herbert, will represent them both. We are not acquainted with young Herbert Somersall as yet. I'm told he is a very pleasing young man and has been well educated, but he will doubtless follow his father at the pit.'

Rose's eyes grew round. 'He will mine coal? Himself? With his own hands?'

'No, Rose. His role will be managerial. In time he will supervise the pit, the men, the entire business. Like you, he has but lately completed his education and returned to Yorkshire. I suppose his father will begin to induct him into the business immediately.'

Rose lost interest in young Mr Somersall. 'And there's another young gentleman, is there not?'

'Yes. A university friend of Herbert is staying at Somersall Grange at present. A Mr Milton. He is an engineer, and is to advise on pumps, props and so forth.'

Rose shook her curls to indicate that nothing could be of less interest to her. 'I shall not be seated next to either Mr Herbert Somersall or his engineering friend, shall I? What on earth could I talk to them about? I know nothing of mining.'

'Edgar will take you in to dinner,' Mrs Eagerly said. 'You are too young to be entrusted to a gentleman whose acquaintance we have only just formed. Unless you feel you could trust yourself to Mr Golightly?'

Rose screwed up her face. 'Mr Golightly the grocer?' she said. 'No, I should not like that.'

'The tea merchant,' Mrs Eagerly corrected, as though this was an entirely different and far superior occupation. 'Yes. He is to bring his wife and daughter. You know Miss Golightly, I think? She assists at the Sunday school. They are a very worthy local family.'

Rose frowned. Flossie Golightly was a lumpen girl, with far too carnal an interest in unmarried ploughmen and sheep drovers for Rose's liking. Their few attempts to make friends had foundered. 'And the tenth?'

Mrs Eagerly shot Rose a look. 'Our dear Miss Harlish, of course.'

Recollecting Beth's presence, Rose went to stand beside her. 'How nicely you embroider, Miss Harlish,' she said. 'I have not the patience for it. Or for anything, in truth! Oh! How I wish my father and Edgar would return. I counted scarce a dozen worshippers going into the service. I wonder Papa does not cut out a hymn or two and abbreviate his sermon for so few.'

'The Bible says that when only two or three are gathered, God is there amongst them,' Beth said. 'I am sure He wishes to hear the entirety of the vicar's sermon.'

Mrs Eagerly sighed. 'So many of the villagers have departed for the towns. A quarter of the pews were empty this morning. The parish shrinks, and Moorside was never very affluent to begin with.'

Rose toyed with the silks in the sewing box. 'This blue is perfect for the harebells you're working,' she mused. 'It is the blue of Edgar's eyes, I think.'

'Indeed? I had not observed.' Beth reached for the scissors and cut her thread. She addressed her next remark to Mrs Eagerly. 'Migration is not all *towards* the towns and cities, ma'am. The MacAllister sisters have lately moved into Laurel Cottage, and Mr Slade is spending ever so much on Clough Farmhouse. I do not think he would go to the trouble if he did not intend to be there a great deal.'

Mrs Eagerly frowned. The MacAllister sisters were impoverished; they would add little to her husband's income. And as for Mr Slade—a merchant apparently, and well-to-do, but with a dubious reputation—so far, he had not been seen at church. Nothing could matter less to the vicar himself than money—he was more interested in ministering to the poor and needy in the parish—but someone must encourage the more genteel amongst the residents to do their duty and Mrs Eagerly had taken that task upon her own shoulders. She had visited the lawyer's wife, only to be turned from the door—the lady was indisposed and not able to receive callers. The professor had no wife so the vicar must call on him. The doctor and his wife were good enough people in their way but really, the church needed the patronage of quality ...

'I wonder the Talbots never visit Tall Chimneys,' she said. 'Or his cousin, Mrs Stockbridge, to whom I understand the house is given over for her lifetime. They say it is a very fine house, though rather oddly situated.'

'I cannot say why they do not come,' replied Beth. 'The house is kept in readiness; although, to tell the truth, it often feels like so much wasted effort. And the place has a desolate air about it, as though it were lonely.'

Rose gave a delighted sigh. 'How romantic! It pines for its master and mistress. If I were in your place, Miss Harlish, I would take up residence myself.'

'But that would not be right,' Beth said. 'Frank and I are its custodians, not its owners. We would not presume so far.'

'I am sorry Mr Harlish will not join us this evening,' Rose said, 'for he is an intriguing figure when I see him at a distance across the moor or toiling in the churchyard. But,' with a sigh, 'it would make the numbers uneven if he did.'

'That is not the reason he will not attend, Rose. My brother is shy. He is awkward in company. It is not his milieu.'

Rose considered this. 'He is a solitary soul,' she mused, thinking of the romantic heroes of Sir Walter Scott's novels.

'He is a countryman, very dedicated to his work,' Mrs Eagerly said, 'and not one given to small talk.' It was charitable of her to put it so. Her few encounters with Frank Harlish had left her with the impression of a taciturn, not to say surly man. The same could not be said of Beth, who was personable—the perfect companion for Rose. She said, 'I should be interested to see Tall Chimneys one day, if you would care to show it to me. Rose, would you not like to visit the old house in the hollow?'

'Oh yes!' Rose clapped her hands in glee. 'I fancy it very like the castle in *The Castle of Otranto*.'[iii]

'It is not at all like that,' Beth said with a smile. 'The original part of the house is very ancient—as much as two hundred years old—but the wings are recent, built by Mr Talbot only ten years ago. No. You must not think of it as a crumbling medieval place. It is comparatively modern, in fact. Light and comfortable.'

'Oh.' Rose wandered back to the window.

'All the more shocking to leave it unoccupied,' Mrs Eagerly muttered. 'But I should still like to see it.'

'By all means, Ma'am. I shall be happy to oblige you.'

A bustle in the hallway announced the return of the clergymen from church. The parlour door opened to admit a tall and well-looking young man, fair-haired, dressed in clerical garb that managed to be decorously sober and also rather debonaire.

'Why do you hide yourselves away in here?' he enquired brightly, his blue eyes alight, 'when Mr Somersall's carriage is visible on the moorland track, and the Golightlys can be seen passing the lychgate as we speak? Get up, I say, and make ready to meet our guests.'

He came further into the room and regarded Rose. 'My, my,' he said, looking approvingly at her dress and hair, 'how pretty you look, Sister. Young Mr Somersall is doomed.'

He looked away, perhaps to give Rose the opportunity to become mistress of her evident pleasure in his compliment, and addressed his mother. 'The vicar sends you his compliments, Mama. He has gone upstairs to wash his hands and will be down directly. Is the Somersalls' carriage to call for Miss Harlish? Or shall I walk down the lane to meet her? It will only take me a few minutes. I do not like to think of her walking the lanes unaccompanied. Oh!' A small movement at the back of the room caught his attention and he turned to see Miss Harlish herself in the middle of tidying away her silks and needles. He gave a self-deprecating laugh. 'But here she is already! Conjured as though by very thought! Good evening, Miss Harlish. How delightful to see you. I trust you were not accosted on your journey?'

Beth smiled. 'By no means, sir. My brother escorted me and will come again to take me home.'

'We will not trouble him to come out so late,' Edgar declared. 'I shall send a boy with a note. One way or another, we shall see you safely home.' He lifted his hand to forestall Beth's objection. 'No. No. It will be our pleasure. Come now, Rose, let us greet your guests.'

With that, he swept his stepsister from the room. His mother followed closely on his heels with Beth in her train.

Chapter 4

The vicar, Oscar Eagerly, was a thoroughly genial man who exuded good humour through every pore. His hair—once ink-black and shiny as treacle—had greyed but was still as thick as ever. His eyes were bright and kind, though etched around with lines, and his smile was wide and remarkably white. He was unmistakably Indian in his appearance but nothing Indian in manner or address remained—he had been in England these forty-five years—and his parishioners had long since got over their suspicion of him. He was well-liked. His passion for ministry was unmistakable and his compassion for the poor very genuine. Though able to converse on an equal footing with men of quality and fortune, he made no pretence of either for himself.

Indeed, for himself he had no ambition at all beyond the preaching of the gospel and the bringing of souls to Christ. But being left in sole charge of a young daughter, he had been forced to think beyond his own wants. Rose, though a good and obedient girl, was by no means equipped for a life of religious service or pious obscurity. Poor rented rooms, mean streets, the sick, the sinning and the forsaken were not her sphere; she was beautiful, lively and whimsical, but squeamish. She had not the steadiness or selflessness of her father but rather the impulsive and capricious nature of her mother, who had not been the helpmeet Oscar Eagerly had hoped for, though he had loved her very dearly. Thus, after an appropriate period of widowhood, he had sought for and found a second wife who would be equal to the rigours of a rural parish while at the same time having the good sense to rear Rose for life as the wife of a well-heeled, indulgent husband. Mrs Maria Maybury, widow of an army chaplain just returned from India, satisfied all his requirements and had for the past three years been his consort in the parish of Moorside.

Now Rose was home from school, where she had been educated as thoroughly as her flighty mind allowed, Mrs Eagerly had begun the work of finding Rose a husband—rather sooner than the vicar thought necessary. A titled position the girl could not likely aspire to, and of dowry she brought very little, but Mrs Eagerly had persuaded her husband that their daughter's own charms would be more than sufficient to induce a suitable man to make an offer. Naturally, as her parents they saw her mixed blood as no impediment whatsoever and would show the door to any oaf low enough to see it in that light, but they were not so naive as to know that it might be a stumbling block to some. And so, the eligible Mr Herbert Somersall, a man of no particular breeding but raised with all the refinement and education money could buy and heir to a colliery fortune, had been invited to dine along with a local family, to see if he might suit.

The local family, the Golightlys, had been chosen to provide colour and conversation, to dilute what might otherwise be a rather awkward and obvious match-making experiment. They were a jolly, not-at-all sophisticated family, lynchpins of the local community. Now they clamoured up the path of the vicarage arguing good-naturedly, obviously very excited about the evening ahead of them.

The drawing room at the vicarage was small, fashionably cluttered with diminutive tables draped with lace doilies, cabinets stuffed with curios, numerous bookcases and a plethora of occasional furniture. It was soon made to feel much smaller by the arrival of the Golightly family, who were all stout and constitutionally ungainly. They jostled in the doorway for a time, stopping it up like a cork in a bottle before suddenly all popping through the aperture with great velocity, causing Mrs Eagerly's collection of fine china figurines to chime and tremble in their cabinet. The Golightlys laughed very merrily at their clumsiness, looking around them the while with bright and expectant eyes, and their good humour—along with the distinct aroma of the spices, tobacco, tea and coffee that was their stock-in-trade—further filled up the room. Beth found herself pressed breathlessly against a bureau and Edgar had to brace himself against the hearth for fear of being squashed into the fireplace. The Eagerlys stood their ground however, staunchly occupying the centre of the carpet in the face of the buffets and manoeuvrings of their guests, like the last remnant of a battalion at the close of a particularly epic battle.

They all shook hands very cordially, instantly dispelling the combative air. Mrs Eagerly motioned to the maid that drinks should be served.

It was clear that the Golightlys had dressed carefully and in their best, and also that their best had required much mending and making do, trimming and tailoring. Mr Golightly's suit was of a style fashionable some thirty years previously and of the size he had likely been at that time; it strained around his rotund figure, the stitches in its seams quite visible, its buttons threatening to fly off at any moment. Mrs Golightly had compensated for the age of her attire with the addition of a superfluity of lace at the bosom and cuff; but no amount of trimming could eradicate the distinct whiff of camphor that mingled with her natural body odours. Miss Flossie Golightly had eschewed any accessory apart from a transparent fichu, which she soon removed, declaring the heat in the room so overpowering that she was 'sweating cobs.' Her dress displayed a vast expanse of fleshy shoulder and only just contained a large swell of bosom. The act of removing the wrap caused her to knock over a small table. Mrs Golightly, seeking to right the table, succeeded in upsetting a chair. Edgar dashed to restore the furniture. Beth discreetly removed a vase of flowers from harm's way.

Mr Golightly puffed and panted and mopped his brow with a large handkerchief and swallowed in one gulp the glass of Madeira handed to him by the maid. 'My word,' he gasped out, his face very florid, 'I'll swear the vicarage is a full half mile further from the shop than it used to be. The walk has half killed me. Let me sit down.'

He swept a quantity of supernumerary cushions from a low sofa and had begun to lower himself into it when his wife cried, 'Algernon! Don't sit there, lad. It is too low. We'll need a winch and tackle to get you out of it.' But she was too late. With creaking seams and a ricochet of buttons, Mr Golightly beached himself upon the sofa.

Flossie scrabbled to retrieve her father's fastenings, her bosoms perilously at risk of escaping their meagre restraint and joining the buttons on the carpet. She knocked the fire irons over with a clatter but even this cacophony did not drown out her grunts and wheezes of effort and her grumbling. 'You must stay where you are now, Father, or your britches will be round your ankles.'

Blushing, Rose knelt to assist.

Mrs Golightly lunged towards her husband, tripped over the rug and landed in an ungainly heap at his feet 'There now. That's both of us aground, and no mistake. I suppose you've a needle and thread about the place, Mrs Eagerly? Algernon will have to be sewn back into his clothes.'

While his wife went to get her sewing box, the vicar threw open the French doors. As an attempt to make the room larger, it was in vain, but the additional air did relieve the sense of suffocation somewhat, and it offered an egress from the mayhem wrought by the Golightlys in the few minutes since their arrival. Edgar took Rose by the arm and indicated to Beth that she should follow them into the garden while the Golightly womenfolk repaired the grocer's clothing.

Thus, they were on the vicarage lawn when the Somersall party arrived and indeed, such was the pleasantness of the summer evening—and such a relief from the correspondingly airless and chaotic atmosphere within—that Beth was glad it should be so. She was not a young woman who enjoyed being indoors when she could be out, and the rose beds and borders, the old church beyond the hedge, with its quiet graveyard and old yews, and the view of the moor on the other side of the lane all offered far more scope in the way of conversation than did the cluttered interior of the vicarage. Also, these occasions always wrought within her a consciousness of playing a part, a role, of going through the motions of something she despised, or perhaps more accurately that she despised herself for so doing.

When Herbert Somersall and his companion were halfway up the path they spied the others and diverted their steps across the lawn.

Herbert Somersall might best described in terms of all the things he was not. He was neither tall nor small, measuring just above the middle height. He was not heavily built, but perhaps would be in time. He was not at all ill-looking without being what was considered handsome. His hair was of no distinct colour, just an indeterminate sandy brown, and it already showed signs of receding; he would be bald before he was forty. His eyes were not quite grey and not quite blue and had a staring, myopic, rather astonished look about them that was quite endearing. His mind was not particularly sharp and yet a carefully cultivated expression of intelligence that he assumed whilst engaged in conversation disguised this very effectively. What Herbert lacked in wit he made up for by impeccable manners and a modest, unassuming air. He was gentle and kind, but not very confident.

Finally, Herbert was by no means ignorant of the purport of his invitation to the vicarage, or of his father's intention in sanctioning his acceptance of it. He eyed Rose closely as he approached across the soft, yielding lawn. She was certainly very beautiful, surrounded by flowers and bathed in the glow of the sunset that at last cast its soft, blushing light across the land. He understood she was not wealthy—but *that* did not matter. Nevertheless, she was a lady, or would be when the last clinging

25

tendrils of girlhood that now still adhered to her air disappeared, and when her form had ripened and matured. He had been made to understand that she had been delicately reared, shrewdly educated, and her family was unexceptionable. She was a vicar's daughter and what could be more refined, more respectable than that? There was apparently some tangential connection with a wealthy and influential family—merchants, shipbuilders, railway magnates, landed—he forgot the details, but his father had made much of them.

He shook hands with his host and the curate and then with Rose, bestowing upon her what he hoped was a winning smile. It was explained to him that Mrs Eagerly and the remainder of the party were detained indoors by a crisis of a sartorial nature and would be with them presently. Beth was brought forth from the obscurity of an arbour and introduced in her turn as 'Miss Beth Harlish, Rose's very good friend,' which reminded Herbert of his own friend, who loitered a pace or two behind him, pretending interest in a group of topiary obelisks.

Herbert swivelled and motioned his acquaintance forward. 'Let me introduce Mr Milton—Stephen—an associate of mine, a fellow alumnus of Balliol College. He's a true scholar, unlike me.' He gave a self-deprecating laugh. 'I'm a thorough dunderhead, I'm afraid. But if you want brains, Stephen's your man.'

Stephen Milton shook hands crisply with the vicar and the curate. 'Very good of you to include me,' he said in a low gruff voice.

To the women he gave a stiff bow, saying only, 'Charmed,' and 'Ma'am,' before turning back to the shrubbery.

Tall, slenderly built and dark haired, Stephen Milton was very handsome in a brooding and sullen way that did not entirely impress. His clothing was good, but not exceptionally good, and not new. His eyes were dark and moody, deep set beneath heavy brows, and his forehead somewhat furrowed, as though his mind was perpetually occupied with profound and important conundrums.

Rose gave a trill of laughter and said, 'What a terrifying man,' threading her arm through Edgar's but looking up through her lashes at Herbert so as to include him in the joke.

Herbert said gamely, 'Oh yes, he *is*.'

The vicar said, 'Edgar, would you be so good as to go indoors and see how matters progress?'

With visible reluctance Edgar disentangled himself from Rose and strode away, glancing over his shoulder frowningly when Herbert held out his own arm as a substitute. Rose could do nothing but take it, which she did tremblingly but willingly enough.

'Do show me the garden, Miss Eagerly,' Herbert said, 'before the light goes. Do you know the names of all the flowers? I suppose you do. It seems to me that young ladies have an encyclopaedic mind for these things. For myself, I hardly know a dahlia from a dandelion.' They strolled off towards one of the herbaceous borders.

The vicar gave Beth a meaningful look before joining Stephen Milton and, indicating the various cones, cubes and globes of the topiary, embarked upon a discussion of geometry that seemed to both surprise and energise the young man.

Beth answered the vicar with a small nod before following the young people at a distance calculated to afford some small degree of privacy without at all allowing them to consider themselves alone.

Rose, somewhat panicked at being so precipitately borne off to the shrubbery, and wishing to include Beth in the conversation said, 'Miss Harlish has invited us to visit Tall Chimneys, the house of which she is the steward. Is that not so, Miss Harlish? It is a very fine house, I believe ... the architecture ... and so forth. Perhaps ... but probably it is presumptuous of me to mention it ...' she tailed off, throwing a flustered look at Beth.

'By all means,' Beth said, suppressing a sigh. 'If Mr Somersall has any interest in seeing the place.'

'I should like it of all things,' he cried. 'Only tell me the day and the time and I shall be present, and I shall make so bold as to accept on my friend's behalf also. Stephen admires a flying buttress more than any man I know.'

Presently, the Golightlys spilled out of the French doors. In the course of their hasty basting and embroidery they had consumed the entirety of the Madeira on the drinks tray. They tripped over a paving stone or two and shambled across the lawn to meet the other guests. Mr Golightly guffawed and the Golightly ladies laughed and clutched at each other, their glee metamorphosing into a kind of hysteria as Herbert Somersall and Stephen Milton were introduced. Flossie Golightly indeed nearly convulsed with delight, simpering and quaking beneath the bewildered gaze of the two gentlemen and erupting into shrieks of uncontrollable giggles. In vain did her mama and papa admonish her, and indeed their own mirth was only slightly less irrepressible than hers.

The maid circulated once more with the tray and, as the church clock struck the half hour, dinner was announced.

As arranged, Edgar took Rose into dinner. The vicar took Mrs Golightly's arm and Flossie undertook to steer her father safely to his chair although her ability to do so was seriously in doubt—she was as

27

tipsy as he was. Herbert found himself assigned to the mama rather than the daughter, but played his part with good grace.

Beth and Stephen remained on the lawns. The longest day was not far away and the late sunset across the moors was particularly beautiful. A soft fragrant breeze met them from across its expanse, unspeakably refreshing after the heat of the day. Stephen ran a finger around the inside of his collar. Beth breathed in deep draughts of the invigorating air. It was clear from their lingering there that neither was ready to relinquish the brief relief afforded by the evening breeze in favour of the dining room, where the shifting of chairs and the crash of a tumbling *jardiniere* indicated that some leisureliness on their part could do no harm. It would be mere speculation to wonder if they both felt their very attendance at the party was spurious, that they were unwelcome additions invited more out of kindness than for the pleasure or prestige of their company. As minutes passed and they made no move to follow the others, such speculation gained traction.

For her part, notwithstanding her appetite—which was by this late hour quite acute—Beth would much have preferred to be at home at the gatehouse, to sit upon the small garden seat that would give her the best view of the sunset across the moor, to hear the contented noises of the hens as they settled to their roost, and the whispering susurration of the wind in the trees behind her. She had a sudden craving for the aroma of Frank's pipe and the soft scrape of his knife as he whittled at a stick, the simplicity of bread and cheese and homegrown greenery laid out on the oak table. She dragged her mind's eye from these things to see that Stephen was likewise lost in his own reverie, but the nature of it she could by no means discern. He was inscrutable.

But then, abruptly and without turning his head, without looking at her at all he asked, 'What are you thinking of?' and she was surprised that his accent was local, Yorkshire—though, like hers, a refined, softened version.

'Of home,' she replied.

He nodded. 'And where's that?'

She motioned with her head. 'Down the lane, there.'

'A pleasant spot, no doubt. You live with your ...?'

'With my brother. Yes. In our childhood home. Much quieter now with only two. At one time there were six of us living cheek-by-jowl! And you?'

He breathed in deeply, then out again through his nose. 'I have no home at present,' he said. 'If the work at the colliery suits, I suppose I shall settle. But I am not sure I can get on with Mr Somersall.'

'With Mr Herbert Somersall? I understood you were friends.'

'Oh no. Not with *him*. I like Herbert well enough. But his father rules the roost. You are acquainted with the elder Mr Somersall?'

'I never met him in my life.'

'Count yourself lucky. He is a despot of the worst kind. And his mine is in a shocking state. It's dangerous for the men. If I *do* remain …'

'… you can improve things?'

He turned to look at her then, fixing her with eyes that were intensely dark. 'Undoubtedly.'

'But perhaps, in time, Mr Herbert will take control.'

Stephen gave a harsh bark of a laugh. 'Not until the old man is six feet under,' he said bleakly. 'He isn't the type to retire.'

Beth felt their conversation had veered rather closer to gossip than she was comfortable with. 'Perhaps we ought to go in?'

Stephen sighed. 'If you like. What foolery it all is! I'd as soon have a plate of bread and cheese than whatever has been cooked up for us here.'

This sentiment so exactly echoed Beth's own that she gave an involuntary smile.

'Oh, there it is,' Stephen said, softening a little and at last proffering his arm.

Beth laid her hand on it lightly. 'There is what?'

'Your smile. You. I knew it was in there somewhere. What manner of lady are you, if you don't mind me asking? Excuse me, but your attire … and your situation here … I can't fathom it.'

Another woman might have objected to his enquiry, to have felt insulted, but not Beth, who was as conscious as anyone could be of her anomalous situation, that she was neither fish nor fowl. They passed the last of the rose beds and lingered on the terrace before the French doors. 'I am no kind of lady at all,' Beth said, 'in the same way I surmise that you are no kind of gentleman. I mean no slight, I assure you. We are both ordinary people who have been given opportunities to better ourselves. But … oh! I sometimes wonder …'

'… whether it would not have been better to have stayed where we were? Ah yes. A fish, be it in ever so small a pond, is still happier than a fish out of water.'

Beth nodded.

He handed her into the drawing room, where the candlelight was no substitute for the purple twilight they left behind them, and they made their way into the dining room.

Chapter 5

After dinner, Mrs Eagerly and the young ladies returned to the gardens, where a full moon poured pearlescent light over the flower borders and onto the churchyard, illuminating the old graves almost as brightly as day. Mrs Golightly got as far as the drawing room, where she lingered so as to ease her stays, but then sank down onto a settee and was soon asleep and snoring.

'What a spread!' Flossie remarked with a hiccough, smacking her lips in remembrance of the feast they had consumed, 'and so many courses. In general, we have only two.' Her speech was slurred, and if it had not been for Beth's firm guidance she would undoubtedly have fallen into the herbaceous border.

'So do we, in general,' said Mrs Eagerly, 'but cook was anxious to try some new receipts. The syllabub, for instance, was an experiment. But one I think we shall urge her to repeat.'

'I never tasted anything so good, did you, Miss Harlish?' Flossie turned glazed eyes on her companion. 'Would your brother like it?'

'I thought it very good,' said Beth, 'but I think Frank would not. He does not have a sweet tooth. And in any case, we have no convenient means of keeping the cream chilled. Watch your step there, Flossie, or you will knock the sundial over.'

'I found it somewhat sickly, truth be told,' said Rose, 'and I noticed that Mr Somersall hardly touched his, nor Mr Milton either.' They passed the open windows of the dining room, where the low hum of masculine conversation could be heard. 'What do the gentlemen do, when the ladies retire?' she asked. 'And why *must* we retire and entertain ourselves, when their conversation is so much more engaging?'

'That is not very complimentary to us!' Mrs Eagerly remarked, ushering her stepdaughter away from the window lest any of those within should hear Rose's complaint.

'But true, all the same,' said Flossie, making a lunge towards the window. 'Let us listen in!' she hissed in a stage whisper. 'They may be speaking of us!'

'If so, I would not for all the world hear them,' said Beth, yanking Flossie away. 'But I expect they speak of politics, of business and of international affairs.' This being the case, she likewise would have preferred to remain within. From her limited conversation with Stephen, she had gathered he was well travelled and well informed. Not that he had been overly forthcoming. Indeed, he had spoken little, but what he had said had been interesting.

Herbert's earlier conversation had diverted Rose and Flossie exceedingly: anecdotes of undergraduate japes at Balliol and misadventures in the metropolis in which he always cast himself in the role of clown or dupe so that the slightly risqué nature of the escapades appeared to result from his own foolishness than from any inherent evil or reprehensible excess.

'Also, they drink wine,' said Flossie. 'More wine, that is. I hope Papa doesn't overindulge. We shall not manage the walk home. I shall have to send for Johnny to bring the cart.' Johnny was the Golightlys' son, a boy of twelve who managed the deliveries.

Mrs Eagerly shared Flossie's hope. It seemed to her that Mr Golightly, like his wife, was close to soporific intoxication. 'The night is so warm. I am sure they will not sit long,' she said. 'But I would not have any of you take a chill. Let me fetch our shawls.'

The church clock struck ten. This was the hour Beth had named to Frank for her collection, and very willingly would she have made her excuses. She was no more used to late hours than she was to late dinners, and the next day's agenda would require her to rise early. But a note had been sent along to the Plough and so she could look for no reprieve from that quarter. Resignedly, she bent her lips into a smile and tightened her grip on Flossie Golightly. 'The moonlight is so delightful, is it not? Let us

31

recall lines from our favourite poets that mention it while we wait for the gentlemen to join us.

> *Sleep sweetly, tender heart, in peace,*
> *Sleep Holy Spirit, blessed soul,*
> *While the stars burn, the moons increase.*[iv]

Do you know that one? It's Tennyson. Or what about this?

> *Lo! where the Moon along the sky*
> *Sails with her happy destiny;*
> *Oft is she hid from mortal eye*
> *Or dimly seen,*
> *But when the clouds asunder fly*
> *How bright her mien!*[v]

That's William Wordsworth.'

But Rose shook her head. 'I cannot recall any,' she said.

Flossie, having read no poetry, sang a few lines of a rather bawdy song that concluded with

> *While the sun shone, she scrubbed the floors*
> *But when the moon came up, down dropped her—*[vi]

'Flossie!' Beth hissed.

They continued their moonlit perambulations in silence.

Within the dining room, Mr Golightly congratulated the vicar on his claret. 'From London, I suppose. I wager I can get you a dozen cases as good as this, and at half the price. Unless you prefer brandy. French brandy. That, too, I can get—under the counter, if you get my meaning.'

'The embargo on French goods is quite over,' said Stephen. 'The war is distant history and the need for smuggled goods is a thing of the past.'

'Import duties and excise are not, though,' Mr Golightly grumbled. 'By the time the revenue has taken its share there is precious little profit to be had in wine and spirits from the continent.'

Conversation turned to the encampment of the Irish families on the moor.

'We passed them on our way here,' Stephen observed.

'They are a rag-taggle cohort,' said Edgar darkly, avoiding the vicar's censorious eye. 'I am surprised they are permitted to remain. The bailiff should send them packing.'

'I am surprised they choose such an itinerant existence, when there is plenty of work in the mines and the mills,' said Herbert. 'Father is always lamenting the shortage of labour.'

'The Irish folk on the moor are not suited to industry of that kind,' the vicar said pointedly. 'Though they work hard enough when they get suitable employment. And there are women and children amongst them, and the elderly.'

Mr Golightly harrumphed something about them making themselves useful about the parish, but admitted to locking and bolting his doors with especial assiduity. 'There is one of their number,' he growled, 'a sharp-nosed, squint-eyed rascal, that I would not trust as far as I could throw him.'

'I know the man you mean,' said Edgar. 'He is indeed an evil-looking fellow. They are *all* a bad influence, if you ask me. Dancing and gambling … the parish needs little encouragement to sin.'

'I am sorry to say that the parish at large has not been kind to them,' said the vicar with a frown. 'It is not as though they take work from others, but they seem different—foreign, I suppose, and strange—and this has excited some suspicion. Also a kind of fascination. They are viewed as curiosities in a circus might be. But I think they are to be pitied, poor souls, rather than suspected.'

Stephen looked as though he did not quite agree, but remarked only, 'Innocent of crime they might be, yet they seemed wild and scarcely civilised. Do you not fear for the women of the parish?'

'Indeed,' said Edgar. 'And that is why we must see Miss Harlish safely home. During the day she goes about unchaperoned, but at night … it would hardly be wise, I think.'

'She goes amongst the Irish people distributing aid, when she can,' the vicar said. 'She has nothing to fear from them.'

'Her brother should not allow it,' said Stephen darkly.

'Indeed not,' echoed Edgar.

The vicar smiled. 'I think Mr Harlish is not in that authoritative position with regards to his sister.'

Stephen raised his eyes, which had been fixed on the cloth with a brooding, morose air throughout the conversation. 'She is independently-minded then, Mr Eagerly? I like that in a young lady.'

'Miss Harlish is an extraordinarily gifted lady, very well read. I like her exceedingly. I wish I could do more for her.' The vicar threw a covert glance at his stepson, but Edgar did not acknowledge it.

Mr Golightly's chin and its ancillary jowls concertinaed onto his collar. He was asleep.

Herbert, having used up his stock of amusing anecdotes on the ladies, now surrendered himself to a gentle interrogation from his host. The niceties of romance were all very well for the ladies, but the gentlemen made no secret of his purpose amongst them. Herbert admitted to being three and twenty years of age and declared himself entirely free of obligation to any lady, either romantical or contractual. He was irrevocably committed to the colliery—could conceive of and indeed would be permitted no other professional outlet—and quite resigned to the necessity of learning every aspect of it. One day he would assume command of it so far as 'the governor'—by which he meant his father—would allow, which might not, he intimated, be very much at first or even for some considerable time.

'My father is so very tenacious, sir,' he explained with a gloomy sigh. 'His occupation of his seat of power on the board has been so comparatively short. Not much above fifteen years, sir. I was not ten years of age when he bought the first mine. And for a man of his ambition and talents, it is really no time at all. He has so much more he wishes to achieve and so I fear … that is I expect—that it will be some time before I am so fortunate as to step into his shoes. Should I *be* so fortunate. But in the meantime, I have a salary and some shares, and although I currently reside at my father's house, I could easily take my own if … that is to say, in short, I am amply supplied should I wish … should my circumstances be altered, *improved*, that is, by …' but he trailed off, unable to presume so far as to utter the word 'matrimony.' Up to this he had hardly tasted his wine, but now he resorted to his glass and drank off the full measure, blushing to the roots of his hair.

Mr Eagerly smiled, and passed the decanter.

Stephen had remained silent during this part of the discussion, concentrating on his wine, consistently swallowing two glasses to the other gentlemen's one, but exhibiting not the least sign of inebriation.

Edgar said, 'What delightful company the ladies were this evening! I do not think we should tarry long before we join them. I fancy they are strolling in the garden. The moon is full up.' He made no move to rise, but levelled his gaze at Herbert.

'Yes, indeed,' that gentleman stammered. 'Delightful. Miss Rose is winsome. As beautiful as a rose! Her name is most apt! But hardly yet budded. You must be so proud of her, Vicar.'

'She is young,' the vicar conceded. 'Mrs Eagerly and I are considering a removal to town in October. Rose would benefit from a season—at least one—to widen her acquaintance. Our good friend Mr Talbot has been so good as to intimate his willingness to put his house at our disposal. It is in Grosvenor Square. Perhaps you know it?'

Stephen gave a strangled cough and emptied his glass. 'A very superior address,' he choked out.

'Indeed, yes! Much *too* superior for us, I fear! Of course, circumstances may arise which preclude the necessity of the trip altogether.' He paused before continuing. 'But in fact, my brother is most insistent that we lodge ourselves with him, and I think that if we do go, we will be more comfortable in Harley Street. We will not presume to move in the first circles. That would be beyond our scope. But I am assured there is, these days, a thriving and very respectable society of mercantile and professional families such as your own, Mr Somersall. Lawyers and architects, engineers, physicians, merchants and governmental officials. Rose will find herself at home in such company, I think.'

'Do not forget the church, sir,' said Edgar vehemently, revealing a passion he had perhaps been at pains to suppress, 'where Rose has *always* been at home.' He mastered himself quickly, however, and turned to Herbert to enquire, 'Do you expect to be in town at all this autumn?'

Herbert crumbled a morsel of bread that had been left on the cloth. 'I doubt it,' he said. He fully understood the import of the vicar's words. If he wished to win Rose's affections, he had until October to do so. And he thought he understood the curate's import also. If he—Herbert—were to enter the field for Rose's hand, he would not be unopposed.

'No,' Edgar said, sitting back in his chair, his urbane air firmly restored. 'No more shall I. I shall assume the parish duties while my stepfather is away. But there is sport, I assume? Though a clergyman, I have no objection to sport. Do you hunt? Or shoot?'

Mr Golightly let out a loud snore and another percussive sound of a gastric nature that roused him from his slumber and caused the four other gentlemen to rise to their feet with great alacrity.

'Let us join the ladies,' the vicar said loudly, leading the way from the room, which was suddenly very stuffy.

Stephen could not quit the room fast enough. 'Miss Harlish. She will not accompany you to town, I presume,' he said to the vicar as they made their escape.

'Oh no,' the elder man replied. 'Unfortunately, it would be beyond my power to include her in the party, fond though Rose is of her. Miss Harlish has been educated and designed for a wider sphere than this, but I am sorry to say she must find it herself.'

Chapter 6

The party reunited itself briefly on the moon-soaked lawns of the rectory, but the Golightlys soon betook themselves, yawning and swaying, to the lane and thence home.

Rose, though drooping with fatigue, walked beside Herbert on a further tour of the shrubberies and borders long enough for him to request that she do his mother the great honour of a visit, 'for she has no acquaintance in the country as yet, and her health precludes her from making calls in the ordinary way. You really would be giving her the greatest pleasure.'

Rose glanced over her shoulder to where her father and stepmother strolled in their wake, and at the slightest nod of ascent from that quarter whispered that, yes, she would be delighted, if Mama or Miss Harlish were at liberty to bear her company. At length she could conceal her weariness no longer, and Mrs Eagerly declared that it was time for the young woman to retire. Having gained the promise of a visit to Somersall Grange, Herbert made no protest, and bid Rose a good night with a brief but meaningful clasp of the hand.

It was promptly mooted that the gentlemen should accompany Miss Harlish home.

'Let us go in the carriage, since it stands by,' said Herbert. But Beth would not countenance such thing and indeed Mrs Eagerly thought it unwise for a young lady to enter a closed carriage alone, even with two such respectable gentlemen as Messrs Somersall and Milton.

Beth said she would walk, very happily, and quite alone. The moon was bright and she feared nothing, nothing whatsoever.

Naturally, this line of argument was not to be permitted and in the end it was agreed that Stephen and Herbert would take the stroll along the lane, the carriage following at a distance. The vicar insisted that his stepson be of the party, and so in the end Beth had the protection—quite unnecessary in her opinion—of three attendants along the brightly lit and entirely benign lane to the gatehouse.

The curate took her arm at first, and the two others followed, but Edgar lost his possession of her when he stopped to light a cigar, and it was Stephen who quickly took his place at her side.

They walked in silence for a few moments, Stephen surveying the dusky expanse of moor to either side of them, then training his eyes to the left, where the flickering light of a fire identified the location of the Irish.

'I hear you are quite at home amongst them,' he said, only the direction of his gaze making clear to Beth the object of his remark.

'I have visited them,' she acknowledged. 'The children have no schooling, and there is one woman amongst them who is near her time. I would not be a Christian if I did not do what I can.'

'And are there only women and children there?'

'Some older men, rather past the peak of their physical capacity for labour, and yet they do what they are able. One of them plays the Irish harp. His fingers are still nimble enough. One of the women dances and they earn a few pennies that way.'

'And are there no young men?'

Beth glanced at his face but it was inscrutable, so she did not answer for a few moments.

'I mean, I suppose, are there not men who could labour at the colliery, for instance? I am sure their remuneration would surpass whatever they earn hereabouts. And that would ameliorate the condition of the whole group. They would not need to trespass on your good nature then.'

'It is no trespass,' Beth protested. 'There are men who are hale, but for their own reasons they choose not to take up employment in mines or mills. They have not the constitution for it. One has a susceptibility of the chest. The doctor calls it asthma. Coal dust, or those fibres in the weaving sheds, would be injurious to his health. He does better in the fresh air. Another has only one arm, but he has a knack with horses and Mr Slade employs him in the stable. Others work variously as peat diggers and shepherds. They are not workshy.'

Stephen gave a cynical grunt, stinging Beth into temper. 'They are not malingerers!' she insisted. 'They are honourable people, honest and diligent. It is not their fault that the potato harvest failed! What would you have done, in their place? Stayed on some miserable patch of blighted ground and starved? Do you think they are any less attached to their homes than we are to ours? We spoke earlier about having been removed from our natural places, you and I, Mr Milton, without being given the means or the opportunity to gain acceptance in another. So it is for them! You might look down on them, but you—and I—are not so different to them. Not really.'

In her ire, Beth had begun to walk more quickly, and Stephen had been forced to increase his pace to keep step with her. A considerable distance had opened up between them and the others, who strolled in a very leisurely fashion some way behind, smoking cigars and sparring in a desultory manner.

'Forgive me, Miss Harlish,' Stephen burst out. 'I see I have touched a nerve and you're quite right, I know nothing about these people. I oughtn't to judge them. I admire your altruism. But ... but I fear ...'

Beth's anger evaporated slightly in the soft air of the moor. 'You think, because I am a woman, I am not a sufficiently good judge of my own safety. My brother is the same,' she said, reluctantly, because she did not wish to criticise Frank to a stranger. 'Because he is a man, he disregards any danger for himself. It is only *me* ...'

'He does not like you to associate with them?'

Beth shook her head. 'No. But,' with a defiant lift of her head, 'I am not ruled by him.'

She stopped in the road and turned towards him. Her face, illuminated by the low slanting moonlight, heated from her passion of a moment before, was vibrantly lovely, the tilt of her head and the set of her chin so proud as to be almost regal. Her eyes, which had seemed mild to him before, retained an ember of fire. In that moment he thought she was very beautiful.

Stephen had his back to the moon, which was now setting, and his face was obscured. She could not read his expression and his eyes were dark pools, lost in the shadow of his hair which fell down across his brow. She could sense him fighting an inner battle with himself.

'Oh,' he cried out at last, 'I am a misanthropist. I expect the worst from people. It is a fault of mine, I do own it. I am sceptical and bitter because ... but never mind that. These people on the moor—I can tell you see a species of honour and fortitude amongst them. You admire their resilience and perhaps you envy their freedom. Perhaps *you* would like to dance in the market square to the tune of an Irish harp! But do not mistake. Do not allow them to play *you*, Miss Harlish. They will not return what they receive from you. And one day they will go away.'

Beth considered his words. The gatehouse was in view now. A thin line of smoke rose from the chimney, stirred into whorls by the slight breeze that whispered across the moor—a brushstroke of charcoal against the pewter sky. Frank would have left the kettle on the range ready for her bedtime cup of camomile tea. Her slippers would be warming on the fender. She felt suddenly weary, sick of conversation and company, and ready for home.

'You are quite right,' she said quietly. 'I will receive nothing back. I *expect* nothing. That is the nature of charity. And yes, one day they will leave. For now, the moor is pleasant enough, but we all know what winters are like here. They will have no option than to move on. Now I will say goodnight. There is my house and my brother waits within. Goodnight, Mr Milton.'

She offered her hand and he took it, but a moment later the hand was gone and so was she, lost in the darkness that now rushed across the moor like a tide across a beach. He looked up to see the moon had sunk below the horizon. The sky was ink black, and spangled with innumerable stars.

In the village, the church clock struck one.

In the gatehouse, everything was as Beth had predicted, the kettle simmering, her slippers on the fender and a covered plate with a slice of pie on the oak table.

But of her brother Frank there was no sign.

Chapter 7

An hour or so earlier on that same evening—the evening of the vicar's dinner—while the full moon still poured down a light of translucent brilliance on the Irish camp, a half dozen women moved listlessly to complete their chores now the heat of the day had been replaced by the cool of night. One stooped over the fire and stirred the contents of a large iron pot. Two others folded sheets that had dried on the bushes and rocks. A fourth made her way towards the lean-to where the animals were tethered. A crone, aged beyond any kind of work, sat in the camp's only chair. It might at one time have been very fine, but now— like the woman herself—was all but derelict, held together by the last remnants of its upholstery. She mumbled her gums around the stem of a slender pipe.

The sixth woman perched on the bottom step of the *vardo*. She sat just on the periphery of the firelight and was shadowed from the moon by the bulk of the wagon behind her. Her skirts were hitched up to her knees, showing naked and remarkably clean feet and very shapely shins, bare of stockings. The skin of her legs glowed in the firelight, and her jet-black hair sparked with its own embers. The glimmer lent her clothes colour and quality that daylight—or even the moonlight, had she placed herself in its way—would have denied. But her eyes were of such a fathomless black that no illumination, not even the radiance of heaven, could have plumbed them. She kept her face down however, and occupied herself with hacking slices off a stale loaf and smearing them with some grease or dripping from a tin at her feet before piling them onto a trencher.

A couple of men beyond their middle years sat on upturned crates and sharpened their tools for the following day's labour—one with some difficulty, since his left arm was missing above the elbow joint. Their faces were lined, their eyes hooded, their lips pursed in concentration on their task, concealing teeth that were broken and awry and stained brown with tobacco. Nearby, the old man about whom Beth had made reference earlier plucked the strings of his harp in a medley of traditional airs, very wistful.

Ten or so children between two and eight years old sat cross-legged on the ground close to the cooking pot, their hungry eyes flicking between it and the growing mound of bread in the trencher. They were ragged and threadbare but not undernourished. Seated amongst them was a man—a man, that is, if his wide burly shoulders and broad jaw, bristly chin and deep voice were to qualify him as an adult male. But if his open guileless expression, wide wondering eyes and ingenuous smile were to be believed, he was another child, playfellow of those others who lay tumbled and expectant on a worn piece of carpet. His eyes—blue, and of a remarkable clarity—stared unblinkingly, not at the pot or the bread, but at the woman on the *vardo* steps.

She spoke to him testily. 'Dónall, why do you not go and help with the animals? You unsettle me when you stare at me like that.'

But Dónall remained seated and his eyes did not waver.

Some of the dogs lifted their heads and uttered a warning growl as two men strode into the camp. They carried buckets they had filled with water at a tiny spring some quarter of a mile distant. They proceeded to pour the water into troughs for the various animals.

One of them, a diminutive man with a thin, shrew-like face, aimed a cuff at the head of a tow-headed boy of about twelve who was occupied in grooming the shaggy ponies. 'You were told to fetch water, Conn,' the man wheezed out, his voice high and constricted. 'Do you not think I've enough work with hauling the stones all day?'

'And so I did, Da,' Conn replied, indignant, 'but it was all used for the cooking and ...' He threw an unconscious look across the camp at the dark-haired woman on the step of the *vardo*. '... and suchlike.'

His father hawked and spat on the ground. 'If Aoife wants to wash herself like an Egyptian whore she should fetch her own water. Or find an ass to milk. It isn't for you to do *her* bidding,' he whined, before disappearing with his companion back to the spring for further supplies.

'No, Da,' Conn said to his retreating back.

The woman distributing a dole of oats amongst the livestock said, 'Don't mind your da, Conn. He's tired. A plate of stew and a nip of spirit will set him right. And recall, he doesn't know that it's rabbits from your own snares in the pot. I'll be sure to tell him when he gets back.'

For all the man's complaint of fatigue, his wife looked weary enough to drop. Not even the kind flicker of firelight could energise her dull skin and lacklustre eyes. The moonlight was merciless, revealing hollowed cheeks and the lifeless straw of the hair that had escaped the restraint of a filthy scarf. Her belly was large with child, her ankles—above dirty, bare feet—swollen to gargantuan proportions.

'Dónall helped with the snares, Ma,' Conn mumbled, reluctant to relinquish a share of the praise, but wishing to give his friend his due.

'To be sure. And so I shall tell Ruairi, when he returns.' A scuffle amongst the children by the fire made her grimace. 'That'll be your sister causing trouble. Here.' She thrust the sack of oats at her son and went to see what the matter was, but by the time she arrived at the place where the children were Dónall had distracted the little girl, whose tears had turned to laughter.

Presently, Conn's father and his companion—a rangy, gangling man with wispy grey hair and the tattered remains of what might at one time have been a priest's habit—returned with more water, and the people began to gather a bizarre medley of plates and dishes and such cutlery as they could muster from their various living quarters. The supper was ready. The old harpist laid aside his instrument and one of the women handed him a shallow saucepan and a wooden spoon and tied a kerchief under his chin. Conn took his place on the rug with the other children and pulled his sister onto his lap, ready to share his food with her while their mother attended to their other siblings. One of the older men brought his crate to the side of the ancient chair and prepared to assist the very aged woman with her meal. Imperceptibly, the children edged closer and closer to the cooking pot until it was a wonder that their toes were not roasted in the fire along with the potatoes that nestled in the ashes. Conn's mother passed amongst the entire company with the water bucket and a ladle so that they could drink, not because any complained of thirst but so that their stomachs would be tricked into feeling fuller than their rations would allow.

The meal was ready, but no one made a move to serve it. They sat around the fire and stared into the flames as though made of the same

42

primeval stone as the obelisk that threw its shadow across the turf. The moon crossed the sky impassively above them and the moor grasses were petrified in absolute stillness.

Then the dogs gave tongue, not in warning but in joy, scampering across the grassy platform.

'Here's Ruairi,' said one or two of the company, exchanging nods and smiles.

A tall, well-made, dark-haired man strode into the camp, his cry of greeting seeming to lift the strange enchantment of a moment before. The dogs leapt up at him, capering like puppies. Dónall, likewise, got to his feet and ran over to greet the man, his arms held open as widely as the smile that stretched his large mouth. The man returned Dónall's embrace and acknowledged the salutation of the dogs before pushing them all good-naturedly aside.

Conn, who had also risen, stood diffidently in the shadow of one of the wagons, ready to bring whatever the man might require.

'Ah! I'm late,' Ruairi said, seeing the empty plates and the children's hungry eyes. 'You shouldn't have waited. Indeed, you shouldn't. I was detained at the Plough. I'm sorry. Let the children be fed without delay. Father, you'll say the grace?'

The gangling man rose to his feet, but reluctantly, throwing an agonised look at the newcomer before mumbling, '*Benedic, Domine, nos et haec Tua dona, quae de Tua largitate sumus sumpturi. Per Christum Dominum nostrum. Amen.*[vii]' He resumed his seat on the grass. 'But 'twas not God's bounty,' he spat out, 'but yours, Ruairi, and young Conn's, and Dónall there, and the womenfolk and these men here alongside of me. *They* are the authors of this feast.'

Conn's mother began to divide out the stew amongst the clamouring children. Aoife handed round the bread and Dónall used a stick to roll the potatoes from the ashes while Ruairi passed amongst the company enquiring about the work at Clough Farm, where those who were able had been employed clearing stones that day. 'And you were given vittles? Vittles at noon were agreed upon. That's good. And,' he turned to Conn's asthmatic father, 'the dust did not irritate your chest, so? And you,' he clasped the harpist's shoulder, which was thin, the bones fragile as a bird's, 'you took good care of the women and children? No one came to trouble them, I hope? For tis only you who stands between them and any mischief, should it come.'

The old man sat up the straighter at this remark, frowned and shook his head to suggest that had any miscreant been so foolish as to disturb the peace of the camp he would have been garrotted by the strings of the harp should no other weapon have come to hand.

Ruairi divested himself of a long coat and began to rummage in its several pockets, bringing out a twist of tobacco for the old woman and a pot of salve for the expectant mother. 'For your swollen ankles,' he murmured, palming the treasure into the pocket of her dress. 'And I spoke to the doctor today. He'll come and you need him, when your time is upon you. I assured him there'd be ready money down.'

She opened her mouth to declare that no doctor's assistance would be required on this occasion as on any of the other six, but Ruairi had already turned away to dole out other gifts: a block of salt; a packet of tea; a new coil of fine wire for Conn's snares; a skein of darning wool, and sugared plums for the children, who had already devoured their share of the food. He waved away their thanks, busying himself with turning up the sleeves of his shirt to reveal thickly muscled arms.

Conn, who had not yet eaten his portion of food, brought a half barrel and upended it so that Ruairi could seat himself, then produced a pewter plate and spoon, and watched jealously to make sure that the newcomer received his share of the food. He loitered shyly at Ruairi's shoulder while he ate, saying nothing, but looking on with eager, adoring eyes until Ruairi said, 'Eat, Conn. They're your own rabbits, I suppose? But these ladies could make good stew out of shoe leather.' He smiled his thanks at two women who sat on the rug, sopping up gravy with bread and feeding it to their children. They were widows, their husbands having died of sickness the previous year.

'Dónall helped me,' Conn said loyally, but taking up his bowl of stew. 'And I hear tell of a fishpond down in the hollow where the big house is,' he said, wolfing his food. 'Teeming with bream and perch they say. But I have no hook or line—'

'And we would not *take* what does not belong to us now, would we?' Ruairi interrupted. 'The lady who minds the house has been good to us. And her brother, who likely tends the pond, is in the way of doing us a service. It would not do to get on the wrong side of him.'

'Oh. No,' Conn mumbled, blushing. 'I didn't know.'

"Twas a good thought, Conn,' said his mother, passing her boy more bread. 'Down beyond the town there's a broad river. I suppose anyone may fish *there*.'

'Come to that,' said the squint-eyed man whom Mr Golightly had identified as particularly untrustworthy—and indeed he *was* an opportunist, with a history of petty thievery, 'these rabbits must belong to somebody, and to my mind there's not much difference between a rabbit and a fish.'

Ruairi frowned. 'There's all the difference. Rabbits are wild. A fish that is kept like that, in a pond, is like a sheep or a cow. It is husbanded for some purpose by its owner, it is livestock, and the owner will take it amiss should his livestock disappear. We do not want the bailiffs upon us, do we?'

'I can outsmart a bailiff,' the man said under his breath.

'But the boy there may *not*,' Ruairi hissed. 'Would you see him transported for poaching?'

'You've been at the Plough?' Aoife asked brightly, deftly turning the conversation. 'It's a pity they do not allow music and dancing on Sundays. We had a goodly haul of sixpences last night.'

'Music, dancing and billiards are banned on Sundays^{viii},' Ruairi acknowledged, 'but,' with a wink, 'not five-and-ten^{ix}, if discreetly played.' He rummaged in the pocket of his britches and brought out a fistful of coins, which he passed to the priest. 'Here are my winnings, Father Fearghal, to go into the communal chest. In any case,' he went on, 'I do not think it wise for you to dance too frequently, Aoife. Anything too commonly available loses its allure.'

'Tell that to the village swains,' one of the older men grumbled. 'They do not tire of Aoife's smiles no matter how often she bestows them. Aye, and I suppose she is free with other favours too, but not here. *We* have too few sixpences.'

Aoife gave him an artificial smile and said, 'A smile costs nothing.'

'Soap is costly though,' Conn's mother remarked. 'I wish *I'd* had time to bathe *my* feet today.' She looked down at her filthy feet and swollen legs.

'I helped with the supper,' Aoife returned, snappishly, 'and I think I earn more than all your posies and palm-readings put together.' She gave Ruairi a fiery look. 'Do I not? What is my tally, in comparison with theirs?'

'Oh! The men shower their shillings on you, Aoife, we all know that. But what for?' said Mícheál, the grumbler.

'We all earn and contribute what we can,' Ruairi said mildly. 'It's what we agreed.'

'You will sail too close to the wind one day, Aoife,' warned one of the widows. 'Some men can only be played on so far. A smile, to some, is as good as a promise.'

Dónall stepped forward, his brow dark and his fists clenched. 'I ... I ...' he stuttered, 'I won't—'

'Oh! We know, Dónall. Do not fear. No one will annoy Aoife while you are by,' Ruairi soothed. 'You are her knight, are you not?'

Conn's father nudged Mícheál. 'When he is *not* by ...' he gasped breathily.

Mícheál grinned. 'Aye. That is a different story. She does not have the look of being much 'annoyed,' does she?'

Supper over, the children were hustled to bed, which in most cases was no more than a blanket beneath a stretched canvas awning. The old woman was helped to bed on one of the sleeping platforms within a wagon by her son and his wife, and the harpist quickly moved to occupy her chair. Conn and Dónall set off to set their snares amongst the low-growing shrubs of the moor, with Conn's mother, Brónach, cautioning both to take care not to fall into a bog, and to go speedily to their rest as soon as they returned. Wearily, the women gathered the dishes and rinsed them in one of the buckets before stumbling off to their beds, bone tired. Aoife measured oats and water and a shaving of salt into the cooking pot, not troubling herself to clean out the remnants of the stew beforehand, and put it back over the ashes of the fire to make the following day's porridge. Then she resumed her seat on the steps of the *vardo*, taking out a tortoiseshell comb and drawing it languidly through her long, black hair.

Fionn, the squint-eyed man who did not fear bailiffs, got out a flat board that he placed upon his knee, three small cups and an acorn. He began to practise a trick, hiding the acorn beneath a cup and then moving the cups around with swift dexterity so that it was impossible to keep track of the acorn, which had, in any case, usually been palmed.

Soon, with the exception of Aoife, only men remained by the fire. Conn and Dónall joined them once the snares were set, in defiance of Brónach's decree. The men passed a flagon amongst them—by-passing Conn and Dónall, and spoke in low voices.

The man with the missing arm said, 'I wish we could afford better vittles for the children—fruit, and fresh bread. But I suppose we must husband our resources against the winter.'

'There will be fruit enough in the hedgerows in another month or so, Lorcán,' someone said. 'And come apple-harvest time, the children will have their fill.'

'God willing, the weather will hold until then. We cannot remain here beyond the autumn,' his neighbour agreed. 'Mother is too frail. I hear Kent is milder. But if we are to get there in time for the hops, we would have to set off before the end of July. 'Tis a long trek.'

'I'm for staying in Yorkshire,' said Lorcán. 'We have encountered less distrust here than elsewhere. There are vacant cottages in the village. Or, the women and children might get work in a mill. They are sometimes preferred. Their fingers are more nimble.'

'Brónach and me shall not go into a town,' her husband wheezed. 'I cannot work in a mill or factory—'

'No more can I,' said Lorcán, raising his stump.

'I, for one, would not wish to take up the tenancy of a cottage,' said another man. 'It would be too permanent. Too comfortable. Being in England is necessary *now*, but it isn't forever. I want to go home.'

'There are better opportunities in the town,' Fionn said, but not looking up from his board where the little cups moved so quickly they were blurred.

'For cheating and thievery, you mean? But I will not be supported by my wife and children. I'd rather we all starved.'

'No one will be allowed to starve,' said Ruairi. 'It is not yet the longest day. There is plenty of time for us to decide about our winter quarters. In the meantime, there is haymaking tomorrow for those who are able, at Drystone Farm. The farmer expects us as soon as the dew is dried from the grass. But Cillian,' he turned to the asthmatic man, 'the chaff will be too much for you. You'll take Dónall and Conn back to Clough Farm and continue with the stones. 'Tis backbreaking work, I know. But Dónall is strong and Conn is a quick learner. It's time the two lads took their share in the labour.'

Conn suppressed a sigh. Dónall was no more a lad than Ruairi was. In terms of age he could easily have been as old as three- or four-and-twenty, but in mental capacity he was as young as Conn's little sister and sometimes as difficult to manage. Yet it often fell to Conn's lot to take Dónall under his wing. However, to please his father he said, 'I'll work hard, Da. I don't want to be left with the women and children.'

Dónall didn't look so sure. He would not object to moving stones. He was strong, and mechanical repetitive work did not trouble him. But he understood that stone-moving at Clough Farm would separate him from Aoife. 'But ... but ...' he began. 'What about ... the market?'

Aoife routinely danced on market days in the local town, while the other women sold posies of heather, eggs if there were any, and fortunes that they made up, none of them having 'the sight.' Occasionally one of them would pick up a day's work laundering, but this was rare; the townsfolk did not trust the Irish in their houses. On market days Dónall watched over Aoife, fending off local lads who tried to take liberties, and guarding the hoard of farthings and halfpennies that were thrown into the case of the harp. So long as he did not speak, kept his face impassive and suppressed his natural smile he presented a convincingly intimidating figure; sturdy, broad-chested, with fists like hams.

'It isn't market day tomorrow,' Ruairi said. 'Do not fear, Dónall. Aoife and the others will be quite safe here. Now I think you should go to bed. Someone will rouse you at dawn.'

Conn and Dónall went to their rest, but Aoife and the other men remained by the fire.

Fionn began to pack away his cups. He said, 'I shall go into town tomorrow and look about me. I am not so sure I would not do better on my own. I have no wife or children to consider.'

'You must do as you think fit,' said Ruairi. 'But take care.'

The moon began to set. Darkness, kept at bay by its light, began to encroach at last across the moor. The shadow of the standing stone faded into the grey of the turf as though the stone itself was sinking into the peat of the moor, its black form enveloped by the dark until the two were indistinguishable.

The turfs of the fire glowed beneath the cooking vessel. Soon they were the only source of light apart from the canopy of stars that now glimmered in the vastness of space.

The village clock struck one, its mellow clang sounding clearly across the moor. The men exchanged glances. Aoife collected the flagon and put it beneath the steps of the *vardo* and brought out from the same location a number of shillelaghs[x], which she handed to Ruairi. Lorcán got up from his seat and crossed the clearing to where the horses drowsed in their stall. Silently, he put one between the shafts of the cart, muffling the rattle and chink of the bridle, disturbing the dogs who were snoring beneath the cart. Two of the men went to their respective wagons and returned wearing dark caps pulled low over their ears, and black coats. Fionn and the priest stowed rope and canvas into the cart. Aoife used a taper from the fire and lit two covered lanterns, which she passed to the men.

Ruairi shrugged his coat back on. He said, 'A prayer for us, Father? That we meet with no evil?'

'For all the good it will do you. *Benedicat tibi Dominus, et custodiat te. Ostendat Dominus faciem suam tibi, et misereatur tui. Convertat Dominus vultum suum ad te, et det tibi pacem.*[xi]'

The men stood around the clearing.

Someone—but who, in the darkness, it was impossible to say—said, 'You're sure he'll come?'

'He'll come,' said Ruairi.

They all tuned their ears but the silence was absolute, all sound sucked up into the vast dome of the night sky.

Aoife, close at Ruairi's side although he had not heard her approach, said, 'What time shall you return? I shall have tea waiting.' She drew a dark shawl around her shoulders.

'About four o'clock, if all goes well. Before dawn anyway, God willing.'

One of the dogs growled, swiftly hushed by one of the men.

'Here he is,' said Ruairi.

Lorcán and Mícheál climbed into the seat of the wagon. The others perched themselves behind, on the flatbed.

Ruairi strode forward a few paces to where a man stood outside the faint glow of the lanterns. 'Mr Harlish,' he said, extending a hand. 'We've a fine evening for it. You've no lantern?'

'I need none,' said Frank Harlish. He looked past Ruairi at the little group gathered round the cart. Seeing Aoife amongst them he snatched off his hat and began to mash it in his hands. 'Miss,' he said. 'I hope you do not ... that is, this is no work for a lady.'

'Pah!' Cillian, Conn's father, spat on the ground. 'Aoife is no lady!'

Frank looked as though he might make objection to this, stepping forward a pace and fixing Cillian with a glare, but Ruairi said, 'Let us go. It wants barely three hours to dawn and we've a long way to travel.'

Frank turned his eyes to Aoife and she favoured him with a dazzling smile and an elegant curtsey. For a moment his expression was the perfect picture of hopeless desire and naked admiration, such as Aoife saw dozens of times a day from virtually every man who laid his eyes upon her. She was used to it, though she did not discount its power. For Frank, however, the feelings that engendered the expression, and the expression itself, were new and foreign. He allowed himself to gaze upon her for a few seconds, blinked and swallowed, then turned and led the way along the close-cropped bridleway. Ruairi made a signal and Lorcán clicked his tongue to urge the horse forward. In a moment they had been absorbed into the night.

Aoife, Cillian and the priest returned to the fireside where the harpist slumbered in the old woman's chair.

'I'll sleep for a few hours,' said Cillian, turning towards the wagon where Brónach and the children slept.

'So will I, if I can,' said the other man, throwing himself down onto the carpet where the children had sat earlier. He closed his eyes and was almost instantly asleep.

Aoife returned to her seat on the steps of her *vardo* and took up her comb once more. She stared into the glowing embers of the fire. A small smile played on her lips.

Chapter 8

Conn and Dónall lay together beneath the wagon and watched the men depart on their clandestine business.

'Where're they going?' Dónall asked.

'They go to do some moonlight work,' said Conn knowledgeably. 'Poaching, perhaps.' He lay on his pallet with his hands behind his head and looked up at the underside of the wagon, dimly illuminated by dying firelight, tracing the faint line of the axle, the knots that tied the canvas awning in place. Somewhere not far away he could hear some insect making its way through the grass.

Dónall creased his brow. 'Rabbits?'

'Deer, more likely, or pheasant. Go to sleep, Dónall. We are to work alongside the men tomorrow.'

'There is no market,' said Dónall, yawning.

'No, not tomorrow. When we are done, shall we try for some fish by the river? I can try and fashion some tackle.'

Dónall made no reply, and Conn thought he was asleep until he said, 'Brónach has a baby in her belly.'

Conn sighed. 'Yes.

'How did it get there?'

Conn turned his head. Dónall's pale eyes shone in the darkness. 'I suppose my father put it there. Do you not know about such things?'

Dónall shook his head. His face creased this way and that as he tried to get his thoughts into a shape he could manage but in the end he only said, 'Aoife would not say.'

'You have seen the dogs do it often enough,' said Conn. 'It is like that, I suppose, but Father Fearghal says that people must wait until they are married, or it is a sin. I would not trouble yourself about it.'

'Aoife is not married,' Dónall said, partly comforted. But then the image of the dogs copulating came to him, vivid as day. In relation to Aoife it distressed him; but also, in a way he did not understand, it fascinated him. Something in his groin roiled. He pressed it down with his hand but that only made it worse.

'Not yet, anyway.' Conn yawned. 'Good night, Dónall.' He turned on his side, but Dónall rose up onto one elbow.

'Aoife can't … No. She mustn't …' His hand moved furtively beneath the blanket, making a delicious ache that must be stroked before it would go away.

Conn turned back to look at him. 'Mustn't get married?'

'N… no. And not … like the dogs.' He swallowed thickly. The more he tried to stop it the worse—and the better—it got. 'And there mustn't be … a baby,' he said through gritted teeth.

Conn settled himself back down. 'I know what you mean. There isn't enough to go around as it is. But babies do come once the vows are exchanged. They do not seem to be able to stop themselves. What are you doing? Have you got an ant down your pants? Stop twitching and go to sleep, Dónall.'

Dónall continued to fidget, however, squirming restlessly until at last, with a little cry, he went still.

Conn heard the church clock strike the half hour and the old woman's snores and a faint whicker from one of the horses. He thought about the day to come—how hard the work might be, how he would like to impress his father, and wondered if he would get a larger share of food. His stomach felt hollow. It always did.

Above him he heard one of the little children cry out and a woman's voice soothing it back to sleep.

Dónall said, 'My mother … she died …'

Conn sighed. 'I thought you were asleep. Yes, I know, Dónall. It sometimes happens. And sometimes the baby dies. Father Fearghal says it is God's will. Is that why you don't want Aoife to have a baby? Because you worry that she will die?'

Dónall thought about it for a while. 'No,' he said at last. 'It is because … because … I do not want to share.'

51

Chapter 9

It was past two o'clock when Herbert Somersall and Stephen Milton returned to Somersall Grange. Two braziers smoked and guttered either side of the impressive sweep of steps where the carriage decanted them before proceeding beneath an archway and into the stable yard. Other than the braziers the house was entirely dark, its shutters fastened behind the dozen or so windows that flanked the front door on either side. The house was flat-fronted, dour and raw in its newness, as though freshly flayed. No creeper or weathering had had the opportunity to soften its façade and Mr Somersall had not cared to pay for the ornamentation of stonework, the elegance of mullion or the nicety of architectural embellishment that would have added beauty to the sheer size that was the building's only boast. Piles of dressed stone and heaps of gravel made dark mounds on the rough, unseeded apron at the front of the house that would one day be lush lawns and ornamental shrubberies. Scaffolding still clung to the house's east gable, where the chimneys were but half built and the leading incomplete.

A weary footman opened the door at the gentlemen's knock and handed them their chamber sticks, imparting the information that Mr Somersall had departed early in the evening for his house in town, so as to be at his desk in the colliery offices at cockcrow.

'The master expects to see you both there,' the footman said. 'Shall I send word to the stables that your horses should be made ready?'

'I shall not go to the works tomorrow,' said Herbert recklessly, yawning to conceal his daring. 'A man does not woo *and* work. The old man must be made to understand that if he sets me to this task, I shall go at it until it is done.'

'It is no very arduous work though, is it?' asked Stephen. 'I thought the young lady pleasant enough.'

'She is pleasant,' Herbert agreed. 'But the curate has already staked a claim that must be undermined before I can make my move. The lady must be willing. I will not have any wife, be she ever so pretty, against her own wishes.'

'I have not your excuse to avoid work,' said Stephen gloomily, and gave direction that his horse should be saddled and ready by six.

The two men mounted the wide, sweeping stair to the upper floor, their wavering candle flames illuminating large canvasses, pedestals with marble busts and the skeleton of an enormous chandelier suspended from the lofty heights of a frescoed ceiling. Although frugal of adornment outside, Mr Somersall had not quibbled at the expense of furnishing the interior of his house, reasoning that these movable appurtenances were investments and could be sold if necessary, while exterior columns, pediments and entablatures—be they doric or ionic—being fixtures, could never give any pecuniary return.

'What a dreadful, artificial and pretentious place this is,' Stephen remarked, his voice strangely amplified by the vast proportions of the place. 'It seeks to establish generations of family history, grand tours, proud annals of ancestral derring-do ... when in fact your family tree—like mine—is but a sapling. Indeed, mine is hardly more than an acorn as yet.'

'You are right,' Herbert said good-naturedly. 'Five minutes would more than encompass the reading of the Somersall exploits. No wonder my mother has not the brass neck to go out and call upon her neighbours. She was much happier in Ferret Street. Here's my room, or the room I suppose to be mine. With all these doors it is almost impossible to be sure. Good night, Milton.'

The two men parted company. Happy coincidence had led Herbert to the correct door and his valet was within, dozing in a chair by the fire. In five minutes Herbert was in his warm bed and in two more he was fast asleep.

Stephen Milton had no valet. His room was dark, the fire long since gone out, his bed neither turned down nor containing a warming pan. He

53

flung off his clothes and climbed between the chilly sheets, disgruntled at his bed's lack of comfort, but even so not relishing the need to get up from it so soon. He lay on his back for a while, his hands clasped behind his head, and thought about Herbert's prospective bride—insipidly sweet, a porcelain doll which would likely break or cry if confronted with even a suggestion of hardship. What good would she be to a man? Unlike Beth Harlish. Now *there* was a woman who would make herself useful, who would not expect a soft life but who would labour alongside her husband, who had a mind to understand and a heart to care and—yes, he was sure he had discerned it—a core of molten passion. There was a woman worth the winning. He considered the sharp surge of defensiveness—of jealousy, even—that had risen up in him over her, in relation to the Irish people. He couldn't justify it. What was she to him? And she had a brother to protect her. But as he mulled the matter over he felt it again—a hot, involuntary rush of possessiveness.

At half past five a footman brought hot water for shaving, a pot of coffee and some bread and cold meat to Stephen's room, and by six he was mounted and half a mile from Somersall Grange.

It was a full five hours later when Herbert was roused by his mother, who brought him a tray of breakfast.

Mrs Somersall was a small fine-boned tremulous woman, perpetually astonished by her husband's precipitous rise in the mercantile firmament and, to be truthful, not at all comfortable amongst all the great evidence of that rise. Of the abundant and choicest foods with which her table was these days supplied she could not partake, due to severe dyspepsia. Fine wine brought on the migraine. Her closets were full of beautiful gowns for morning, afternoon and evening wear, lace collars, stiff petticoats, leather boots and silk slippers, cambric nightdresses, embroidered shawls and wraps of the softest cashmere, but all of these hung off her bony frame like rags from a scarecrow. Similarly, her jewellery—rings and brooches, collars and tiaras—would better have adorned the maid than they did the mistress. She had not the bearing, the figure, the confidence or the pleasure in them that would make them truly her own. Like the Turkey rugs, the ornately carved chairs, the heavy draperies, fine china and solid silver that proliferated throughout the house, she felt that her clothes were temporary, on loan, likely to be recalled. Fundamentally, she did not feel worthy; and her husband—full of hubris and spleen—did nothing to encourage her. As mistress of this great new house and of the town house—equally fine if not so large—she felt utterly cowed by the weight of stone and timber and slate. She had not dared to enter more than a dozen of the rooms of Somersall Grange, confining herself mainly to a sitting room that appended her bedroom, and betaking herself to the dining room and the drawing room only when her husband's presence in the house required her ministrations there.

Her son had spoken truly when he said she had been more comfortable in Ferret Street, the first home that she and Mr Somersall had occupied upon their marriage. A good house, squeezed in between the chambers of a barrister and the premises of a wine merchant, with a dining room and a scullery on the ground floor, a parlour and a bedroom above and, in the attic, room for Mrs Somersall's maid-of-all-work, advisor, friend and bastion, Ida Plim. A comfortable house, a house suitable for a colliery foreman and his wife, a house very fit for the evening entertainment of those within their social sphere—not the barrister or the wine merchant, to be sure, but the draper, the chandler, the curate and his sickly wife, the bailiff and the captain of the customs men. Many was the happy hour spent with Ida in that cosy scullery, buffing up the little pieces of brass that were the house's pride-and-joy, hemming pillowcases and crocheting antimacassars and, in due course, making the layette for baby Herbert. And what was she—Mrs Somersall—to do *now*, when all the pillowcases came ready hemmed and the bits of brass had been dispensed with alongside the antimacassars and the services of poor Ida Plim?

Mrs Somersall, in her new situation of Lady of the Grange and wife to the successful colliery owner, was lonely, fretful and disposed to melancholy; so very glad was she, that June morning, to find her son in residence at Somersall Grange. She brought in the breakfast tray with her own hands and opened the curtains just sufficiently to rouse the sleeper to wakefulness. She smoothed the hair back from her darling's face, kissed his cheeks and helped him sit up against the pillows before handing him tea.

'Now,' said she, perching on the edge of a chair, 'tell me of your dinner at the vicarage.'

'Oh,' he yawned, 'it was very nice. I suppose you have not heard from Father. I rather think he expected me at the works today. He has not sent any message?'

Mrs Somersall flinched at the idea, her wary eyes darting here and there as though a message might come shrieking from the cornice or fly like a Valkyrie down the chimney. Her husband's messages could be quite as upsetting as the man himself. 'Nothing has been brought to me,' she squeaked. That much was true. Even if a messenger had galloped the eight miles from the colliery with Mr Somersall's vitriol stinging its flanks, how could she help it if the message had not been brought? There was such a fuss about these things. The footman must have the receiving of the message, and the butler must put it on a silver tray, and then there were the long corridors to be navigated, and the innumerable stairs, and the doors … one room led into another in such a very confusing way … she was sure there must be a dozen servants at this very moment lost within the labyrinth of antechambers and retiring rooms, galleries and landings. 'Perhaps you ought to send a word,' she suggested, 'to explain … that is, to request …'

'Oh! I shall not trouble the groom,' Herbert said, swallowing a thickly buttered muffin. 'And, after all, if I were to get up now and set off, I could not be there before two, and by that time my father will be at the docks. Tell me, Mother, is there a hot house here?'

'A hot house?'

'Yes, with flowers and such like. I should like to send a bouquet to Miss Eagerly.'

'Well, I believe there is a room with plants and flowers. A glass room. With a fountain. I went in once, but I could not tell you where it is. A bouquet for Miss Eagerly? She was nice then, was she? She was not *very* brown?'

'Brown? Well no. Not noticeably so. She is dark, that is, her hair is dark, and her eyes. But I would say her complexion was very pleasing. She was nice. Very pretty. Young. I invited her to call on you.'

'Oh!' Mrs Somersall's hand flew to her mouth. 'You did not! Oh, Herbert! How could you? What for? How will I know what to say? Will they expect tea? But I cannot—'

'The butler will serve the tea, Mother. Or perhaps the housekeeper. You need only sit and smile and talk about the weather.'

Mrs Somersall looked doubtfully out of the window. 'It has been very fine,' she said under her breath, practicing. 'We have been enjoying very fine weather of late.'

'Perfect!' Herbert threw back the covers and got out of bed. 'Please ring the bell, Mother. I will bathe, I think. And in the meantime, you can make enquiry as to the location of the hot house and gather the flowers for me, and I will take them myself to the vicarage. Have the groom saddle my horse.'

Chapter 10

The morning after the vicar's dinner, when Beth got downstairs there was still no sign of Frank. His mattress remained rolled and stowed neatly behind the settle. The fire was almost out and the kettle cold. The dog raised his head from the hearth rug and thumped his tail.

It was still early. Mist lay over the moor in a pale lilac haze, but above it the sun and the cloudless blue sky—just visible through the whorls of mist—promised another hot day. Bejewelled cobwebs, like finery discarded after a ball, covered the garden. The path was a network of silvery snail trails. Beth went to let the hens out of their coop, scattering feed before reaching into the laying boxes, but it was too early for them to have laid. She visited the privy and then filled the kettle at the pump, squinting down the lane in the expectation of Frank's long-legged, loping figure coming through the mist towards her—but the lane was empty.

She stirred life into the fire, made tea and cut bread for breakfast, laying Frank a place and leaving it *in situ* after she had eaten and cleared her own cup and plate away. She left his, not as an accusation, but in the same spirit in which he, the night before, had left her slippers by the fender and the last slice of pie on the plate. His plate and cup and knife on the table said, 'You were missed. I am worried.'

Frank's and Beth's was a kinship of action rather than words, their mutual affection demonstrated by acts of kindness. Frank was, anyway, a man of few words; such conversation as he had was pithy and to the point. He would be embarrassed by verbal assurances of fondness. So far as Beth could recall she had never kissed her brother, or held his hand, but that did not mean she did not love him. His care for her was demonstrated in his protection over her, in his undertaking of the hard labour of the garden and down at the house, in fetching of water and bringing in of logs and peats for the fire, in his unquestioning acceptance of that restlessness of spirit that he did not share but that he knew clouded her soul.

Lately his introspection had increased, and he had been missing for hours—but never the whole night long. She thought she knew the cause. It worried her, but she trusted Frank. He was steady, and would do nothing rash.

Beth made dough and left it to prove in the alcove above the fire while a pot of hot water came to the simmer. Then she washed Frank's shirt, her stockings and some few other small items, which she hung on the line in the garden. Then, before the sun had fully burned away the mist, she let herself out of the gatehouse, leaving the key behind a loose stone in the wall and lifting an admonishing hand to the dog, which would have liked to accompany her. 'You must stay and watch the hens,' she said, latching the gate in place. 'But this afternoon, you shall come with me to see the women by the standing stone; and if you can catch a rabbit or hare on the way, all the better.'

She rounded the building and was surprised to see that the ornate gates, usually closed and padlocked shut, were open. She had not heard their rasp and creak, nor the passage of any horse or vehicle. Panic clutched at her throat. Had the family come? Would she arrive at the house to find the Talbots or the Stockbridges there, a posse of servants carrying in trunks and boxes and provisions? Why had they not written to let her know they proposed a visit? The furniture was covered in sheets! The rooms were not aired! The chimneys had not been swept since the previous winter! There had seemed no point, when month had followed month and year had followed year and still nobody had come.

She quickened her pace, half-running down the steep incline of the drive, which switchbacked left and right down the thickly forested slope. There was a quicker way, a secret way—a path through the trees, over rills of running water and round moss-encrusted boulders. She and Frank had run up and down it all their lives but it was very steep, and while the morning mist was dissipating up on the moor, here in the hollow it was still thick; she might turn an ankle or worse. Finally, that path would bring her out in the garden, by the stone fountain—an area reserved for the family's use. For her to be there while they were in residence would be an intrusion.

It was chill under the canopy of the trees—the mist a damp shroud—but noisy with birdsong and the sounds of other scuttling, rustling things that lived in the hollow. Beth tuned her ears for the noises of human activity, the whinny of horses, the running feet of children on the gravel sweep, but heard only her own, labouring breaths and the skitter of her feet on the lose shale of the path.

She felt—as she always did when descending into the combe—a sense of entering some mysterious realm, a primeval place where the ordinary rules did not apply, a domain of dryads and nymphs. A forgotten place, enslaved by loneliness. But she shook off these fancies. If the family had come there would be work to do, perhaps tempers to soothe, arrangements to be made with the coal merchant, the butcher and the purveyor of game, for the icehouse was empty apart from a last flitch of bacon. Would the furnace work? For they would surely want hot water. Frank had not tested it since Easter ... her thoughts ran on as her feet covered the ground.

And then the trees thinned, and the shale of the drive gave way to the finer gravel of the sweep, and the house was before her. It wallowed in a thick grey soup of mist but Beth did not need her eyes to see the solid edifice of stone with its portico and datestone, blank inscrutable windows and proud towering chimneys. So well did she know it that she could conjure its smallest detail in her mind's eye, could have made her way from room to room blindfolded.

No carriage stood before the door, which was shut fast as she had last left it. There was no tumble of trunks and portmanteaux, no hurry of servants, no fluster of flapping dust sheets. The house stood as it always did—grandly enigmatic, beautifully neglected, keeping its secrets.

Poor old place. Forsaken still. But not by her.

Beth stood, breathing heavily, jealously surveying the beautiful stonework of the house, its lovely symmetry, the classical balance of its windows.

She murmured, 'I see you. I have not forgotten you.'

Through the miasma of greyish vapour, as through a dirty window of memory, she wrought a vision of herself and Frank and their siblings as children, with little Georgina, playing—as they had been permitted and even encouraged to do—on the lawn and along the terrace. Mrs Orphan, the housekeeper, tending the vegetable and physic garden. Mr Burleigh, the groom, showing her brother Arthur the workings of things in the stable yard. And Miss Jocelyn, who became Mrs Willow and was now Mrs

59

Stockbridge, who had not been like any real lady but who had worked alongside them, getting her hands dirty and not caring. If Beth squinted her eyes through the brume of recollection she could almost see her father disappearing into the plantation with a bow saw or a bag of feed for the pheasants he reared there, though no one ever came to shoot them. And her mother, like as not sitting in some patch of sunshine and humming contentedly to herself, neglecting the chores ... and the calling to mind of these scenes gave Beth such a pang of nostalgia and grief, especially for her beloved father, that tears sprang into her eyes adding more mist to the morning haze.[xii]

Voices drifted through her woe and distraction, from the direction of the stable yard.

She walked quickly along the drive as though, were she fast enough, she might glimpse the ghosts of her childhood. She passed around the north wing of the house to where a cobbled enclosure connected the kitchens to the stables, smoke house and other ancillary buildings, and there stopped abruptly.

A man stood by the water trough with his back to her. He was stripped to the waist; his grubby shirt hung from the pump handle. His shoulders were wide set and corded with sinew and muscle, the skin tanned. His back was long, tapering to the waist. He stood immobile, as though petrified by some enchantment, a carved statue that—impossibly—she had never noticed before. The voices she thought she'd heard were silenced. Beth dashed her arm across her eyes and shook her head to dispel the fancy because while surely the ghosts and visions she had invoked were only that—whims and daydreams—this was a solid, breathing, flesh-and-blood man.

Something about her action broke the spell. As though released, the man bent and submerged his head and upper torso in the cold water, coming up again gasping, scrubbing at his face, neck and body with a piece of soap before dousing himself again, shaking his head to dislodge the water from his thick, black hair.

Then a woman emerged from the kitchen door. Beth recognised her. It was Aoife, the Irish dancer, but dressed now in a sober skirt and modest blouse with a thick knitted wrap tied close across her body against the chill morning air. Her long, lustrous hair was bound back, tamed by a strip of material. She carried two mugs which added their steam to the vapour that still lingered, and beneath her arm was a bundle of linen.

Aoife saw Beth and stopped abruptly, slopping the tea over the sides of the mugs.

The man, following Aoife's gaze, turned. Unwilling to look and yet absolutely unable to look away, Beth eyed the whorls of black hair that covered his broad chest, narrowed to a vee and disappeared into the waistband of his britches. She dragged her eyes to his face. Dark brows over blue eyes. A strong nose and wide, passionate mouth. His jaw and chin were shadowed; he needed a shave. It was Ruairi Connolly, the leader of the Irish folk. Although *they* were the intruders, unaccountably present at Tall Chimneys having opened the gates and gained access to the kitchen—Beth could by no means explain this circumstance to herself—it was Beth who blushed, who felt as though she trespassed.

'I'm … I'm sorry,' she stammered, turning to leave.

The two interlopers looked at one another, some agreement passing between them. Aoife handed Ruairi the linen—a clean shirt—and Ruairi began to pull it on.

'Oh, but Miss Harlish,' said Aoife with tooth-jarring sweetness, placing the cups on the edge of the trough and coming across the cobbles, 'it is we who must apologise. What must you think of us? And you're as white as a sheet, as though you'd seen a ghost!'

She guided Beth towards an old mounting block and bid her sit on it. 'I'll fetch you tea. They say it's good for shock. And then we'll explain everything. Your brother—'

'Frank is here?' Beth got out.

'Of course he is!' Aoife laughed, musically but not very authentically. 'You do not imagine we'd have the gall to make free without him?'

The sun was at last dispersing the mist and Beth could see, beyond the trough, the door of the coach house standing open and Frank on its threshold, wiping his hands on a rag, disturbed from whatever work he was engaged upon by the voices in the yard.

'Betsey!' he cried, throwing the rag aside and coming quickly to where she sat. 'Are you well? What is amiss?' He squatted beside her.

Aoife retreated, murmuring about another cup of tea, and discreetly Ruairi followed her into the kitchen.

Beth hissed, '*You* are amiss, Frank! Where have you been all night? And what is afoot *here*? Why are these people here?'

'Oh.' Frank stood up and his eye slid away from hers. 'Their cart lost its pin. I'm just making a repair. We had to manage the thing between us halfway across the moor.' He showed her his arm and the side of his hand, which were grazed and bruised from where he'd had to press against the cartwheel to keep it in place.

'But why here?'

'Well.' He shrugged. 'The forge is closed, you know.'

Beth clicked her tongue. 'Don't be obtuse, Frank. You know what I mean. What business were you about? With them? In the dead of night?'

Frank was saved the requirement of giving her an answer by the arrival of Ruairi Connolly, bearing a cup of tea balanced with painstaking care on its delicate saucer. She knew the china had come from the dresser in the servants' hall, altogether superior to the earthenware mugs the Irish people had chosen for themselves. The significance of this small differentiation softened Beth somewhat. Even more of her distrust was undermined by the disarming brilliance of Ruairi's smile.

'That will restore you, Miss Harlish,' he said, handing over the tea. ''Tis good strong tea. Best Assam, I'm told.'

Beth sipped the tea. It was excellent. But she knew that no tea of such quality would have been left in the kitchen at Tall Chimneys. 'Where did it—'

'A grateful customer,' said Ruairi. 'People often pay us in kind rather than in coin. And Aoife was so fortunate as to meet with the dairyman on her way, so it's fresh milk you have. Now I must beg your forgiveness for my state of undress just before, Miss Harlish. I wouldn't embarrass a lady for the world, but it's a hard night of it we've had, is it not, Mr Harlish? And your man here worked harder than any to navigate our way and to keep the wheel on! But I thought to refresh myself while he fixed the pin, for I've to go straight from here to the haymaking at Drystone farm, and I'd no notion you would be witness.'

His charm was almost irresistible—his blue eyes so sincere, his smile wide and genuine—but Beth clung to her purpose. 'And what, precisely, was the nature of the business you had with my brother?' At her side, she felt Frank cringe with awkwardness.

But without a moment's hesitation Ruairi said, 'We went to the lime kiln across the moor. Mr Slade requires lime to make mortar and I undertook to collect it. Your brother was so good as to act as guide. The paths, you know—'

'Of course I know,' Beth interrupted. 'But why at night?'

'So much cooler for the horse,' Aoife said lightly, joining them. 'Not to mention the men! And we cannot afford to lose a day's labour on the farms, miss. We must work while there is work to be had. I hope you do not object to my using your kitchen to make breakfast. Your brother said it would be alright.' Aoife took a pace closer to Frank, as though sheltering herself from Beth's possible remonstrance. Frank drew himself up but seemed at the same time to become less substantial, as though the least breath of air from Aoife's lips would disperse him like a dandelion clock.

Aoife said, 'There's bacon in the skillet, and I brought bread. I am sorry it isn't fresh.'

Beth said, 'Bacon? You've brought out the last flitch?'

Frank coloured, and dug the toe of his boot about in the gravel. 'It would not have lasted much longer,' he mumbled. 'The ice is all gone.'

'So kind as you are,' Aoife observed sweetly, 'to share what you have with those in need.'

Awkwardness hung in the air. Ruairi drained his mug. Aoife looked up at Frank through her lashes. Beth kept her accusing eyes on her brother.

'It's no different to the potatoes, I suppose,' Frank flung out defensively to Beth, and marched back to the coach house.

'Perhaps, after all ...' Ruairi said, 'it would be better if we breakfasted back at the camp. If the cart is repaired?'

'Oh no!' Beth, stung into remorse, got to her feet. 'Forgive me. I am tired and ... I was taken by surprise to find you here. But now everything is made clear, and of course you shall have the bacon, and take such of it back as you can use. Thank you for the tea. I must get on with my chores. Excuse me.'

She walked past them, using the kitchen door to gain access to the house, noting the neat air of the kitchen and the economical little fire lit in the range, just enough for the kettle and the skillet of bacon that sizzled and spat on the hotplate.

She mounted the stairs and went from room to room, flinging open shutters and sliding open the casements to admit the morning air, which was fresh now, the earlier mist having been burned away by the summer sun. She cleared dead flies and moths from the window ledges and dusted spider webs, checked the fireplaces for soot falls and turned the mattresses in the principal bedrooms. She examined the linen presses carefully for signs of moth, placing bags of dried rosemary, thyme and lavender between the layers of sheets and pillowcases.

Chapter 11

Two hours later, her chores completed, she returned to the kitchen to find everything neat and orderly, as though no one had been there at all. The earthenware cups that Aoife and Ruairi had used were already washed and dried and back on their shelf exactly where they ought to be, and the china cup and saucer was back amongst its fellows on the dresser. There was no sign of the skillet and the coals in the fire had been carefully raked; they were already cold. She glanced into the housekeeper's rooms and the butler's pantry, and tried the door of the strongroom, where the silver and plate and the house's more valuable artefacts were secured, and then felt guilty. It was wrong of her to harbour suspicions of the immigrants—and hypocritical, for hadn't she just the previous night defended them to Mr Milton? She felt ashamed of her inhospitable behaviour—she must have appeared so rude—but could not deny the sense of satisfaction she felt that the house had been restored to her. It was not hers. She knew it was not hers. And yet, if she did not love it, who would?

She went into the pantry and found a bottle of elderflower cordial she had made earlier in the summer and prepared a glass for Frank.

She found him in the coach house where the Irish cart still stood, a brightly burnished pin in place to secure the wheel.

'They've gone?' She placed the glass of cordial on his workbench.

'Long ago.'

'But they haven't taken the cart?'

'Nor the horse. Poor thing is exhausted. It's in the stable yonder.'

Frank continued to work at something on the bench. She could not see what it was. He kept his head down, his shoulders hunched, working some tool. A shaft of sunlight illuminated his injured arm and hand. 'Shall I bring you some salve?' It was a gesture, an olive branch, but he did not take it.

He said, 'It'll do.'

She wandered around the coach house. Bags of coal were stacked in one corner. A ladder led up to the hayloft where she could glimpse various crates and tools. In the furthest corner of the space there was another heap she didn't recall having seen before, covered over with a thick canvas. She lifted the corner of it to peer beneath.

'Leave that,' Frank barked.

Beth dropped the canvas instantly, but turned a questioning face towards him.

'It's the lime,' Frank mumbled, not meeting her eye. 'It's caustic. If it gets in your eyes it can blind you.'

'Mr Slade didn't need it today?'

Frank shrugged. 'I know nothing about it. I was asked to guide them, and I did.' He seemed to struggle for a few moments, wanting to say more but apparently not knowing how. 'I thought you'd be glad,' he said at last.

'That you'd helped them? I am. But I wish you'd told me. I worried when you were not returned this morning.' Beth went to stand beside him, as Aoife had done earlier.

'I would have been, but for the wheel.' His tone was still gruff, and he did not look up from his task, but she sensed a softening.

She pressed it. 'I'm sorry about the bacon,' she said. 'I shouldn't have questioned it, especially not when ... not when they were here. It's as much yours as mine—'

'It isn't ours at all!' he interjected with a trace of dry humour. 'Not really. But who's going to eat it if we don't? And I gave them some apples out of the store. They are beginning to wizen, and are more than we will eat.'

'That's good. But still ... Miss Connolly ... Aoife ... I think you like her, and I embarrassed you.'

Frank's activity intensified and he turned away from her, purportedly to find some better light for his task, but she knew he was hiding his flaming cheek and her heart contracted within her. Frank was in love! But oh! with such an unworthy object! She wanted to reiterate the warning she had received the previous night from Mr Milton, that the Irish people would not return what they received and that one day they would go away, but she had not the heart to do it. 'They are brother and sister, are they not? The Connollys? Like us.'

Frank nodded.

'And the other young man. Dónall. Is he also her brother?'

Frank shook his head. 'A cousin, but brought up along with them. His mother died in the labouring, and the surgeon was overlong in his business. In the delay, the boy was denied breath. Indeed, I'm told he was not expected to be alive at all, so long was it. Ruairi—Mr Connolly—has a vague recollection of it though he was barely five years old himself. Anyway, once he was born the boy was placed in the cradle with Aoi … with Miss Connolly, and by some miracle he lived! Their mother nursed them both. But the damage was done, and they say Dónall's mind will never compass more than it did when he was a child. He is over-possessive of her … of Miss Connolly. But harmless, so long as she is let alone.'

It was a long speech for Frank, indicative of his intense interest in the young Irishwoman.

Beth said gently, 'But she is not let alone, is she? When she dances, she attracts every eye.'

She heard Frank swallow—a hard, dry gulp—and nudged the glass of cordial closer to his hand, but he said no more, as though his day's allocation of words had been used up.

Beth knew better than to press him further. The little breach in their accord was healed and she did not wish to risk another rift and so changed the topic by saying, 'Mrs Eagerly expressed an interest in going over the house, Frank. I can hardly refuse when they have been so hospitable to me, and the vicar has put me in the way of supplementing our income. Miss Eagerly took it upon herself to extend the invitation to the gentlemen who dined with us last night. But it would hardly be proper, would it? To show the house as though we owned it. And I know you would dislike it.'

Frank moved two or three tools around on the workbench while he considered. 'You must ask permission of Mrs Stockbridge. If she refuses, that would be reason enough to tell the vicar's wife you cannot oblige her.'

'I could write,' Beth said slowly. 'But Frank, if permission were granted, wouldn't you hate it?'

He shrugged. 'I would have little to do with it, I suppose. You would show the people around and then they'd go away. What would it be to me?'

'I would have to give them refreshment. And of course we have no one to wait upon them but ourselves. I can manage a light luncheon, but who will serve it?'

'That would be your own affair,' he said, making it clear that *he* would not assist. 'I suppose some of the Irishwomen might oblige,' he added. 'If the weather holds—which it will—you can use the terrace, or the lawn.'

'Oh, Frank,' she said, smiling. 'That is an excellent idea. There will be no need for the formality of the dining room. I should not like to set myself up as mistress by presiding there.'

Her pleasure softened him. 'Ask Mrs Golightly to provide the fare,' he said recklessly. 'You are as good a cook as she is, but I suppose you will not wish to receive your guests with flour in your hair, and the cost will not be more than we can manage. I was well compensated for my work last night, and I am told there is more of the like to be had if I wish. This day month, shall we say? That will be the third week in July. But do not get your hopes up. Mrs Stockbridge may say no.'

'Of course. But oh! Thank you, Frank.' Because she wished to repay his kindness she added, 'I thought to go to the camp this afternoon to see the woman who is with child. I have made some little garments and hemmed some cloths. Shall you accompany me? Perhaps, by then, the horse will be rested and we can return the cart.'

Frank grunted his assent. 'But first I must tend to the sow,' he said grimly. 'I never knew such a brute of a pig in my life. She almost bit me this morning, and makes daily attempts to escape her pen.'

'She will be cured and smoked before long. Then you will have the last laugh!'

Chapter 12

Mr Somersall's newest acquisition was the colliery at Ellingbeck,[xiii] and it was to this location that Stephen Milton rode to undertake his day's work, bleary with lack of sleep and fulminating with a sense of injustice.

In its comparatively recent historical iteration, Ellingbeck had been a place much like Moorside—that is to say a rural settlement with some farms and cottages, a mill, a smithy and an inn. It had been quite pretty in an artless, unconscious way until early in the second decade of the century, when the discovery of a seam of coal—deep and plentiful—had metamorphosed it into an industrial town with narrow, mean streets housing miners in terraces that had been thrown up with little care as to their attractiveness and none at all as regards their comfort. A dozen or more households shared a privy and a pump, and a communal cookhouse was the only means of producing a hot meal. Families were squashed into single rooms. Noise, filth, stench and sickness travelled unhindered by the thin partitions that separated one miserable little tribe of humanity from another.

Coal, naturally, was supplied at a discount for heating, making already-airless rooms more airless still and dirty to boot; the miners' meagre belongings, bedding and sticks of furniture were grimy with a greasy residue that was no sooner cleaned off than it materialised once more. The chimneys above the terraces spewed forth plumes of black noxious smoke, joining the smoke from the mine's engines and the steam locomotives that made their laborious way into the station. Summer and winter, smoke hung in a pall over the sorrowful place unless the wind dragged it, like a dirty curtain, briefly away. So utterly did it obscure any view of the moors, hills and green fields that still existed just a mile or two above the town, and so downcast were the inhabitants of Ellingbeck by the drudgery of their work in any case, that the fresher air and the soft green hue of the land might as well have been a hundred miles away or something they once dreamed to be true.

Nevertheless, above the town the beck after which the town was named—the Elling—still burbled over rocks and between green flower-strewn banks, all innocent as to its fate to be boiled in vats or used to sluice thick black greasy grime from the new-hewn coal. Below the town, to one side of the railway line, its waters were turgid and bitter, poisoning fish and leaving a slick rime on the flattened riverbanks. The countryside was decimated by piles of rubble and spoil, discarded machinery and several camps of would-be miners and hangers-on—washer women, midwives, apothecaries and barber-surgeons, pick-pockets, preachers, prostitutes and purveyors of illegally distilled gin.

Stephen Milton rode his horse along the rough streets of the little town and arrived at the chaotic collection of sheds and engine houses of the colliery just as the eight o'clock claxon sounded, summoning those fortunate enough to have employment in the offices of the colliery to their work. He threw the reins of his horse and a penny to a boy, with instruction that the horse should be taken to a certain livery stable and not to the place where the poor nags that pulled the coal trucks were housed. He quickly mounted some rickety wooden steps that led up the side of a building to a door located on the first floor. He paused for a moment, tidying his dress, wiping his face with a handkerchief and removing his hat to smooth down the thick waves of his hair before grasping the door handle and going inside.

He entered a large office where several desks were already occupied by sundry clerks, the colliery manager and Mr Somersall's man of business, who oversaw the finances of the concern. All looked up briefly from their work before reapplying themselves to their ledgers and letters with only the barest possible nod of acknowledgement to his 'Good morning, gentlemen.'

Stephen strode across the room to his own desk—or rather broad, sloping shelf—on which were laid the several large engineering drawings and blueprints that purported to describe the mine workings below ground, the rag-tag collection of buildings above, and the various pumps, engines and other pieces of machinery upon whose efficient and reliable operation the very lives of the miners depended. Since arriving in the north with his friend Herbert and accepting a temporary contract of employment from Mr Somersall, it had been Stephen's labour to compare the schematics of the mine with its actuality, and in many particulars had he found significant discrepancies between the two. Accordingly he had begun to produce his own accurate diagrams. Now he removed his coat and hat, rolled up his sleeves and recommenced the work he had left off the previous Saturday.

Two other rooms opened from the large general office, separated from it by a glazed partition. One, considerably the smaller, was the office allocated to Herbert. Inside it, a clerk busied himself with correspondence and filing, having ascertained by a brief glance that Herbert had not accompanied the young engineer.

The other room was occupied by Mr Somersall himself when he was in attendance at the colliery in Ellingbeck, which was by no means every day since he had other mines as well as interests in Whitby docks, and must frequently be in York or even Leeds for the pursuance of his other mercantile affairs. The office door was always kept closed and a blind pulled down over the window to hide the activity of the colliery owner from view, so whether he worked diligently reading reports, writing letters, perusing accounts and directing affairs until the sweat stood out on his brow and the fervour of his application rendered him into a blur of industry, no one knew. Likewise, if he spent his days with his feet upon the fender, a cigar between his lips and a romantic novel in his hand, no one knew that either.

On this morning, however, no visual confirmation was required to know what passed within. The glazing of the partition absolutely quivered and quaked with the sound of Mr Somersall's voice as he dressed down some poor underling in a deep, gruff and altogether unmusical voice, like the barking of some rough dog half strangled by a chain. His accent was broad and unashamedly Yorkshire, his language unadorned by any nicety of expression, being plain, matter-of-fact and unarguable. Unarguable in one respect, in that his lengthy soliloquies allowed for no interruption or reply; he spoke indefatigably, loudly, on and on without taking breath. Unarguable also in that he spoke in statements, in declarations, in pronouncements and decrees that asserted his own indisputable authority on all matters. Nobody was better informed, more thoroughly master, had looked into and acquainted themselves to better effect than he had—he contended. Even when he was factually incorrect—as he not infrequently was—any suggestion to that effect was proved by a misapplication of mathematics, an invention of statistics, an on-the-spot conjuring of new laws of physics, the rearrangement or even the creation of historical facts, to be erroneous.

All the men in the outer office shifted uneasily as Mr Somersall's rant continued, for they all knew that once commenced his ire was unlikely to be satisfied with the *hors d'oeuvre* of a single victim but would seek richer meat, and none wished to become the hapless *entrée*. One of the clerks left the office altogether, carrying a bundle of documents to some unspecified location. The remaining clerks spread out a file of correspondence and pored over it with exaggerated concentration. Their fellow, the man in Herbert's office, looked on with envious eyes because, without Herbert, he had in truth not much to occupy himself. Presently Stephen took pity on him and pressed a sixpence into his hand, sending him in search of a hot pie and a jug of coffee and saying in a low voice, 'No need to hurry, Jack. And on your way back, see that my horse is properly stabled at the livery, will you?' The clerk squashed his hat onto his head and scampered thankfully from the room.

Mr Somersall's diatribe sawed relentlessly on. Another five minutes, then five more ticked by on the clock.

The colliery manager made a show of consulting his pocket watch before hurriedly shrugging his coat on and walking purposefully from the room as though late for an important appointment, and the man of business was quick to follow his example when, at last, Mr Somersall's invective seemed on the point of conclusion. The man of business succeeded in exiting the office just as Mr Somersall's door opened and what remained of his interlocutor limped out.

It was the colliery foreman, a man known by Stephen to be able and experienced in the role, but a quietly spoken man who had struggled to gain the respect of the miners. Now he was white-gilled, barely able to put one foot in front of the other. One hand clenched his hat so tightly that it was a thing unrecognisable; his hand, even through its deeply ingrained grime, was white and bloodless. He reached out the other hand— trembling as though palsied—to close the door of Mr Somersall's office and began to navigate his way between the desks, faltering here and there, dizzied and dazed by the eviscerating interview he had just endured. Stephen threw him a look loaded with sympathy and crossed the room to open the outer door, stooping as the foreman passed to murmur that if he could locate the young clerk, he would find pie and coffee also, and that he should use both to restore himself before returning to the pit.

The two remaining clerks shrank even closer to their task, but it was Stephen's name that Mr Somersall shouted from his office, so loudly that the finely-wrought instruments on Stephen's desk shook.

'Mr Milton!'

Stephen sighed and pulled on his coat before crossing the office and entering the sanctum of his employer.

Chapter 18

Mr Somersall's office was comfortably appointed, with a large desk empty of anything that could be called work, a leather chair, a Turkey rug upon the floor and a bookcase containing leather-bound books which had surely never been read—certainly not by Mr Somersall and probably not by anyone else. He had a fireplace but it was empty since the weather continued to be so warm. A second even more comfortable chair sat before the fireplace and beside that stood a low round table containing a silver tray with a crystal decanter, two glasses and a silver filigree covered soda siphon.

Mr Somersall sat behind his desk. He had pushed his chair back slightly so he could extend his legs. Stephen took this attitude to be a good sign. Mr Somersall looked more like a satiated man than one hungry for more. In physical appearance Mr Somersall was rather ugly, with a large domed head from which a sparse fuzz of iron grey hair stood out, untamed by any comb or grease. What his head lacked in hair his cheeks and jowls more than amply made up for. He wore thick grizzled whiskers that extended from his beetling eyebrows, swarmed over his mottled cheeks and met on his upper lip. The column of his chin and neck—the one indistinguishable from the other—were clean shaven and, just now, a dark puce in colour. His eyes and nose were small and his mouth, or what could be seen of it as he had a habit of pursing his lips very tightly together, was thin and mean. He was corpulent, the good living of his recent successful years having added extra layers to his chest, stomach and thighs, but expert and expensive tailoring—in particular richly embroidered silk waistcoats—did their best to mitigate any suggestion of inelegance.

Now, Mr Somersall sat back in his chair, puffed on a large, expensive cigar and regarded Stephen narrowly through his small bloodshot eyes. Stephen closed the office door with studied care and came to stand on the carpet a foot or so in front of the desk with his hands behind his back. He returned his employer's look with unwavering directness and fixed an expression of polite and attentive interest across his features.

He said, 'Good morning, sir.'

Mr Somersall motioned towards the silver tray and Stephen mixed a glass of brandy-and-soda, which he placed carefully on the blotter on the desk before resuming his former stance. He did not make the mistake of pouring himself a drink, and this seemed to satisfy Mr Somersall.

'My son does not accompany you, I take it?'

'No sir. I believe he remained at Somersall Grange today. We returned rather late from our dinner at the vicarage.'

'Hmph.' Mr Somersall took up the glass and gulped the brandy-and-soda down. 'Another. Take one yourself, if you like.'

Stephen refilled the glass, but indicated by a slight shake of the head that he would not partake himself.

'*You* managed to rouse yerself from your bed though? I wonder *he* did not. But in fact I do not wonder o'er much, for he is lazy, that son of mine.'

Stephen made no response to this remark but said, 'I hope to inspect the sump today. As you know, I'm concerned—'

'And how was your dinner?' Mr Somersall enquired. 'Who else was there?'

'The grocer and his wife and daughter, the curate, and a Miss Harlish. She is housekeeper at Tall Chimneys, the great house.'

'The Talbots' house? Is she indeed? I find that very interesting. A "great house," you call it? I doubt it compares with mine, but we will let that go. What mention was made of the Talbots? They are the vicar's patrons. Mr Talbot is godfather to the girl. He is sure to do sommat[xiv] for her. That would be a connection I should like to make. I hear much of Mr Talbot on the exchange. You cannot move nowadays without passing a mill or a shipyard or a railway line but that they have a hand in it. The young lady, she was comely?'

'Miss Harlish?' Stephen was teasing, but Mr Somersall took his bait.

'The vicar's girl,' he roared, spraying spittle. 'You don't think I have the least interest in a housekeeper, I hope? My son will make a grave error if he looks in *that* direction.'

'I believe Herbert found the young lady most delightful. I understand she is to call on Mrs Somersall in the coming days.'

'Is she?' This seemed to interest Mr Somersall. He shifted in his seat and his eyes widened. 'I should like to see her myself. When is she to call?'

'As to that, I cannot say. I don't believe anything was fixed. But Mr Somersall, as to the sump. You know I believe the pump to be insufficiently powerful to empty it. If the bottom levels were to flood—'

But again Mr Somersall interrupted him. 'Flood? *Flood?* Look about you, Mr Milton. There has been no rain for weeks. The sump is as dry as a bone. "As dry as a bone," so the foreman tells me. Those, Mr Milton, were his exact words to me not ten minutes since. Why, he says you could not get half a cup of water from it if you was dying of thirst. No, sir, not if you was dying.'

'And so that may well be *now*—' Stephen attempted.

Mr Somersall leaned forward in his chair. 'Where weather is concerned, weather here, in Yorkshire, where I have lived all my life, where man and boy I have lived and laboured, well, I believe I may say that I am somewhat acquainted with it. No one, it seems to me, could be better acquainted. Indeed I go so far as to say that no one *is* better acquainted than I am myself. And so, as to rain, you can take it from me as a certain fact that we shall have none, none of significance I say, until August or even September—I will allow myself so much flexibility in my prediction—September, let us say. And by then the ground will be so desiccated—that is the proper meteorological term, and also the correct geological term—that it will soak up the rain like a sponge, like a sponge, sir, and I'll wager that sump will be as dry in December as it is now. But, it may be that by December the condition of the sump, its utter dehydration or otherwise, may not be your concern, Mr Milton. For my understanding is that your sojourn with us is not contracted to last beyond November. Am I not correct? I am sure I *am* correct for I am very rarely wrong and never, *never* am I wrong on matters of business, and so I say with a certainty that your contract was for six months, beginning in May and concluding in November.'

'That is quite correct, sir.'

'Of course it is! Naturally it is correct, and so you should not trouble yourself with it. The strength and capacity of the pump is my business, sir. My own. If you will be so good as to complete the drawings I have requested, that will be quite enough. If, in pursuance of that task you need to visit the sump, the seams, the stope or anything else, you are quite welcome to do so; but as to the pump, leave that alone.'

Stephen sighed. 'Very well, sir, but I should like—'

'I do not much care what you would like,' Mr Somersall interjected. 'I know what young men want, having been a young man myself and having known a great many young men. I think there are few who have known as many young men as I have in their career and therefore I feel myself peculiarly well qualified to speak on their predilections. But I am sorry to inform you that in this case I can take no notice. None at all. To be blunt, your preferences are nothing to me—' and no doubt Mr Somersall would have continued to apprise Stephen at length as to the utter irrelevance of his partialities had it not been for a timid knock upon the door.

'—oh, what is it, *now?*' Mr Somersall bawled, as though he had been subject to constant interruptions in his work from the moment of his arrival.

One of the clerks opened the door just sufficiently to allow him to insert the smallest portion of his face into the room. 'Begging your pardon, sir, and so sorry for the intrusion, but you requested your carriage at nine, and it is just nine of the clock now, sir, and your carriage awaits in the yard.' Having delivered his message the clerk withdrew so hurriedly that it was a wonder he did not trap his nose in the door.

Mr Somersall consulted his pocket watch and then hoisted himself from his chair. Stephen lifted the colliery owner's coat from the hook where it hung and helped that gentleman into it. Perhaps the gesture reminded Mr Somersall that whilst he had the undoubted authority of an employer for an employee over Stephen, he had also the duty of a host.

'I am sure Mrs Somersall expects the honour of your company at the Grange this evening,' he said, panting slightly at the exertion of being shoehorned into his outerwear, 'unless you would prefer to stay in town. Either house is at your disposal, sir, while you are my son's guest. But of course, you will inform Mrs Somersall of your intentions.'

Stephen bowed. 'Where do you intend to dine, sir? If you intend returning to the Grange, I will do myself the honour of sending Mrs Somersall a note to expect us both.'

Mr Somersall considered. 'I shall remain in town,' he said at last. 'That is, if I do not go to York. But if you hear when the lady from the vicarage is to call, perhaps you will be so good as to let me know.'

Stephen acknowledged the request without absolutely agreeing to comply with it, and it may be that Mr Somersall was sensible of his prevarication for he turned a gimlet eye on Stephen and said, 'In fact, let it be known that she is *not* to visit until I can be sure to be at liberty to meet her. My son's social dalliances cannot be allowed to dictate *my* calendar, do you understand?'

Stephen said that he did, and Mr Somersall departed the office to the relief of everyone he left behind.

Chapter 14

The rest of the day passed in what was almost a holiday mood. The clerks threw open the windows and propped open the door to admit what small breaths of fresh air were to be had in that dank and sulphurous place. The man of business had ale and sandwiches brought in at noon for the general consumption of the office staff. In the afternoon, Stephen descended the mine to the sump to find that the "half a cup" of water there was actually as much as would reach above the knees of the average man, but still below the level when the pump was required. An inspection of the lower levels found no significant moisture and he was satisfied with the positioning and soundness of the props although the air was very foul just there, which gave rise to questions of ventilation and of gas. On returning to the surface he went into the building that housed the ventilation engine and determined that it too was below ideal capacity.

Stephen stood in the yard. The air was thick with dust and fumes, the heat almost unbearable. Trucks of coal trundled past him towards the washing sheds, boys led pit ponies about, smiths' hammers rang out repairing tools, and women and children—debarred from work below ground since the act of 1841—undertaking whatever tasks they could that would supplement their family income, shrieked and shouted to be heard above the din. He needed to think, to go over his calculations, but the noise was so clanging and cacophonous as to drive a person demented, and he swept off his hat and ran his hands through his hair, almost tearing at it. But feeling soot and dust amongst his locks, and his own sweat, made his gorge rise. Mr Somersall would hear no reason on the subject of the pumping engines, which had both been designed and installed when the mine had been a much smaller affair and were now too small to offer sufficient insurance against flood or explosion.

Stephen was seven-and-twenty, without family and almost without friends. He had been born to an out-of-wedlock mother who was pitied by a local clergyman, given scullery work and allowed to sleep with her child in a draughty attic. The child—Stephen—had shown intelligence and discretion, and so was permitted to join the lessons of the clergyman's children, soon outstripping them all in achievement. While pleasing the vicar, this precocity had displeased the vicar's wife, and she had insisted that Stephen be removed to a school where his brilliance would not eclipse the dull glow of her own children. Her spite extended to Stephen's mother, who was cast off without a reference and soon died. The school was cruel and cold, but a schoolmaster—later headmaster—recognised Stephen's talent, took him in hand, and in due course arranged for a scholarship whereby he could advance to Balliol. There had been a promise of a teaching post back at the school, but this came to nothing on the headmaster's untimely death. And so Stephen found himself alone in the world again, with only himself, his engineering expertise and his ambition—which was not small—to rely on. He was constitutionally distrustful. People had promised, and then reneged. A general sense of being badly treated accounted for the chip on his shoulder.

He believed that, were he to request it, his contract with Mr Somersall could be extended almost indefinitely; and no doubt the salary would be reasonable. He narrowed his eyes for a moment to envisage what such a life might look like. Whitby and the surrounding countryside were pleasant and he imagined establishing himself in a modest house and living contentedly—as contentedly, that is, as a man like Stephen ever could. Herbert was by no means an uncongenial companion and *he,* no doubt, would remain in the vicinity. Were both to find agreeable wives— and here, unbidden, came Beth Harlish's face to his inner eye—the two families could establish a very pleasing intercourse, a social as well as a business connection that would satisfy anyone, even Stephen, who knew himself to be a man not easy to please.

But Mr Somersall threw his shadow over this pipedream. As Stephen had told Beth, the old man would not relinquish control of his empire until the laying-out women prised it from his cold, lifeless hands. The idea of contending with Mr Somersall's hubris for any extended period of time was more than Stephen could contemplate. He would lose his reason or,

79

if he did not lose that he would certainly lose his temper, which was short and fiery. Mr Somersall was exactly the kind of man to ignore sound advice and then, when things turned bad, to blame those whose counsel he had disregarded. Stephen found his hands clenched into fists, and that he was grinding his teeth.

It was past four o'clock, and when he returned to the office he found everyone else had tidied their desks and gone home, even the colliery manager, who was supposed to remain until the six o'clock claxon brought the day shift up from the mine to make room for the night brigade. In his stead he had left the poor, brow-beaten foreman who had suffered at Mr Somersall's hand earlier that day whose name, Stephen now recalled, was Jessop. Mr Jessop occupied the manager's chair in the office, but uncomfortably, cowed by the ledger before him into which he was to enter the tally of the day's work, and the quill, which was awkward in hands more used to a pick axe.

He looked up as Stephen entered. 'I thank you for the pie and the coffee,' he said. 'I had not breakfasted. I'd been roused from my bed at two to see to an accident on the second level and had not been home since.'

'Is that what Mr Somersall wanted to see you about?' Stephen enquired, not looking at the man as he tidied away his own engineering drawing tools.

'Aye. A lad had his foot crushed by a wagon. The surgeon had to amputate. But the master wasn't interested in that. "How long was production halted?" was all he wanted to know.'

'And even that, I wager, *he* told *you*,' Stephen said wryly.

The man gave a dry laugh. 'To the last second of time and the nearest tonne of coal,' he agreed, 'with a lecture on efficiency thrown in for free.'

'I'm concerned about air quality down on the bottom level,' Stephen said. 'The ventilation engine isn't up to the job. The air smelled noxious to me. The men use their Geordie lamps, I hope? They're not tempted back to the candle?'[xv]

Jessop looked shifty. 'They are not permitted candles, sir, but some of the men dislike the lamps, even now. And Mr Somersall will not issue replacements, sir, if lamps are lost or damaged.'

'Will he not?' Stephen sighed. On impulse he rolled up his drawings and inserted them into a cylindrical leather valise, determining to spend the next day working on them in peace and quiet in some sequestered room at the Grange. Surely in such a vast place, there was a study or a library or some such room he could appropriate for the purpose? He wished the foreman goodnight.

He collected his horse and rode back towards Somersall Grange, though with reluctant steps. It was further by two miles than the town house in Whitby, but *that* had been rendered an impossible prospect from the information that Mr Somersall himself might spend the night there. At present Stephen had nowhere else to lay his head save some inn or other, where he supposed he might take a room, sending his excuses to Mrs Somersall and requesting that his bags be sent along. But his stipend would not stretch to that indefinitely, and he did not wish to desert Herbert.

He rode up, out of the town and onto the moor, where the air—hot, and heavy with the smell of plants and alive with insects that pestered him—was at least free of dust and smoke. He contemplated the wider moorland carriageway that would lead most directly to Somersall Grange or, if he were to continue on it, to the market town of Brayton, and past that to the standing stone and thence to Moorside and the snug little gatehouse at whose gate he had last spied Miss Harlish. He had a mind—an almost irrepressible impulse—to spur his horse forward, to pound the carriageway, to gallop the dozen or so miles to that abode where he pictured Beth, busy about some mundane task that she would instantly abandon at the sight of himself, tired and dusty but smiling at her door. But no. It was ridiculous. And how could he, so filthy and dishevelled as he was from the mine, and so out of sorts? So he eschewed the broader way and took instead a narrower track that followed the course of the Elling, a meandering and rugged route that took him around boulders and along the edges of vivid green hollows of sulphurous bogs.

The river water, reduced in capacity because of the drought, was still plentiful and here and there, formed deep pools where little waterfalls had hollowed out a lagoon. At a rise in the ground he halted his horse and looked around. For miles and miles he could see no person, no habitation, nor any sign of any living creature apart from himself. He breathed deeply, in and out, of the hot perfumed air, willing it to quieten the tumult of discontent and angst that boiled in his soul. At the next pool he dismounted and led his horse to drink, drank himself of the sweet cold water and, after a little hesitation, stripped off his clothes and submerged himself in the pool.

Chapter 15

About that same time, Frank and Beth led the Irishmen's horse across the short-cropped turf of the moor towards the standing stone. The horse—refreshed now, and probably better fed than it had been for some while—tossed its head and side-stepped skittishly, eager to run. The cart behind it was empty. Beth had declared herself quite willing to assist with loading the lime but for some reason of his own that Beth could not fathom, Frank had refused her offer, apparently deeming it best to leave the lime until Ruairi or some of his fellows could collect it. He had closed and locked the door of the coach house and almost bundled her onto the cart to hurry her away from the place.

He had trudged in silence up the steep switchbacks of the drive, refusing to climb up next to her, speaking quietly to the horse as a way of avoiding the need to speak to his sister, and she wondered at this strange changeableness in his character. Reserved he had always been, but not moody nor yet subject to such odd swings in his mood. Lately he had seemed unwontedly light of spirit but would then plunge into some slough of despond. Only him being in love could account for it. It was new and unsettling. Frank was the mainstay of her life, the constant. If he married, she would have to give place to his wife, remove herself from the gatehouse and live elsewhere, though she did not know where. It would be terrible, but for Frank's happiness she would do it in a heartbeat.

Whether Aoife could make Frank happy ... ah! *That,* she doubted, but she buttoned up her doubt and tucked it away.

They stopped at home for an hour, leaving the horse tied up just within the throat of the drive, where the trees gave shade. Beth stoked the fire, put the loaf into the oven to bake and wrapped a pat of butter and a jar of preserves in a cloth. Then, carrying a bowl of hot water up to her room, she stripped off her dress and shift and washed herself, brushed her hair and looped it back off her neck before putting on a clean frock. The little things Beth had made for Brónach's baby were in a coffer at the end of her bed, soon lifted out and made into a bundle.

When Beth returned to the kitchen the loaf was done and added to the basket with the other things. She stepped out into the garden. Frank had washed at the pump, and now wore the shirt she'd hung on the line that morning, and a clean neckerchief. His hair was slicked back off his face, but she knew that in a few moments it would dry and fall again over his brow. He had shaved, and his chin was raw from the scraping of his blade. He had dug some potatoes and was busy putting them into a sack as she stepped out of doors. He feigned not to see her smile of approbation as he loaded the sack onto the flatbed of the cart.

It had been another warm, cloudless day but a breeze blew across the moor as they struck out towards the camp. It teased the locks of Beth's hair and she turned her face towards it, breathing in the scent of plants and peat. Frank plodded beside the horse, but she sensed his eagerness—and his fretfulness—as they neared the camp. Something roiled in Beth's stomach. Was it just disquiet at Frank's distraction? Or the prospect of opening Tall Chimneys to the gaze of outsiders? She was revisited by the vision—brief but vivid—of Mr Connolly as he had stood just that morning, stripped to the waist. Or perhaps she was just hungry? She had not eaten since breakfast.

Beth squinted across the moor towards the camp. The children were engaged in some game. Two or three of the women gathered in washing from the bushes and some of the dogs squabbled over a bone. The Harlishes' dog quartered the moor to either side of the track, scenting rabbits but finding none. He would not demean himself by fighting over a bone, but should one of the immigrants' dogs be in season, he would fight to the death.

There it was again—a strange clutch in her stomach, a stab of something ... not anxiety ... she shook it off.

From beside her covered wagon, one of the women—Caitlin, Beth identified—waved a hand in greeting and the others turned to see who approached. At the same time, from the other side of the standing stone where a path led towards the village, another group came into view. On foot, slow and clearly very weary, the men who had been haymaking made their way into camp.

Aoife descended the steps of her *vardo* and pushed a kettle over the glowing peats. Her hair was loose around her shoulders and the wind winnowed it like the riffle of a raven's feathers. The standing stone uttered a subdued continuous hum, like the low growl of warning in a dog's chest.

Frank stopped abruptly and made a show of attending to the horse's traces while the workers greeted their families. Caitlin's husband, Cormac, bent over his mother—the aged woman who sat in her usual chair—and then kissed Caitlin. She pointed to the Harlishes where they loitered on the periphery of the camp, then ushered her husband into their own wagon, snatching a clean shirt from a guy rope as she passed. Mícheál and Father Fearghal paused only long enough to put their scythes out of the children's reach before collecting buckets and heading towards the spring, nodding greeting to Frank and Beth as they passed. Lorcán crossed the ground to where Frank held the horse.

'She's fed and watered,' Frank said, handing over the leading rein and reaching up to help Beth down. 'And the cart's in good fettle now. We won't intrude. Only Beth has something for—'

'Come along now and join us,' Lorcán said, waving away Frank's excuses with his stump. 'Don't we owe you a debt of gratitude after your help last night?' He turned to Beth. 'We'd all have been drowned in a bog or crushed by the wagon or worse, miss, if not for your brother. Come now, and share what we have. There's tea in the kettle, I think, or something stronger if you've the taste for it.' He turned and called across to the children. 'Come now, you scoundrels. Where are your manners? Come and take this lady's basket, will you? And find something for her to sit upon.'

The children ran, clamouring, and took Beth's basket, and although they peered eagerly into it, she noticed they did not remove anything. A boy of about eight years of age shouldered the sack of potatoes and carried it across to where they stored the provisions. A little girl of about three took Beth's hand and led her across to the circle around the fire, where a wide pallet was hastily covered with a rug and she was bidden to sit.

The old woman spoke to her, but her toothlessness, or the pipe between her lips, or the impenetrable strength of her accent made it impossible for Beth to decipher her words. Beth smiled and took the mug of tea that was handed to her and ached to get up and help as the other women, in instinctive concert, chopped vegetables to add to the stew, or wiped the children over with damp rags to clean the worst of the dust and grime from their faces and hands, folded laundry or collected peats. Beth missed the informal camaraderie of women's company, wondered how she could miss something she had never known then recognised it was more that the communal effort reminded her of her childhood.

Presently Brónach came and eased herself down beside Beth. 'It's good of you to come, and thank you for the things you've brought, miss,' she said, clutching Beth's hand briefly. 'You're a fine needlewoman, so you are. I've baby clothes from the others, of course, but they're so old and patched, and so much had to be left behind.' She stroked her belly. 'I did not think this one would have such a good start, indeed I didn't. And I told Cillian this would have to be the last, or the baby things would be nought but threads. But I fear he would have taken no notice. He's a man, after all, and …' she stopped herself and turned wide eyes on Beth. 'But I shouldn't be speaking thus, and you still unmarried, miss. We womenfolk here have got used to a certain frankness I suppose. There's not much privacy here.'

'That's alright,' Beth said, drinking tea as a means of hiding her blushes, but wondering if Aoife—also unwed—had been exposed to the unfiltered exchanges of the married and widowed women. She thought it likely. Aoife was certainly no innocent.

She said, 'You've had a good day's work, it seems? Haymaking at Drystone Farm, I think?'

'Yes. And Cillian took the boys back to Mr Slade's place. Conn was rare pleased to be counted as one of the men, and Dónall, of course. He has twice the strength of Cillian, truth be told, though he's loath to leave Aoife unguarded. But for such work as moving stone, he can do as much as two others.' She sighed. 'Fionn did not lend his aid to either undertaking. He has been absent the whole day. I hope he does not return full of drink. He has a temper on him.'

Beth looked around the camp. 'And Mr Connolly?'

'He'll be back presently. Doubtless he's gone to Clough Farm to see Mr Slade about last night's business. Now *that* was a stroke of luck, and no mistake. That's good trade to be in, if you're quick and quiet, and we're led to believe there's as much of it as we care to undertake.'

'Moving lime?'

Brónach laughed. 'Lime, is it? Well, if you say so, miss.' She turned to look at Beth to better share the joke, but the genuine confusion in Beth's eye gave her pause. 'And look at me *again,* speaking out of turn,' she said, half to herself. With difficulty she rose to her feet. 'I'd better be after seeing to the little ones,' she said. 'Excuse me, miss. But you'll stay to supper, you and your brother. There's plenty, and not rabbit, saints be praised. Sick to death we are of rabbit, though glad enough of it when there's nothing else. A flitch of bacon has come our way, and a rare treat it is when cooked up with some onions and apples, and welcome you are to share it.'

Across the moor the church clock struck six, and although the sun was nowhere near setting, it seemed some of its heat loosened its grip on the moor. The little breeze strengthened and set the herbage whispering. The birds that had dozed in the shade of the undergrowth all day took to the wing once more.

A little girl brought one of the books Beth had delivered on a previous visit, and scrambled onto Beth's lap. The book was a poor ragged thing by this time, its pages torn, its print smudged with damp and grubby fingerprints; it was almost indecipherable. But Beth knew the story and made up what she could not read in the text, and soon had a circle of avid listeners around her as the adults went about their tasks. The smell from the cooking pot grew richer and more enticing. From time to time she encouraged the older children to spell out a word or to read a line or two of the story, and to the younger ones she showed the pictures and had them explain to her what took place in them. When the story was read, and read again, she found her tea mug had been replaced by a vessel of some strong spirit, and when she looked around all the adults were imbibing freely. Their chores were done and there was a relaxed, almost dissipated holiday mood about the camp that Beth found slightly unnerving. Anxious for reassurance, she sought out her brother and at last spied him apart from the rest, across the clearing where the animals were corralled. He was seated on the back of the cart and close beside him, confidential and smiling up coyly, was Aoife.

Beth sipped at her drink. It made her eyes water, but it was not the raw, illegal spirit she had expected. She believed it was brandy, and good brandy at that. What could these itinerants be doing drinking such fine liquor? It sent a warming glow through her stomach that somewhat settled the disquiet that had been her companion since the morning, when she had discovered Frank's bed unslept in. She took another sip and the uneasiness retreated still further.

Then, from a distance of about a hundred yards, a loud hallooing could be heard, and everyone turned to see Ruairi Connolly approaching the camp. His white shirt was open to the chest, his sleeves rolled to the elbow and his dark hair bound back by a bandana. He strode purposefully, shoulders square and head erect, apparently not at all fatigued by his day of haymaking after a sleepless night hauling lime. The unaccustomed sensation in Beth's stomach returned with a vengeance, and the brandy burned her heart.

Ruairi had his arms around Conn on one side and Dónall on the other, and behind them came Cillian. They were dusty and drained. Even Dónall showed by a weariness in his gait that the day's work had exhausted him, and it was clear that Ruairi's energetic demeanour was calculated to buoy the spirits of the others.

At his cry of greeting—or warning—Aoife slipped from the back of the cart and made her way quickly to the steps of her *vardo* where she began to slice the loaf that Beth had brought. But not quickly enough to prevent Dónall from seeing the place from which she had moved. His eyes were keen and she was always his focus, and he had espied her sitting with the Yorkshireman. He shrugged off Ruairi's restraining arm and increased his pace to a shambling run. He covered the last twenty yards into the camp, burst through the circle around the fire and hurled his weight towards Frank. His ham-like hands were curled into fists and he yelled accusations, though these were largely unintelligible. Frank—a peaceable man who, although strong and well able to defend himself, would always avoid violence if possible—put up defensive arms and dodged Dónall's flailing fists but did still take a blow to the temple before Lorcán and the other men pulled Dónall away.

'What are you about, man?' cried Ruairi, hurrying up to the fray, a deep frown corrugating his wide forehead. 'Dónall, I'm ashamed of you. This is no way to treat our guest, and our confrère. Did I not tell you what a help Mr Harlish was to us last night? And look, he has brought his sister with him. What must she think of us?'

Dónall's ire seemed to cool as swiftly as it had boiled, and Ruairi's disapproval was as wounding to him as any blow could have been. He hung his head and mumbled, half crying in his distress, but then flung an arm out to the *vardo* and cried 'Aoife' in a voice that was broken with confusion and shame and the hot burning sparks of his jealousy.

'Ah, Dónall,' said Ruairi, replacing his arm about Dónall's shoulders and speaking confidentially, but in a voice that carried to the entire camp. 'Aoife has many protectors here. Father Fearghal, look, and Tadhg,' indicating the elderly harpist, 'and she herself is no one's fool. If I am to entrust to you the work of a man then she must be out of your sight and you must trust to God to watch over her when you cannot.'

Dónall knuckled the tears from his eyes and leaned against Ruairi as a child would have done after being separated for even a few moments from a beloved parent's affection, and allowed himself to be led towards the circle and seated on the upturned barrel that would normally have been Ruairi's own preserve.

'There now,' said Ruairi. 'You shall have a man's seat and a man's portion of supper and a glass of grog to wash it down with since you have done a man's work today.'

Dónall nodded and tried a watery smile, but the look he threw over his shoulder at Frank was cold with venom.

Chapter 16

The Irish folk were keen to gloss over the unpleasantness of Dónall's attack. More brandy was doled out and Tadhg brought out his harp and played a medley of cheerful songs accompanied by Mícheál on a flute and Cormac on a bodhrán[xvi]. The children joined hands and danced, singing the words of the song in a language neither Beth nor Frank understood.

Frank had made a cautious approach to the circle and now perched on a bench formed from a plank of wood supported by two stumps. It was as far away as possible from Aoife's *vardo* where she remained, singing snatches of the song and clapping her hands, her face very animated and seemingly unconcerned by the altercation that had taken place. Fearghal and Cillian sat on either side of Frank and engaged him in conversation and presently Eistir and Elíse, the widows, served the bacon stew, bringing Frank the first helping.

Fionn sloped into camp and settled himself on an upturned crate, but when Cillian and Ruairi made a point of emptying their pockets of the day's wages, he contributed nothing.

'You met with no success in town?' Ruairi asked. 'Did you not win at cards, or earn some coppers with your conjuring?'

'Or pick a pocket?' Cillian added. 'I do not see why you should eat what you have not earned. It's the rule here.'

But Fionn kept his counsel, and the matter was allowed to rest.

The sun at last began its slide down the dome of the sky, setting fire to fine ribbons of cloud that had laid themselves across the horizon like idle strokes from an artist's brush. The light across the moor was hazy with pollen and dust, pale violet. The shadow of the standing stone began to lengthen, throwing itself like a pointing finger across the turf and over the three men on the bench. Its hum of earlier had given way to the slightest possible crack and fizz as the stone cooled in the evening air. Beth gave an involuntary shiver.

'You're chilled,' said a voice behind her, and she felt her shawl being draped around her shoulders. 'May I?' Ruairi indicated the vacant side of Beth's pallet and, at her nod, seated himself beside her. 'I'm sorry about this morning,' he said in a low voice, 'and for Dónall, just now.'

'There's no need to apologise for either,' said Beth. 'Perhaps I should apologise to you. I was rude this morning, and it may be that our being here now has upset the young man.'

Ruairi turned and smiled, a wide smile that revealed white teeth. 'Shall we say we're even, then?'

His body beside her exuded warmth, and she smelled the sweet hay of his day's labour on his skin and clothes. His eyes were blue, but in this light took on a darker hue, the colour Beth imagined the sea might be, though she had never seen it other than at a great distance. She was drawn into their depths and the urge to close her eyes and drown was strong. The brandy sang in her veins.

She dragged herself with difficulty back to reason and returned his smile. 'I'd like that,' she said, 'for I have a favour to ask of your womenfolk, if I may. I might be in error, but it seems to me that you're the leader here, the guardian of these folk … I do not know if that is the correct term, so forgive me if I misconstrue, but it appears that you stand in some authority over them, and so it is to you that I make my request.'

Ruairi gave a wry smile. 'As to authority, I have none. I am a simple man, as they are, thrown upon his own resources. There was a time when I might have claimed some superiority. I have a small farm of my own. I could have called myself a landowner, whereas these men were labourers, or tenants of smallholdings. I was better educated, my parents having the means to send me to school, whereas these could pick up only such learning as was thrown their way, and even that was given but sparingly. Their overlords preferred to keep them in ignorance, the better to keep them under the boot. The exception is Father Fearghal, of course. He was educated in the seminary, has Latin and Greek, and would be our natural leader in things spiritual as well as temporal, but he resigned all claim to lead us when he lost his faith. Tadhg is the oldest amongst us—the oldest man, I should say—but he has no desire to lead; all his strength was stolen, along with his wife and children, by the famine. The famine, I am afraid, took everything we had. It was the great leveller. And so we all use what gifts we have and we contribute them to the common good. I negotiate work and remuneration, having some understanding of what farmers require and when, and perhaps a little pride remains in that I can speak to them on an equal standing. But what was the favour you wished to ask? I am sure that if it is within our power, we will be happy to oblige.'

Beth explained her scheme to open Tall Chimneys to the vicarage family, Mr Somersall and Mr Milton, only realising as she did so what a great undertaking it was. 'Of course, nothing can be done until we hear from Mrs Stockbridge. But if she is agreeable, we shall have to light the furnace,' she said, half to herself, 'for the making of tea, and for washing up afterwards. It will need to be serviced and the flue cleared, for Frank has not done it so far this year. Chairs must be carried to the terrace, and tables. I shall have to find such napery as Mrs Stockbridge will not mind us using, and although I do my best to keep the place free of dust, of course I cannot do it efficiently on my own ... Oh! But I run on, and none of this is to the purpose, for I only wish to know if three or four of the women would come down and assist. Of course I shall pay them, and give them luncheon. And since the furnace is to be lit, perhaps they would like to avail themselves of hot water.'

Ruairi laughed. 'For a quantity of hot water I believe the women would work for nothing,' he said. 'Some of the children have never had a bath in their lives. They will be afraid they will drown! I think I can say with certainty that you will have all the help you require, and more. And Cormac is good with machinery. He will help with the furnace.'

Their stew arrived and they ate without speaking. The bacon was very good, sweetly flavoured with the apples Frank had brought from the store, where they had been laid by the previous autumn.

Soon after supper the children and the old woman were hustled to bed. Conn announced that he would go and check his snares and Frank offered to accompany him. 'I know some good spots,' he said.

'Will you come with us, Dónall?' Conn asked, but Dónall glowered and shook his head. He had moved to sit on the steps that led up to Aoife's *vardo*, pressing himself closely and possessively to her side, not to be moved. With a sigh, Aoife collected the book that Beth had read to the children earlier and began to turn its pages, murmuring the story in a low voice, showing Dónall the pictures.

The men began various chores around the camp, feeding the animals and fetching more water. Those like Lorcán, Cormac and Mícheál, who had been up all night, took themselves to their rest. Fionn, who had also gone the last day and night without sleep, remained, practising his sleight of hand, but not very efficiently since he had drunk more than his share of the brandy; he lolled on his seat and kept dropping the little cups. Once, when Eistir passed close to him on her way to her wagon, he grabbed her skirts and would have pulled her onto his lap, but she slapped his hand away sharply.

The women collected the dishes to carry away to the stream for washing but when Beth rose, offering to help, she was waved back to her seat.

Ruairi sat on, savouring the brandy, his long legs stretched out to the glowing peats of the fire, which echoed the flaming sky in the west. Apart from Aoife and Dónall, whose head now drooped and rested on Aoife's shoulder, and drunken Fionn, they were alone.

'Such fine brandy,' said Beth, sipping from her cup. 'Another payment in kind, I suppose?'

Ruairi nodded. 'Coin, to be honest, would be more useful. But we must take what we are given.'

'It is a very egalitarian camp you have here. My patroness, Mrs Stockbridge, would approve of it.'

'Oh?' Ruairi turned his eyes from the fire and looked at her.

Beth swallowed and finding her mouth dry, finished the brandy in her cup. She was a little inebriated. She had been intoxicated once or twice, notably as a child when the lax oversight of her mother had left young Betsey alone with a flagon of cider. The experience had rather cured her of the taste for strong drink; and yet the brandy on this night was part of the strangeness of the entire evening—wildly unexpected, affecting and potent with heady vapour and underlayers of flavour she could not plumb. The man beside her was integral to her sense of disorientation. She summoned equilibrium. 'Yes,' she said. 'When we were children—Frank and I, and our brother and sister—our parents were employed at Tall Chimneys, and Mrs Stockbridge—but she was Miss Talbot then—was the only person in residence. We were never quite sure why she had been sent here all alone. It was as though she had displeased her parents, but we could not tell how. We were sure Mrs Orphan knew. She was housekeeper …' She was conscious of rambling, but Ruairi kept his eyes fixed on her, and his rapt attention seemed to draw the words from between her faltering lips. She took a deep breath. 'As time went on, Miss Talbot—we were to call her Jocelyn, though it never felt comfortable—dispensed with the proper separation that normally exists between servants and their mistress. She was lonely, I suppose, and had only my parents and the housekeeper for company. It was very odd, but at the time I had no notion of its oddness. Only now do I see it.' She frowned, and ran her tongue over her lips.

Ruairi reached behind him and brought out the bottle, then refilled both their cups. 'Go on.'

Beth drank, then said, 'In time, she … Miss Talbot … was as likely to be found in the servants' hall as in the drawing room, and we children were given free rein of the house and gardens. It seems strange now, though it never did then, that we returned to the gatehouse each evening though there were empty rooms by the score at the big house. I suppose my parents liked their privacy. My father, in particular, liked his independence.'

'All men do,' Ruairi murmured.

'Anyway, what I wanted to say was that we all of us—including Miss Talbot—had our responsibilities, as you do, here. Mine was to assist the housekeeper, and to play with the baby, and to feed the hens and collect the eggs. Then, as I got older, Mrs Orphan taught me more duties of the household. Miss Talbot did her share—more than her share, especially in the garden. She came to believe that the idea of 'mistress' and 'servant' had no meaning.'

Ruairi nodded. 'It is an interesting concept,' he said. 'But in the end, Miss Talbot owned the house, and paid the wages I presume. She was at liberty to go elsewhere and not return. You have not that freedom, unless I mistake. And even now, you are reliant on her.'

'You speak truth,' Beth said slowly. 'I was sent to school and educated to be a gentlewoman. At one time I wished very much to be a teacher. But I had to return and now I do not know, if I *had* the freedom, that I would take it. Home is …' she sought for the right words, '… so powerful a draw,' she concluded. 'But …' she did not know how to explain what she wanted to say, how the heartstrings that tied her to Tall Chimneys felt sometimes like restraints that she must fight against. That this home—no matter how secure or comfortable it might be—felt like a prison. That she was capable, was *ready* for so much more. And that this contradiction caused her, sometimes, to feel both restless and afraid.

She lifted her gaze to his, and it felt that even though she had not expressed the heart of her dichotomy, he had understood it.

He said, 'Indeed. But not so powerful that one would remain to die. Whether that be a physical death, or an emotional one. Either way, the instinct to live is stronger.'

Beth thought about Tall Chimneys as it lay below them in the quiet hollow; its stately chimneys, its patient pride, its watchful waiting silence.

'I think, if I had to leave here, I might die,' she said, very low, 'but sometimes I think I will die if I *don't.'*

The look of empathy that crossed his features was intense, a mirroring of her own tormented soul, and Beth felt the great balm that comes from being seen and understood. But then, with an inrush of compassion and eyes full of guilty sorrow she said, 'How thoughtless and cruel you must think me. When you have been torn from your home and have no idea of when—or if—you might return. You must think about it, in its neglected state. Your childhood memories, I suppose, are all there, and you left behind the ones you loved.'

'Oh no,' he assured her, allowing his eyes to travel to where Aoife and Dónall sat across the fire. 'I brought away the ones I love, to save them. They ... *they* could not withstand it. Could not watch their neighbours starve, sicken and die. The ravening wolf of hunger took many forms, Betsey.' He had used her familiar name, the one that made her feel like a child, but Beth did not care; they were so aligned in spirit and like-mindedness that there was no space for nicety between them. 'You would not conceive the ways people will prey on those who are desperate. Aoife is not constituted for hardship,' he went on, 'and Dónall is too ...' he groped for the word, but it evaded him. 'Life is confusing enough for him. But for them, I would have stayed. Oh!' He turned back to face her, and his eyes were alight with passion. 'I understand you when you speak of the power of home. My roots were deep in the soil, as yours are, and had I been by myself I believe I could have endured any hardship for the sake of that patch of ground that was mine and mine alone. No landlord could take it from me, and I had not mortgaged it, as so many had. But the land, Betsey, was poisoned, and anything that grew was foul. While I might have scratched a meagre living for myself, I could not feed three and so I tore myself from it as a tree is torn from the ground, as that stone there,' he motioned to the standing stone, which was a monolith of shadow now, for the sun had set and night had come, 'as that stone was ripped from where it belonged.' His voice broke, and he pressed his hand to his eyes.

'I am sorry. I am sorry,' cried Beth, sick at heart.

He reached out and took her hand and held it tightly, and they sat side by side in the glow from the fire, speaking no more, until at last her head drooped and rested upon his shoulder.

The night slipped around, over and past her. She was conscious of low voices, of the lilt of the harp as it played a haunting air, of the snap of the fire and the crackle of sparks as they rose into the night sky. Then even that remote consciousness left her, and she slept.

Chapter 17

June passed, one splendid dry warm day after another. Hay was gathered in, sheep were sheared and dipped. The strawberries in the Harlishes' garden ripened and were sweet. Beth made preserves, which she took as gifts to the MacAllister ladies, the professor and the lawyer's dejected wife.

Frank was away under cover of darkness 'fetching lime' on three further occasions—such, apparently, was Mr Slade's voracious need for it—and thrice did Beth hear in the dead of night the grind of cartwheels on the lane that passed the gatehouse. She made no mention of it, however, and pretended not to notice the mysterious consignments that were stacked in the stables for a few days, and then disappeared.

The Harlishes' stock of coin, which they kept behind a panel under the stairs, increased.

Frank began to nurture Dónall's trust. It was hard at first—the lad was jealous and suspicious—but Frank was used to dealing with skittish creatures; he had a natural way with the wary and the damaged. He invited Dónall and Conn to see the place in the woods where he reared the pheasant poults. By this time in the year they were leggy and adventurous, eager to be out of their enclosure. Frank showed the lads how to check the fences for holes, to examine the birds for injury or disease, the importance of regular feeding and fresh water.

Dónall was standoffish at first, looking on moodily while Conn crawled into the shelters to spread fresh bedding or sat on the ground with a half dozen birds nestled against his legs. Frank ignored Dónall's sulks without ignoring Dónall himself, and promised both boys that when it was time to release the birds into the wild they should be the ones to do it.

'After that,' Frank said, 'they are fair game. If you can shoot one, you can take it for the pot. At one time that would have been a hanging offense, but no one comes to shoot these birds now. I only raise them for my own satisfaction.'

'Why do you not keep them confined, and wring their necks one by one when you are hungry?' Conn asked. 'That is what we do with our chickens.'

Frank considered. 'I could do that. But it would not be fair. Pheasants were wild birds. They have been domesticated only for the sport of gentlemen. They can survive in the wild, whereas a hen cannot.' He looked at Dónall. 'Do you not think that things should have a chance to be free?'

Dónall shrugged, but then pointed to where a hen bird had raised herself from a nesting box. Beneath her, nestled in the straw, was a new-hatched poult.

Frank said, 'This is a late clutch. I doubt the others will hatch. This one is weak. The older ones will pick on it. It might be kinder to kill it now.'

Dónall, suddenly moved, said, 'N... no.'

Frank raised an eyebrow. 'No? What shall we do then?'

Dónall squatted down beside the nest box. 'We must l ... look after it. Will its mother not ...?' He frowned.

'She might.' Frank stood up. There were about fifty adolescent poults in the enclosure. 'But she cannot protect it against so many. What do you suggest?'

Dónall rubbed his eyes with his fists.

Conn began, 'What about—'

But Frank raised a finger. 'Let Dónall think of a way,' he said.

Dónall looked around him at the rough sticks and poles that formed the birds' enclosure, the row of nest boxes and the low, open-sided apexes where the birds roosted at night. He held out his arms to indicate the entire arrangement. 'Like this,' he said, 'but small.'

'To keep them separated?' Frank stroked his chin. 'Yes. That might work. Will you lads help me build it?'

Later that night Frank described the incident to Beth. 'Dónall would make a decent woodsman, I think. It's more instinct than brain, and he has a natural desire to nurture.'

She poured him a cup of ale. 'Do you think it is that characteristic that makes him so protective of Miss Connolly?'

Frank nodded. 'Perhaps.' He fiddled with a knot in a piece of string. 'Will you go back to the camp, Betsey? You could befriend him also.'

Beth had not returned to the camp at the standing stone, feeling too ashamed of her behaviour on the previous occasion, and conflicted about her feelings for Ruairi. She had felt so akin to him; it had been like speaking to a twin soul. Only with the house, Tall Chimneys, had she felt such empathy before. She had never spoken so unreservedly with anyone before as she had with Ruairi that night by the fire. Except perhaps, she qualified, with Stephen Milton. With him there had been a profound— though fleeting—accord. But she reminded herself that Ruairi Connolly was an itinerant. His sojourn at Moorside would not be long. And he was a charmer; she must not allow herself to fall under his spell.

Not that she did not encounter Ruairi. She saw him frequently in the village, going into or coming from the Plough, and quite often in company with Flossie Golightly, who hung on his arm making no secret of her feelings for him. In addition, Frank's clandestine business seemed to involve much discussion and planning, and many was the afternoon that Beth returned to the gatehouse to find Ruairi and her brother—and sometimes Aoife also—in the garden sharing a jug of ale. It was strange to see a social side to Frank; he was a loner, generally. Ruairi seemed to do most of the talking while Frank nodded, or put in the occasional suggestion. Aoife wandered round the garden, looking at the flowers and taking no part in the talk. But all conversation would cease at Beth's approach. Both men rose and Ruairi picked up his hat. His smile was warm, his blue eyes full of pleasure and laughter, without a trace of the melancholy she had witnessed before. He strode quickly to open the gate for her, and might offer to take her basket from her arm, but she would shake her head and hurry indoors, intent on some invented task.

Ruairi never failed to mention her friends at the camp. 'They miss you. The children fall behind in their learning. Brónach would enjoy your company.' But Beth could only smile and mumble some excuse, and try to quell the fluttering in her heart.

Aoife rarely spoke at all, or if she did it was only to murmur some remark about the flowers.

It was therefore from a distance that Beth noted signs of increased prosperity amongst the Irish people. The children had new clothes and the ragged canvasses that covered the wagons were replaced. The old cart that Frank had repaired was joined by another that materialised one day in the yard of Tall Chimneys. Frank was at work for several days, sawing and hammering, adapting it to use. Beth chose a moment when he was elsewhere about the property to walk around it curiously. It was larger and newer than the old vehicle, and cleverly equipped with various compartments and ingenious partitions presumably for the transportation of goods of … a delicate nature.

Every week Frank drove Beth to Brayton in a little gig they hired from the Plough, to purchase commodities not available more locally. Aoife and her friends were always at the market place, placing themselves on the wide shallow steps of the church. The women moved amongst the crowds selling posies or little items that the men had spent the evenings whittling from sticks. Sometimes they would examine a palm, and invent some vague prediction. Aoife had traded her much-patched dancing dress for a new red flounced skirt with extra layers that she twitched and twirled with her hands as part of the dance. Of drawers, stockings, corset or petticoat there was, astonishingly, no sign at all, but the skirt itself was very pretty, Beth allowed. Tadhg, Cormac and Mícheál played their instruments slowly at first, and Aoife's movements were correspondingly graceful, her bare feet hardly seeming to move on the polished granite steps. Then the tempo of the music would increase and the dance was more energetic, her skirt swirling like flames around her. Her hair, loose and lustrous, took flight as she whirled, her feet were a blur as they skipped and leapt. The crowd clapped, urging her on until she danced so quickly it seemed impossible she could stay upright, her whole body a writhing, spinning dynamo and the material of her skirts no more than a shimmering haze. Then, abruptly, it was ended, and Aoife stood like a statue, only her shoulders and bosom labouring as she panted from her exertion. Dónall, the while, moved through the crowd and pushed back those who would press too close. When the dance was over he would hand Aoife her shawl or fetch her water.

On these occasions Beth caught Dónall giving Frank a hesitant smile, but generally Frank's attention was too rigidly on Aoife and he did not notice. He watched her transfixed, a curious melding of desire, disgust and delight marking his features. Afterwards, in seeming to make his way randomly through the stalls, he would succeed in exchanging a word or two with her, bending down so that he could catch what she said between heaving breaths. Beth saw Aoife's hand sometimes touch Frank's sleeve as she smiled up at him and they might seem to agree upon something, nod, then move apart.

Beth believed—though she did not know for sure—that Aoife's evening performances at the Plough were different to the ones in the marketplace, where women and children were amongst the spectators. At the Plough, there were only men. She pictured them standing three or four deep at the bar, or seated at the long tables with their pewter tankards in hand, all raucous with drink. Beth's imagination was not equal to conjuring the kind of extravagance, innuendo and even salaciousness to which Aoife might go on those occasions, but she knew that Aoife drew spectators from far-flung villages, farms and hamlets and even the colliery towns, and particularly entertained the men of the Mounted Guard[xvii].

The Guard regularly stopped at the Plough on their way through the villages in search of contraband goods, though they never found any in Moorside. It was understood—but not stated—that Ned Widderington managed matters, plying the Guard with drink and greasing the palm of their captain. With this insurance, Mr Golightly had expanded his range of wines and spirits, which nowadays included Geneva[xviii], cognac and champagne. His stock of tobacco, tea and sugar appeared almost limitless, was of excellent quality, and yet was suspiciously cheap.

Chapter 18

Brónach's baby was delivered on the first night of July but not by the doctor, who arrived too late to do more than declare the child undersized and unlikely to thrive. Father Fearghal baptised the baby—a girl— immediately. Kathleen lay listless in her mother's arms and seemed little interested in the breast, in the curiosity of her brothers and sisters or in the surprisingly tender embraces of her father. She gazed unblinkingly up at the sky, where skylarks sang and tumbled for her entertainment, and at the end of a week she heaved a heavy sigh and slipped away to join them. Brónach and the other women wept, and the vicar allowed Father Fearghal to conduct a burial in a quiet corner of the churchyard. Cillian got drunk, Conn got a black eye and—for the first time—reciprocated his father's gesture with a split lip. A brawl ensued and there was enmity for a while between Cillian and the other men of the camp, but then life—as it always must—went on.

The vicious sow gave birth to a litter a few days later, but motherhood did not improve her mood. Frank forbade Beth to go near the pen and only approached the animal himself when armed with a long stick and a broad board.

He said, 'We will choose one of her litter to brood next year. She is too unpredictable for safety. I shall be glad when she is hanging from her feet in the yard.'

Beth waited anxiously for a reply to her letter to Mrs Stockbridge. In her mind she planned the event at Tall Chimneys: which rooms she would open, the artefacts she would display, the food she would serve. She walked slowly through the house, peering beneath the coverings that shrouded the furniture, looking up at the spaces where the portraits and mirrors used to hang, recalling which glowering Talbot ancestor had hung where.

'It is only right,' she murmured to the house, 'that you should be shown off, for you are very beautiful, you know.' And it seemed to her that the house sighed, and the longcase clock in the hall chimed the hour. She kept the clock wound and it maintained good time. Beth liked to hear the steady tick-tock, tick-tock of it as she moved through the rooms. She thought of it as the house's heartbeat. She dusted and dreamed, swept and schemed, but her ideas were all theoretical until Mrs Stockbridge should sanction—or veto—the proposal.

To Frank, Beth said nothing. In her heart she knew he hated the very idea of opening the house, of welcoming guests, of being 'on show'.

In the meantime, she went on as before: visiting, encouraging and aiding; tending to matters at the big house; cooking and cleaning for Frank; working in the garden at the gatehouse and down at the big house where they used the glasshouses to nurture more exotic fruits and to extend the growing season so they were provided with tomatoes and cucumbers and salads long after the gatehouse garden had succumbed to frost.

In the later evening hours, when the sun threw its setting flames across the moor, her eye was drawn to the camp, and in the stillness she could hear drifting snatches of the refugees' conversation as they gathered around the standing stone to eat their meal. She felt drawn to them, but was conscious also of a strange barrier that separated her. She was not one of them. She did not belong. But this, too, was a familiar sensation, and so her association with the Irish people was just another facet of the generality of her life.

From time to time she was asked to chaperone Miss Eagerly and Herbert Somersall. She was taken driving in his carriage. They walked along the river bank and explored a ruined abbey. She drank tea at the vicarage and sat by with some sewing while Rose tried to teach Herbert a card game she had played at school. But it seemed to Beth that her attendance was hardly required, for usually Mrs Eagerly was also of the party, and frequently Rose's stepbrother Edgar, the curate, would happen upon them as he returned from visiting in the parish. Beth discerned no great passion in either Rose or Herbert—the two laughed and frolicked more like playmates—but she supposed a merry friendship was as good a basis for a happy marriage as any.

Stephen Milton did not accompany Herbert on these visits. When Beth enquired after him Herbert said, 'Oh! Stephen is conscientious. He is paid to do a job and he does it, though I tell him the old man will hardly know if it is done or not. My father is not a man to allow for any expertise that is not his own, you know.'

'Why then does he employ Mr Milton? It seems to me that one man wastes his money and the other man wastes his time.'

'You are quite right, Miss Harlish! Indeed you are. But it suits me to have Stephen near me just now. My mother is glad of his company at the Grange, you know, with my father being in town. And poor Stephen has nowhere else! That's the sad truth. His mother is dead, and so is the patron who arranged for his education. It seems likely to me that Stephen will go to South America or the Transvaal. No end of possibilities there for a chap of Stephen's talents; he will probably make his fortune. There are gold mines and diamonds and I don't know what else. Things that are worth digging for. We only have coal, you know.'

'I believe there is gold in Wales,' Beth said.

'Is there? You astonish me. Well, perhaps Stephen will go there. Oh! Miss Eagerly! That fellow is selling puppies. Do let me buy you one. Should you not like a puppy as a companion? That one with the patch over his eye is so amusing, is he not? Like a pirate!'

At last, when July was already in its second week, a reply came to Beth's letter. It came not from Mrs Stockbridge but from her son, Lucas Willow, who explained that in his mother's absence abroad, he was charged to manage her affairs. Regarding the scheme proposed by Miss Harlish and her brother, he gave his unconditional consent—as he was sure his mother would do. He enclosed a generous bank note to cover expenses.

When Frank returned home Beth showed him the letter.

'So we may proceed, Frank?'

He sighed. 'If you are absolutely determined on it, then yes. You will speak to Mrs Golightly? Then I suppose I shall arrange things with Mr Connolly. Unless you had rather?' He raised an enquiring eyebrow. 'You avoid speaking to him. You have not visited the camp by the standing stone. Your absence has been noted.'

Beth busied herself with their supper. 'I am ashamed, Frank. I made a fool of myself.'

'Connolly will not regard it. If anyone makes a fool of themselves it is Miss Golightly. She has set her cap at him.'

'Miss Golightly is immodest,' Beth said, slicing cheese savagely. 'If that is what Mr Connolly likes, good luck to him.'

Frank poured them both a glass of ale. 'I think he likes *you*, Betsey.' He sipped his ale, ruminating. He had more to say, and Beth knew him well enough not to hurry him.

It was not until they sat at table that he said, 'They are not so different from us, you know. And if he asked for your hand I would not refuse him my permission.'

'You would have no say in the matter.'

'Perhaps not. But I like the man.'

'You like his sister, more to the point.'

Frank fed bits of his piecrust to the dog, and avoided her eye.

Presently he said, 'We have much in common with the Connollys. They are people of the land, as we are; they are gentlefolk; educated—as we have been—but not thereby in any way entitled. Only the famine brought them from their home—'

'And they will return there as soon as things improve, Frank. Mr Connolly is as wedded to his patch of ground as you are to this one,' said Beth, exasperated, rising from the table and putting the kettle over the fire.

Frank began to carry their dishes to the scullery, but even so she heard him say, 'We will see,' beneath his breath.

Beth sighed. Poor Frank. He was besotted.

Chapter 19

In the month that followed the vicar's dinner, Mr Somersall was constantly away—detained in York, then journeying to Leeds and finally being eagerly requested by sundry very respectable businessmen to give his attendance in Liverpool where, by his own assertion, his was the only advice they would tolerate on certain pressing mercantile matters.

Accordingly, Rose's call upon Mrs Somersall was postponed but Herbert was daily in the young woman's company, pursuing with assiduity the task of winning her heart. Like the entire household at the Grange and probably the staff at Ellingbeck, Herbert relaxed, blissfully freed from the tyranny of Mr Somersall's overbearing presence. He spent the mornings lounging around the grounds of the Grange taking idle potshots at the jackdaws that flapped and cawed around the house. In the afternoons he had his horse saddled so as to ride across the moor to the vicarage.

Stephen Milton's desk at the colliery also remained empty, but unlike Herbert, Stephen did spend the days at work on his calculations and schematics, having found within Somersall Grange an excellently appointed library with a large table where he could spread out the sheets, and good light from an easterly-facing window.

Mrs Somersall expressed astonishment on being informed of its existence, and had to be led down the passageways to be shown its location. 'It is just three doors away from the dining room,' she said, 'and

I must have passed this window on my walks along the terrace a dozen times. And yet I have never thought to look inside. Well, Mr Milton, it is indeed a very suitable place for your endeavours I should think, and you are most welcome to use it, at least until Mr Somersall should state his opinion. I am sure *I* shall not disturb you. I am not one for reading such weighty tomes as these.'

But in fact Mrs Somersall found herself rather drawn to the library, in spite of her assertion that she would not disturb Stephen at his labours. Indeed she did not disturb him, creeping in and seating herself on a sofa and turning the pages of *Godey's Lady's Book*[xix] or *The Ladies' Cabinet*.[xx] True, he could sometimes hear her talking softly under her breath, but when he asked her to repeat her remark she would say, 'Don't mind me. I am speaking to myself. Only to myself. It is a habit I have acquired since Ida went away. When one is alone so often, you know ... but if I disturb you, I will return to my sitting room.' Of course he denied that he was in any way discomposed, and so the two went on companionably and, on the whole, Mrs Somersall was happier and more comfortable than she had been since taking up residence at the Grange.

One Monday morning, Herbert sauntered into the library to find Stephen and his mother there. By way of greeting, Mrs Somersall lifted the magazine in her hands and said, 'Poor Ida used to enjoy this so much. Oh! I do miss Ida. I wanted so badly to bring her here with me, but Mr Somersall said she would not do. She is in York now you know, in a tolerably good situation at a school for little girls.'

'You could order the carriage and visit her,' Herbert said, strolling along the shelves with his hands behind his back, not lifting any volume out for closer inspection. 'Nothing would be easier. Or you could take the railway from Whitby.'

'Oh no.' Mrs Somersall shrank from the suggestion. 'I could not. The grooms are so very frightening you know, and as for the train ... I am sure the speed would kill me. And in any case, I am to be at home to receive Miss Eagerly, am I not? Though I must say I had expected her call before now.'

Herbert frowned and went to stand on the hearth rug. 'You know it has had to be put off until my father is home. Stephen tells me that the old man is determined to be here himself and, since he is away, nothing can be fixed. Really it is too trying. You can be sure I would have accomplished it 'ere now if it were not for the old man's command. A comfortable visit here with you from the ladies would have been just the thing. But he is sure to frighten poor Miss Eagerly out of her wits. And what chance shall I have with her then?'

'Is Miss Harlish to accompany Miss Eagerly?' enquired Stephen lightly, bending over a drawing of the mine in cross-section and adding a detail. 'I do not think *she* will be cowed by your father, or by any man.'

'I am not to marry Miss Harlish,' Herbert replied sulkily, 'so the question is hardly germane.'

'Are you to marry Miss Eagerly? By heaven, man, you have gone about your work quickly,' Stephen said.

'Oh dear Herbert,' said Mrs Somersall, 'you must not be too hasty. "Marry in haste, repent at leisure," they say. You must be quite sure of the young lady, you know.'

'As to that, I am fairly sanguine,' said Herbert, turning to the mantel and making close examination of a trinket there. 'The old man requires it of me and I have decided to please him. There is no point in *dis*pleasing him, if it can be helped. We all know that. There is nothing whatsoever objectionable about the young lady. Indeed, she is pleasant and pretty, if a little silly. But I do not object to that. I am silly myself. She is very young, but if her people see her youthfulness as no objection I am sure I do not. But the fact is that while her stepbrother is by I make little progress.'

'Her stepbrother?' Mrs Somersall cried. 'Is that not very irregular?'

'They were not infants together. His mother married her father only three years ago. She was at school and he was at Oxford, so really it is only in the past few months that they have been properly acquainted. But,' Herbert concluded gloomily, 'I think I can say his regard is more than familial.'

'And what about hers?'

Herbert made a moue. 'I cannot say. She likes him, but whether her feelings are warmer than that ...'

'And he is always on hand, you say, when you pay your call?'

'More often than not. The grocer's daughter is there sometimes. She is a flirt of the first order, more likely to drive a fellow's thoughts to lasciviousness than to deter him. But the vicar's wife is quite alive to the fact, and she makes her presence felt by passing the shrubbery, where we usually sit, a dozen times. Then Miss Harlish has attended us on a walk along the river bank and an excursion to an old abbey. She had the headache, conveniently, and stayed in the shade of a tree while we strolled about, so that was more satisfactory. But other than that, Edgar Maybury contrives to appear almost every afternoon and it is all I can do to take one of Miss Eagerly's arms while he affixes himself to the other. So,' with a heavy sigh, 'I have made little headway.'

'Poor lamb,' crooned Mrs Somersall, adding a tremulous, 'your father will be disappointed. I believe he has quite set his heart upon it.'

'He has set his pride upon it, which operates more powerfully than his heart,' Herbert muttered. Then he burst out, 'I wish you would come with me, Milton. There is no need to closet yourself as you do with your nose to the grindstone. I shall not tell the old man you neglect your work. And in fact, if you played your part that would be as productive as all your calculations. You could occupy the curate while I woo the girl.'

'I have been to morning service with you every Sunday,' Stephen said, 'and sat through the curate's sermon for your sake. It is a wonder the church roof did not come crashing down on me, for you know I am a confirmed atheist.'

'I wish I'd accompanied you, rather than attend St Mary's in Whitby,' said Mrs Somersall, surprising both young men, for she rarely expressed anything so daringly individual as a personal preference. 'Nobody speaks to me, except yesterday the wife of the rural dean asked for a donation to some fund or other. Once she had my sovereign in her hand she bustled off to where Lady Riding stood. I bade the coachman drive past Ferret Street, just for old time's sake, but he said the way was too narrow for the coach and so we came straight home.'

'You shall come with us next week mother, if you wish,' said Herbert rashly. 'Father cannot keep you from church, and if we encounter the Eagerlys there without him, he has only himself to blame.'

'I do not know,' said his mother shrinkingly. 'He would not like me to be absent from St Mary's, where he has paid for the pew and has his name on the roll of benefactors. I ought to consult him before I alter my routine. And he would not like me to form an opinion of Miss Eagerly before he did.'

'We are all thoroughly under his thumb,' grumbled Herbert. He consulted his pocket watch. 'It is time I was away. There is to be a picnic this afternoon. Miss Harlish is to open the great house in the hollow. You will not accompany me, Stephen?'

Stephen looked down at his plans. They were complete, to the first and second seams. He would need to visit the lower levels and take some measurements before he could proceed further. 'I have not been invited,' he demurred.

'That does not signify. It is to be quite a party. Half the village is to attend, so has the affair mushroomed from Miss Harlish's original intention. The entirety of the gypsy camp is enlisted to serve, for naturally the Harlishes have no servants; they *are* servants, if you come to that! I believe many people have more interest in the gypsies than in the house.'

'They are not gypsies, Somersall,' said Stephen. 'They are Irish. Itinerants. Immigrants. But not gypsies.'

'I do not see the difference. But have it your own way. More to the point, Miss Harlish's brother will be there. Miss Eagerly says he is something of a recluse. I imagine a bearded hermit in sackcloth. Should you not like to see such a spectacle? And I am told the house is a very curious place, quite hidden away and secret. Mother, you should put on your bonnet. I can have the carriage brought around in a quarter of an hour.'

'Oh no, Herbert, I will not venture,' said Mrs Somersall, but with a light of regret in her eye. 'But you should take a half-holiday, Mr Milton, indeed you should. You have worked without let this month past, and I fear for your health if you do not get some exercise. I ...' she summoned great daring, 'I will tell Mr Somersall that you went with my sanction, if it comes to question.'

'Very well,' said Stephen, putting his drawing implements away in their case. 'I will go and change my boots and see you in the stable yard in five minutes, Herbert, if you will order the saddling of my horse.'

When he had left, Mrs Somersall said to Herbert, 'I beg you will send my compliments to Mrs Eagerly, and tell Miss Eagerly that I hope to see her at the Grange as soon as your father returns.'

Chapter 20

The reader will apprehend from Herbert's remarks that Beth's plan to open the house had considerably expanded in scope from the small private tour she initially intended. Mrs Golightly was delighted to be asked to provide the refreshments, and equally delighted to spread abroad the news that the old house was to be opened up for viewing to a very select few—naturally including herself—and to Miss Harlish's other particular friends about the parish. Beth found herself besieged by requests—some veiled and very diffidently proffered, some quite blatant—to be included in the party. It transpired that her 'very particular friends' were more numerous than she had imagined. Soon the doctor, his lady and their numerous children were added. The Misses MacAllister could not be excluded; the musical Miss MacAllister—Miss Felicity—was particularly desirous of playing the grand pianoforte. The lawyer begged permission to bring his lachrymose wife. The retired academic could hardly be omitted and neither could the schoolmaster. Mr Slade requested an invitation and, as he was funding the lime transportation, Frank agreed to include him, and also—most reluctantly—a couple of other local farmers.

'The affair is getting out of hand, Betsey,' he complained.

Ned Widderington, the publican, declared his intention of 'going down to see the place' whether invited or not, though Frank absolutely drew a line at this, avowing that Ned should not get within a mile of it.

Frank was appalled by the increasing scope of the scheme. Nothing could be more horrifying to him than the idea of playing host. He reminded his sister repeatedly that they were mere custodians, that they had no right to behave otherwise. When she tried to discuss the arrangements with him he had nothing to say. For the first time in years, they argued; Frank saying with his anxious demeanour, taut jaw and more than usual reticence far more than in words how troubled he was. Beth was sympathetic and equally awed but unable now to halt matters. More than once their discord resulted in Frank absenting himself from the gatehouse for a long period, but Beth was used to that; he had always been a person to whom the woods and moors were more of a solace than the comforts of home—although she suspected that a certain Irishwoman had become, to Frank, a better consolation than either. She was sure they met each other in secret; she dared not imagine how far things had progressed.

At last, reading again the letter from Lucas Willow, reassuring and comforting herself with its *carte blanche,* she decided to let the thing have its head with or without Frank's involvement. She would trouble him no more with it. And so she proceeded with her preparations.

The Irishwomen declared themselves more than ready to assist. Brónach, in particular, welcomed the distraction and took upon herself to lead and organise the others, under Beth's supervision. Many were the carpet beatings, dustings, floor scrubbings and window polishings that went on during the days leading up to the event. Likewise, in the garden, beds were dug over, shrubs pruned, gravel weeded and the lawns cut. Cormac assisted with the servicing of the furnace, and a wholesale laundering of Irish garments and bedding took place. All the women and children and some of the men bathed, either in the tin bath in the servants' scullery or in the huge copper claw-footed bath that had been installed in an antechamber off one of the principal bedrooms.

Aoife, in particular, insisted upon the privacy and extra decadence of this location for her ablutions. She, more than any of the others, was enchanted by Tall Chimneys, wandering in quiet awe through the rooms, gently touching the window draperies and gazing up at the portraits that were being rehung in the long gallery. She was drawn to the pianoforte in the music room, which she played with great reverence if indifferent skill. It was badly out of tune, but Tadhg soon remedied that, spending several hours with his tuning lever until the instrument sang sweetly.

Of all the women, Aoife was the least useful, disappearing for long periods of time and giving no very clear explanation for her absences, which invariably occurred when Dónall was away from Tall Chimneys, moving stones at Clough Farm. Her disappearances accorded also with periods when Frank was mysteriously not to be found in the workshops or gardens. Beth sighed. She knew which way the wind blew. But she did not allow this state of affairs to trouble her. She had other things on her mind.

Once the date for the opening of the house was set she saw Ruairi Connolly frequently. He came to visit *her* in these days, not Frank, every day bringing some fresh enquiry, the need for some question to be settled regarding the works that would bring the big house to a state of readiness. He brought Brónach first, that they might go down to the house and look over the tasks in hand. Brónach took the opportunity to return the little garments Beth had made. They were laundered and tenderly folded; some had not even been used.

'There may be another baby,' said Beth tearfully, pressing the things back on her friend.

But Brónach shook her head and said, 'No. No. There must not be another.'

One day Ruairi brought Fearghal and Mícheál, who were to help to tidy the grounds. The more she observed Ruairi's genial larger-than-life self and basked in the whirlwind of laughter that always accompanied him the more she began to suspect that the profound well of homesickness she had glimpsed was only a phantom of the brandy she had so unwisely drunk. His eye was unclouded, his manner untroubled. If he felt any remorse at his unreserve he certainly displayed none. But perhaps, she reasoned, he did not recall it. He smiled at her often and behaved confidentially, more in the manner of a friend than an acquaintance, and she could not help revelling in the glow of his charm. He illuminated and energised. He was all positive thinking and animation. Where *she* doubted, *he* was sure and, particularly in view of Frank's reserve, Beth found herself looking to Ruairi for reassurance.

Even so, she was wary. Ruairi Connolly was a professional charmer, with a twinkle in his eye, rugged good looks and a warm smile that few women could resist. It would not do for her to be ensnared in the net of his charisma.

So, although he addressed her directly, and was the mouthpiece of the Irish folk when direction or clarification was required, she schooled herself to be businesslike and almost cold, answering no more than 'I will discuss it with Elíse' or 'I shall ask Frank to show Mícheál' before excusing herself and hurrying away. She allowed herself no opportunity to observe how he took her abrupt answers and evasive behaviour and strove to master the strong enticement to rest her gaze upon him whenever he was near.

One day however, a few days before the house was due to be opened, it happened that the two of them were left behind when the others rode the trap back to the camp. Frank had been missing since they had drunk a cup of tea in the yard at three o'clock and it was left to Beth to close the windows which had been opened to air the rooms, and to see that the outhouses were locked tight. She threw a pail of scraps onto the compost heap and watered the plants in the glasshouse, leaving the vents open. She thought herself alone until she turned from her task to find Ruairi leaning against the side of the smokehouse, his arms folded across his chest, regarding her with a look she could not decipher. His brows were slightly contracted as though in concentration or puzzlement, but his lips were quirked into the suggestion of a smile.

'You have been avoiding me,' he said, pushing himself upright and coming to take the empty watering can from her. 'Since the night we sat at the fire in the camp.'

'Oh well.' Beth bent to pull a weed from between the bricks of the path. 'I have been busy.' An automatic hand went up to her hair, which was half loosened from its fixings. She tried to tuck it back into tidiness, but felt his hand on her arm.

'No,' he said. 'Let it be. It is prettier so.'

She gave a little laugh she hoped was mocking. 'As if I have time for such things,' she said, but nevertheless left the tendril of hair where it was.

She allowed her eyes to rove the garden—the raised beds, the unused chicken coop, the empty fish pond and, mined into the slope of the crater, the entrance to the icehouse—at anything at all but Ruairi himself, who regarded her discomfiture with cool amusement. The sun had left the hollow and although the air was still warm, she gave a little shudder.

Ruairi said, 'Come, let us leave if your work is done.' He stood aside to let her pass, but not so far that her skirts did not brush against his legs or that she could not smell the aroma of him—a delicious scent of warm cotton and cool charm, soap, tobacco and some unidentifiable aroma that made her insides melt.

She made her way back to the yard and thus to the sweep, but the idea of walking side by side with him up the drive was suddenly more than she could face, so she turned and crossed the lawn instead.

'Let me show you this way,' she said. 'There is still enough light to navigate by.'

She led him down to where the fountain stood, still and flat in the shadow of the trees, and then plunged into the plantation using a path

112

that was hardly discernible. It wove between the trunks of trees and her feet made no noise on the carpet of fallen pine needles. She was critically aware of him behind her and lengthened her stride to put distance between them yet was always conscious of his breath on her neck.

'We children ran up and down here all the time,' she said, by way of breaking the silence. 'My father used it too. I sometimes fancy I see him up ahead between the trees, or hear his steps, or smell the tobacco of his pipe.'

Ruairi said, 'Does that trouble you?'

'No,' she replied. 'It comforts me.'

The path rose steeply, wound between mossy boulders and sometimes crossed little rills of water, leaving the hollow's shadow and gloom and raising them up to where the slanting rays of afternoon light made the leaves above their heads glow like green jewels. From time to time the canopy overhead opened a little to allow streams of golden light to pour onto the forest floor creating glades where, in springtime, wild primroses grew in abundance, but now there was only lush grass.

In one of these glades he reached out and took her elbow. 'Let's sit a while,' he said quietly, 'and talk.'

She turned. Having the advantage of being slightly higher on the slope than he was, she looked him directly in the eye. 'I should get back. Frank—'

'Will be from home a while yet. Betsey,' he said, smiling almost shyly. 'Won't you give me a quarter of an hour?' He motioned to where the grass rose into a little hummock, then spread his coat onto it. 'Please?' A small stream laughed and tinkled between stones, and above them birds flapped and chattered amongst the branches.

Beth's resistance melted. 'Very well,' she said, and lowered herself onto the ground. 'It *is* very nice here beside the stream.'

He sat beside her. His hair, in the late afternoon sunbeam, was full of lights and glints. His chin was shadowed with stubble, but his eyes were like vortexes of starlight, pulling her inexorably into them.

'I like to hear about your childhood. There were four of you?'

She nodded. 'I'm the youngest, and Frank comes next to me. Frank takes after our father. He was a deep-thinking man.'

'You are deep-thinking too, Betsey. I think I have never met such a profoundly meditative woman before.'

She smiled. 'I have had plenty of time for thinking. Our mother was a spontaneous, frivolous person. My sister is like her. My brother Arthur has her lightness of spirit, but my father's intelligence. Our childhood was wonderful, really, but as I have told you, very unorthodox.'

'Yes. I recall all you told me of it. And you spoke also that night of your feelings toward this place. Of being allied ... and also ensnared.'

'Yes.' She plucked a few blades of grass and began to weave them together. 'But it is academic; for how am I to leave?'

'Very easily.' Ruairi lay back and put his hands behind his head. 'You could marry and go wherever your husband would take you.'

'And leave Frank?'

Ruairi narrowed his eyes at the sun. 'Not necessarily.'

Beth's heart beat like a trapped bird in her chest. What was he going to suggest?

'It may be,' said Ruairi languidly, 'that where you go, he finds he also wishes to make his home.'

'But we are committed to Mr Talbot,' said Beth, her voice tight.

'You are *employed* by him. 'Tis not the same.'

She thought about it. 'I suppose not. But Frank declares that he will not leave.'

Ruairi made no reply, and she thought he had perhaps drifted into a doze. She shifted slightly on the grass.

'Why do you not lie down beside me, Betsey?' said Ruairi, turning his head slightly to look up at her through his thick dark lashes. 'It is very comfortable and pleasant, with the song of the birds above and the little brook running by. We cannot always be working, and at the camp I am so often called upon to settle and decide between them. They are like children some of the time, and there is always the worry of where the next day's work might come from, how we might manage.'

'You have all the responsibility of it,' said Beth, feeling a scruple about lying herself down but unable to resist the temptation of it. 'That is a great deal for one man's shoulders.'

Even such broad ones as yours, she wanted to say.

His shoulder pressed against her own, the heat radiated from him. His hand brushed hers and suddenly their fingers were entwined. For a working man, his hands were smooth. She stiffened slightly but he made no further move and gradually she relaxed.

'I suppose,' she said presently, attempting a note of levity that she did not feel, 'that you have lain with many a girl like this, side by side in some secluded pasture or woodland dell. I must tell you that it would be most frowned upon should we be discovered. My reputation would be beyond rescue.'

He turned his head towards her and met her gaze, eye-to-eye. 'Not so very many,' he said, in a voice so low she could barely catch his words. 'But I assure you, Miss Harlish, that I would not permit your reputation to be brought into question.' He lifted a thumb and began to stroke the side of her hand with it, a languid sensuous action that fired bolts of pleasure up her arm. 'So,' he said, 'have you been avoiding me? And why?'

She turned her head back to the patch of sky that showed between the trees. 'Yes,' she said with a sigh. 'I was ashamed. To become intoxicated and then to be carried home like a common dairymaid.'

She felt him chuckle. 'You were a very decorous drunk,' he said. 'No swearing, no lewd suggestions, no bawdy singing and hardly any snoring.'

'Hardly any?' She turned to look at him, appalled, but saw the laughter in his eyes. 'You're teasing.'

He raised himself up on one elbow to look down at her but he did not relinquish her hand, and in fact used his other hand to part and stroke her fingers. 'Such tiny hands that you have, Betsey,' he said, looking down at them briefly. 'I liked holding your hand that night. If anyone were to be ashamed, it would be me. I behaved in an unmanly way.'

'It is not unmanly to have deep feelings,' she said, lifting her other hand so that the four—his hands and hers—were enmeshed and intertwined in a complex arrangement of fingers and feelings.

'It is unmanly to let them show,' he suggested. 'But with you I find my feelings are hard to rein in. There is something about you, Betsey ...' Now it was his turn to avoid her eye. He frowned and swallowed and looked very hard at their hands. At last he raised his gaze to meet hers. 'You have a way of drawing a man out. Is it a trick? Some kind of sorcery? When I am with you I feel that all the flummery—the niceties and conventions—are needless, and that we are just two naked souls—twin souls—standing in the light of God. Do you feel it, too?' he said huskily.

Beth made no reply, but bathed herself in the intensity of his eyes, which were now the colour of dark sapphires. Her breathing was very shallow. His head was so close to hers that she breathed in the air he breathed out.

As she did not reply Ruairi went on. 'There is a star in you, Betsey. A rare star. You shine. When you are near, I cannot keep my eyes from you, or my hands, or my lips.'

The slightest possible lift of her chin would have invited him to suit his action to the word. Time stopped as she trembled on the brink. Then she took a deep shuddering breath, summoning resolve.

She withdrew her hands from his. 'I think,' she said, falteringly, 'that it would be a mistake to remain here much longer. Look,' she continued, more firmly, 'the sun has gone and our way is steep and tricky. We must not linger.'

He gave a heavy, heartfelt groan and then got to his feet, holding out a hand to help her up. 'Very well.'

Chapter 21

The day of the open house dawned bright and clear, yet another glorious summer day. Beth and Frank were at the big house almost before dawn. Beth had determined—in the face of Frank's patent but unspoken reservations—that a very few of the house's treasures—normally kept under lock and key in the butler's safe—would be brought out for display, and that none but their own hands could be trusted in the bringing out, burnishing and placement. The least ostentatious candlesticks were to be placed upon the dining table and the everyday silver was to be used for the serving of tea on the lawn, together with such china that they had in sufficient abundance but not, on any account, the oriental tea bowls brought from the far east by a Talbot ancestor.

They opened the rooms, throwing wide the shutters and adjusting the draperies so that the furniture—uncovered for the first time in half a dozen years—should not be faded by the sunlight. Beth brought out some of the more ancient folios and maps for display in the library. Moodily, Frank unpacked the exquisite collection of classical figurines from their straw-lined crates and arranged them in the music room. The gilded mirrors and more manageable oil paintings had already been rehung. Neither of the Harlishes had a clear idea of the monetary or artistic worth of these artefacts, but chose and placed them based on their childhood recollections.

'It's right that these things should see the light of day once in a while,' Beth told Frank as they unrolled a large Persian carpet in the music room. 'How else will we know if they have the moth, or are damp?'

Frank agreed, but grudgingly. He pointed to a spot at one edge of the rug. 'Do you recall when Arthur spilled candle wax there? We thought Miss Jocelyn would be angry, but she laughed it off.'

'Mrs Orphan was angry,' Beth recalled. 'But she got it off with a hot iron and brown paper. You can scarcely see the mark, now.'

'It was very strange, I suppose,' said Frank, adjusting the rug so that it sat square with the hearth.

'It seems so now,' agreed Beth, 'but at the time we did not think so. We were happy, were we not?'

Frank shrugged. 'We were lucky. Luckier than most. We were never cold nor hungry; and we were allowed to stay, you and me.'

'You did not envy our brother and sister?' Beth hardly needed to ask the question of Frank, addressing it more to herself. But thinking of her late conversation with Ruairi she said, '*Could* you ever leave here Frank?'

He shook his head. 'Never.'

'No,' she said. 'I thought not.'

Through the open window they heard the wheels of a cart and the sound of voices.

'Here are the Irish people,' said Beth, dusting her hands on her apron. 'They are early, as they promised they would be. You should ask the men to begin bringing tables and chairs onto the terrace, if you have finished cleaning off the moss. I will take the women upstairs so that we can make up the beds in the principal bedrooms, then I will cut flowers in the garden to arrange in vases.'

'Do not take too many,' said Frank. 'If all the flowers are in here, there will be nothing to interest people in the garden.'

'I shall not,' said Beth. 'And those I do cut I shall give to our guests to take home. There is no point in them remaining here when the house is shut up again tomorrow.'

'When are the people to come?' Frank asked.

'Not before two.'

He nodded. 'Very well.'

She met Ruairi in the grand hall. He wore a freshly brushed coat and a shirt of fine Irish linen, open at the neck. His hair was pushed back off his face and his chin clean-shaven. He gave her a wide bright smile.

'Good morning to you miss,' he said, sweeping a gallant bow. 'The fine weather I promised you has arrived and we are all assembled below for your inspection. Even Dónall has been scrubbed raw though it took

118

three of us to hold him down.' This final remark was spoken in a voice designed to carry to Frank, who could be seen through the double doors of the music room, adjusting the furniture over the newly laid rug.

'Good morning,' Beth returned. 'You are *all* assembled? Even Caitlin's mother-in-law? And the children?'

Beth's panic must have shown on her face.

Ruairi said, 'The children were not to be denied their holiday. But the old woman remains at the camp, with Father Fearghal. Do not worry. We will not embarrass you, and neither will we encumber you. Everyone knows what is expected.' There was a tightness about his jaw; his gaze, usually so bold and direct, dropped to the floor. 'We will not impose ourselves on the genteel company.'

Beth was filled with remorse. 'Mrs Stockbridge would recognise no distinction and neither do I,' she said. 'Who am I to say that one is better than another? I hope you will all enjoy yourselves.'

'Ah! Miss Betsey,' Ruairi said with a soft smile, lifting his eyes once more to meet hers. 'You're a rare one, and no mistake. Now,' stepping forward so that he was right before her and looking down at her with his keenest and most penetrating gaze, 'what would you have me do for you?'

Involuntarily, Beth took a step backwards and almost stumbled into a settle. He shot out a hand to steady her. 'Careful,' he said in a low voice, 'it will not do for you to fall and injure yourself, Betsey.'

She removed her elbow from his grasp. 'I am *Beth*,' she said severely. 'And I am in no danger of falling.' She moved away. 'I will go down to the kitchen. I am sure Frank will appreciate your help in the music room. There is furniture to be moved.'

She left him and descended to the kitchen, pausing a moment in the stairwell to steady her breathing.

In no danger of falling? What a fool she was to tell herself so!

The Irishwomen were gathered in the servants' hall, neatly groomed, with clean hands, and wearing the freshly starched aprons Beth had issued to cover the worn and patched condition of their dresses; they, at least, were ready to work as well, Beth hoped, as to enjoy themselves. Unlike the others, Aoife wore her finest attire: a bright red overskirt and tightly laced bodice, a fine lace shawl, earrings and a number of beaded necklaces. Her hair was loose and gleaming, and her eyes were bright.

The children were everywhere about the place. They, too, were tidy enough, but busy peering into larders and climbing on the long benches that sat either side of the servants' table.

Caitlin said, 'The children will be no bother, miss, and we hope that the fine folks will like to see them dance. Traditional Irish dancing, miss, such as all the girls and boys at home do learn. Not the …' she threw a glance at Aoife, 'not the dancing that does for the market or the men at the pub, you understand.'

'*That's* traditional,' Aoife retorted.

'No, it isn't,' Caitlin hissed back. 'It's shameful.'

Aoife only shrugged and tossed her head.

'I see.' Beth prevaricated. As she pondered, she noticed Dónall hovering in the doorway. She had not forgotten his attack upon Frank. He was intimidating, and his volatility unnerved her. On the other hand, Frank seemed to be wearing down the lad's defences and she did not wish to undo that good work.

She said, 'Good morning Dónall,' in a determinedly bright voice.

As Ruairi had said, Dónall was scrubbed and groomed, his unruly hair slicked back with grease, and he had shaved—or been shaved—his chin showing the nicks of the razor. He wore a coat and breeches that were probably borrowed and that fit him ill, but which were cleaner and more presentable than his usual work clothes.

He smiled, a wide guileless smile that further tempered her doubts, and she added, 'My, don't you look handsome?'

His grin expanded still further. His gaze travelled to where Aoife stood against the dresser, drawn to her as though magnetised, craving her agreement, but Aoife picked at a fingernail and did not meet his eye.

Beth felt a sudden stab of genuine sympathy for him, a boy within a man's body. The ferocity of his feelings for Aoife were probably unsettling and all but incomprehensible even to himself. He was perpetually innocent and at the same time, inherently—because of his obsession—a danger.

She quickly instructed the women on the tasks she wished them to accomplish. Dónall's expression as the women got on with their work was hard to read—eager, but also anxious and uncertain; wanting to play a part, but not knowing how.

Inspiration came. She said, 'Dónall, if you would be so kind, there are quoits and skittles and ropes and such like in a crate in the stable. I believe there is also a croquet set. My brothers and sister used to play with them when we were small. I wonder if any are still fit for use? If they are, if the children would like to play with them, can you set out the games on the lawn? It may be that any other children who come today will enjoy them, and it will be nice for you all to make friends.'

His brow cleared and he immediately set to work, the children following in his wake.

Alone in the servants' hall, Beth took a deep breath. Her plans were made and the helpers all knew what to do. There was nothing now but to watch the day unfold.

She fetched her secateurs and went out into the garden.

Chapter 22

As it turned out, Herbert was to have unimpeded access to Miss Eagerly that afternoon. Both the vicar and the curate were engaged to attend some diocesan convocation in York and could not return until the evening. Not wishing to miss out on the rare opportunity to see the house, the ladies of the vicarage had been forced to make their own arrangements. Mrs Eagerly was to drive a little trap she kept for going about the parish, but had been urged by Mrs Golightly to accept the assistance of her boy Johnny in the management of the pony.

'The way is terrible steep, ma'am,' warned that good lady, 'and since I am to provide the victuals, Johnny will have been up and down it a dozen times, for there is to be a firkin of ale, as well as a dozen bottles of champagne—real champagne, ma'am, just got from the continent—and some very superior tea, also just procured. And indeed, ma'am, if you should wish me to add a pound or two to your order I can easily do so. Not to mention the ham Miss Beth has requested, and any number of pies ... oh! But I run on and forget the thrust of my remark, which is that Johnny will be as familiar with the drive as he is with the inside of his own nose, and can guide your pony without the least difficulty if you will trust yourself to him. And a sixpence will keep him there to bring you back whenever you are ready. I shall have him present himself at one-thirty sharp.'

Mrs Eagerly had agreed to this suggestion—indeed there was little opportunity to do otherwise. At the appointed hour, both ladies were dressed and ready, the horse between the shafts and Johnny fortified with bread and cheese from the vicarage kitchen. But hardly had the horse been urged into motion when Herbert and Stephen arrived.

Mrs Eagerly sighed. She had hoped to use their drive to interrogate Rose as to the condition of her feelings for her suitor.

The day was very warm, and both men had removed their coats for the ride across the moor. Mr Milton's superior height and elegance of deportment could only overshadow Herbert's, but Mrs Eagerly saw that Rose's eyes were all for the slighter rider, and this had to be sufficient reassurance that things were progressing in the desired direction.

The two gentlemen swiftly restored their coats.

'Good afternoon ladies,' cried Herbert, lifting his hat. 'What a fine day for an excursion! I see you both have parasols. A splendid idea, but that from the elevation of our mounts they prevent us from seeing your lovely faces. I shall dismount and walk alongside you, if I may?' He did so, leaping lightly and landing with aplomb, throwing the reins of his horse to Stephen.

Rose blushed and drew her parasol further down, but Mrs Eagerly raised hers sufficiently to favour Herbert with an ironical eyebrow that communicated more effectively than words ever could that he should concentrate his flattery on its single object. He went around to Rose's side of the gig.

In a voice so low that Herbert had to lean close to catch her words, Rose said, 'Mrs Golightly has quite frightened us. She says the drive is steep and very dangerous. That is why we have Johnny to guide the horse.'

Herbert placed his hand on the back of her seat. 'I shall not allow you to tumble, Miss Eagerly.'

'No danger of *that*,' snorted Johnny. 'I 'ave t'orse's 'ead and can 'aul on t' brake if it comes to it.'

But Herbert ignored the remark. 'A squire is very well,' he said, 'but a knight is far better. Is that not so, Lady Rose?' and was rewarded by a delighted smile.

They proceeded down the lane and took the turn that would lead them past the gatehouse.

'The vicar and the curate do not attend today?' Herbert observed. 'I am heartily sorry to be denied the pleasure of their company.'

Behind them, Stephen smothered a bark of laughter with a cough. 'Indeed,' he concurred after clearing his throat. 'Very sorry.'

'Papa and Edgar are in York,' Rose confided. 'The Archbishop required their attendance. They hope to be back in time to join us later.'

'Excellent,' said Herbert, moving his hand slightly so that it brushed Rose's arm. 'But in their absence I hope you will allow me to attend you. Are you more interested in the interior or the gardens? Milton, I know, is avid to examine the exterior architecture. Give him a gargoyle or a gable, and he is in his element.'

'Perhaps, the interior,' Rose murmured. 'One would like to imagine the lives of the early inhabitants: Jacobite rebels and cavaliers. The men wore luxuriant wigs, I believe, and hats decorated with feathers.'

'You have your history muddled, Rose,' said Mrs Eagerly. She retained the reins but in reality Johnny had the full management of the horse and there was nothing for her to do. 'The cavaliers fought for King Charles I in 1642. The Jacobites came much later.'

'Not so very much later,' Milton muttered. 'Seventy years or so.'

Mrs Eagerly gave an affronted sniff; she did not like to be corrected.

'The house may have seen both but, I grant you, not together,' Stephen amended.

Rose pressed her lips together and lowered her eyes, pretending interest in the fastening of her glove.

'Milton is a perfect compendium of knowledge,' said Herbert. 'I do not know my Saxons from my Stewarts. But what we lack in information we can make up for with imagination, Miss Eagerly. I will happily conjure chevaliers and caballeros, damsels and dragons for your amusement.' And he was favoured with another grateful smile.

They passed the gatehouse.

'This is Miss Harlish's abode,' cried Rose, half rising so that she could peer over the wall. 'What a charming house! So romantic. I wish we could see inside! Oh! But I wonder how they arrange things, Miss Harlish and her brother? There hardly seems room for two.'

'I think Miss Harlish said that at one time the house accommodated six,' said Milton, also taking a great interest in the hexagonal house and its neat gardens.

''Ere's the gates to the big 'ouse,' Johnny announced. 'Now it do get quite steep from 'ere, and suddenly rather dark, on account of the trees. We can take it at a lick, if you like. I did this morning, though I got a clip round the ear for it. Father said the beer would be all shook up.'

'We will take it very steadily, if you please,' said Mrs Eagerly, tightening her grip on the reins. 'If you shake *me* up, you shall forego your sixpence.'

124

The way was indeed very steep, the drive zigzagging left and right down the slope, but Johnny had good control of the horse, which was in any case a steady and surefooted creature. Herbert had more difficulty keeping his feet than the mare did, as the gradient necessitated an increase in speed, his boots slithered on the loose shale of the drive surface and sometimes came dangerously close to the sheer drop. Notwithstanding, he remained staunchly by Miss Eagerly's side and was rewarded once or twice when she grasped his arm, but whether this was in response to the gig's bouncing or to keep him from disappearing beneath its wheels, was moot.

From time to time Herbert gasped out, 'There now. I have you. I have you, Miss Eagerly,' though he sounded increasingly unsure, and at last Mrs Eagerly said, 'Why do you not ride, Mr Somersall? Four legs are better than two, you know.'

But Herbert was not to be moved. 'By no means,' he declared breathlessly. 'I am not so easily to be turned from my purpose.'

Milton plodded behind the gig, looking right and left through the thick plantation of firs and green-leafed trees, catching sight of bright runnels of water, mossy boulders and enticing glades.

'A very curious spot,' he said at one point. 'Whyever was the house built down here?'

'Miss Harlish does not know,' replied Rose, over her shoulder. 'Whoever did so must have wished it to be a secret.'

'What a strange hush there is,' said Mrs Eagerly. 'Hardly a bird sings. I hope Tall Chimneys does not turn out to be a gloomy place. One hardly relishes a whole afternoon in a dank hollow. I am glad we brought our shawls, Rose, for although the day is warm, here it feels chill.'

But just then the trees began to thin out, and filaments of warm sunshine began to filter through the canopy, and birds could again be heard chirping in the branches. The drive levelled, took a sharp turn and they were out of the trees altogether, in a wide pleasant clearing at the centre of which stood Tall Chimneys, bathed in sunshine, its windows gleaming and open, its door thrown wide. Before the house was a lawn, which extended round to the side where the sound of music could be heard.

Rose gasped. 'Oh! How beautiful!'

Miss Harlish and a fellow Mrs Eagerly did not recognise stepped forward. The fellow took charge of the gentlemen's horses. Though he had but one arm, he managed both with ease. He would also have taken the vicarage horse in hand, but that Johnny—with an eye to his sixpence—retained it.

Herbert said to Stephen, 'That will be one of the gypsies.'

Stephen hissed, 'Irish,' but Herbert had already repeated the remark to Rose, adding, 'Shall we have our fortunes told? They all have the sight, you know. Should you like to know what the future holds, Miss Eagerly? I own that *I* would.' He gave her a significant look, and took her hand to assist her in descending. He pressed it warmly and was rewarded by feeling it tremble in his.

The horses were led away towards the rear of the house.

'Mrs Eagerly,' Beth cried. 'And Miss Rose. How pleased I am to see you. And Mr Somersall too. How are you? And Mr Milton. I am happy to see you again.'

The gentlemen bowed and Herbert said, 'A pleasure, Miss Harlish. I hope we are not ahead of our time. Milton's enthusiasm for the venture was not to be contained, I do assure you. He has been straining at the leash since daybreak.'

Stephen Milton frowned, but could hardly contradict his friend for fear of causing offense. 'I own I am eager to see the place,' he said, gazing up at its façade. 'The original structure was Jacobean, I apprehend. Probably just a tower. You can tell from the steep pitch of the roof, and the decorative stonework. These other wings are later.'

'You already know more than I do,' said Beth with a smile. 'I wanted to make it clear that my brother and I are merely custodians of the house. Factotums only. Servants. Of its history we know little. We are happy to welcome our friends today—all our friends.' She glanced significantly at the little knot of men and women from the camp who stood diffidently waiting to be of service. 'But there is to be no misunderstanding as to our position.'

'That's quite understood, Miss Harlish,' said Herbert, misunderstanding completely. He invited Rose to take his arm. 'Miss Eagerly and I prefer fiction to fact, and are ready to invent its history to our own design. May we go in?'

Beth gestured them forward. 'By all means. You will find refreshments on the terrace, when you are ready. The doctor and his family are already there. I hope the children have not eaten all the cake! Oh! Here are the Misses MacAllister. You must excuse me.'

Another gig had emerged from the drive and she hurried to greet its occupants repeating, as they stepped down, her disclaimer as to proprietorship or authority, but at the same time feeling immensely proud. In the absence of the Talbots or Mrs Stockbridge, who else could claim greater connection to the house than herself?

126

Stephen watched her go with regret but then, seeing Mrs Eagerly without an escort, could do no less than offer his arm. 'You'll do me the honour, ma'am?' he muttered.

They went together into the house, finding themselves in a large hall where the well-polished, honey-coloured oak planks on the floor and the darker wood panelling around the walls gave a warmer welcome than they had expected. An enormous fireplace stood opposite the door. Herbert had seized an ancient sword from its fixing above the mantel and did battle with an imaginary assailant, to the pealing pleasure of Rose.

'Mr Somersall,' cried Mrs Eagerly, aghast. 'That sword could be hundreds of years old. Put it back!'

Herbert gave a last lunge with the weapon, impaling the fantastical villain.

''Twill not be the first blood spilt on this ground,' he said theatrically, replacing the sword with a flourish, 'and by God, should Lady Rose require it, it will not be the last!'

Rose attempted to smother her laughter, but unsuccessfully. Herbert had hit on the juvenile playful manner calculated to appeal to her.

Mrs Eagerly said, 'Silly boy,' but not unkindly, and they all walked into the library where an elderly gentleman was busy perusing the folios. He stood up at their approach, removing spectacles from his nose. He was short of stature and wide of girth with tufts of grey hair that grew above his ears but from nowhere else on his head, not even above his eyes. His face was round and purple with thread veins, his eyes small but bright with intelligence and, due to the lack of eyebrows, had a perpetually astonished expression. That he had no wife was apparent from the dirty, unbrushed state of his coat and the stains on his shirt, but there was no mistaking him for a poor man. A large diamond shone from a ring on his little finger and a heavy gold watch and chain dangled from his breast pocket.

'I do not think I have had the honour,' he said gruffly. 'I am Bissel. Professor. Of Bracken Lodge.'

Herbert introduced the vicarage party. 'And I'm Herbert Somersall, of Somersall Grange. This is Milton, my friend and associate. Pleased to make your acquaintance.'

'I do not think we have had the pleasure of seeing you at church,' observed Mrs Eagerly pointedly.

'No ma'am,' said the professor. 'I am not an adherent. I am examining this extraordinary cartography.' He indicated the documents. 'If I am not mistaken, these are early maps of the Americas.'

Stephen Milton would have enjoyed looking over the maps but the pressure on his arm indicated that Mrs Eagerly wished to move on in pursuit of Rose and Herbert, who had already gone into an adjacent room.

'A pleasure to meet you, sir,' Milton said with some regret.

The next room was the music room but the doctor's children, thumping discordantly on the pianoforte, made lingering there impossible and they moved across the passageway to the dining room. Here Mrs Eagerly swallowed down an envious lump in her throat. Her own dining chamber, in comparison, was minute. Here was proportion! Here was elegance! Here was capacity! The table—gleaming mahogany—was easily twenty feet long, with a thumb moulded top of highly figured hand cut timbers. 'Two dozen people could sit down with ease,' she murmured. She relinquished Stephen's arm and sauntered along the sideboard, where a number of priceless Dutch Delft tureens and platters were on display, along with various gilded trays and bowls and a canteen of solid silver cutlery. 'Rose,' she said, 'come and look at these. They are exquisite.'

Herbert said, 'I wish Mother had come. It would do her good to see that she is not alone in having nice things.'

'I doubt hers are as nice as these,' said Mrs Eagerly. 'These are over a hundred years old.'

'Of course ours are new,' Herbert allowed. 'But equally fine, in their way. I must say the old man has spared no expense.' He glanced down at Rose to see if his words had struck a chord, but she looked bored. 'Come, Miss Eagerly,' he said, offering his arm once more. 'Let us go upstairs and see if we can find the ghost.'

Rose shrieked—but delightedly—'A *ghost?*'

'But of course,' Herbert assured her. 'Old houses always have ghosts.' He looked to Mrs Eagerly for permission. Over their heads, the doctor's children had abandoned the piano and were running amok along the landing. The pair would not be alone.

'Very well,' she said with an indulgent smile. 'Go and find your ghost.'

The two ran from the room, laughing as unconstrainedly as the children above.

'I cannot think,' said Mrs Eagerly slowly, 'that Miss Harlish can quite understand the value of these things. No doubt she has an eye for beauty …'

'There *is* Miss Harlish,' said Stephen, seeing her pass the doorway with two elderly ladies in tow. 'Shall we join them?'

They followed the sound of Miss Harlish's voice down the long gallery and found her in a small but very elegant sitting room. 'Miss Talbot preferred this room,' she was saying to her companions. 'Oh! Here are Mrs Eagerly and Mr Milton.' She effected the introductions before proceeding. 'Miss Talbot never used the larger rooms. There was never any company, you see. There is a small table under the window where she wrote her letters but sadly she never received any reply, poor lady. She was disowned by her family, for what fault we never could discover. I believe she wrote a sort of journal also. She must have been lonely. She took her meals here too, at one time. But latterly she ate with the rest of us in the kitchen, and spent her days at work about the place, and she appeared much happier. It seemed normal to us after a while, her joining us. But I know it was singular.'

She went on to describe the room to one of the ladies, who was blind. 'A powder blue paper upon the walls, figured with a trellis of roses in white relief. The curtains are brocade, a darker blue, the colour of the sea, or so I am told. I have never seen the ocean ...'

Stephen lingered in the doorway and observed her. The sun was off the room, which was east-facing, but still her hair had golden lights within it. He admired her neat figure, her simple dress, the way she brought the room to life for the blind lady.

She reached down to a low shelf where a number of children's books lay. 'She read these books to the children. I ought to give them to the Irish children. They can do no good here. I do not suppose there will ever be children in this house again.'

'The Talbots do not have an unmarried son about them?' Miss Felicity MacAllister enquired. Her voice was reedy. 'It would be so fitting for you to become *chatelaine*.'

'There is a son, I believe, Mr Rafe. He is about my own age. But as to his marital state, I cannot say. And in any case, I would not presume so high.'

'You show proper diffidence,' Mrs Eagerly observed.

Stephen opened his mouth, ready to make an angry retort. Miss Harlish needed no diffidence nor any false modesty. She would not be kept confined, if he could help it. But he swallowed his spleen. It was not his place. He met Beth's eye, however, and they understood one another.

'I wonder,' said Beth, 'if I might leave the Misses MacAllister in your care, Mrs Eagerly? If you make your way to the terrace, there are refreshments. I must return to the drive. Mr Milton, could I prevail on your assistance for a moment?'

She left the room and Stephen followed behind her. He said, 'What assistance can I lend, Miss Harlish?'

When they were out of earshot of the sitting room she turned and said, 'None at all. But I thought you would like to be unencumbered. Mrs Eagerly can manage without you. Do you not wish to join Mr Somersall and Miss Eagerly?'

'By all means, if you will accompany me. I believe they have gone upstairs.' He motioned towards the staircase.

'Regretfully, I must return to the drive—that part of my statement was true! Perhaps later, we might have some conversation.'

'I hope so,' he replied, but she had already passed through the doorway and he was left alone in the sun-dappled hall.

Chapter 28

The day progressed with the arrival of the lawyer, his wife pale and drooping on his arm, and then of the schoolmaster, who had no wife, drooping or otherwise but who brought instead his very aged mother. She was surprisingly sprightly however, and extremely loquacious. Indeed, she spoke without ceasing from the moment of her arrival to the time of her departure, but she was well informed as to the house's antecedents, having lived in the village for her whole life, and found a ready audience amongst those who, though living in the vicinity a good while, had never visited the house.

'A solitary woman lived here for many years,' she said, blinking up at the splendid façade of the house. 'Old Mrs Talbot, that was. The place was much smaller then. I do not recall these additions, but then I came here only once or twice, with Papa. Papa was the vicar, then, before dear Mr Eagerly and before Mr Foley, whose wife went quite mad. Papa brought me when I was quite a young girl. Mrs Talbot's husband and her son were in India, we were told, making mountains of money. Every so often a wagon would come bringing treasure, or so we were led to believe. The husband died on his voyage home; and though the son survived the voyage, he never returned to this house, though by then his mother had become a cripple. How a boy can neglect his mother I do not know!' with a fond look at her own son. 'In truth, we saw little of the woman, for she rarely ventured forth, and then only in a closed carriage. She lived here all alone apart from a maid girl and a manservant. The gatehouse was made over for them, for they married, or they *said* they married. That was in '80, when I had the rheumatic fever, for I recall that when I fell ill it was a ruin, but by the time I recovered it had been restored, and Papa carried me down the lane to see it. They were a surly disreputable pair, those servants. And in fact Mrs Talbot died months before we heard of it. How long she lay mouldering here I do not know. That was in 1805, the year my dear brother died in the battle of Trafalgar. The servants cleared out. Foul play was suspected; you can imagine the gossip! She was quite at their mercy. No doubt they starved the poor old woman to death and took vast quantities of gold. But then Miss Harlish's parents came, and all was well ... now I do recall Mrs Harlish ...' She continued to speak as her son led her into the house, followed by the lawyer and his wife and a couple of farmers and their families, who had arrived in the interim. But the remainder of her discourse was lost to Beth, who stayed on the sweep to greet her guests, and on the whole she was glad not to overhear what a slovenly will-'o'-the-wisp her mother had been thought.

Now she looked up at the house. How it seemed to bask in the attention, the clinging ivy and wisteria positively shivering with pleasure. She could hear the hum of voices on the terrace, the thwack of croquet mallets on the lawn and the laughter of children, so much more vibrant than the faint ghostly echoes that sometimes drifted to her ears.

She did a quick count in her head. The only guest yet to arrive was Mr Slade. Probably Frank ought to be the one to greet him. But where *was* Frank? She had not seen him since much earlier.

She walked to the yard. Several grooms and some of the Irishmen were gathered around the beer barrel. She saw that Mrs Golightly had provided fare, which was set out on a trestle table just within the coach house. Beth was rather angered, for she had not wished there to be a division. Ruairi was with them. He leaned over Miss Golightly, who was seated on a mounting block, a mug of ale in her hand. They seemed to be sharing a joke. The charismatic smile so often bestowed on Beth was now all for Flossie Golightly.

Seized with jealousy, Beth said, 'Miss Golightly. I am sure your mother has need of you on the terrace.'

'Oh no, she has not,' said Flossie saucily. 'I am to ensure the working folk are fed for now. When the music and dancing begin, I shall go to the terrace readily enough,' she cut her eyes at Ruairi, 'so long as I have a partner.'

Ruairi smiled and took a pull of his beer. He said, 'Is there something I can help you with, Miss Harlish?'

'Why do you not mingle on the terrace?' she enquired.

Ruairi gave her a twinkling grin. 'Because you are not there.'

'Charming,' snorted Flossie, draining her ale.

'I'm looking for my brother,' said Beth. 'Have you seen him?'

'No, not this hour gone,' said Ruairi. 'In fact, I think he disappeared the moment your first guests arrived.' He quirked an eyebrow. 'You did not expect him to play *mine host?*'

'I expected him to be *present.*'

'I will endeavour to make good by my presence your brother's truancy. You can be sure of *me.*'

When she got to the terrace, however, she saw that Frank's absence had not been remarked. The guests sauntered on the lawn watching the children's games, or sat beneath awnings drinking tea or champagne. Herbert and Rose played quoits by the fountain, the doctor and his wife looking on. Miss Arabella MacAllister engaged Mrs Eagerly in quiet conversation while Brónach had seated herself alongside the lawyer's wife. The two spoke confidentially together, both occasionally dabbing their eyes with handkerchiefs. A coven of farmers' wives and the schoolmaster's mother had moved chairs to the shade of an oak tree, where they ate from plates piled high with pie, cold chicken and slices of ham. The old woman's mouth moved relentlessly, either in chewing or in speaking, or in both. Her audience crammed their mouths and listened to her, wide-eyed, as she regaled them with anecdote and gossip. The farmers stood nearby, the delicate champagne glasses awkward in their hands, their Sunday collars chafing in the heat. Someone was playing the pianoforte—Miss Felicity MacAllister, she identified. The music filled the house and Beth's own soul swelled with joy.

Caitlin and Elíse moved amongst the company replenishing cups and glasses and offering platters of dainty sandwiches and pastries. Just within the French doors she could see Eistir managing the kettle on a spirit stove and tidying the buffet. The professor, the lawyer and Mr Milton stood before one of the portraits deep in conversation.

Everybody is here but Frank. She fumed, but indulgently, until it dawned on her that Aoife was also nowhere to be seen. Her lenience crumbled. That woman was leading Frank astray; she was a bad influence. Frank had not been the same since he'd first seen her. Where could they be hiding? Surely, they would not be so flagrant ...? She stood back and scanned the upper windows of the house. From one of them, two faces looked down at her, their expressions unpleasantly smug. But neither of them was Frank or Aoife.

Beth mounted the stairs feeling her temper ripening. Ruairi followed her, taking them two at a time. She hadn't requested his attendance but he must have seen her surprise and indignation. 'Tis Mr Slade,' he said, catching up with her at the first turn, 'and Ned Widderington, from the Plough. Were they not invited?'

'Mr Slade was,' Beth allowed as she led the way along the landing. 'We heard that Ned had it in mind, but we scarcely thought he would have the brass neck to turn up. He is not to be trusted within half a mile of a silver spoon. They should have made themselves known, rather than roaming unannounced and unaccompanied about the house.' She found that tears were near. Seeing those men, one of whom she knew to be thoroughly disreputable, lolling from the window as though they owned the place, had ignited a flame of jealousy. How dare they? 'Frank should be here,' she said, her voice choked.

'*I* am here,' said Ruairi, touching her arm. He looked down into her face and saw the simmering tears in her eyes. He pressed her arm. 'I am *here*,' he said again with great intensity. Then he strode into the room.

The men were in the principal bedroom, and they were not alone. Fionn lurked by the dressing table, examining a heavy silver dressing table set and an oriental trinket box.

'Don't touch those!' Beth cried, and he sprang away guiltily, his wall-eye raking the ceiling.

Before she could say more, Ruairi stepped towards Ned Widderington and Mr Slade. He held out his hand in a gesture calculated to disarm them and they had both shaken it before he said, 'Upon my word, gentlemen, you rather insult your hostess by poking around in her house without being introduced.'

'I need no introduction,' said the publican. He was a slight, fleshless man with flinty eyes, a mean mouth and an adenoidal tone. 'Miss Harlish knows me.'

'But she did not expect you today,' Ruairi said levelly. 'You ought to have apologised for barging in, before doing so.'

Ned curled his lip. 'This is not *her* house.'

'Miss Harlish makes no claim to anything, other than good manners,' Ruairi retorted, and turned away from him. 'Mr Slade,' he said to the other man. 'Let me introduce you to Miss Harlish. Miss Harlish. Mr Slade, of Clough Farm.'

Beth managed to dip a small curtsey but her animosity to the man could not be extinguished.

Fionn slunk from the room, his hands in his pockets.

Slade was a tall, imposing man but not a handsome one, with a large nose and watery eyes and a preternaturally pale complexion. He had a great quantity of ginger hair both upon his head and worn as whiskers on his cheeks. He was impeccably dressed, however, and had an air of ebullient authority quite at odds with his sneering companion. Beth did not know which she found the most repellent.

Slade smiled to reveal a jumble of yellow, irregular teeth. 'I must apologise,' he said to Beth. 'I met this fellow as I rode down the drive and, finding no one to greet us, we made so bold as to explore the house. I must thank Mr Connolly for reminding me of my manners. How do you do, ma'am? What a pleasure it is to meet you. Though I think I could have picked you out from a crowd. Your resemblance to your brother is uncanny. Where *is* Mr Harlish?' He looked beyond Beth and Ruairi, through the open door and into the landing, as though expecting to see Frank hovering there.

'He is detained at present,' said Ruairi smoothly. 'Let me escort you both downstairs so that you can make acquaintance with some of the local families. There is tea, or champagne if you care for it. Or,' turning to Ned, 'beer, for those who do not appreciate the finer things.'

'The beer is fine,' Ned carped back. 'I supplied it, so I should know. Nothing wrong with beer, unless folks think themselves too high for it.'

Ruairi began to shepherd them from the room. 'To be sure, I like a glass of beer myself,' he said.

Mr Slade said, 'Where is your sister, Connolly? I have a great desire to renew my acquaintance with her. It is some while since we saw her at Clough Farm.' Something about his tone made Beth shudder.

'Ah! She is somewhere about the place, no doubt,' said Ruairi.

Left alone, Beth touched the silver mirror and hair brushes and straightened the counterpane on the bed before opening still wider the casement window, wishing to remove the smell of stale tobacco and sweat that lingered.

She visited the other two bedrooms that had been opened for inspection. Nothing was amiss. Except that still there was no sign of Frank or Aoife.

The afternoon began to wane, the sun leaving the hollow hours before it would slip below the rim of the moor. From an upper window Beth watched shadow slowly engulf the fountain. Beneath its shroud, Herbert and Rose sat close together on a stone seat. Soon the lawn, then the terrace would be swallowed up. The champagne must be all drunk by now, and the food all eaten. Surely the children would begin to tire. The farmers' wives had become somewhat raucous. They had wrested the croquet mallets from the children and begun an inept, inebriated game. One of them tripped on a hoop and lay on her back on the lawn, her skirts akimbo, laughing uproariously. Conn and Dónall rushed to help her up. Mrs Eagerly and even the lawyer's wife lifted their hands to smother smiles. The sighted Miss MacAllister leaned towards her blind sister to explain the cause of the laughter.

At the end of the terrace Mr Milton sat alone, the ankle of one leg resting on the knee of the other. He held a book in his hand and was reading intently—or appeared to do so. Beth watched him for some moments; he never turned a single page.

Suddenly, as successful as the day had been, Beth wanted it to be over, for the horses to be brought out and for people to climb into their gigs and carriages and leave Tall Chimneys to its solitude once more. Even the Irishwomen, as helpful as they had been, were beginning to weary her—their bright, interminable chat, the way they allowed the kitchen door to slam, the crashing of pots and pans as they washed up in the scullery were all becoming intrusive. She would dismiss them. She would rather clear away herself, in the familiar silence. She and Frank, together, could put things back to rights.

But she saw that Caitlin and Brónach were gathering the children, ready to dance. Tadgh and the other men had taken up their instruments. The other guests began to gather in a polite semicircle to watch the performance.

She ought to go down.

On her way, she looked down on the rear yard from a landing window. It would have been swamped in shadow, but that someone had lit a fire in a brazier. Fionn had joined Lorcán and the grooms near the beer barrel. Their number had been augmented by the farmers and Ned Widderington. All drank liberally of the ale. Their jocular talk rose up to her on the still dusk air. Fionn fanned out a deck of cards, enticing the men to part with their change. Flossie Golightly lolled against the stable door asleep, her mouth open, her breasts rising and falling, her empty beer tankard dangling from her fingers.

She would miss the dancing.

Chapter 24

Beth had just reached the hall when she heard the sound of a carriage on the drive. The front of the house was all in shade now, and someone had lit torches along the periphery of the sweep.

The carriage was a brougham, very grand, pulled by four black horses and attended by two men in livery at the rear, as well as the coachman.

For a terrible moment, Beth thought that Mrs Stockbridge or worse, Mr Talbot had come. Her mind flew to the letter they had received from Lucas Willow that might be proffered as proof of permission given.

The footmen descended and hurried to let down the step of the coach and to open its door.

An extremely portly man struggled out. He wore no hat but was otherwise immaculately dressed. He waddled self-importantly towards Beth, leaving his diminutive wife to be handed out of the carriage by the footman.

'I'm Somersall,' the man announced, looking about him. 'Where is your master?'

'Mr Talbot is from home.' Beth faltered, completely wrong-footed.

'Do not tell me Mr Talbot is from home. I *know* he is from home because I left him just yesterday in Leeds. But this house is given over to a cousin of some sort, is it not? Where is he?'

'Mr Talbot's cousin is Mrs Stockbridge, sir. She is away.'

'Away?' Mr Somersall looked astonished. 'Away, you say? So who is in authority here? What other member of the family can you summon to greet me. I am Somersall, I tell you.'

His wife had ventured to join them on the steps of the house. 'Oh, Peregrine,' she said, reaching out a tremulous hand. 'We are not expected. I told you it would be so.'

He shook her off. 'But we will not be turned away, Mildred. Herbert is here, and his prospective bride, and I have Talbot's blessing to look the girl over and by God I *will* look her over.'

Beth began to take stock of the situation and to gather her wits. She essayed a smile. 'I am sorry to say that there is no member of the family present, sir. I am Beth Harlish. I have the honour to be Mrs Stockbridge's representative—'

'Representative!' Mr Somersall blustered. 'Hardly. My man of business, intimate though he is with my affairs, would hardly venture to elevate himself by such a title; and *you*, I apprehend, have not the confidential understanding of your mistress's concerns as he has of mine.'

'I am in charge of the house,' Beth insisted, speaking loudly, 'in her absence. However little I may deserve such an honour.'

Somersall regarded her narrowly, and then took in the drive—gaily illuminated by torches—and the rooms he could see beyond the hallway—candlelit now, and arrayed in all their splendour. 'And you entertain your friends, do you, in her absence and no doubt at her expense?' he asked contemptuously. 'I do not know when I have ever heard of such presumption. I am a man well acquainted with the overreaching audacious impudence of some members of the lower orders; but *this,* I think, takes the biscuit.'

'Sir,' cried Beth, very angry. 'You mistake entirely—'

'Mistake? No, not me. Not Peregrine Somersall. I am no doubt a man who *makes* many things, but I am not a man who makes mistakes. Now, as to my son. Is he here?'

Beth breathed in through her nose, summoning fortitude. 'He is,' she said stiffly. 'And he will be fetched.'

By this time, some of those who had been gathered around the brazier in the yard had come forth to see if assistance was needed. Lorcán exchanged a few words with the coachman, indicating water or stabling for the horses should it be required, but the fellow regarded him with a sneer.

Mr Somersall said, 'Fetched,' you say? I think not. I am not the kind of man to be kept waiting on a driveway. I insist upon being shown inside, and properly received.'

He would have barged past her, but that Beth stepped neatly to one side and said stiffly, 'By all means, sir,' and was able to usher him into the hall. 'Ma'am,' she added to the timorous Mrs Somersall who cowered on the step. 'I am Beth Harlish. I think perhaps your son may have spoken of me.'

'Indeed I believe I have heard your name mentioned, and,' in a very confidential voice, 'I do apologise for the intrusion.'

Mr Somersall yelled, 'Mildred!' and she hurried in his wake.

The sound of music and the children's voices permeated from the terrace. Mr Somersall followed them, but not without crossing the thresholds of the library, music room and drawing room to take quick assessment of their size and appurtenances.

'I do not wonder Talbot never comes here,' he observed. 'What poky rooms. Where is my son?'

They entered the dining room and stepped out onto the terrace, which was the only area of the grounds to have any sun at that point in the afternoon. The children had completed their display, and were curtseying prettily to their audience. The sun was in Mr Somersall's eyes and so he did not immediately see the gathering of people on the shadowed lawn. Only their applause alerted him to the presence of some dozen people, but it faded to silence at his appearance.

He squinted into the sun, raking the company with his censorious eye. 'I don't know you, or what manner of people you are, although by the evidence of these beggarly children I ascertain you are not people of quality. You will know me, no doubt. I am Somersall.' He looked along the terrace, where a table and two vacant seats caught his eye. 'My wife will take tea, if any can be procured, and I will have brandy-and-soda.' He seated himself and indicated the chair opposite, to which Mrs Somersall scuttled and sat down. 'If someone will have the goodness to tell my son I am here—'

'Father,' said Herbert, emerging from the gloom of the lawn and stepping onto the terrace. 'Upon my word,' he said, laughing nervously, 'I did not expect to see you today.'

Caitlin and Brónach hurried the children away with the promise of cake in the kitchen. The doctor's children and those belonging to the farmers also went in search of like refreshment. The other guests, amused and intrigued, lingered in small knots so as to be able to overhear the remainder of the encounter. Elíse brought a cup of tea and placed it onto the table before Mrs Somersall. She gave the gentleman a gimlet look. She did not like to have her child described as "beggarly."

'What manner of maid are you?' he enquired with a curled lip. 'And where is your uniform? Dear me, what a slovenly household is here. My friend Talbot will be glad to know of it. Where is my brandy-and-soda?'

Elíse said, 'I am no manner of maid, sir, though I have manners, which is more than can be said for some. And as for your brandy, I am afraid there isn't any.' She stalked away with her head held high.

Ruairi stepped up to Beth and bent to murmur into her ear. 'There *is* brandy,' he said quietly. 'I will bring it, though I hope it chokes the man.'

But Mr Somersall was oblivious to the stares, the amusement and even the affront of his onlookers. He addressed Herbert. 'This is nice company you keep,' he said. 'I wonder you do not find it more convivial at the colliery. There, at least, is discipline and decorum and respect. If you'd been there, or at the office, you would have known well enough I was expected home today,' he carped. 'But I am told you have not been seen there this entire month.'

'Father, I ...' Herbert, manufacturing at great effort an expression of genial unconcern, gestured towards the end of the terrace, where Rose and her mama stood. Rose was white-faced, her eyes round and glassy with sheer dread. She shrank against Mrs Eagerly, who herself wore a look of revulsion.

But Mr Somersall ignored Herbert's gesture. 'They say when the cat is away the mice will play, and upon my word so it seems,' he said, giving his son a very disdainful glare. 'I do not see why you should draw a salary when you do no work. That is not the way of things. I do not pay the miners, nor the engineers, nor the farriers, nor the banksmen nor the coal-pickers nor yet the lamproom men nor even the clerks to do nothing, do I? Do you think they would expect to receive their stipend for staying at home all day?' He swigged the brandy that had been placed before him, spluttering, for it was undiluted. 'This is not brandy-and-soda,' he said, gasping.

'No, sir,' said Ruairi coldly.

Nevertheless, Somersall held out his glass for more and Ruairi, who had foreseen that this might occur, placed a second glass down.

Somersall looked Ruairi up and down. 'Upon my word, the servants here are no more than churls and miscreants,' he said. 'The house is a den of insurrection and revolt. Servants setting themselves up ... I never heard of such a thing. I shall tell the captain of militia, with whom I am well acquainted. He will clear the place as a terrier clears a nest of rats.'

Ruairi's expression remained neutral; he stared into the middle distance as though the man was no more important than one of the flower urns that lined the terrace. He maintained his position at Mr Somersall's elbow, his considerable height and muscularity saying more than words.

'Sir ...' Herbert appealed. He looked very pained and ashamed, and wrung his hands. Those who had up till now rather enjoyed the spectacle, began to murmur their displeasure; who was this man to so insult them? Did he not see the vicar's lady, the doctor, the lawyer? But more even than their own offense did they feel Herbert's discomfort. They had rather liked the young man, and they did not wish to witness his humiliation. They began to drift away.

The shade had crept onto the terrace and now engulfed it. Only the upper windows of the house blazed with late afternoon sunlight. As warm as the day had been, soon it would grow chill within the hollow. Distractedly, Beth began to think about shawls and wraps for the ladies. But what was the point? Any moment, they would make their excuses and depart. Half an hour earlier she had wanted them to leave. But not like this. She drew herself up, ready to confront her unwelcome guest, but she met Ruairi's eye—clear, level, competent—and she desisted.

The colliery owner turned back to Herbert. 'So, sir. Have you an explanation for your truancy?'

Mrs Somersall screwed up her courage to say, 'Mr Somersall, you forget. Herbert has been most assiduous in pursuing the task with which—'

'Do not interrupt me, Mildred,' said Mr Somersall fiercely, although she had not done so. He banged his hand on the table and caused her tea to slop into its saucer.

Ruairi took a half step closer to Somersall's chair so that he loomed over him.

Somersall said, 'Step away, man.' But Ruairi remained fixed, making no sign of hearing the command.

Stephen Milton stepped forward. His hands flexed at his sides. 'As much as I hesitate to contradict,' he said, although in fact most eager to do so, 'Herbert has been assisting me with the schematics you required. His knowledge of the mine has been invaluable. And then also, of course, he has been such a comfort to his mother, who would otherwise have been left quite unattended. But *this,* sir, is neither the time nor the place for such a discussion.'

'Oh! You are here, are you, sir?' said Somersall, peering around Ruairi with difficulty to eye Stephen. 'You have not been at your desk either, I hear.'

'Not at the office,' Stephen replied whitely, 'but you will find that I have not neglected my duty. In the meantime,' he forged on, 'I think you came here with the intention of meeting Miss Eagerly. Let that be accomplished, and then you need be detained no longer, and what is left of Miss Harlish's entertainment can proceed.' He gestured to invite Rose forward. She came most unwillingly, as a lamb to the slaughter, taking refuge behind Herbert, though in truth he provided very insubstantial protection.

'Mr Somersall, Mrs Somersall,' said Stephen, very stiffly—his temper was barely in check—let me present Miss Eagerly, and her stepmother, Mrs Eagerly.'

The ladies curtseyed, Rose very wobbly, her mama barely bending an iota, so affronted and appalled was she.

Mr Somersall struggled from his chair, bowed perfunctorily and then would have collapsed heavily back into his seat had Ruairi not whipped it away.

'You will not sit, sir, while there are ladies standing,' he said, mildly admonishing, placing the chair for the vicar's wife. Stephen swiftly brought another for Rose, who looked as though she might fall at any moment.

Somersall staggered, almost fell, and only saved himself by clutching at the vines which covered the wall. 'You cur,' he exploded when he had righted himself, but Ruairi had melted from the scene.

Mrs Somersall put out a hand to the young woman who was seated beside her. 'His bark is much worse than his bite,' she said, clutching poor Rose's shaking hand. But Rose was not reassured. A fat tear fell from her eye and rolled down her cheek.

'I think I heard you say that you have met Mr Talbot,' said Beth, in order to expedite the episode which could not now be avoided. 'In Leeds.'

'Yes, indeed,' said Mr Somersall, looking Rose over narrowly as though sizing up a horse. 'A most agreeable man. A man of business. A man with whom to *do* business.'

'And he mentioned Miss Eagerly?'

'His goddaughter, yes.'

'He sent his affectionate regards, no doubt,' Stephen put in. 'The vicarage family is invited to his town house in October.'

Somersall waved Stephen's remark away and addressed himself to Rose, who cringed beneath his regard. 'You are very young,' said Mr Somersall. 'What age are you?'

Rose moved her lips but no sound came forth.

'She is just seventeen years of age,' said her mother tautly.

'Herbert is two-and-twenty.'

'*Three*-and-twenty,' Mrs Somersall murmured. She still held Rose's hand.

'I will not be contradicted!' roared Mr Somersall, making his wife absolutely flinch. Rose began to cry in earnest.

Mr Somersall turned away, almost disgusted. 'She is not what I expected. I must speak with Talbot to see what he will settle upon her. If he is generous, that might make it worth the risk.' He looked up at the house. 'This, perhaps, would be a reasonable dowry. I suppose they must live somewhere, though upon my word, there must be a wholesale routing of these scruffy and impertinent servants. But there must be shares also, and ready money down.' He sighed and wiped his hands on his handkerchief as though he had completed an arduous job of work. 'If Talbot is forthcoming, I will not object.'

'But perhaps I will, sir,' said Mrs Eagerly standing, full of spleen. 'And so might the vicar, when he hears of your unconscionable rudeness.' She opened her arms to her daughter, but to her surprise it was Herbert's bosom onto which Rose threw herself.

'She is a dear sweet girl,' Herbert burst out, finding that the prize he had agreed to win at his father's behest was now very much one he desired on his own account. He enfolded Rose in his embrace.

'No doubt,' said Mr Somersall disdainfully. 'As your mother was. A dear sweet biddable creature. Come, Mildred.' His wife leapt to her feet and followed him across the terrace. He stopped at the French doors. 'You will come and dine,' he said over his shoulder. 'My wife will send a note.'

It was not known who escorted the Somersalls from the premises. Beth certainly did not. Their departure left her feeling both eviscerated and furious. She sank down onto the chair that Mrs Somersall had vacated, filled with dismay. Her day was ruined, the event a failure, her guests—her friends—insulted. The feeling was augmented when Mrs Eagerly announced her intention of going immediately home. She was in high dudgeon, haughty and offended, barely able to say a civil farewell before climbing onto her gig and commanding Johnny to lead the horse on.

Beth returned miserably to the terrace where she was greeted by Ruairi. 'An interesting interlude,' he said, his eyes twinkling, 'but the evening is young. Your remaining guests would like to dance, I think.'

'Really?' She was amazed. She had expected Mrs Eagerly's withdrawal to initiate a smart exodus by all the rest.

'Yes. With your permission?'

She nodded, and looked on with an astonished detachment as the furniture was pushed back, torches brought, the musicians assembled and her guests encouraged and cajoled into forming up into a set.

Brónach called the steps as the Irish folk guided the locals in reels and jigs. More champagne was opened, and the children brought out again to demonstrate the trickier steps: heels and toes, drumming and cuts.

Stephen Milton did not dance, but took it upon himself to refill the champagne glasses so that the Irishwomen could enjoy themselves. Flossie Golightly got a second wind, and squealed with delight as she was hurled around in the *Port an Fhómhair*[xxi] and the *Tonnaí Thorai*[xxii] by Ruairi and then by any other man who would partner her. Mr Golightly— surprisingly light on his feet for such a large man—danced with Miss Arabella MacAllister, Elíse and Caitlin, and even Mrs Golightly was persuaded to take a turn when Herbert requested her hand. The lawyer's wife positively laughed. The professor regaled anyone who would listen with a potted history of Irish culture. The farmers and their wives threw themselves into the dance with abandon. Mr Slade approached Beth, but she declined, sitting next to the sightless Miss Felicity MacAllister and describing to her, as best as she could, the figures and movements of the dance. But when Ruairi approached her and held out his hand, she rose automatically and placed herself into his arms and allowed herself to be guided down the long set, and it seemed to her that they two danced alone on the ancient terrace beneath the starry canopy of the night.

Chapter 25

The longcase clock was chiming nine as Beth saw her guests—some quite unsteady on their feet—into their carriages, laughing and calling out final farewells. The hollow was deeply dark, the sun having long since left it, though the house's windows blazed with light. The vault of sky above them winked with the first stars.

The doctor piled his wife and children into their trap. The lawyer and his wife—more cheerful than she had been this many a day—drove away. The professor in his phaeton, and the farmers on their carts departed, as did Mr Slade, mounted on a fine bay and Ned Widderington, atop a skinny hack. The Misses MacAllister were handed into their hired gig. The schoolmaster and his mother—still talking—prepared to leave. And lastly Mr and Mrs Golightly, with Flossie wedged tightly between them on the seat of their conveyance, joined the train. They all departed at last, their horses disappearing into the tunnel of the drive to begin their slow ascent.

Herbert Somersall and Stephen Milton remained. 'We have not seen your brother,' Herbert said. On the upper floor, someone went from room to room extinguishing the lamps and closing the windows. From the terrace came the grunts and shouted instructions as the Irishmen manoeuvred the furniture back indoors. The children played on, their enjoyment of the toys and games undiminished though they played in darkness—the torches had burnt out. Herbert indicated the women from the camp, who passed back and forth collecting crockery and glasses and packing up what little remained of the food. 'These people are quite able to see to things here, Miss Harlish,' he urged. 'You must be tired. Let us see you home.'

'I cannot leave it to them,' cried Beth. She was, in truth, exhausted—emotionally and physically spent. 'I am responsible,' she sobbed. 'Frank should be here.' She wrung her hands. 'Indeed, I do not know where he can be.' Though the last two hours had passed happily, she had not forgotten the agony of the Somersalls' visit, or her bewilderment at her brother's absence.

'Miss Harlish. Betsey,' said a voice in the gloaming. Ruairi Connolly's voice. 'Brónach has made fresh tea and saved you a plate of victuals. You have neither eaten nor drunk the whole day through, she says. Come.' He reached out a hand towards her. 'Come to the yard, where the fire will warm you. Eat and drink.'

Stephen bridled. '*Miss Harlish* can do better than the yard, I think,' he said.

'The kitchen then, or any room you like,' Ruairi said, shooting Milton a meaningful look. 'Let these gentlemen accompany you. Only do come and sit down before you fall.'

Beth allowed herself to be guided to the hall, where she sank down upon the ancient settle. Behind her, the steady percussion of the clock was a solace. Herbert and Stephen perched either side of her. She accepted the cup of tea that Ruairi brought, though she waved away the food. 'Where is my brother?' she asked.

Ruairi smiled. 'I am sure he will appear. No harm will have come to him, in any case, I can assure you of that.'

'Because your sister is with him?' Beth murmured. She feared the exact opposite. 'Wherever they are, they are together.'

'Exactly so,' Ruairi said. He looked at Herbert and Stephen, but seeing that they were not minded to give place to him, he only indicated the food, communicating to them that they should use their influence to get Beth to swallow a few mouthfuls. Then he strode off towards the dining room.

Milton proffered the plate. 'Eat a little, Miss Harlish,' he said. 'A little of the cold chicken, perhaps?'

To please him, she took a morsel.

Herbert said, 'The day has been uncommonly enjoyable, with one exception. I cannot tell you how sorry I am, Miss Harlish. Up until his advent, I was making great strides with Miss Eagerly. I heartily wish he would confine himself to business. He has no aptitude for society. What goes at the colliery does not do amongst gentlefolks.'

Beth turned to Stephen. 'Do you make any progress at the colliery?'

He was moved that she wished to distract from Herbert's discomfort, and that she recalled the topic of their prior conversation. He handed her a small sandwich before he answered. 'I am drawing up schematics to show that the pump is inadequate, and the ventilation engine likewise. And I have gone so far as to design new apparatus—a large engine that will do the work of both current pumps. But I think I do so in vain. Mr Somersall is not disposed to take my advice.'

'He is not disposed to take anyone's advice on any subject,' Herbert said with a grim face. 'You should not take it personally.'

'I do not, but I fear the men who drown or suffocate may do so,' Stephen said.

'I wish you could meet my brother.'

'Upon my word, we hoped to do so today,' said Herbert.

'Not Frank,' said Beth. 'My elder brother. He is an engineer. He works for Mr Talbot. He would not allow you to waste your talent.'

'I should very much like to meet him,' said Stephen. 'Another sandwich?'

Beth shook her head.

'Very well,' said Stephen putting the plate aside. 'Finish your tea then.'

Beth did so, sighed, and then rose, though the rising was an effort. 'I must see to things,' she said. 'You do not need to stay. I can see myself home, or I will go with the Irish people. Goodnight, gentlemen.' She went into the library and closed the doors.

Herbert and Stephen sat on in the hall. Though the front door was still open it admitted no light, and indeed seemed to draw more darkness in, dimming the light from the single candle that had been left to light the room. The two men could hardly make each other out.

'Did you propose to Miss Eagerly?'

Herbert flushed, though of course Stephen could not see it. 'She said that I may speak to her papa, but that was before my father came.'

'And will you?'

Herbert sighed. 'I suppose so, however hopeless my chances now.'

'Do you love her?'

'I think I do, now.'

'And what about the curate?'

Herbert rose and paced the floor. 'What can he offer her? Nothing! A curate's stipend! But then, if Father cuts me off, I shall have less than that.'

'You can only ask, and accept her answer.'

'Let us go, Milton. The vicar may have returned by now. I can call at the vicarage and get the thing done.'

'You speak of it as though you were having a tooth drawn. You go. I shall remain here and see Miss Harlish home. Tell the man in the stable to have my horse ready, if you will.'

Presently, Stephen heard the sound of Herbert's horse on the drive, but he remained in the hall, waiting.

The clock struck ten, then eleven, but Stephen sat doggedly on.

Beth and her helpers moved around the house almost in darkness, only a few lamps lighting the rooms as they replaced the covers on the furniture and fastened the shutters. When at last the kitchen was put to rights, the glassware and china returned to their rightful places, all the women and children and most of the men departed using one of their carts. Only Fionn, Dónall and Ruairi remained. Fionn and Dónall loaded the other cart and stood in readiness while Ruairi accompanied Beth over the house, ensuring all was locked and secure. The flickering candle that Ruairi held aloft seemed hardly to move the thick darkness, nor did their soft footsteps disturb the cloaking silence. Beth felt disembodied, as though dreaming. When they came to the dining room, Beth gasped. The candle illuminated the treasures on the sideboard.

'We cannot leave these here,' she said.

'All will be well,' Ruairi assured her. 'You must leave something for Frank to assuage his guilt at deserting you.'

'I am very angry with him,' Beth admitted. 'I wish he had told me that this was his intention.'

'Sometimes, we cannot know,' said Ruairi cryptically. 'But the day was a success, yes? With or without your brother.'

'I suppose so,' said Beth, suddenly so wiltingly tired she thought she might simply lie down on the floor and sleep. Perhaps she sagged, or half fell. Suddenly his arm was around her. She could feel the heat of the candle he held in his hand and also his heat as he held her securely to himself. She had not the strength—nor the will—to step away. She allowed herself to lean against him, to breathe in the scent of sandalwood and soap and manliness that exuded from his chest and his shirt. She felt his chin against her hair, the soft rasp of his cheek. She reached an arm around his waist and snaked another up around his neck. He leaned slightly, putting the candle stick down on the table, and then wrapped his other arm around her. She had not been held by a man since she was a child, when her father had carried her or held her on his lap. She had forgotten the wonderful security of it, the sense of being cared for and protected, the sanctuary. But there was something else, now, a feeling that demanded more, that commanded her to press harder and deeper; and his safekeeping contained an element of most desirable danger. The imperative—and the paradox—of it made her tremble.

He moved his hand and brought it to her face, smoothing the hair that had escaped its arrangement hours before and then lifting up her chin.

'Open your eyes,' he said softly.

Then came the sound of brisk footsteps along the passageway— Frank! Ruairi would have retained his hold on her, but Beth sprang away.

But it was not Frank.

Stephen Milton said, 'Miss Harlish. It is almost midnight. I will take you home now.'

Chapter 26

Stephen mounted, and Ruairi lifted Beth up so that she sat across the horse, partly on the saddle and partly on Stephen's lap.

Some half an hour before the three had moved to the drawing room, which was adjacent to the dining room, and free of its romantically charged air. Ruairi argued, charmingly but strongly, that Beth should remain at the house. There were beds made up, he said, and food for breakfast and the drive, in this darkness, would be hazardous for even the most surefooted horse. Plus her fatigue was extreme. Anyone with eyes could see that Miss Harlish was utterly done in.

But Stephen had resisted any suggestion that Beth stay at Tall Chimneys. Alone? Unthinkable! Even with both him and Mr Connolly to stand guard, it would not be seemly, and since the village females and all the Irish ladies had departed, he would escort Miss Harlish home to the care of her brother.

The debate, conducted in hissed undertones, had taken place above Beth's head. In truth, she had been almost beyond caring.

Stephen had prevailed, and now he placed a hand firmly on her waist and took the reins in the other. He urged his horse into motion.

The sweep was impenetrably dark, the house no more than a smudge of charcoal, and only the whiteness of Ruairi's shirt distinguished him from the surrounding dim. Nearby, the harness of the Irishmen's cart horse rattled.

Beth said, 'You'll see to the house?'

Ruairi nodded. 'I will.'

Then the horse was moving, and Beth could only look over Stephen's shoulder to where Ruairi remained on the sweep, a lone figure, his hands in his pockets. Then he was gone, absorbed into the night. And they were gone too, swallowed by the utter blackness of the drive.

'How will you see?' she murmured. Her head had fallen onto Stephen's shoulder. Sleep was almost upon her.

'The horse will manage, and my eyes will adjust by and by. Rest, Miss Harlish, and soon you will be safe at home.'

The motion of the horse beneath her, and Stephen's stolid support, did lull her. His nearness was not like Ruairi's, which had been meltingly tender and inviting, a feather bed she could have sunk into. Stephen was rigid, a fortification of rectitude, and yet she sensed, within that carapace, a simmering vat of magma—passion, but barely contained. He was angry, disgusted perhaps. He did not approve of her friendship with the Irish.

'You do not trust him,' she muttered into the collar of his coat.

'I do not know him,' Stephen replied stiffly. 'I own he seems considerate of you.' He was thinking of the tea and food, she supposed. 'But I have told you, people like him will never repay what you give.'

Beth thought about the extra work that had come Frank's way since the advent of the Irish people, and the other alterations in her brother they had wrought, which she supposed she must count as good since they made him happy, however briefly. And the day that had just passed— none of it would have been possible without their aid. How hard they had worked, and how willingly, with no question of pay, although she supposed Frank would arrange some remuneration.

'I am not sure,' she said through a yawn.

'I pray I am wrong,' said Stephen.

The journey up the long steep driveway seemed to take hours. The night was very still, the motion of the horse so soporific that Beth felt suspended in a state of quasi-wakefulness, anchored only by the firm grip of Stephen's arm and the texture of his coat on her cheek.

At some point they were overtaken by the cart. Stephen moved his horse to the side so that it could pass them. Its wheels were quiet on the shale of the drive—another of Frank's adaptations, she thought blearily. She could not make out Ruairi amongst the hunched figures on the seat.

Whether Stephen's horse laboured under his double burden or whether Stephen himself—desirous of prolonging the exquisite episode—allowed it to amble and dally, can only be inferred. Either way, over an hour had passed before the gap in the trees indicated the end of the driveway, and a single light burning in the gatehouse window showed that Beth had reached home.

'Frank is within,' she said, lifting her head from where it had lain on Stephen's shoulder, and stretching her arms above her head.

'He has neglected his duty today,' Stephen declared, as he assisted Beth to slide from the horse. 'I shall come indoors with you and tell him so.'

'Oh no,' said Beth, 'I beg you will not. He will have some explanation and … I partly know what it is. You do not know his character. I was a fool to think he would wait on our guests today. He deplores any kind of society. It was enough that he allowed me to have my head. I will not chastise him.'

'Well,' said Stephen who had dismounted now and stood with the reins in his hand. His arms—without Beth in them—were empty and useless, so he stroked the horse's neck. 'If you are sure.'

'I am quite sure, thank you. I will wish you goodnight.'

She turned away from him and put her hand on the latch of the gate.

'We did not have that conversation,' said Stephen abruptly, almost sulkily. 'I wish to converse with you, Miss Harlish.'

'Oh?' She turned to look at him, but even with the low glow of the lamp in the window his face was obscure. 'On what subject?'

'On any subject,' he burst out. 'Name it, and I will take it up. Botany, philosophy. Why grass is green, why birds fly, who made the moon … Cervantes, Shakespeare … life, death, love … *especially* …'

'My goodness,' she said. 'That is a wide range. One conversation will not encompass it.'

'Good,' he said, but his passion was vented. He managed a wan smile. 'The more, the better, in my view. You understand me, Miss Harlish?'

She said, 'I believe so, Mr Milton. Goodnight.'

She entered the garden and put her hand upon the door but did not open it until she saw Stephen disappear in the greyness of the lane, and even then she lingered, preparing herself for the discussion she would need to have with Frank. She had passed beyond fatigue. A strange calmness enveloped her. She felt as though she floated at a distance, and watched herself as she stood at the door.

At length, as the church clock struck the half hour, she turned the handle, opened the door carefully and stepped into the scullery. The dog lay across the threshold of the inner door. He raised his head and whined.

She bent to pat him. 'And why have you been shut out?' she asked quietly. Normally, the dog lay at the foot of Frank's mattress, by the fire.

She removed her shoes and hung her shawl on the hook before stepping over the dog and opening the inner door.

The muted lamp threw a sickly sallow light over the interior, and the smouldering coals on the fire added a lurid sheen. Why had Frank banked the fire? The room was suffocatingly hot. Abandoned crockery littered the table: two plates; a board with cheese and bread; a bowl of tomatoes; a flagon of cider—empty—and two drinking vessels, one of which lay on its side. Other elements of the room—usually so tidy—were in disarray. Clothing was draped over the chairs and the banister. Frank's boots had been kicked under the table. The settle was askew. The room reeked of something feral she could not name.

Frank's mattress lay before the hearth, a strew of covers and blankets concealing the man who, no doubt drunk, had collapsed in a stupor.

Beth was shocked. Frank never drank to excess, but then after her over-indulgence at the camp, she had no high horse upon which to climb.

The blankets on the bed began to move, were thrown back, and an arm emerged.

Beth said, 'Frank,' intending to reassure him, to fetch him water if he required it. But the arm was not his. It was slender, the hand small.

'Frank!' Beth repeated, more sharply.

Frank and Aoife sprang up in the bed.

Frank said, 'Betsey,' in a high voice she did not recognise, and clutched the covers to his body. His eyes were bleary, his chin and cheeks rough with stubble. She had never seen him look so dissolute.

Aoife said nothing. Her hair was everywhere, in wild disarray, tumbling over her shoulders and pooling on the pillow behind her. She made no attempt to cover herself; beneath the cascade of her hair, her shoulders and breasts were naked. She levelled a gaze at Beth that was full of knowing and triumph. The smile she offered, through lips swollen from passion, was exultant. She lifted a languorous hand to her hair, pulling her fingers through its knots, and then reached out and ran her fingers down Frank's arm, a proprietorial gesture that offended Beth more than all the rest.

Again, Beth said, 'Frank?'

'We are married,' he blurted out. 'Married today by Father Fearghal.'

Aoife lifted her hand to show a wedding band.

'Is that our mother's?' Beth gasped, appalled.

Aoife held her hand out to admire the ring on her finger. She said, 'Of course.'

'Oh, *Frank,*' Beth cried. 'How could you? What good will it do?' She looked at Aoife. She was feckless, selfish, immodest. 'She will not be a good wife,' she said, 'and this is not her home.'

'It *is* her home now,' said Frank, 'and she is the wife I have chosen.' His hazel eyes challenged but also held a quality of helplessness. He was determined on his course, but needed her aid if he was to succeed.

Despair engulfed Beth. She turned and went back into the scullery without any clear idea in her mind, only too disgusted and appalled to remain in the fetid room any longer. Automatically, she bent to put on her shoes. As she tied them, the door opened and Frank's head appeared in the gap. He had put his shirt and trousers on. 'Where are you going?'

She shrugged. 'I don't know.' She glanced past him, seeing the disarray of the room and catching again the sour whiff—of sex, she realised. She shuddered. 'I cannot stay here.'

'Why not?' He stepped through the door and closed it behind him, but still spoke low. 'This is still *your* home. We will live together, the three of us. Aoife agreed to it.'

'I cannot stay here,' Beth repeated dully. 'No house needs two mistresses.' She wrapped her shawl around her shoulders and put her hand upon the handle of the outer door.

He stayed her. 'But where will you go?'

'I don't know,' she replied wearily. 'If only you had told me, Frank. I would not have prevented you. But we could have made arrangements.'

'It is the small hours,' said Frank. 'You cannot just go—'

'I can. Don't worry. I will find somewhere. It is not so very late. Perhaps the Eagerlys ...'

Frank groaned and raked his hair with his fingers. 'Oh, Betsey. I *wanted* ...'

'I know,' she said, smiling. 'She has bewitched you. But it is done now, and we must find a way forward. But not tonight, Frank. I am bone weary.'

She stood on tiptoe and kissed his cheek, an unusual gesture between them. Then she left the house.

The dog must have slipped out behind her. She felt his nose nudge her hand as she stood, undecided, on the lane. There was no moon, but the night felt benign and oddly comforting. It was not cold. The moor stretched out around her. She could see a reddish glow, which must be the Irish camp. Perhaps they would welcome her. The occasional wink of light from windows in the village suggested that not everyone was abed. She had no intention of going to the vicarage, though, in spite of her assertion. She would sleep in the wood, she thought bitterly. On the moor.

In a ditch. What did it matter? But no. There was only one place she could go, only one place where she would be safe.

She turned, and began to walk down the drive.

A figure emerged from the shadows. 'Betsey.'

She regarded him. 'You knew,' she said hollowly. 'You knew, and you did not warn me.'

'I tried.' Ruairi stepped closer. 'I tried to get you to stay at the big house. Then tomorrow I would have told you. This was *your* day. We all agreed on that.'

Beth shivered, but not from cold. 'You *all* knew?'

'No. Just Frank and Aoife and me. And Father Fearghal, of course. He was needed to officiate.'

Beth continued to walk down the drive. The darkness was intense and yet, as Stephen had suggested, she found her eyes soon adjusted. Ruairi kept pace with her, and the dog trotted behind.

Presently, she said, 'Why did it have to be a secret?'

'Because of Dónall. I fear that, from him, it must remain a secret. At least for a while.'

'He will realise, when you all move on and she stays behind,' she said dryly.

'Ah yes. Then he will know.'

'And before that, I apprehend. If she is to live at the gatehouse, with Frank.' The words caught in her throat.

'These last weeks we have habituated him to her absence. And Frank has frequently been at the camp, so he is used to seeing them together. We have tried to manage matters. No one wants to distress the boy.'

'He is lucky,' Beth said, unable to keep the bitterness from her voice. 'My feelings were given no such consideration. No one gave *me* a second thought.' She sounded churlish, but she could not help it.

'You're wrong there,' said Ruairi, but he did not elaborate.

They walked in silence for a while. Beth's mind was so mazed with shock and tiredness she could summon neither energy nor erudition, but images from the day just gone swirled around like pictures in the zoetrope the professor had shown her one day—the guests, the elegant food and drink, Miss MacAllister's beautiful piano playing, Tall Chimneys—quivering with pleasure. Stephen Milton seated alone at the end of the terrace waiting ... for *her*, she now identified, for the conversation she had promised him. The Irish children dancing. Brónach and the lawyer's wife. That insufferable man—it had amused her to see him stumble when Ruairi removed his chair. The dancing. And then later, in the dining room, by candlelight ...

She stopped abruptly and looked up into Ruairi's face. 'You do not need to come with me,' she said. 'You certainly will not stay with me. Perhaps that was your plan, earlier?' Had it been, she wondered? Had he planned to seduce her, and keep her at Tall Chimneys while Frank … Perhaps *that* had all been agreed, along with the rest. Frank and Aoife would marry, and to keep things tidy she and Ruairi …

'Not in the way you think,' he said quickly. 'I know I can never match Frank's good fortune.'

'Good fortune, you call it?' Beth almost laughed. 'For her, perhaps.' She resumed the path.

'You don't think she loves him?' Within two strides, he had caught up with her. 'Aoife could have any man, but she chose him. Only love could have made her do that.'

'Self-love, perhaps. Or the chance of a ready-made home, security … the devotion of a *real* man as opposed to a doating boy.'

'She has a home back in Ireland, and I can offer her all the security she will ever need.'

'You cannot offer her a husband's love,' said Beth, surprising herself. Until recently she—Beth—had not realised the great difference the love of a man who was not family could make. 'Perhaps she does not believe you will ever return,' she went on. 'She has given up your dream, for one of her own.'

'I do not blame her,' said Ruairi through a clenched jaw. She could tell that he saw the truth in what she said, and was wounded by it.

She pushed the knife home, stopping once more and turning to face him. 'You sacrificed everything for her,' she said, 'and she has not kept faith with you.'

Her eyes were fully adjusted to the darkness now. She could see his face, white and drawn, the muscles of his neck and jaw taut, and his eyes bright with tears.

'By God, you're right,' he cried out, his voice breaking. He raised clenched fists to his head. 'We have both been betrayed, Betsey. I begged her not to do it. I spoke of our farm, the old house where we were brought up as children, the green rolling pastures, the path through the woods to the river … oh! Betsey, if you could see it, so beautiful as it is, the air soft as lambs' wool, the water sweet like honey … none of it moved her. She spoke only of being tired of travelling, of living like tramps, and she spoke of some need …' he pressed his hands to his breast and Beth gathered that Aoife had made a similar gesture in trying to explain herself to him. '… some need that she could not explain to me. But I know she hated being looked at askance, of being different and alien, distrusted. We all

156

do! We have not been treated with compassion, you know. From one place we were hounded, though there was sickness amongst us from the boat and the children were hungry. In another there was no work, or no work that we were permitted to undertake, and the children had to beg ... and Aoife, she has had to subject herself to lewdness from men just to get a few sixpences. She has suffered more than any of us.'

'I know. I know,' she said, appalled at the effect of her cruelty. 'I am sorry.'

'Oh! *You* have no cause to be sorry. You have been kind. You and your brother both. I think that's why ...'

'Yes, yes,' she said. 'I see. Frank *is* kind. He will be good to her.'

Ruairi rummaged in his pocket and brought out a handkerchief. 'I know it,' he said, wiping his eyes. 'But she will never belong here. And now *I* will have to choose *again*.'

They continued. The darkest part of the short night was over, or perhaps Beth's shock had sufficiently subsided and her angst expiated itself in their talk. It seemed to her that the air was paler. She could make out the trunks of trees as they passed. In the depths of the wood, a bird sang a few experimental notes.

As they walked she reflected on the words they had spoken—or not so much the words but of the honesty the words had borne. What had he called them? Twin souls—standing in the light of God. She'd had the same notion, though she hadn't told Ruairi so. But it was undeniable. With Ruairi she felt a kinship, an absence of artifice. They understood one another. What point was there in denying what was as evident to her as it was to him?

The steepness of the drive began to level out and soon the house came into view, veiled in pre-dawn greyness. It waited for her, patiently, as she had known it would, a refuge. It was not hers—she knew it would never belong to her—but she belonged to it, and perhaps that was almost as good.

Her feet crunched on the gravel, Ruairi's beside her as they approached the house, and she felt its welcome.

Ruairi took the key from his pocket and opened the door. They entered the hall.

He looked down at her. 'What will you do now? Will you sleep?'

She sighed. 'I suppose so. And then I must think what I shall do.'

'What do you mean?' He stood very near. She could feel his breath on her hair. She was so weary and yet she felt a flare of heat from within that seeped some unsuspected energy into her core.

She looked up into his face. The blue of his eyes was like the heart of a flame. Her mouth was dry. 'I don't know,' she said.

He smothered her words with his kiss. His lips were soft, practised. The glowing ember of heat within her became an inferno. She felt its white heat, like the fire in the lime kilns, melting her limbs and boiling her organs until she thought they would explode.

She felt his hands in her hair, on her neck and breast. Her own hands tore at his clothing. As he kissed her he lifted her, moving swiftly across the hall and reaching behind her to push open the library door. He swept cushions from a settle and lowered her onto them.

He said, 'I must have light. Just a little, so that I can see you, Betsey.'

She lay in a half swoon, almost delirious, both afraid of and desperate for what was to come. She heard him unlatch the shutters and a pale ray of dawn light showed the well-known appointments of the room as shadows and ghosts, barely there. Only Ruairi was substantial in that dreamlike fantastical brume of desire and shock and sleeplessness that filled the room and Beth herself.

She said, 'Ruairi,' and held out her hand to bring him to her, but he did not come. She heard his feet cross the room and throw open the connecting door to the music room.

He groaned, and when he spoke his voice was low and tight. 'Betsey,' he said. 'Get up, darling. Things are amiss.'

His words were a deluge of cold water. The conflagration in her body utterly quenched. She struggled to her feet, straightened her dress and tucking her hair behind her ears looked dazedly about the room. The precious folios and maps were scattered about the floor. She followed Ruairi to where he stood just within the music room. The figurines were missing from the mantel. One had been dropped, smashed; splinters of porcelain littered the hearth. They moved in horror to the dining room. The Dutch Delft had disappeared; the candle sticks, the gilded trays and the solid silver cutlery—all gone.

'Tell me you put these things away,' Beth said, turning agonised eyes on Ruairi.

'No,' he said. 'I am sorry. I had not thought that we would be leaving the house ...' He coloured a little, and looked at his feet. 'It is Milton's doing. Had he not persuaded you ...'

'No,' said Beth bitterly, her face ashen. 'It is mine. All my own.'

Chapter 27

'You remain here,' Ruairi said, helping her to a chair for she had gone so pale she seemed likely to swoon. 'I will fetch help.'

'There *is* no help!' Beth wrang her hands. 'The things are gone!'

'But the thief may be caught, if we are quick about it,' he said, grabbing his coat from where he had cast it off in their passion of a moment before.

'Ned Widderington,' she spat. 'If I know anything, the treasures will have been transported halfway across the county by now.'

He paused. 'You suspect Ned?'

'I do,' she said. 'He is a thorough villain. Everyone knows it. But he is wily. There will be no proof, and a dozen witnesses will have him behind the bar for the entire evening. The parish constable will do no good—he is doubtless in Ned's pocket. The magistrate will have to be sent for, and the nearest is in Whitby.'[xxiii]

'Then we will send to Whitby. I will fetch your friend the lawyer. He will advise us. And Frank. I will send Frank.'

He disappeared back up the drive he had traversed twice in the last hour, leaving Beth alone.

She found and lit a lamp, for the dawn light was watery, and surveyed the carnage with a mixture of horror and shame. She suppressed an instinct to tidy up the shards of porcelain and to restore the folios to order.

She supposed the magistrate, when he came, would wish to see the house as the thief had left it.

It was cold in the house and she pulled her shawl around her, but nothing could assuage the deep hollow of sick despair and guilt that assaulted her.

She had failed Tall Chimneys and betrayed Mrs Stockbridge. And she had nearly ... oh-so-nearly ... but she would not think of that.

She trailed through the rooms, the light of her lamp throwing weird and grotesque shadows onto the sheeted furniture and the walls. She was assailed by gloom. She would certainly be dismissed, resolving the ambivalence of her relationship to Tall Chimneys. The place she had both loved and resented would be closed to her and she would find out, she supposed, whether she could live away from its sheltering walls and happy—oh! such happy—memories. As the Irish had been banished from their land, so would she be banished. And scorned as they were, for she would receive no reference. People might even suspect her to be complicit. Hadn't she insisted on getting the treasures from their vault? Hadn't she left them here, unprotected? Hadn't she invited all and sundry to look upon them? What hubris, to set herself up! And now, what humiliation, to be cast so low.

Outdoors, the sky was lightening into pearly grey morning. She ached from tiredness but her agonised mind would not let her rest, and she felt too ashamed—too tainted—to rest herself on any of the house's chairs, much less to lie on even the least of the beds. She did not deserve respite. Oh! If only Frank was here. He would comfort her. He would see some way through this dreadful situation. If only he had *been* here, instead of sloping off, beguiled by Aoife's dark eyes and alluring smile. He would not have allowed Ned Widderington entrance to the house.

But the thought of Frank—and of Aoife, his wife—stabbed Beth with deeper remorse. She must save him *because* of her, who must be supported now. He had never smiled upon the scheme to open the house. He had done it to indulge her, and perhaps also to distract her from his assignations in the woods, on the moor ... anywhere, she supposed, where Dónall's gimlet eye would not find them out.

She went to the little sitting room in the east wing that she had shown earlier—oh! with such insufferable pride—to the Misses MacAllister. The sun had not yet risen above the line of trees, yet in this room the first light had a tinge of warmth in it and was sufficient to write by. She blew out the lamp and seated herself at the desk, pulled paper from the drawer and flipped open the lid of the ink well.

Her first letter was to Mrs Stockbridge. She explained the bare facts: which artefacts had been stolen; the timings so far as she knew them; that a magistrate had been summoned. She took the entirety of the blame upon herself, tendering her resignation as stewardess of Tall Chimneys with immediate effect, and stating also her intention to find alternative accommodation. As regards Frank, she exonerated him completely and, mentioning the change in his marital state, recommended that Aoife take her own place as custodian of the big house and its contents. She apologised, describing her great remorse, and finally thanked Mrs Stockbridge for all the good she had conferred that she—Beth—had now rewarded with so ill a return.

The second letter, which she enclosed within the first, was addressed to her brother Arthur. It apprised him briefly of the situation at Tall Chimneys, and then recommended to him an engineer with whom she had lately become acquainted. 'I believe,' said her concluding paragraph, 'that henceforth my word will count for little, and any endorsement of mine might serve more as an injunction, but in you, Arthur, I trust to a kinder heart than I will encounter elsewhere. Mr Milton is conscientious, earnest and talented. He is wasted in his current position with Mr Somersall. Like us, he was not born with advantages, but has received them from others who recognised his worth. I hope you will be able to offer him something for my sake, though I forfeit any claim on your favour.'

As she was folding and sealing her letters, she heard Frank enter the room.

'You are writing?' he said. 'To Mrs Stockbridge, I presume.'

'Yes,' she said, not looking up. 'I will take it to the post, if you will wait for Mr Brock.' Mr Brock was the name of the lawyer. 'I do not suppose the magistrate can be got here before tomorrow.'

'Yes, of course. I will wait,' said Frank, 'But, Betsey ...'

'I wish you would call me Beth,' she burst out. 'Betsey is such a stupid rusticated name.'

'It isn't.'

She rose and turned to look at him now. It was obvious that he had washed and dressed in haste. He was unshaven and his clothes were thrown on anyhow. She almost understood what it had cost him to leave his marital bed.

Unless required to repair something, or to perform some other task beyond her own strength or competency, Frank rarely ventured into the rooms of the house. Now he stood awkwardly on the Persian carpet, his feet close together as though to avoid occupying too much of it. He had removed his boots. There was a hole in the toe of his sock.

Did Aoife know how to darn?

She regarded him coldly, though she longed for the comfort and reassurance she hoped he would offer. The letter in her hand was a leaden weight. 'Yes?'

He mashed his hat in his hands and could not meet her eye. 'About Aoife, and the way things will be …'

'They will be as they ought to be,' she said. 'Is she still there? At the gatehouse?'

'No. She has returned to the camp. Dónall—' Now he did look at her. She saw all her own need for solace and encouragement reflected in his hazel eyes.

But she was no more able to give than he was. 'Yes,' she said. 'I understand. Dónall must be kept in the dark, as *I* was. There must be more sneaking and pretence.'

'I have not enjoyed it,' he said sternly, the amber flecks in his eyes flashing like embers. 'But the boy is so sensitive, and the thing must be broken to him bit by bit.'

'Speaking of bits,' said Beth, 'there are splinters of porcelain in the music room. I thought they ought to remain, so the magistrate can see them. When you do clear them away, be careful not to cut yourself.'

'Very well,' he said, his eyes radiating all the words his mouth could not encompass. 'But *you*, surely—'

'Oh no. *I* will not touch another thing in this house. I am not entitled.' Her voice quavered as she made her declaration, and the sparks in his eyes were swamped by tears that trembled on his lashes but did not fall.

He dashed them away. 'Go home, Betsey,' he said, kindly imperative. 'Go home. Eat, sleep. You are overwrought. Yesterday …' he waved his hand to indicate the party and Tall Chimneys' brief quickening from enchanted slumber, 'it was too much for you. I should have … and you have not slept. Later … tomorrow … things will look better and we will consult with our friends and see what must be done.'

She nodded. 'Very well.'

She had no notion of the time. The day was light but not bright. The circle of sky above the hollow was grey, skimmed over with thin cloud. Summer was over.

The dog had followed her from the house and now shambled after her, hopeful of breakfast she supposed.

She climbed up the driveway, bone weary, her feet plodding and sometimes stumbling. From time to time she glanced into the woodland that bordered the drive. She thought of the glades where clear water ran between stones. Perhaps she could find the very place where she and Ruairi had lain together on the grass and entwined their fingers. She could wet her parched lips and dash her face and perhaps clear the fug of exhaustion that clouded her brain. The moss there was thick and soft, and would make a welcome pillow. But the letter in her pocket importuned her. It must be posted, and quickly.

She let herself into the gatehouse and fed the dog in the scullery before opening the inner door to the single living room. Everything had been left in disarray. The mattress still occupied the floor before the fire, its sheets and blankets tumbled and reeking of sex. The bread and cheese on the table were covered in fat flies; they rose into the air, buzzing with annoyance as Beth entered. There was no fire in the grate, no coals in the scuttle, no water in the pail. The milk in the pitcher was sour. Dust covered every surface—the oak dresser, the little book shelf, the back of the settle and the wooden treads of the stairs.

She picked her way across the room and mounted the stairs, noting an item of Aoife's clothing on the banister as she did so. A scarf, a shawl, or one of the bandanas she sometimes used to tie back her hair? It was impossible to say. Whatever it was, it was exotic and mysterious, and it smelled of Aoife.

Her own room was untouched—that, at least, was a comfort—the bed neatly made as she had left it more than twenty-four hours previously, her clothing folded or hung up on pegs. The curtains riffled in the breeze from the slightly open window. The air was fresh, untainted by what had taken place below. She longed to lie down, could so easily have sunk down fully dressed as she was and slept the day—the week, the year, her life—away. But she stiffened her resolve. She had no right to that oblivion. She found a large portmanteau and began to fill it with underclothes, stockings, two shifts and a clean petticoat. She added a warm shawl, a spare skirt and blouse. Her hair brush, silver and tortoiseshell—a gift from Miss Georgina on the occasion of her marriage to Mr Balfour—was added. A novel she had been loaned by Mrs Eagerly—she would return it on her way past the vicarage. What else? She looked around her. No. There was nothing else that she might need or had a right to take.

Downstairs, she opened the panel beneath the stairs and took a handful of coins from the strongbox. She supposed, strictly speaking, she could claim half its contents, but she could not carry so much coinage, and neither did she trust herself with it.

It was tempting to restore some kind of order to the gatehouse. Frank would not like to come home to *this*. But Frank had made his bed and must be content to lie in it.

She secured the dog in the garden and set out along the lane. The cloud overhead was thicker now, the vivid hues of the moor muted. She saw no movement around the camp; everyone must have gone off to their day's work.

She met neither Ruairi nor the lawyer on the lane and arrived at the vicarage as the church clock struck seven. She doubted anyone would be up, but the maid who answered her knock said the vicar and his wife were at breakfast and she was shown into the dining room.

Mr Eagerly rose. 'Good morning Miss Harlish,' he said, dabbing his mouth with a napkin. He indicated a chair. 'You've breakfasted? Have a cup of tea, at least.'

She refused the chair and the refreshment. 'I have come but to return this book,' she said, holding it out to Mrs Eagerly. But when the lady made no move to take it, she placed it onto the table cloth. 'You are still annoyed by your interview with Mr Somersall,' she said. 'I can only apologise. The man was vulgar and rude.'

Mrs Eagerly's eyes did not quite meet Beth's. 'That, and other things,' she said. 'I was just telling the vicar. We must decide on a course of action. Mr Herbert Somersall was here last night. I suppose you know that?'

Beth shook her head. 'I had no inkling of it. Are things resolved then, between them?'

'By no means,' barked out Mrs Eagerly. 'We cannot contemplate the idea of our Rose allying herself to such a family. If we had known—'

'My dear,' interrupted Mr Eagerly gently. 'Rose will not be marrying the father, and her own inclination is—'

'Where we have inclined her, so we can disincline her,' his wife said severely. 'And of course, if they marry, she must have to do with the father sometimes. More to the point, *we* will be forced to have dealings with him. Oh, Vicar, if you had only seen and heard him!' She appealed to Beth. 'Was he not insufferable?'

'Yes, indeed,' Beth said. 'I was mortified. Mrs Eagerly, since I am here, I wonder if I might mention a circumstance to you in respect of Rose. I find myself in need of—'

'Yes, we have heard all about it,' said Mrs Eagerly. 'News of that kind cannot be kept secret long in a village such as this.'

Beth sighed. 'You know about—'

'Oh yes. We know all about your brother's Popish marriage ... not that it *is* a marriage, Popish or otherwise. That priest is unfrocked, we are told, without authority to perform any religious rite, and the ground was unconsecrated ... the vicar is sore offended, though he is too honourable to say so—'

'My dear,' interposed the vicar. 'I am sure Miss Harlish had nothing to do with it. However ill-advised her brother's actions, she cannot be blamed.' He addressed Beth. 'Was there something you hoped we could do for you, Miss Harlish?'

She'd had a half-formed idea of offering herself as Rose's permanent companion, of occupying, perhaps, some small chamber at the vicarage, but the notion withered as she saw Mrs Eagerly's expression. They would not want her near their daughter. She said, 'Oh no. Nothing, thank you Mr Eagerly. Only to thank you for the loan of the book.'

As though to confirm Beth's suspicions, Mrs Eagerly took a pocket book from her reticule and leafed through the pages. 'I think,' she said, 'we had engaged you to accompany Rose to attend the children's Sunday school concert on Saturday next. I am sorry to say that Rose will be unable to keep that engagement now.' She gave Beth a level look, and Beth understood it all.

'Of course,' she said. 'Thank you. I will trespass no longer on your time.'

She decided to take the moorland route to Brayton. It took her past the Irish camp. Aoife sat on the steps of her *vardo* with Dónall at her side. The old lady dozed in her chair and a few of the children played a game with a collection of twigs and stones. All raised their hands in acknowledgement as she passed, presumably not remarking the heavy portmanteau on her shoulder, and too occupied to invite her to sit a while.

A little breeze had sprung up, refreshing after so many hot windless days. It came from the east. The standing stone murmured, almost purring with pleasure at the refreshment.

Beth knew the moorland byways as well as Frank did. She soon left the wider carriage route and followed smaller tracks between boulders encrusted with bright green lichen, and brakes of heather that would soon be in bloom. The air was chilly and the sky, which had smiled in a perfect cerulean blue for weeks, now frowned with low rain-laden cloud. But the walking warmed Beth who, in any case, was so weary—as well as hungry and thirsty and also in a state of shocked incongruity—that she hardly noticed the cold or her tired legs, aching feet or empty stomach. She trudged on, her mind full of the past twenty-four hours—of her foolishness and pride and what it had cost her. She thought also of the future, though this was a blank to her, a wall of mist she could not penetrate.

She was only half aware of the track or her route. Instinct and memory guided her rather than her senses, which were dull and confused, but she came at last to the bridge which crossed the river and entered the town.

It was market day. The stalls in the market place were all covered by awnings in preparation for the rain that all knew would fall before the day was done. People shopped, or exchanged news. A shepherd drove a flock of sheep to the auction ring. Life went on, Beth mused, as she made her way across the market square to the post office.

There was no sign of the Irish folk. The lilting strains of Tadgh's harp were absent. She could not see the familiar figures of Brónach, Caitlin, Elíse or Eistir moving amongst the people with their posies, nor the children lining up on the church steps to perform. This was odd, but such was her distraction that she did not wonder at it over much.

The letter and the posting of it were her focus.

Then it was done, her penny handed over and the stamp affixed, and the letter gone into the bag, ready for the mail coach that would take it to the train.

Now that she had completed her obligation she found herself at a loss, without a plan of any kind, without destination, without a friend to whom she could turn. Without hope.

The bag dragged at her shoulder. For all the world she would have laid it down and walked away, but that it was her last tenuous connection with Frank and home.

Thinking of Frank brought to mind a place the two of them had frequented in their childhood days. Arthur had been too eager to help Mr Burleigh in the making and repairing of tools to play with his siblings, and their sister too squeamish to risk the brackish water of the bogs or the multi-legged insects that swarmed on the moor. Beth and Frank, though, had spent hours exploring and playing make-believe, often under the watchful gaze of their father as he husbanded pheasant that no one would ever come and shoot, dug peats for the fires or stalked deer to supply the table. But then, as they became older and more cognizant of the moorland tract, he had trusted them to wander alone. And they had found a place right in the centre of the moor—a sheer outcrop of rock that reared up from the moor, from the top of which you could see, on a clear day, the town of Whitby and the shimmering sea beyond. And at the base of the cliff there had been a cave, with a little brook running by. They had lit a fire and toasted bits of bread begged from Mrs Orphan. Frank had snared a rabbit, skinned and gutted it, and they had roasted it. It tasted foul—

burned—and the bones had almost choked them … she smiled at the memory.

She walked through the town in a dream, lost in her memories, and crossed the bridge again as the first fat drops of rain began to fall.

The day closed in, low cloud and curtains of rain ushering in what looked like evening though it was barely noon. Looking up, she could make out nothing through the sheets of water. The landscape melted and merged into a grey-green smudge and soon the track was awash. Somehow her feet knew the way and she kept her head bent, noting tussocks of grass running now with silvery beads of water, phosphorescent green bogs with their surfaces disturbed to reveal the black depths beneath. She saw hefty boulders, their moss oozing, and the very occasional stunted tree. She herself was soaked, water pouring from her head, weighing down her dress and the bag that she carried, and filling her boots. She stumbled on, sure that soon she would see the great crag rising up through the miasma and, in its lee, the little shelter where she could rest at last.

Her way was very erratic. She stumbled often and almost fell. Her legs were so weary, the bag on her shoulder a leaden weight. The grass and stones, the scrub and bracken were a blur; it was hard to tell one from the other, her vision mired by rain and utter fatigue. Perhaps she even slept, consciousness giving way momentarily as she tripped and blundered across the moor.

Then suddenly a splash, and she was knee deep in some horrible and evil-smelling bog. The bag slipped from her arm and disappeared beneath the greenish surface. Her feet sank deeper into the slime, and by no amount of struggle could she find purchase. She flailed and floundered, her dress all tangled, sinking until the water reached her waist, the swamp around her turning turgid and emitting noxious fumes of decay and dead things. She reached out to grasp the milk grasses that grew on the bog's periphery but they were wet, and slid from her grip. With her last reserves of effort she managed to pull herself to firmer ground, but the water was so cold it had turned her numb and her lower limbs ceased to obey her. She could not stand. Eventually she stopped struggling and laid her head on the wet ground.

Part Two

Chapter 28

When Beth awoke it was to find herself in a small sloped-ceiling bedroom. The coverlet, the yellow roses on the wallpaper and the sprigged muslin of the curtains were all strange to her. The window was small yet admitted a flood of light so bright she could barely manage to keep her eyes open.

She raised her hand to filter the sunbeam, and someone said, 'Oh! You're awake.'

A chair creaked. A door opened and softly closed again and she heard light footsteps descending stairs.

When the door opened again it was to admit Frank. He had to duck his head to get through the tiny doorway, and then crouch, as the ceiling was too low to allow him to stand upright. He carried a cup and saucer, a teapot and a plate on a tray, which he placed on a small dresser.

'Can you sit up?'

'I think so,' she said, struggling.

She felt his arm behind her, lifting, and settling the pillow behind her head.

He poured tea. 'Here,' he said. 'Drink.'

She thought the hands that reached out were too thin to be hers and she examined them wonderingly for a moment before taking the cup.

The relentless light poured into the room. 'Where is this place?' she asked, and, 'Could you adjust the curtain please?'

'Alright,' he said, 'but it is a pity. This is the first half-fine day we have had.' Nevertheless he did so, and the room was plunged into a soft yellow dimness. 'This is the attic of Laurel Cottage. You have displaced the Misses MacAllisters' maid.'

'And how did I come here?'

'That is someone else's story. How is the tea?'

She drank. 'It is very good,' she said. 'What day is it?'

'I hardly know. Thursday, I think.'

'I have been asleep two days?'

'You have been asleep for over a week. You have been very ill, Betsey.'

She stared at him, seeing now his grey, exhausted face, his unshaven chin. 'You had better tell me.'

He laughed, a hard dry sound. 'Perhaps first, you had better tell *me* what on earth you were thinking of. Where were you going?' He was frowning, angry, but she knew him too well—his anger was really relief.

She thought about it. 'I wanted to go to the place where we played as children. Do you recall it? The high crag, and the little cave at its base. I thought I would feel safe there.'

That softened him. He folded himself and sat gingerly on the edge of a small spindle-backed chair. 'Yes,' he said, so quietly that she could hardly hear him. 'Yes. I remember that place. We cooked a rabbit.'

'We *cremated* a rabbit.'

He smiled. 'And after that?'

She shrugged. 'I had no course of action in mind, only that I could not return home.'

'You are determined then, to leave Tall Chimneys? To leave the gatehouse. To leave *me?*'

'How can I stay?'

He dismissed that, and would have commenced some line of reasoning that had occupied his mind during the long days and nights of his vigil, but she cut him off. 'So. Now you.'

He steepled his hands and looked down at them.

'The lawyer came, and then the next day the magistrate. But by then the culprit was known.'

'Ned Widderington?'

Frank shook his head. 'No. It was Fionn, the Irishman. I do not know how he did it beneath your nose, and Ruairi's and that other man's—'

'Mr Milton's?'

'Yes. But somehow, while you talked—'

'Yes.' She settled her head back on the pillow, trying to remember. It was like reaching back into a nightmare. 'There was a long discussion in the drawing room. Ruairi wished me to remain at the big house. I suppose he wished to save your blushes. But Mr Milton insisted that I went home.'

'Well then, while that was in train, Fionn and Dónall spirited the things from the dining room and the music room onto their cart. The thievery had been done before you even left the house.'

'Dónall was involved?'

Frank nodded. Her cup was empty so he took it from her and passed her the plate, on which two dainty sandwiches nestled on a doily.

She shook her head, 'I don't think I can—'

'Yes,' he said. 'You must. Just try.'

She took a tiny bite. Her teeth felt too large in her mouth. 'So,' she said when she had swallowed. 'Dónall?'

'Of course he had no understanding. He had unloaded a cart in the morning and he loaded one up in the evening. He did not question what was in the sacks and boxes.'

'Then, how do they know Fionn was the culprit?'

'He deposited Dónall at the camp. Everyone else was in bed by then, Aoife's *vardo* in darkness—'

'Though, she was not in it.'

'No. But Dónall didn't know that. He went to bed. At dawn when Ruairi roused them, Fionn, the horse and cart were missing. And so was their strongbox. All their accumulated earnings. They are destitute.'

'Oh no!'

'Yes. And now no one but Mr Slade will give them work. Fionn's mischief has made them all suspect. And they are three men down: Fionn, and two who have gone in pursuit. They cannot move on. The old woman is ill, and not expected to live long. The wet weather has got to her chest …' he trailed off. 'I have been told I mustn't tire you.'

'I am not tired,' she said, although she was. It was hard to concentrate. Her mind kept wandering. When she looked at the plate the sandwiches were gone, though she had no memory of eating them. Then, by some sleight of hand she could not follow, the plate was gone and the cup and saucer back.

'Has there been word from Mrs Stockbridge?'

Frank shook his head. 'Not so far. But then, I have not been at the gatehouse since you were found. I have been here.'

'Here?'

He gave her a rueful smile. 'Of course,' he said. 'Where else?'

There passed a night. The soft patter of rain against the window restful, and reminding her of the gatehouse. Then a day. The drip-drip-drip of the gutters a sort of torture. The doctor came and took her pulse and declared her out of danger.

'What danger?' she wanted to know, but he gave her no reply.

The Misses MacAllister came and went with cups of gruel, with tea and elderflower cordial, with sponges and hot water, with the chamber pot. She began to recall, as from a dark memory, their ministrations during the worst of her fever—gentle hands lifting her, changing her nightclothes, spooning water. Now she protested, but in the end was forced to allow them to tend her; she had no strength, and the least movement or activity exhausted her.

More nights. More days. A week? The only constant was the rain, which peppered the roof above her head and guzzled down the gutters until she was sure the whole of Yorkshire must be afloat.

Frank was almost always there, but he was not a man who was comfortable indoors. He would sit awhile and sometimes read aloud from a novel, but his restlessness and her own lack of concentration made it futile. He told her that he spent the hours away from her in tending the MacAllisters' garden. 'Although I don't know why,' he concluded, gloomily, 'it is all quag.'

She lay and listened to the house. Beneath the constant assault of rain it was quiet; she sensed the ladies below shutting doors very quietly, muting their voices. She did not hear the piano, although she knew that in general Miss Felicity played every day. At the same time, she was conscious of movement and concerted activity. She heard a dray or cart outside the house, grunts and shuffles as something heavy was moved. She was curious, but not avidly so, as though her little room was a million miles from ordinary life, and anything that happened there could not affect her.

More days and nights. She calculated that August must be a week old. She pictured the heather on the moor; it would be in full bloom, an ultraviolet haze of purple and pink stretching as far as the eye could see. But when she got up from her bed and bent to see it from the window,

171

she found a gauzy curtain of moisture that made the view of the moor grey and dull. Her legs trembled and she had to cling to the dresser for fear of falling. Suddenly she felt cold, and climbed back into bed.

That night she was woken by the sound of rain hitting the roof just above her head like musket fire, and throwing itself like pebbles at the tiny window. The sound dredged up some feverish memory that morphed into her dreams so that she awoke hot and weeping.

She thought of the people at the camp, damp and cold; those covered wagons would be no protection against Yorkshire rain, which, as everyone knows, is harsher, wetter and more penetrating than any other. Aoife's *vardo* would offer better shelter than those converted drays, but of course the pretence must be kept up that she slept in it every night. What nonsense! No wonder Cormac's mother was ill. No doubt the children would suffer too. How hopeless, lost and beleaguered they must feel! Her anxiety for them became part of her own sense of destitution.

She wished Ruairi would come, but she supposed he had gone in pursuit of Fionn. A pity. With that peculiar sympathy between him and herself, they would understand each other's pain.

One day she said to Miss Felicity, who sat on the chair and knitted some shapeless indeterminate garment, 'How did I come to be here?'

'A young man brought you,' she replied. 'We knew you were sought. Patty heard of it in the village when she went to collect our provisions. News, also, of the burglary was abroad, and the talk in the shop! Oh, my dear, we were incensed. Arabella was all for going straight to the village and giving Mrs Golightly a piece of her mind—'

'Mrs Golightly?'

'Oh yes, indeed. That lady was of the opinion that the robbery and your disappearance were connected. That you, in short, had stolen the things and then run away with that Irishman.'

Miss Felicity paused in her knitting and Beth watched the older woman's fingers moving like a drunken soldier along the needle, counting stitches—but missing many. 'Dear me,' she murmured. 'This is very odd. There should be one hundred and fifty. But no matter. It always seems to come out right in the end.'

'Mrs Golightly is a gossip,' Beth murmured. 'Where there is no truth, she will provide a facsimile.'

'And no one gives anything she says the least credence,' asserted Miss Felicity, resuming her work, though Beth knew this to be an untruth. There were many in Moorside who took everything Mrs Golightly said as gospel.

Miss Felicity went on. 'But the day passed, and we had no news that you were found. And that night, oh! The storm was so fierce, the rain absolutely in torrents along the lane, according to Arabella, and the noise of it … and the thought of you … I was awake all the night long.'

'So that would have been Tuesday night,' said Beth, speaking to herself.

But Miss Felicity, whose hearing was acute, said, 'Yes, for we had brawn. It is always brawn on Tuesdays. Fresh brawn from the butcher in the marketplace is not so very disagreeable if fried and served with plenty of onions. It is cheap anyway, and if there is any left over Patty adds it to pork trimmings to make a pie, which does us for Wednesday.'

'And so it was Wednesday when I was found, and brought here?'

'Yes dear, I recall that Patty had but just taken the pie from the oven. It smelt very nice, for all that I dislike pork trimmings. They are so very gristly sometimes. But the pie was ready, the day all but gone, when we heard a horse outside the house and then there came a loud hammering upon the door, and I almost shrieked, but Arabella went to the door, taking the precaution of seizing Father's old walking cane from the umbrella stand in the hallway. I knew, because I heard the rattle of it as she drew it forth. She opened the door and there on the doorstep was a young man, as wet as could be, with you in his arms. He must have been young, for he had carried you a great distance. That he was very wet I would have needed no telling even if it hadn't rained cats and dogs for the last day and night, for Patty complained afterwards that the hall rug was quite saturated, and his boots left mud on the staircase as he carried you up.'

'It was very good of you to take me in,' said Beth.

'Oh, my dear, there was no question about that,' said Miss Felicity, turning her work and commencing another row. 'Only we could not at first agree on which room to put you in, for Arabella and I each have our own, and there are only two, but then Patty, so good and kind as she is, said, 'Take her up to my room,' and so it was done. And the young man departed immediately to fetch the doctor.'

'And, the young man,' ventured Beth, knowing it was pointless to ask for a description, 'what manner of man was he—a gentleman?'

'As to that, I couldn't say. Arabella says he was handsome, tall, and dark.'

Ruairi! Beth closed her eyes and recalled standing close to him in the candlelit dining room, the feel of his warm solid body against hers. And then, the next morning, their stumbling and tumbling, tearing at his clothes … she thought of him searching for her through the storm, though his own little enclave must have been so decimated by Fionn's betrayal, and all the while trying to keep news of Aoife's marriage a secret from Dónall, despite the whole village knowing of it. Her eyes filled with tears at his courage and tenderness. They rolled down her cheeks, but Miss Felicity knew nothing of them. She knitted in great complacency and the rhythmic, homely sound of her industry comforted Beth, and lulled her into sleep.

When Beth came back to consciousness, Miss Felicity had departed, and the smell that drifted up the stairs told her it must be Wednesday— pie. Not that she would be permitted to eat any of it. She was fed boiled white fish, beef soup, minced chicken, arrowroot, eggs, and milk puddings. The purport of Miss Felicity's words suddenly assailed her. They were poor. How was her invalid diet being afforded? And what about the doctor? He had called on half a dozen occasions.

Next time Frank came to her she said, 'I do not wish to be a financial burden on the Misses MacAllister.'

'You are not.'

'But the food, Frank. And the doctor. After the expense of the party … and you will not have been able to fetch any … commodities for Mr Slade these past weeks. Our coffers must be almost empty. I took some coins, but not more than a guinea.'

He gave her a little smile. 'It has not cost us a penny. You are not entirely friendless, Betsey,' he said.

She was perplexed. She could not think who would fund her recovery if Frank did not. The Eagerlys thought the worst of her. The Golightlys also. The lawyer, perhaps? Or Professor Bissel? Thinking of friends, Ruairi sprang into her mind, as he increasingly did now. 'Mr Connolly has not been to see me, nor any of the Irish.'

'They have not forgotten you,' Frank replied. 'Imagine how they feel, to have placed you in such a predicament.'

'I should never have pursued the scheme of opening the house,' Beth burst out. 'All this trouble has stemmed from that ill-conceived idea. I almost feel worse about them than I do about Mrs Stockbridge. She has much, so what she has lost will not signify in the wide scheme of things. But they have lost everything.'

'And you have thrown everything away.'

'I have *not*,' she said tearfully. 'I have paid the price that was due for my mistake, and very dear has it cost me, I assure you. But it had to be done.'

After a while Frank said, 'You blame yourself too much. The Irish, at any rate, do not accuse you.'

That made her cry more, but Frank had never been able to deal with tears and when her paroxysm was over, he had gone.

The next day he did not come at all, and Beth was ill again with a malady more of the mind than the body. The doctor came and bled her, and afterwards she heard him instruct the MacAllisters that they should deny any visitors for the next few days.

Sometimes her mind was blank, thinking of nothing, lost neither in memory nor dream but in a vast echoing drum of depression.

Sometimes she tried to remember the day she had been lost, fumbling in her subconscious to conjure up the moment of Ruairi finding her, presumably lying insensible on the moor, to imagine his arms lifting her, the long walk to Laurel Cottage, which must have been the nearest habitation. Of him standing, pouring water, on the Misses MacAllisters' doorstep, then bringing her up to this room and lying her on the bed. It was frivolous. Romantic. Very silly. And yet how else could it have been?

Sometimes she tried to think of the future. When she felt strong she formed schemes by which she could earn her bread. She would write to an agency she knew of in Whitby, seeking work as a housekeeper or even as a maid. But she did not feel strong very often, and in her weak moments she considered an approach to Mrs Burleigh, who lived now in Wiltshire. Her husband bred fine horses. They were comparatively wealthy, their sons at Oxford, their daughters already married. Mrs Burleigh might appreciate help and companionship. Or Miss Georgina, who was now Mrs Balfour. There were two or three children in the nursery who might soon need a governess. Oh! But how could she ask for *more* from those who had already given so much? Wasn't it time she stood on her own two feet?

When next she saw Frank, he looked tired.

She said, 'What is amiss? Is there news?'

He waved her concern away. 'We were about Mr Slade's business last night,' he said. The fiction of lime-moving had been utterly abandoned. 'The Irish are desperate for funds and so we made the attempt, but it was heavy going. The ground is so wet and the cart got stuck a dozen times. And we almost encountered a division of the Mounted Guard. They were lost. One had strayed into a bog. We had to lie low while they extricated horse and rider.'

'But you were not apprehended?'

He shook his head.

'Mr Connolly was with you?'

'He is still away, trying to run Fionn to ground. We were short of hands. Dónall proved surprisingly useful.'

'Dónall went with you?'

175

Frank nodded. 'I am … earning his trust, I think.'

'When Mr Connolly does return, I hope he will come and see me. I wish to thank him.'

Frank looked puzzled. 'I am sure he expects no gratitude.'

'Nevertheless,' she said.

Later, she said, 'News of your marriage was known the very next day. The Eagerlys had heard it. I assume Dónall does not know of it.'

Frank passed his hand over his face. 'No. He is still in ignorance, even if every other Tom, Dick and Harry knows my business. That is why I am trying to build a rapport, so that when the scales fall from his eyes … but he will not take it kindly. Father Fearghal revealed our secret not an hour after we were married. He went to the Plough and got drunk and spoke of it. He is like many a man who, lacking something themselves, envies those who have it still.'

'I don't know what you mean.'

'Faith. Father Fearghal lost his faith. But Aoife still believes and wanted to have the sacrament to bind us, so she insisted.'

'I did not know that—that she is so strong in her faith,' mused Beth thinking perhaps rather better of the young woman than she had done.

Frank frowned. 'What else had she? When home, parents, friends and all security had been taken from her?'

'She had her brother,' said Beth vehemently.

'As you have. And yet you despaired. Where was *your* faith, Betsey?'

'It is in myself that I have lost faith,' she said faintly.

After a week—or possibly two—Beth was allowed downstairs to sit on a sofa close to the fire, which had been lit in the grate to counteract the damp, gloomy day without. It was almost September now, often a beautiful month of sparkling frosts and night skies so clear that the whole glittering canopy of heaven can be seen, but this year only cloud and unremitting rain had come.

The room was the one where she used to sit and sew for the MacAllisters, but there was something different about it. She looked around. The pianoforte had gone, as had a dresser and a side table. The walls were bare of pictures and the cabinet that used to contain all their little family mementoes and precious curios was vacant.

'You have not been robbed?' she cried, taking in the empty sideboard and mantel.

'No dear,' said Miss Arabella, tucking a quilt around Beth's legs. 'All is well. But, to tell the whole truth of it, we have been asked to go to my brother's in Leeds and we have decided to go. He is well set up now Papa's affairs have been put in order, and there is room for us and, in short,

Felicity and I have not felt the countryside hereabouts is quite conducive to us. I fear we will not cope with the winter.'

'You are leaving?' Beth breathed. She looked about her again. 'And I have delayed your departure.'

'Your being here has meant a small postponement in our arrangements, but you must not worry about that. We have been delighted to take care of you; and Patty is very pleased for it has meant she was kept on when, by now, we would have had to let her go. My brother has his own staff and we could not take her with us.'

'No wonder she was so willing to give up her bed,' said Beth. 'But really, I must impose on you no longer. I am quite well now, and ...'

'Your brother is eager to have you back at the gatehouse as soon as ever you are well enough. But the doctor says that time has not yet come.'

'I shall not go there, in any case,' Beth said. 'You must know that the situation there has changed.'

'Yes dear, we know all about it. You must discuss it with him.'

'I have tried,' Beth said with a sigh. 'He does not understand.'

Miss Arabella took up a skein of knitting identical to her sister's but that this one was identifiable as a crossover wrap.

'You are knitting in the same yarn as your sister,' Beth observed.

Miss Arabella lowered her voice. 'Oh yes. When she is done, she will believe this to be the result. Her own work keeps her hands occupied and she believes herself to be useful, but sadly her knitting is fuller of holes than of stitches. I usually unravel it and do it over.'

'You are very kind.'

Miss Arabella said, 'There is a special kind of bond between siblings, do you not agree? They are the ones we know for the longest in our lives. Longer than our parents, longer than a spouse, longer than children, should we have any. Our brother is married, but yet look how he has made arrangements to take care of us! He is having a suite of rooms in his house adapted for Felicity's needs. I am sure your brother will make some provision for you, Beth. You should trust yourself to him.'

Beth had been restless in her bedchamber, and had looked forward very much to being allowed downstairs. But she found the effort of dressing and descending had tired her. Miss Arabella's counsel stabbed her to the quick, but she could not argue against it. There was a unique bond between siblings. Hadn't it caused Ruairí to leave his home? There was nothing he would not do for Aoife. Perhaps, similarly, Frank would make some provision for her, but if it involved sharing the gatehouse with Aoife, that could not be borne.

Chapter 29

Stephen Milton stepped out of the engine shed, wiping his hands on an oily rag. It was hot in the shed, the heat generated by the inferno of the furnace and sealed tank of boiling water. The din of the grindings and windings, the thumpings and bumpings only seemed to add to the temperature, making the air suffocating. Stephen had removed his jacket, waistcoat and shirt and worked—like the other men in the engine houses—with a bare-torso. His skin was slick with sweat and the greasy grime that comes off coal, his hair plastered across his brow. There was no doubt that the heat of the machinery affected him, but he had also lately had a fever and did not know if some residue of that remained.

Outside of the shed the air was shockingly cold but the rain, mercifully, had ceased—at least for now. The ground was awash with oily puddles, mud, horse ordure and slime, but Stephen stood and allowed the frigid air—grimy though it was with smoke and coal dust—to cool his body.

Presently, he walked to a trough and soused himself in cold water, then took the cup that hung from the pump and jerked the mechanism to dispense clean water that he drank thirstily.

The rain that had begun the day after Beth's party had not at first threatened the mine. The ground was parched, the peat of the moor fissured and dry. For the first week it had absorbed the rain like a sponge, the gasping grasses and scrub reviving from their wilting state, flowering and sending out exuberant new growth though the season was over. The excess had found its way to the underground network of channels and grottoes that characterises the limestone landscape, as well as filling up the streams and rivers, which had dried to barely a trickle. But then, inevitably, the mine—an unnatural cavern but quite as effective as its primordial kin—began to fill. Stephen had risen from his sickbed and presented himself at the mine with the fixed intention of remaining there to do what he could to avert disaster, and he had been there ever since.

It was evening, though what the hour might be Stephen had no idea because his pocket watch was with his clothing in a locker. Braziers burned in the cobbled yard of the mine, throwing a mixture of lurid, almost hellish light and grotesque shadows onto the shambolic collection of sheds and warehouses. He had been working on the engine since just after dawn, as he had done every day since the sump—as predicted—filled to the point when it had to be deployed. It had taken his unremitting efforts to keep the machine operating at sufficient capacity to prevent the lower levels from flooding. He had initiated a twenty-four hour running program of maintenance—the adjustment of valves, the oiling of parts and the calibration of instruments—but it could not go on indefinitely. The pump was simply insufficient, and too old. He had sent express to Mr Somersall requesting—even demanding—permission to abandon the lower levels of the mine; if the rain continued, they would certainly flood.

His only reply had been a terse, 'Under no circumstances.'

Soon Jessop would come and relieve him. He was not an engineer, but he understood the working of the engine and, like Stephen, he cared enough about the men on the levels to exert himself. The two had alternated in twelve-hour shifts since almost the beginning of the deluge, taking it in turns to sleep on a cot in Herbert's office, eating what food could be got from the pie shops in the town. Surprisingly, Herbert had thrown himself into the crisis, finding perhaps that occupation was as good a remedy as anything for a heart in limbo, a heart that had been offered but neither accepted nor rejected. He had been acting as Stephen's eyes and ears below ground, surveying the levels, measuring the water in the sump and making close enquiry of the men as to the quantity of water generally. But he would not take it upon himself to issue the order for the lower levels to be abandoned in direct opposition to his father's decree to the contrary, and at the end of the day shift he generally betook himself home.

The yard was quiet. Some dozen or so men worked above ground during the period of the night shift, urging the exhausted ponies to pull

179

the laden trucks from the shaft head to the washing sheds. But the washing sheds did not operate at night, and neither did the freight trains come to take away the washed coal so there was, at last, a blessed diminution in the usual racket. A few women and children quartered the ground, picking up stray lumps of coal to feed their fires and, within the engine houses, stokers shovelled coal to feed the insatiable furnaces. But now Stephen was alone, and he sank onto a makeshift bench and put his head in his hands and thought of the night brigade below ground, hard at work. They must know all too well that the failure of the pumping engine would result in an immediate and cataclysmic rise in the water levels. The lower seams would be inundated. There would be no time for men to be lifted to safety.

The smart clip of boots crossing the yard caused him to look up. A man, well—but not flashily—dressed, tall and bearing himself with confident authority, approached. Wearily Stephen rose.

'Good evening, sir,' he said. 'Can I be of any assistance? I am Milton, colliery engineer. I am sorry that there is no one here of greater moment just now.'

The man smiled—and his smile reminded Stephen of someone, but he could not just then think who—and held out his hand. 'You are the man I seek then. You are husbanding the pumping engine, I believe?'

'I am,' said Stephen, astonished. He held up his own hand—grimy still despite its dunking in the trough. 'You must forgive me, sir, if I do not reciprocate your gesture. You have come from Mr Somersall? I had almost given up hope.'

'I have been in his company,' said the stranger, 'and I overheard him speak of your efforts here. He is expected in a few days, but I decided to come ahead and see for myself what can be done, if anything can.'

'You're an engineer?' Stephen could have wept with relief. He had hoped for a new engine—not that it could have been brought into service immediately, it would come in parts and need constructing on site. But the assistance of a fellow engineer would be invaluable. There might be something he had neglected that would nurse the engine through the current crisis.

'I am,' said the man, with a genial smile. 'Will you show me inside?'

The two entered the shed, the newcomer removing his coat and rolling up his shirt sleeves. 'You're Stephen? Call me Arthur,' he said. 'Now.' He rubbed his hands together gleefully, and let his eye rove over the machine. 'What have we here? What's her maximum head?'[xxiv]

'A hundred and fifty feet. And we're working at all of that.'

Arthur stroked his chin. 'I see. How are the valves?'

180

'Ground down in the summer, and new piston rings fitted.'

'That's good. Did you rebore the cylinder at the same time?'

'I did. We are regularly greasing all the moving parts, and I have adjusted the speed governor as far as I dare.'

'Good. But you must not push it too far or the sleeve bearings will give way.'

'I know. Left to myself, I would close the lower levels, but Mr Somersall will not hear of it.'

Arthur made a tutting noise. 'That is playing with fire.'

'I am sorry to say he is careless of the men's safety. The ventilation engine is at capacity, which is a worry in itself, but add to that he refuses to replace the Geordie lamps. If someone were to make a flame ... I despair. But my hands are tied.'

'And you're exhausted,' observed Arthur, turning his attention from the engine to the engineer. 'When did you last sleep? Or eat?'

'The foreman and I are working twelve hour shifts. He is due any minute. I suppose I might find one of the pie shops still open, if I'm lucky.'

Arthur furrowed his brow. 'What about the oil?' he asked. 'When did you last change it?'

'You're right. I might squeeze a degree or two more efficiency from her if I change the oil, but I can't do that without shutting the engine down, and I dare not do that.'

'I agree,' said Arthur. 'Six hours to cool it sufficiently, and then the oil change, and a couple of hours to get it back to temperature. It's too risky while there are men underground and more rain threatens. But come. Let's go over the engine together. Two pairs of eyes are better than one. Hand me a grease gun.'

Inch by inch, they went over the mechanisms, lubricating working parts and checking seals. Arthur was older than Stephen and more experienced, and occasionally he made a suggestion for improvement, but never in anything other than a spirit of helpfulness. Soon his clothes were besmirched, but he seemed not to care.

Presently Jessop entered the engine shed. He was wet from the waist down. 'I am sorry to be behind my time,' he said. 'I decided to go down and see the state of things. The sump is overwhelmed and there is rising water on the bottom level. What am I to do?'

'How many men are down there?'

'Forty-eight and seven boys. The boys are wet to their thighs.'

Mr Jessop and Stephen exchanged agonised looks. Arthur took a step or two back to allow them some privacy for their deliberations but he watched the exchange narrowly, and he especially watched Stephen.

Above their heads, on the galvanised roof of the shed, they heard the sharp percussion of more rain.

'Another deluge,' said Jessop. 'It is unrelenting.'

'We must evacuate the lower level,' said Stephen at last. 'The pump is at its absolute capacity. I will not be responsible for fifty-five lives. If Somersall burns me at the stake, so be it.'

Chapter 80

The two Ellingbeck men made their way to the mine head, stopping only so that Stephen could snatch a thick coat and a Geordie lamp from the stores and despatch a note to Somersall Grange. It was a few moments before he realised that Arthur was also shrugging into coveralls.

'You do not intend to accompany us?' he asked in astonishment.

The equipment store was well lit, and now Stephen was able to see the stranger more clearly. Brown wavy hair, honest hazel eyes, a determined chin. A friendly open face—the kind of face a person could grow to love. The smile was grim, but not the less resolute.

Arthur said, 'Of course I do. You two cannot clear all the galleries alone.'

'But sir, I cannot allow you to involve yourself. You have been kind, but I gather you are here on your own account. You are not an employee of Mr Somersall.'

'I am here on account of another person,' said Arthur. 'There will be time later for explanations, but for now let us get below ground.'

They splashed through puddles to the wheelhouse, soaked to the skin in seconds by rain that fell like arrows, and entered the cage which would lower them into the mine. The winchman released the brake and they began to descend. The rattle of the gear faded as the cage dropped deeper into the ground. They passed the first level. All was dark; the men must be working in the far galleries. The air was thick and hot, the blackness like a dark throat; the meagre light of their lamps barely penetrated it. On the second level they saw two boys, stripped to the waist, waiting with a barrow of coal to be sent up to the surface.

Stephen called out, 'Good work, lads,' as they passed.

At the third level a group of men called out for the cage to stop, and Mr Jessop hauled on the emergency brake.

Stephen slid open the door. 'What's amiss, lads?'

Two men supported a third between them. "'E's taken bad with 'is chest,' said one fellow. The man in the middle gasped and flapped his mouth like a landed fish. His breaths came chokingly. 'We need to get 'im up top,' said the second supporter. 'Can you gents wait till we send t' cage back down?'

Stephen, Arthur and Mr Jessop looked at each other. 'The bottom level is the one below,' Mr Jessop said. 'We can use the ladders, if you're game.'

'By all means,' said Arthur ushering the wheezing man and his friends into the cage and pulling the bell cord that would tell the winchman to bring the cage back up.

Stephen said, 'You two take the easterly seam. I'll take the other. We will cover more ground if we split up.'

Arthur looked as though he would have preferred to accompany Stephen, but Mr Jessop said, 'You're a man with an air of authority, sir, and I'd be glad if you'd come and back me up.'

Stephen watched them as they disappeared into the utter blackness of the gallery, then he turned and hurried off in the other direction. The gallery was relatively high at this point so close to the main shaft, and so he ran upright, but soon the roof closed in and he had to duck his head. He came to the first stairway—a rickety wooden affair that connected this level with the one below—used only for emergencies but vital at the times when the cage was being used to haul men or loads of coal. He dangled his lamp below him, looking for the glint of water that would tell him they were too late, that the lower level was already flooded. He could make out nothing, so he grasped the ladder and began his descent.

He landed in water that reached his thighs. It was cold and viscous, thick with oily residue. He held his lamp aloft and shouted, 'Hello there! Hello!' but got no reply. He turned west, having decided to penetrate the gallery to its furthest chamber and then return, sending the men that he found on his way down the various side tunnels and into the chambers to alert their fellows, and thus shepherd everyone to the ladder or the cage.

He waded through the flood, shouting and then pausing to listen. The mine had an eerie way of deadening and absorbing sound, but the water gave a low rumble, sinister and threatening.

The gallery opened out to its first chamber but there were no men working there and he forged on. Then he heard the shrill voice of a boy, and encountered two lads struggling with a barrow of coal, though its sides were almost overtopped by the level of water and they themselves were waist deep. More water dripped from the roof, so their hair was wet and their faces—usually covered with coaldust—were washed pale and looked almost ghostly in the feeble light of Stephen's lamp.

'Leave that,' he said, 'and make your way to the stairs. Climb to the next level up.'

The boys looked at him, round-eyed. 'What about our da and grandda?' said one.

'And we'll be leathered if we don't tally this barrow,' said the other.

'I'll fetch them, and mark the barrow to your account,' said Stephen. 'You're Bernie and Jack Carter, are you not?'

They nodded. 'Run along boys, and tell any you meet to do the same. Gather at the stair head so that I can make sure all are accounted for.'

They left their barrow willingly enough, and waded into the darkness. They carried no lamps, but their eyes were so accustomed to the dark they seemed able to navigate their way by some sixth sense.

In the next chamber Stephen encountered the Carter men, one of whom hewed at the roof of the gallery with a pick axe while the other tried to steady the barrow, which bobbed like a boat on the water, to catch the coal.

'Your lads are waiting,' Stephen told them. 'They are safe. Now who works in the tunnels that lead from this one?'

The Carters reeled off the names of some two dozen miners and undertook to inform those men that the level was to be evacuated.

'And how many men in the furthest cavern?'

'Five sir, and a boy. The Taylors work that part of the seam.'

Stephen stated his intention of pressing on to reach them.

'The gallery slopes down steep,' said the elder Carter. 'It'll be deep, sir. But the far cavern is on a rise. The men should be dry enough, though the way to them be wet.'

'I understand,' said Stephen. 'And so far as you know, along with the men you named, those are the last on this side of the level?'

They nodded and strode off.

Stephen pushed further into the labyrinth, crouching almost double now, and with difficulty holding his lamp out of the water, which got deeper as the gallery gradually descended into the depths. There was a flow to the water, a current that tugged at his legs, and at times it was difficult to keep his feet. He felt cold, assailed by a strange fatigue, and wiped his hand across his face to dislodge it. He had not slept in eighteen hours and had not eaten since breakfast at six that morning. Clamping his teeth tightly together to prevent them from chattering he continued to call out, trying to banish the tremor from his voice. But his words bounced back to him, distorted by the cavern walls and by the water that slid and slithered around him and seemed to penetrate his bones.

Then the floor of the gallery dipped sharply and he lost his feet, floundered, thrashed, felt the water close over his head and only just managed to keep his lamp aloft while he scrabbled with his feet to find a purchase. He emerged spluttering from the water and gave his head a glancing blow on the roof. He could not crawl without submerging his lamp, so was forced to continue bent over so that his chin and sometimes his mouth were in the water and his back scraped along the low roof. He hoped this was the lowest point of the gallery, but the way sloped still further beneath his feet until he was forced to squat, the lamp and his head only just clear of the water in the nine inches or so of space between its surface and the roughhewn roof.

At last the way rose steeply and the roof also, and he entered the furthest chamber of the level.

The Taylors were fully alive to their predicament, and had ceased to hew coal. They sat with their backs against the far wall, though their bodies were soaked, the water being about eighteen inches deep in that slightly elevated grotto. The father and four sons and a grandson sat close together, not speaking, but scrambled to their feet when Stephen appeared.

'We did not know if we could get through,' said one of them. 'We did not wish to risk the boy.'

The lad, even through the grime of coal dust, was ashen-faced, his eyes glassy with terror. His teeth chattered, though his father and uncles had provided him with their vests.

'We can get through, but time is short,' said Stephen briskly. 'Pass the boy to me. What's his name?'

'Billy,' said one of the men, lifting the boy and placing him in Stephen's arms.

'Follow closely. At one point, for about ten or fifteen yards, the water is almost to the roof but there is a head height, or there *was,* ten minutes since.' He looked down at the boy lying passive in his arms. 'I bet you can swim, Billy, can't you? I bet you're as fast as a fish in the water, aren't you? And I'll wager you can outdo Bernie and Jack Carter.'

The child looked doubtful, but Stephen continued in a tone of supreme confidence. 'I am sure of it. What they did, so can you do, and without the fuss they made of it either. Come now. We shall soon be warm and dry. You shall hold my lamp, Billy, and light the way for us all.'

He strode back along the gallery with the child cradled in his arms, hearing the splash of the other men as they followed behind. Though he was not a man of faith, he prayed that the breathing space in the lowest part of the route might allow them safe passage.

The water was rising inexorably minute by minute, the low rumble of it now a roar. The current was very strong and contrary as it thrashed and scoured against the walls of the tunnels, seeking exit. It buffeted them this way and that, sending them careering into the walls, rocking them backwards and then pushing them ahead. The surface was agitated into a foam, and carried flotsam—buckets, timbers—that they had to dodge for fear of being knocked off their feet—or worse, unconscious. As the woebegone little party waded along the passageway and began to descend to the lowest part, Billy must have felt the water all around him, lifting and even trying to tug him from Stephen's arms. He began to struggle, turning so that his arms were around Stephen's neck so tightly that Stephen feared he might choke, and wrapping his skinny legs around Stephen's waist. The boy looked with all his eyes at his father, who followed Stephen, and beyond him to his grandfather and beloved uncles, and would have opened his mouth to cry out, but that the water would have instantly filled it.

'This is the worst part,' said Stephen, who was now crouching, shuffling forward inch by painful inch, the boy clasped tightly to his chest and held as far aloft as possible without hitting his head on the roof. But even so it was impossible to stop liquid getting in the lad's mouth and eyes, and Stephen could feel him retch and cough and eventually vomit. Stephen himself could only breathe sporadically—his mouth and nose being below the level of the flow. The burn in his knees and thighs was excruciating. Behind him, the men gasped for air, their faces pressed against the slimy rock of the roof as their bodies struggled for purchase amidst the spuming surges of the torrent. The child's body stiffened, and then went limp. The little limbs were ice cold.

'Talk to me, Billy. Shall you have mutton stew for your supper, do you think? What will your ma have on the stove? Or bacon perhaps, for it will be morning soon.'

'He's gone!' Billy's father cried out, reaching around Stephen to snatch the child, an action which threatened to pull them all under. 'His eyes are staring. Oh! My boy has drowned. Give him to me!'

But Stephen placed his hand on the boy's narrow little chest and felt a flutter beneath his fingertips. 'No,' he gasped out. 'He lives. I can feel his heart.'

At last the floor beneath their feet began to rise, and the ceiling likewise, and they could stand, if with difficulty. The water surged around them still, chest deep, as they fought their way to the ladder. Once there, Stephen passed Billy to his father, who put him over his shoulder and began to climb. The grandfather and the uncles went next.

Stephen called up, 'Is everyone accounted for?' and heard Mr Jessop's voice reply, 'Forty-eight, sir, and seven boys.'

Stephen began to climb the ladder, leaving the pitch dark and the terrible subterranean river behind him, up to where he could see the glow of fifty Geordie lamps. Suddenly his legs began to tremble. It was uncontrollable. He could feel the rattle of the flimsy ladder against the rock. He gripped with his hands but could not trust himself to lift his foot to the next rung. He closed his eyes and took a few deep breaths, though the air was foul and damp.

Then close by, someone said, 'Take my hand, Stephen,' and he looked up to see the face of the engineer above him. What was his name? Stephen blinked and shook his head, dispelling confusion and an overwhelming weariness. A large strong hand reached out to him. He grasped it, and stumbled up the last few rungs of the ladder.

He was up, but the quaking in his legs persisted. The man retained Stephen's hand in a firm grip and placed an arm, for good measure, around his back. 'I do not think we were properly introduced,' said the stranger, so lightly that they might have met at a whist club or a *soiree*. 'I'm Arthur Harlish.'

Chapter 81

Frank and Dónall sat companionably on a fallen log just beyond the pheasants' enclosure.

'You have done well, Dónall, to husband the birds while I have been away.'

Dónall turned his face to Frank. 'What is "husband"? Is that not ...'

'Just a figure of speech,' said Frank, looking away. 'It means to take care of something. As ... well ... as a husband does a wife.' He groped in his pocket and brought out a knife and a small piece of wood and began to whittle.

Dónall said, 'Cillian beats Brónach. Is *that*—'

'Oh no,' said Frank quickly. 'That is not proper husbandry. *I* would not treat a wife so.'

Presently Dónall pointed to the small enclosure they had made for the late clutch. 'The mother bird is ... good,' he said. 'I did not see my ... my mother.'

'Ah, Dónall.' Frank left off his carving to place a hand briefly on the young man's arm. 'I'm sure she would have been good. Aoife and Ruairí have been like parents to you. But you do understand, Dónall, a mother— a surrogate one—is not the same as a wife.'

Dónall turned his pale gaze on Frank once more. 'Surr ...?'

'A replacement. A stand-in. Aoife has stood in place of your mother, though she is not much older than you are.'

189

Dónall frowned. 'N… no,' he said at last. 'She is not like a mother.'

'A sister then?'

Dónall shook his head impatiently, as though to shift the thoughts that jumbled in his head like broken crockery that he might fit them together somehow even though some of the shards were sharp. They would scratch. 'No,' he said. 'I love her like … like Cormac loves Caitlin. He does not beat her. Or like Elíse loves Eister.'

Frank suppressed his astonishment. 'Elíse loves Eistir?'

'Oh yes. But in secret.'

The birds in the enclosure scratched amongst the leaf mould of the woodland floor. Their feathers were glossy with health.

After a moment Dónall said, 'Your sister has been ill.'

'Yes. But she is getting better. I hope she will come home soon.'

'Conn's little sister died.'

'Yes. That was sad. But my sister is not a baby. She is strong. It is not her time.'

Dónall's thoughts made one of the tangential leaps Frank was becoming accustomed to. 'You will let the birds out soon?'

'Aye. You shall help me, if you like. We will continue to feed them. They will return here at night for some weeks but, in the end, they will find their own roosts.' He looked up through the canopy of branches, which was beginning to turn gold and russet. 'Dónall. What do you think about love that is kept secret?'

Dónall shuffled his feet around in the dirt. 'I don't understand it.'

'No more do I,' said Frank. He took a deep breath. 'Dónall,' he began, but just then Aoife came through the trees to join them. Her hair fell about her shoulders and she wore her exotic dancing clothes. Dónall leapt to his feet, his face wreathed in smiles, hopping from foot to foot with pleasure.

'Here you are,' said Aoife, sitting beside Frank on the log. 'What are you doing?'

Dónall pointed at the birds. 'Watching,' he said. 'Soon they will be let out. I am to help.'

'Oh.' Aoife was unimpressed. 'They will be more interesting plucked and stuffed and cooking on the spit.'

Dónall's face clouded. 'I shall not eat them.'

Aoife laughed at him. 'You *will*, Dónall, if you are hungry enough.' She gave a little shiver, although the air beneath the trees was still and a little humid. 'I have forgot my shawl,' she said. 'Dónall. Will you run and fetch it for me?'

He looked as though he did not want to. He pointed to the wood in Frank's hands, from which a pheasant was emerging. 'I want to see him do that.'

Aoife gave Frank an imperceptible nudge. Frank laid the carving down beside him. 'I will not continue until you return,' he said. 'And when it is done, you shall keep it.' His cheek had bloomed with a blush. He rubbed at it roughly as though he could scrub the guilt away.

'Please, Dónall,' wheedled Aoife.

Dónall chewed his lips but at last consented. 'Alright,' he said. 'But do not move from here.'

Aoife hugged her knees and flashed her eyes at Frank. 'No,' she said. 'We will not.'

Dónall had hardly disappeared from sight before Aoife began to hitch up her skirts. 'Oh, Frank,' she said, panting slightly, 'I am mad for want of you.' She reached out and began to loosen the fastening of his shirt, but he stayed her hand and got up from the log.

'We must talk,' he said. 'Betsey will be well enough to come home soon. We must think about how we will arrange things.'

Aoife sighed and righted her dress. 'Nothing simpler,' she said. 'She can remain at the gatehouse. You and I can remove to the big house.'

Frank frowned. 'I do not think so.'

'Why not? There is plenty of space! We could sleep in a different room every day of the month and still not have used them all.' Aoife rose and went to where Frank stood, winding her arms around his waist. 'Would not that be exciting?'

He looked down at her. Her dark eyes were mysterious, her lips moist and tempting. As he regarded them he saw the flick of her tongue as it wetted them. His groin stirred. He put her away from him. 'If we did,' he said gruffly, 'we would not live where the fine folks belong. The housekeeper's apartment, perhaps. Or above the gunroom.'

'Pah!' Aoife was dismissive. 'You do not think I am good enough. I have lived in a gentleman's house from my infancy. I know how to behave in one.'

'Aye,' said Frank, 'so I gather, from your last suggestion. You did not marry a gentleman, Aoife. We cannot live in the grand house and wait upon ourselves! Or would you have me employ a butler and a cook and a groom?'

Aoife cocked an eyebrow. 'The butler and the groom I could manage,' she said coyly. 'The cook would have to shift for her herself, unless you would undertake to satisfy her.'

'Aoife!' He spun to face her. 'You talk like a common—'

'A common whore? And why should I not, since I have been all but forced to *be* one?' Her face was a mask of fury but then it melted, leaving an expression of woundedness. She pouted her lip. 'You know how I have suffered, Frank. How I have been ill-used. I made no secret of it. You said you would take care of me.'

'And so I will,' said Frank, softening, and taking her again in his arms. 'But not at the big house, Aoife. It is no good pretending it can be ours when it never can be.' He rested his cheek on her hair and tried to ignore the burrowing of her hands beneath his shirt, the soft rake of her nails across his chest. 'Perhaps Betsey could take up residence in Mrs Orphan's old rooms,' he murmured. 'She *is* the housekeeper, after all. She would only be alone at night. I do not think she would be discomposed by that. That would leave us with the gatehouse to ourselves. Would that not be a good compromise? Ouch!' He started away from her. 'That hurt.'

'Good,' said Aoife mildly. 'It will teach you to elevate your sister over me. I'm your *wife,* Frank.' She began to wrench at his belt. 'Now, quickly, before Dónall returns, or I shall burst.'

Chapter 82

It may be that a fine diet and the assiduous care of the Misses MacAllister wrought Beth's return to health, or it may be that her own determination to trespass for as short a time as possible on their hospitality brought it about. Equally likely, her youth and healthfulness dictated that no malady could afflict her for long. Either way, her strength returned, and she began to look about her.

She sent a note to the lawyer so that he would know she was ready to resume attendance on his wife, and also to the professor since the cataloguing of his books was only half completed.

The note to the lawyer was returned unopened, enclosed within a short—and ill-spelled—letter from their maid, who told Beth that Mr and Mrs Brock had departed to Bath "for the benifitt of some society and helthful warters" and would not return until spring.

Professor Bissel's reply informed her that in the light of recent events he felt wary of allowing those with unsavoury connections access to his house and particularly to his library, and had therefore engaged the services of a secretary, a man with unimpeachable testimonials and no association whatsoever with dubious local characters.

Beth tore the letter into shreds and threw it into the fire and, in a fit of fury and resentment, wrote immediately to the agency in Whitby requesting work as a lady's companion, a housekeeper or perhaps—if neither of these could be found—as a governess. Even in writing she knew that the attempt would anger Frank, but no letter had come from Mrs Stockbridge and until it did—assuming it carried forgiveness and a refusal to accept the proffered resignation—she would not contemplate a return to Tall Chimneys. Perhaps she was being very stubborn. When her frenzy had passed she was prepared to admit as much. She felt the professor's snub very keenly but she did not altogether reproach him for his caution. He apportioned some degree of blame to her and why not, when even she indicted herself?

The letter despatched, she assisted her hostesses with the packing up of their books and personal effects and encouraged them to think of their new home with their brother in every kind of positive light. As to her own future? The doctor had decreed that she could remove to the gatehouse and the care of *her* brother, but she prevaricated, day by day, finding some excuse for this to be inconvenient—she must assist the MacAllister ladies in their packing; she must complete the hemming and mending she had undertaken to accomplish; she must teach Patty the method for making elderberry cordial.

Her real reasons were several.

The answer to her letter to the agency would come to her at Laurel Cottage, and so she must delay in removing herself from it.

Her stubbornness—and bitter self-blame—made the idea of returning to the gatehouse impossible, even without the prospect of being, as it were, Aoife's guest. What changes—for good or ill—the new mistress of the gatehouse might have made Beth could not contemplate. And how awkward it would be, to intrude herself upon the two lovebirds! Should she offer them her bed? At least they would have privacy. It was not that she was too proud to sleep on the floor, as Frank had done these many years. No, it was not pride that made the idea of return abhorrent, but a sickly kind of disgust for the underhandedness of their *ménage*. Beth could not forget Dónall—that he was being deceived, and that she would have to be complicit in that deception. And she feared the consequences of him learning—as inevitably he must—the truth.

And she disliked the idea of taking a backwards step. In her mind, the catastrophe of the robbery had produced one single good—it had unbound her from Tall Chimneys, breaking the bond she had described to Ruairi. Sometimes it was like a hawser that secures a ship to the shore, and sometimes more like a fetter, such as restrains a prisoner in a cell. But now she was adrift, and now she would discover if she would float or sink.

The final reason was harder to admit to. It had been some six or seven weeks since the ill-fated open house at Tall Chimneys and still there

194

had been no word from Ruairi Connolly—no word, that is, that had come to Beth. She felt entitled to a word from him based on the fever pitch to which their relations had escalated—and how close she had been to giving herself to him entirely. It may well be that word had been brought to the Irish people or even to Frank, but no hint of it had come to her. Frank visited less often now that she was well, or almost well. She knew Mr Slade's nocturnal business had resumed, and although she worried Frank might fall foul of the Mounted Guard, she knew that the immigrants depended on that money more than ever. They had no other work. Much of the harvest had been ruined by rain, and no ploughing could take place until the ground dried. Mr Slade and his legitimate and illegitimate business was all that kept the wolf from the door.

That Ruairi had failed to apprehend Fionn was obvious, or he would have returned. And no doubt the spoils of Tall Chimney and the contents of the strongbox were all sold, gambled or spent by now. Beth conjectured that Ruairi's last hope was to capture Fionn and hand him in to the authorities; it would be the only sign he—a man of honour—could make to show that Fionn and Fionn's actions were utterly disowned by the rest of his countrymen. She was sure of Ruairi, though rumour was rife that he had been in league with Fionn all along, that he had only pretended to go in pursuit of him. Beth herself had no doubts about Ruairi—the intensity of her feelings for him, and the fact of his rescuing her from perishing alone on the moor made her faith in him ironclad.

At some point, she conjectured, he would return. Her fluttering heart and a sudden deluge of heat told her that this was of no small consequence to her. There was unfinished business between them that only his return could conclude. She was sure he felt it as she did. And when he returned—as she was certain he would—he would come to the place where he had delivered her. He would come to Laurel Cottage.

The rain ceased at last, and the moor glowed in its autumn hues. Copper-coloured bracken vied with dusky pink, deep purple and white spears of heather. The peat was richly dark, like bitterest chocolate, and limestone boulders wore velvet lichen cloaks. Sphagnum mosses oozed with moisture, and everywhere the secret trill and trickle of water underlay the squawk of geese as they arrived from foreign climes. Beth walked out every day in company with the MacAllister ladies but, as grateful as she was to them, she began to find their inconsequential conversation and their continual worry over trifles to be wearisome. They were both inveterate gossips, and it was from them that Beth heard the aspersions cast over Ruairi Connolly's character. It made her angry, but she could not chastise them. The shortening days were full of endless debate as to petticoats and pincushions, tippets and talcum boxes. They whittered endlessly about the safe transportation of their trinkets, distracted only by long fond anecdotes of childhood days occasioned by the discovery of some mouldering family heirloom. Beth bore with it and pretended interest, but by the late afternoon gloaming she usually found a restlessness upon her and would fetch her shawl and lace up her warm boots.

The sun might be setting in a glorious symphony of colour leaching down from the sky, setting the heathers ablaze in the west while, in the east, shadows crept across the far-flung moor. She was not afraid. Her misadventure in the storm had been simply that, brought on by exhaustion and shock. She knew the moor as well as anyone, even as well as Frank. She walked briskly, breathing in the thin cold air and enjoying the sensation of it against her face, even loosening her hair from its bonnet and pins and allowing the wind's fingers to tug and toy with it. She felt an odd combination of breathless exuberance and restless yearning, of having it all and wanting more.

The moor rose up behind Laurel Cottage to a sort of crag, smaller than the one she and Frank had visited as children but similar in nature. Here a limestone pavement provided a stage from which she could look across the endless moor. One late afternoon she occupied this position, her bonnet dangling from its strings in her hand and her hair caught up by the wind so that it roiled around her head like Medusa's snakes. The sky was a palette of wonder, every colour smeared and smirched into a sunset rainbow. She held her hand up like a visor to scan the vast tracts of desolate heathland.

Two riders caught her eye, a mile off but coming at a canter in her direction. Gentlemen, their tail coats flapped behind them. Both had removed their hats. One had dark-hair, the other's was lighter—Frank's colour—and much about the brown-haired rider reminded her of Frank. He was of Frank's height and build.

She said aloud, 'It *is* Frank! But what is he doing on a horse?' And then she looked more closely at the other man. Could it be Ruairi? She clapped a hand to her breast. Every hoofbeat brought them closer. She narrowed her eyes, squinting in the low-slanting sunlight. The hair was right but the build was wrong, she decided. This rider was too thin, but then Ruairi had been away a long time and had perhaps lived rough, gone without food …

The riders drew nearer, and their road would have passed below the bluff on which she stood and gone off towards the village, the standing stone and the Irish camp.

Frank and Ruairi were going home! But oh! They would not see her, and the idea that they would pass so close without seeing her was intolerable.

Impulsively she raised her hands and hallooed, her voice clear and high, carrying across the quarter mile that now separated them.

Both men reined in and looked up. She waved, heedless of her unbound hair and her dishevelled dress. 'It's me,' she shouted. 'It's me! Betsey!' She used her familial name instinctively. It felt both odd and comfortable on her lips.

The riders exchanged a word, then turned their horses to a narrow track that took them temporarily out of sight but would bring them up the side of the buttress to where she stood.

She waited breathlessly. He had come at last! Had Frank fetched him? But where was the other man who had set out to find Fionn? Oh! But that did not matter. Ruairi was here!

She turned to see their approach, the sun at her back now, slipping down past the rim of the moor like a penny disappearing into a slot, but enough rosy light remained for her to see immediately that the riders were not Frank and Ruairi. The dark-haired man she identified immediately as Stephen Milton. He *was* thin—thinner even than usual—and had a wan, washed out look to his face that even the bracing air and the sunset's glow could not disguise. It was not that she was not pleased to see him, but he was not Ruairi and she could not help a little groan of disappointment. She turned to the other man. Not Frank, but so like ... could it be ...?

He brought his horse right to her, reached down and swept her onto the saddle with him, his eyes alight with pleasure.

'Arthur! Arthur!' she cried, wrapping her arms around him. 'Oh, Arthur! You are home!'

Chapter 88

Arthur turned his horse in the direction of Laurel Cottage and Stephen followed suit.

'But shall we not stay and watch the last of the sunset?' Beth asked.

Arthur shook his head. 'No, for you have been ill, and so has Stephen. The night will cool too rapidly for two invalids to be out in it.'

Stephen disliked being characterised as an invalid but as they walked their horses over the spongey turf Beth made no enquiry about his illness, exclaiming instead over Arthur's superior riding coat and his figure, which had apparently expanded since his marriage. The dusk light enveloped the moor and Stephen was glad of the obscurity it lent. She leaned against her brother, obviously relishing the solid comfort of his presence. Stephen walked his horse alongside and tried to suppress his envy. He allowed himself to steal glances at Beth, but spoke no word.

'But how come you here, Arthur? And with Mr Milton?' asked Beth at last.

'My story will be soon told,' Arthur said. 'But let us get into the warm, with a fire and some hot tea. I presume your hostesses can stretch to that?'

'They have been all generosity,' Beth told him. 'Though I don't know how it has been afforded. Their income is very meagre, and they live frugally. But nothing has been denied me.'

'That is good,' said Arthur, casting a glance at Stephen. 'You have some kind benefactor, no doubt.'

'I must have. But I do not know who I need to thank.'

They were soon seated in the little parlour of Laurel Cottage, the fire stoked and tea brought. Beth introduced her brother to the Misses MacAllister. Stephen was known to them from the ill-fated open house at Tall Chimneys.

The two spinsters assured themselves that everything was cosy before withdrawing to a different room.

'Now. Tell me everything,' said Beth

'Not until you tell me your story,' Arthur said. 'I know of the robbery. You should not blame yourself. Mr Talbot does not; and neither, I am sure, will Mrs Stockbridge.'

'But she has sent me no word,' said Beth. 'And in any case, Frank has Aoife now. *She* can manage the house. It does not need two of us.'

'She may not have your skill,' said Arthur.

'It takes little skill,' Beth protested. 'In truth, it is a thankless task, keeping a house ready for people who never come. I feel that I would like a change.'

'You shall come to us then. Petunia would be glad of your company. And the children ...'

'No,' said Beth sharply. 'I know there are those who would put a roof over my head, and do not think I am unappreciative. But I have long felt the desire to be independent. I am hopeful of gaining a situation. I have applied to an agency in Whitby.'

'*Have* you? Well, that is enterprising.'

'A situation?' Stephen murmured lightly, conscious that he had no right to enquire.

Beth tilted her chin. 'As a lady's companion, or a housekeeper.'

'And how will that be different,' Arthur wanted to know, 'from housekeeping at Tall Chimneys?'

'There will be *people*. A family, perhaps. Those who will *see* what I do. I get ...' she cut her eyes at Stephen and he knew his presence made it difficult to confide in her brother as she might have done had they been alone. 'I get very lonely,' she concluded.

Her confession brought a lump to Stephen's throat. He coughed and lifted his cup to his lips.

'And I cannot intrude upon Frank and Aoife,' Beth went on. 'There isn't room for three at the gatehouse. Now, Arthur, your turn.'

Arthur paused, clearly turning Beth's words over in his mind, but he did not challenge her. He drained his cup. 'Well,' he said, 'my story is really very easily told. I was in Leeds with Mr Talbot to look at a foundry he wishes to buy. There we met with Mr Somersall. I should say that we were sought out by that gentleman—hounded, almost. He presented himself at the hotel, pursued us to a coffee house and invited us to dine with him at the Leeds, a gentlemen's club just lately opened[xxv].'

'He is not a man who understands rejection,' said Stephen dryly, sipping his tea.

'Indeed he is not,' said Beth, and Stephen knew she recalled Mr Somersall's behaviour at Tall Chimneys. He looked up, to share the reminiscence, but Beth's attention was fixed on her brother.

'The man wished to interest Mr Talbot in his business dealings,' Arthur went on. 'Not so much as to involve him, I do not think—he seems to have plenty of capital—but more to impress. He is certainly very proud of his empire. Then the talk turned to Miss Eagerly, Mr Talbot's goddaughter. It seems an alliance is in the offing and he wished to know … it was quite astonishing, the way he *presumed* … what Mr Talbot intended to do for her. In the way of settlement, I mean. Mr Talbot fielded the enquiries. I suppose he will wish to consult Mr Eagerly before making any absolute reply. But, while we were in Somersall's company, I received your letter.'

'Oh.' Beth had clearly forgotten the letter of recommendation she had written to Arthur. She blushed. Perhaps she regretted the action? Stephen rose abruptly and went to poke the fire.

Arthur said, 'Here. You two must eat this good cake. You are both as thin as laths.' He cut large slices and put them on plates. 'Naturally,' he went on, 'such a strong recommendation could not be ignored, and I began to make discreet enquiry of Mr Somersall. He spoke highly of Stephen, but then he received an express regarding the situation at the mine. *Then* he was not so complimentary.'

'The mine?' Beth turned to Stephen.

'All this rain,' said Stephen, crumbling the cake on his plate. He could not meet her eyes. 'The pump could not cope, and I'd asked permission to close the lower levels.'

'Stephen is quite the hero, though he will be the last to allow it,' said Arthur. 'He kept the pump in operation by sheer strength of his will, and got up from his sickbed to do so. Afterwards, once he had rescued fifty miners with his bare hands, he was taken ill again. I have been staying at Somersall Grange with him. This is his first outing.'

'Taken ill *again*? You were ill *before*?'

'As you were, yes,' mumbled Stephen, taking up some trinket from a side table and turning it in his hands. 'Some pernicious vapour from the marsh, perhaps, or just the drenching we both sustained.'

Beth frowned. 'I last saw you on the night you carried me home from Tall Chimneys. There was no rain and we passed no marsh. I'm sorry,' she said, 'I do not understand.'

'It doesn't matter,' said Stephen, mortified that she did not recall events that had haunted his every sleeping and waking moment since.

'Oh! My friend,' said Arthur, laughing. 'You will get nowhere if you hide your light under a bushel.' He turned to Beth. 'It was Stephen who found you after your misadventure on the moor. He caught sight of you in Brayton, and when the heavens opened he pursued you back towards Moorside, thinking he could carry you home and save you the worst of it. But he did not pass you on the way, and of course was soon apprised of events. He spent the rest of that day and into the night searching for you.'

'I was not alone,' Stephen put in quickly. 'The Irishmen searched also, and of course your brother. Your *other* brother.'

'But it was you who found her at last,' said Arthur, clapping Stephen on the shoulder, 'late on the second day. And since *you* will not say so, *I* will tell Betsey that you left sufficient money here with the ladies to pay for her care. Of course, I will reimburse you.'

'There is no need,' said Stephen, staring fixedly at the carpet and wishing it would swallow him whole.

'Mr Milton,' Beth said wonderingly. 'I am sorry. I had no notion. The ladies described only a tall dark man and I ...' she swallowed thickly. 'I could not think who they might mean.'

'Upon my word, that is not very complimentary to you, Stephen,' said Arthur. 'But let me go on with my story, to cover your vexation. I knew nothing of your disappearance Betsey, and by the time Stephen's note came to Mr Somersall you were here, and your recouperation well underway. But I made enquiry as to the engine at the mine—how and why it might be inadequate—and requested permission to come and make inspection. Of course, it was not the engine I wished to inspect, but rather the engineer. I suspect Mr Somersall will be seriously displeased to find that I have poached Stephen from beneath his nose.'

'He takes no notice of anything I recommend,' said Stephen. 'I do not suppose it will inconvenience him in the slightest.'

'His loss will be my gain then.'

'So you will go to London, then, and work with Arthur?' said Beth.

'And further afield than that,' said Arthur heartily. 'I wish Stephen to go to America. Their locomotives are so much more robust than ours, and already being imported. We cannot allow that. I want Stephen to visit their engine sheds and pick their brains. Then we will begin to manufacture our own locomotives, amalgamating best practice from both sides of the Atlantic. Before long we will reverse the tide of trade and send our engines over there.'

'Oh,' said Beth. 'And,' addressing Stephen, 'shall you like to go?'

Stephen raised his gaze to Beth and looked at her properly for the first time since their meeting on the moor. She had not tidied her hair and it lay on her shoulders, its burnished strands glowing in the firelight. She was thinner but, to him, not the less beautiful. He had thought of nothing but her for weeks; and the dearest memory of all was of carrying her through the storm to sanctuary. She had lain along the bank of a bog, and he thought at first the strew of her dress was no more than a saturated log, but the pale oval of her face and the slight shift in her arm had caused him to wheel his horse back. She was as wet as possible, her dress pouring water, her limbs chilled and larded with black mud and slime. He wiped the dirt from her face to find it bloodless and her lips blue. Next he placed his own mouth over hers to breathe warmth into her, and chafed her arms and legs all careless of propriety. What had it mattered? There had been barely a whisper of life left in her. Then she coughed and made a low moaning sound, and he swept her up. She was delirious—had looked at him with vacant, unseeing eyes. It did not surprise him that she had no memory of it and now he thought about it he was glad, for he had covered the mile or so to Laurel Cottage talking to her all the while of his plans— a good position, a steady income, a small house and *her*. He had poured out his love, knowing she could not hear him and he was therefore able to express himself with an erudition he could never have summoned otherwise. Even the raging storm, with its fervent wind and trenchant rain, could not equal his passion, and when he had delivered her to safety he was emotionally spent and physically exhausted.

Now, he wanted to reprise his ardour, to go on bended knee before her and offer her his hand, to ask that she accompany him to London, to America, to wherever in the world that Arthur and Mr Talbot might send them. What could they not endure, together? What obstacles could they not overcome? Were they not two kindred souls, born in one situation but bred for another? Why should they not find out—even establish— that new sphere in tandem?

But the opportunity was not meet with her brother being by, and although the passion was as hot as ever, the words would not come.

He put down the bauble in his hands and said, 'Yes, indeed. Very much.'

Chapter 84

Mildred Somersall was in a perfect agony of apprehension. Her husband had commanded her to hold a dinner for ten guests. This could not be as in the old days in Ferret Street, when a collation of cold meats, a selection of cheeses and a jug of hot punch had been sufficient to entertain the chandler and the draper and the curate with the sickly wife. This was to be an affair on an altogether grander scale, such as Mrs Somersall had never provided—nor yet even attended—before.

Mr Somersall was away from home yet again, and had been for several weeks. The last time she had laid eyes upon him was the day after the unpleasant interlude at Tall Chimneys. That had become a dim and uncomfortable dream to her now, though Mr Somersall's departure immediately after it made him seem part and parcel of that very nightmare.

In the interim she had been busy and relatively happy, taking care of Mr Milton in his fever, and cheering Herbert from the doldrums of his romantic uncertainty. She had liked the look of Miss Eagerly very much, declaring her a tidy, shy but very pretty girl, and good-natured to boot. Perhaps, come to that, a little *too* good natured—Mrs Somersall would like to have seen in the girl just a spark of resistance to Mr Somersall's brusque address—but she told herself it did not matter. Herbert was not like his father and the young woman would have no cause for fear. And Miss Eagerly's affection for Herbert had been very plain to see. That had pleased Mrs Somersall especially, though naturally it did not surprise her. What girl could be immune to the charms of her darling Herbert?

The weather, of course, had been excessively dreary. It had kept Herbert indoors and Mr Milton had been too ill to venture out, so things had been rather cosy until a crisis at the mine had required them both to go to Ellingbeck. And then she had been alone again. The rain had not inconvenienced her, even then; Mrs Somersall rarely took more exercise than a turn or two along the terrace and she never required the carriage except for church. She was told there were several persistent leaks in the roof of the still-unfinished eastern wing of the house. She instructed the servants to place buckets and to remove the furnishings from any danger of harm but did not herself go and inspect. Those rooms were in any case beyond the scope of her general usage and would not be required for the dinner.

Oh! The dinner! How her thoughts would fly back to it and what nervous paroxysms they caused her. Missives came daily from her husband; she almost dreaded the step of the butler with yet another letter upon his silver salver. Mr Somersall told her to expect copious deliveries of wine and champagne. He decreed the number and constitution of courses, stated the quantity of candles and the livery of the footmen, and even dictated which of her jewels she should wear. There was to be music. A piano tuner had been sent for from York to tune the grand pianoforte upon whose keys no fingers had yet been laid. A maestro pianist was to entertain the company with the assistance of a soprano of some renown. Whether these personages were to be part of the dinner guests, or in addition, or were not to be provided with food at all he did not specify so Mrs Somersall's table plan was in a state of utter disarray.

Then, the invitations. Mr Somersall of course ordained the names of the guests. The vicar and his wife and their daughter were to be invited as a matter of course, and the other young lady whom they had met at Tall Chimneys. Mr Somersall had been vociferous in his low opinion of *her*, yet allowed that they ought to return such scant hospitality as she had meted out. In any case, he said, they would need a spare lady to make up the numbers. The great honour of Lord and Lady Riding's company was to be sought, along with their two unmarried daughters whose names he did not know but told his wife she must contrive to find them out. His design in including the Riding girls was quite clear—he would teach the Eagerlys that Herbert had more than one string to his bow. That Herbert had never even met the honourable ladies Riding—did not probably know of their existence—was quite immaterial. Their mere presence at Somersall Grange would be quite sufficient. Then there was to be Mr

Talbot, who would come with Mr Somersall from Leeds and be accommodated within the house for as many days as he cared to remain. Despite the superior rank and great *éclat* of the Ridings, it was clear that Mr Talbot was to be the premier guest and nothing was to be left undone that could possibly add to his comfort or enjoyment.

Stephen Milton and Talbot's engineer, Arthur Harlish, would complete the party.

Mrs Somersall's cook, who had perhaps over-egged her qualifications to be cook in such a great house as Somersall Grange, was as full of qualm as the mistress, especially when she saw the menu required.

'Two soups? Oh, ma'am, that can hardly be necessary. A green turtle soup[xxvi] will be quite sufficient, will it not?'

'Mr Somersall requires two: green turtle and mulligatawny. I shall partake of neither. A clear broth does for me, but I shall not require you to provide it. I will pretend to eat whatever is served to me. Now, as to the fish. He says stewed eels in anchovy sauce is much in vogue. The idea of it makes me sick, but if he says we must have it … can you attempt it, do you think?'

The cook looked doubtful. 'What are anchovies?'

'I have no idea, Mary.' Mrs Somersall was on first name terms with most of her staff. It did not come naturally to her to make a distinction of rank between them and herself. In the absence of any other, she had made them her friends. 'You must find out. I suppose the fishmonger will tell you. And some simple fried sole. Mr Somersall does not list it here, but I think we should offer an alternative to the eels, do not you, Mary?'

'Fresh sole is dear, ma'am.'

'Shockingly dear! The cost of it quite frightens me. But then it is the only thing that sits comfortable in my stomach. Send one of the men to Whitby quayside early on the day of the dinner Mary, will you? So that they be as fresh as possible. What about the roast? Beef, perhaps? Mr Somersall does not specify and if I choose it is sure to be wrong.'

'What about mutton?' The cook felt comfortable with mutton.

'Very well, and a fowl of some kind. He suggests croquet of fowl with a piquant sauce.'

'A fowl *as well*?'

'So it says here. As to vegetables, I will leave that to you. Oh dear, the list goes onto the other side of the page. We must speak of dessert. Mr Somersall lists several here. A Charlotte russe, a lemon tart, blancmange and a mincemeat pie. Then there is to be cheese—'

'Oh, ma'am! I do not think I am equal to it!'

'No more am I, Mary, but what can we do? I suppose I must send for Mrs Max.' Mrs Max was the cook at the Whitby house, a person to whom Mrs Somersall had never warmed, a harridan who cowed everyone apart from Mr Somersall. 'Surely, between the two of you?'

'Oh, no, ma'am,' the cook mumbled. Mrs Max's reputation was well known. 'There is no need of that. I will contrive, somehow.'

'There's a good girl,' said Mrs Somersall. 'Now send Elsie to me, would you?' Elsie was the housekeeper. 'There are bedrooms to be allocated. Mr Talbot is to stay here and I am to suggest to the Ridings that they may stay also. That will mean accommodating at least one maid and a valet, as well as their grooms. How I am to entertain Lady Riding I do not know. She has never so much as looked at me. She is a cold, proud woman. I almost hope they decline the invitation, but then Mr Somersall will be so angry, and the table plan will be all put out. Oh, Mary! How I wish Mr Somersall had not conceived this scheme. It is quite beyond my powers!' She burst into tears.

Mary, in sympathy, also wept. 'And also mine, ma'am. We are all of us uncommon put about by the master's notion.'

'It is much more comfortable when we are left to ourselves, is it not?'

'Excepting the young gentlemen,' said Mary, wiping her eyes with her apron. 'They are no trouble to us.'

Mrs Somersall was of the same opinion. She had taken Arthur to her bosom since the day he arrived from the mine with a drooping and exhausted Stephen Milton in a hired gig. Arthur was of just that level of society in which Mrs Somersall felt most comfortable. He was easy, demanding nothing of her and indeed wishing to do as much as he could for her. He had no airs, had been perfectly happy to take his meals in the small breakfast parlour where she, Milton and Herbert—when he was at home—usually dined.

The recurrence of Stephen's malaise had been worrisome but had not lasted long, and had required only one visit from the doctor. How glad she had been of Arthur's presence, for Herbert had been summoned to Leeds to attend his father and answer—no doubt—for the closing of the lower levels in direct contradiction of his father's order. Now Mrs Somersall was pleased to see that with the judicious encouragement of Arthur Harlish, Stephen was well on the mend. There was no danger of him leaving an empty seat at her dinner table and ruining the table plan.

So it was to a house in a state of flux that Arthur and Stephen returned after their encounter with Beth on the moor. Mrs Somersall had the footmen in the dining room trying this and then that arrangement of chairs, place settings, glassware and napery.

'Oh do advise me, gentlemen,' Mrs Somersall called as they entered the hall and handed their outerwear to a footman. 'As to the dinner service. Do you think the Minton[xxvii] too ostentatious? Wouldn't we be better with the Rockingham? And where should Lord Riding be seated? Please don't say he should be at my right hand; I shall have nothing to say to him. Mr Milton, you'll take Miss Harlish into dinner. Shall you mind that? Mr Harlish, I hope you will escort one of the Honourable Lady Ridings. I must discover their names, I suppose. Upon my word! This is a world of trouble and I do not know how I shall get through it. If only Ida was here. She knows as little as I do of how grand folks carry on, but she would be such a comfort to me. Yes, yes, very well, James. That will do for now. We will use the Minton, I think, as many glasses as there will be types of wine, though how I shall know which to use I do not know. Oh! I suppose it will not signify, since I shall do no more than touch my lips with them.'

Now Arthur Harlish had found in his heart a great sympathy and tenderness for Mrs Somersall because she reminded him of another poor put-upon lady of his acquaintance.

He saw that the beleaguered woman was close to collapse with all her woes. 'Come, Mrs Somersall,' he said. 'Let us go into the small sitting room and have some hot milk sent up. If the kitchen can find some vanilla and sugar, I shall mix you a little toddy that my wife finds particularly soothing.' He guided the distraught lady to a chair and placed a stool beneath her feet. 'Now then, we shall be cosy. Stephen, fetch the whisky decanter. We shall lace our toddy with something a little stronger.'

Soon the hot milk and other ingredients arrived and they sat over their toddies, and Mrs Somersall felt comfortable for the first time that day. 'And where did your ride take you?' she enquired. 'I hope you have not been outdoors this long time, Mr Milton.'

The young engineer was lost in thought and only stared fixedly into the fire. Arthur knew Stephen to be a man who did not bare his heart to the public gaze but did not need to be told the name that was writ large on that organ. Arthur leaned forward and poured a little more of the toddy into Mrs Somersall's cup resolved to do both Stephen and his hostess a favour

'Our ride took us to a surprising place,' he said, 'for quite by chance we encountered my sister.'

'Your sister? Oh yes, the young lady at Tall Chimneys. Did you ride as far as that?'

'We did not, for she is at present the guest of the Misses MacAllister, who reside at Laurel Cottage. Do you know it? It is slightly set back from the drovers' track, about halfway between Brayton and Moorside. My sister has been unwell, but is now almost recovered. She has reasons of her own for not wishing to return to the gatehouse and so, Mrs Somersall, I find myself with a small request to make of you.'

'I am sure I will do anything in my power to assist you, Mr Harlish, but you must understand my powers are very small; Mr Somersall decides everything.' The sweetness and strong vanilla in the toddy disguised a hefty slug of whisky, and Mrs Somersall was beginning to feel pleasantly mellow.

'I perceive as much, but I think that he will not begrudge you this indulgence, since it will relieve you of much of the burden of entertaining his friends.'

'Well I would give a good deal for that,' said the lady lugubriously. 'What is it you suggest?'

Arthur threw a glance at Stephen, who had dragged his gaze from the fire and now looked intently at Arthur. Arthur lowered one eyelid in a wink before turning back to his hostess. 'She is most desirous of finding a position as a lady's companion,' he said, 'or perhaps a housekeeper. She has taken care of Tall Chimneys since she returned from school, and although there have rarely been any guests, you will have seen for yourself how well maintained the house was.'

'Indeed,' Mrs Somersall murmured, 'But I have a housekeeper. I could not turn Elsie out.'

'And she was trained by a lady who had the management of a very large house, where entertaining on a large scale was commonplace.' Arthur sipped his drink while he allowed this allusion to settle in Mrs Somersall's mind.

'Well,' she said after a few moments, 'that would be very useful at present.' Her eyes were almost closed, but she was not asleep.

Arthur went on, his voice so velvety as to be almost soporific, but not so soft that his words would miss their mark. 'I was thinking that my sister might be a companion to you, Mrs Somersall. A friend, even.'

Stephen, apprehending Arthur's intent, said, 'Poor Ida is beyond your reach, but Miss Harlish could go some way towards compensating for her loss. Should you not like to have a friend about the place?'

A large tear oozed from the corner of Mrs Somersall's eye. 'Oh yes,' she said fervently. 'I should like that very much.'

'That is what I thought,' said Arthur. 'I suggest you write to the agency in Whitby without delay for I think … that is … my sister's present determination is to obtain a position without the aid of any … friend. I am sure you understand me.'

'I think I do,' said Mrs Somersall.

Chapter 85

Hardly a week later, Beth Harlish was established at Somersall Grange.

Her own understanding of her position was very clear. She was to be higher than a servant but not by any means equal to the family. She was not a guest and yet must make herself as agreeable as one if required. She must assist and advise, comfort and counsel, encourage and entertain. She must know when to speak and when to be silent, when to remain and when to withdraw. This, in her own mind, was her new role and with the one—but considerable—reservation posed by the looming spectre of Mr Somersall, she had accepted Mrs Somersall's offer without much hesitation, and even with relish. What it would be, she exclaimed to herself, to have to do with *people*. To be in a house that was *alive*.

Of course the looming spectre was substantial. From her own brief encounter as well as from Mrs Somersall's shrinking demeanour whenever her husband was mentioned, Beth understood the man to be an ogre, a bully and a tyrant. But there remained in Beth such a quantity of self-denigration at her loss of Mrs Stockbridge's artefacts that she told herself that a situation without disadvantage of any kind could hardly be fair. She did not deserve to walk a velvet path.

Mrs Somersall, it quickly became apparent, had quite other notions. *She* was eager to supply as much velvet—also silk, satin and lace—as possible. Miss Harlish was to be to her what Stephen and even Arthur, in the brief duration of his stay, had become: a surrogate child, a young person like Herbert, to be fed, humoured and indulged. She saw in Beth not only a friend but a daughter, almost a plaything—but one which, unfortunately might have to be put away when Mr Somersall was at home. She greeted Beth with ingenuous elation, as though welcoming a long-lost child back to her bosom. She pressed Beth to occupy a principal suite of rooms—almost the best that the Grange had to offer—but these were gently rejected in favour of a small bedroom and smaller sitting room at the far end of a corridor, with an unprepossessing view over the stable block.

'Oh but my dear Miss Harlish,' Mrs Somersall objected, 'this is too small—it is not much bigger than a closet—and you will be so far away from me. I shall not know how to find you.'

'I shall not hide myself away, ma'am, unless it be politic for me to retire,' Beth said. 'It is but a turn or two, a short stair and a length of landing, and I can be at your side whenever you have need of me.'

'Which will be all the time,' said Mrs Somersall, sighing happily. 'I must say that this arrangement fills me with joy. I am so glad that—'

But here a discreet cough from Arthur, who accompanied them, stopped Mrs Somersall from revealing his interference. '—that the agency recommended you. Is it not a happy coincidence? And to think that we should have met each other already, and that your own brother should be with me! Now let us unpack your things.' Mrs Somersall moved towards Beth's box.

'Oh but that will hardly be necessary, ma'am,' said Beth, ashamed of her paltry belongings. Her favourite dresses had been lost in the bog, and the clothing that came from the gatehouse was hardly suitable for life as a lady's companion in a great house such as Somersall Grange. 'I can do it myself.'

But Mrs Somersall could not contain her enthusiasm, and threw open the lid. Immediately she saw the nature of Beth's difficulty, closed the box and sent for her dressmaker, her milliner and her haberdasher and also her bootmaker.

'Of course, the cost must be deducted from my salary,' said Beth humbly.

Later, Arthur said, 'Do not deny Mrs Somersall the pleasure of equipping you. You will soon understand her circumstances. You have met her husband so you must be able to guess something of her life. She reminds me of dear Miss Trimble, who was companion to Mr Talbot's wife. Such a put-upon little body, and quite in awe of Lady Jane[xxviii]. Let

Mrs Somersall have her fun, Betsey. While the cat is away, the mice may play.'

So Beth permitted the measuring and fitting, the leafing through pattern books and examination of fabric swatches, the choosing of ribbons and stockings, the provision of crisp lawn nightdresses and cool muslin shifts and even the daily arrival of a little maidservant for the tightening of stays and the brushing and arranging of her hair, because she could see what delight it gave her employer. But she did not let Mrs Somersall's indulgent misconstruction of the situation turn *her* head, and she reminded herself that Mr Somersall's advent from Leeds, which was daily expected, might have her bundled from the house bag and baggage.

Arthur remained at Somersall Grange attendant on the arrival of Mr Talbot from Leeds, and Stephen did not return to the colliery because he was uncertain of the continuation of his employment there until word should come from his employer. As the days passed, the men's friendship and mutual respect deepened. They spent their mornings in the library together. Arthur was full of admiration for the scope and accuracy of the mine blueprints Stephen had drawn, and particularly fulsome in his praise of the ambitious new engine Stephen had devised. They discussed new technology—*The Great Britain*, the iron steamship that had just completed its first transatlantic crossing; the expansion of the telegraph, which would revolutionise communications; and the Pratt truss, a specialized bridge design using revolutionary new Y- and K-shaped patterns.

Beth was closeted with Mrs Somersall in the forenoons and gradually unravelled for her the practicalities, etiquette and likely programme for the upcoming dinner. She knew the names of the Riding girls because she had been at school with them, and so the invitations were worded, printed and despatched. The seating plan was decided upon, with Beth calling on her recollection of Mrs Orphan's teachings, and the two practised the kind of unexceptionable, elegant drawing room and dinner conversation that would get Mrs Somersall through the ordeal of being seated beside Lord Riding or finding herself on a sofa beside his even more intimidating lady.

'As to the serving of tea, you can safely leave that to me,' Beth said. 'I shall be glad to make myself useful and I would not wish the company to think I pretend to be a real lady.'

'You are fortunate,' said Mrs Somersall with a sigh. 'I must contrive to carry off that deception somehow.'

'You are the host,' said Beth gently, 'and therefore you cannot be wrong in your own home.'

'Oh, my dear, what a comfort you are! But Mr Somersall so often finds fault, and I know I shall be sure to drop my spoon in my soup or trip over my own trimmings. I might have led the guests into a broom closet had you not taught me the way from the grand salon to the dining room. Must I really go first?'

'I am afraid so, on the arm of Lord Riding, and your husband will bring Her Ladyship in the rear. The other guests are harder to rank, but I think Mr Herbert had better take the Honourable Lady Veraminta, and Mr Talbot her sister, Lady Petronella. Mrs Eagerly will have to come behind them with Mr Milton. My brother must take Rose, though I am sure her mama will object, and Mr Eagerly will be left with me. Hopefully, he will not mind. I do not think he will, and perhaps when she sees in what esteem Mr Talbot holds her husband, Mrs Eagerly might not protest.'

Mrs Somersall looked bewildered, ready to lose the small quantity of assurance it had taken Beth so many days to foster.

'Do not worry,' Beth said. 'We will write it down and place the note discreetly, so that you can refer to it immediately beforehand.' She placed her hand on Mrs Somersall's. 'All will be well, ma'am.'

In the afternoons they took their exercise. September was well advanced by this time, and the rain that had bedevilled the past six weeks had departed to leave clear skies, frosty mornings and slanting sunlight. The party walked together a few times along the terrace until Mrs Somersall went inside, and then Arthur, Stephen and Beth would extend their walk around what would be the park of the Grange but which was then still a terrain of rough heath, with the occasional stand of ancient trees and natural rivulets of clear, cold water.

'I will miss you very much when you are gone,' said Beth to Arthur one day as they stood on a slight rise and looked back to where the house lay in golden late afternoon sunshine. 'I suppose that will be almost immediately after Mrs Somersall's dinner?'

'I am at Mr Talbot's disposal,' said Arthur, lighting a cigar, a luxury to which he had recently become accustomed.

'And I am at yours,' said Stephen, 'supposing Mr Somersall is prepared to release me. I am contracted to him until November, though of course I tendered my resignation immediately I was well enough to do so. But if I know the man, he will insist upon holding me.'

'You do not know Mr Talbot,' said Arthur, puffing on his cigar. 'He can be persuasive. You will not smoke with me, Milton? Betsey does not mind.'

Stephen shook his head. 'I dislike the things. But do not mistake me. No one would be happier than me to see the old man give way ... in one way, anyway. But I warn you, he is as stubborn as a rock.'

'In what way would you wish him to stick to you?' Arthur asked, kicking leaves around with his feet but keeping a twinkling, mischievous eye on Stephen the while. 'Why would you wish to remain here a week, a day, even an hour longer than you need to? You say yourself that the man is impossible, your expertise squandered as pearls before swine, your labour utterly wasted. I cannot think of a single reason why you would wish to remain.'

Stephen picked up an acorn and examined it closely. 'There is something about finishing something one has started,' he said.

Beth wandered away beneath the trees and Stephen followed her with his gaze. She looked altogether different than the homely little brown bird of a woman he had first seen at the vicarage. She wore a new walking habit of very superior quality; its sage green suited her nut brown hair and hazel eyes. Something about the shape of her person—Stephen blushed to think of it—was altered; she was more structured, better engineered. Her shape resembled society ladies. Indeed, now she looked like a lady. Had he met her now, he would not have been confused by her, would not have asked, "What manner of lady are you?"

'Harlish,' he said suddenly, 'why do you and your brother call your sister "Betsey"? She was introduced to me as Beth.'

'She was always Betsey amongst the family,' Arthur said. 'But she was teased for it at school. I suppose the name was very humdrum beside the Amelias and Adelaides. So she reinvented herself as Beth, and stuck to it even when she was forced to return to the gatehouse.'

'And why was she forced?'

'Our father died, and our mother lost her wits. Their work at Tall Chimneys had to be continued, or we would have lost our home. I was away by then, and our other sister had a good position as a school teacher. Frank and Betsey were the most suited to take on the work and so Betsey relinquished her ambitions and returned to the gatehouse.'

'She and I have spoken of being born in one sphere but bred for another.' He raised a questioning eyebrow. 'Perhaps now she is free of Tall Chimneys she will be able to pursue her dreams?'

Arthur put his hand on Stephen's arm. 'I think,' he said seriously, 'there is not a braver, more sensible or more resilient woman in England. She appreciates the finer things in life but can live without them. She can endure hardship. I think that, as a travelling companion abroad, no man could do better.'

Stephen made no reply, but he understood very well what Arthur had told him.

Chapter 86

About the same time as the exchange related in the previous chapter, the Eagerlys and Edgar Maybury were in the vicarage drawing room. The maid had been told to admit no visitors. The vicar's sermon remained half-written on his desk and the curate neglected his parish visits. They were at counsel, for a schism had opened up amongst them.

The vicar sat next to his daughter on the sofa. Mrs Eagerly occupied a chair by the fire on quite the other side of the room. Edgar stood close by her, on the hearth rug, with his hands behind his back. And so by their various dispositions within the room might the factions of the schism be inferred. The fire was unlit, despite the day being cool, and neither were any lamps lit. The drawing room was therefore cold and inhospitable and rather gloomy, and so was the atmosphere.

Rose turned a tear-streaked face to her papa. 'I do not understand,' she cried.

Her father passed her his handkerchief but spoke no word.

'Your papa and I have discussed it,' Mrs Eagerly said. 'We both feel that a season in town will be the best thing.'

'As to the season in town, my dear, I have nothing to say against it,' said the vicar. 'But as to the other matter, I fear I cannot concur with your own opinion.'

'But Herbert and I wish to marry,' sobbed Rose. 'And if Papa has no objection—'

'Having no objection is not at all the same thing as giving his sanction,' said Mrs Eagerly. 'He is very far from *that*, I believe.'

The vicar creased his brow. 'Well ...'

'We wondered if young Mr Somersall might suit,' said his wife briskly, as though disposing of a trifle, 'and indeed he is a very dear boy. We are very fond of him. But upon reflection we think that you should meet a great many more young men before fixing your affections.'

'It is too late!' Rose wailed. 'I *have* fixed them.'

'That's nonsense, you know,' put in Edgar. 'You have barely known each other a month—'

'Almost three months,' Rose retorted. 'Ninety-eight days.'

'But he has not been near us for half of that time, since the rains began,' her stepbrother went on. 'And in any case, it is no time at all upon which to base a decision that will last a lifetime. I have always felt—though it was not my place to say so—that our parents were precipitate in their sponsorship of the alliance. We knew nothing of the Somersalls.'

'Indeed we did not,' said Mrs Eagerly with a shudder. 'If we had, we would certainly not have promoted the acquaintance. And now this!' She flapped the card that had been delivered that morning, which was their invitation to dine at Somersall Grange. 'I do not think I can spend a single minute in that man's company, let alone an entire evening! You did not see him, Oscar. If you had, nothing on earth would persuade you to a continuance of our acquaintance with Herbert. Did you not see how I trembled on my return from Tall Chimneys? Did you yourself not have to bring me a restorative before I could utter a coherent word? And as for Rose! She was ill for a week afterwards!'

The notion of restorative sherry was very tempting, and the vicar eyed the side table where a decanter stood, but he took a deep breath and summoned what patience might be forthcoming from another source.

'You are right, my dear. I did not see Herbert's father. But I did see Herbert, as you did not. He called upon me that very evening, as you know, and I think I have never heard such out-and-out honesty nor been privileged to receive such frankness from any young man. Herbert knows his father's faults. He neither denies nor excuses them, and believe me when I say that he came without the smallest hope. He knew his father's behaviour had been unconscionable. But yet the strength of his feeling for Rose overcame. He does love her, as ardently as his nature will allow, and I found myself unable to send him away comfortless.'

The vicar waited to see if his words would soften the heart of his wife. There was more he could say—much more. That Herbert had come into his study in such a drooping and disconsolate state that the vicar had at first feared for his health. That Herbert had abjectly used words of disgust and shame such as no man should ever have to utter about his own father. That Herbert had related, in confidence, incidences of past cruelty, bullying and cold-heartedness that had caused tears to fill the vicar's own eyes, and that Herbert himself had wept—positively sobbed—at the recollection of them. Mr Eagerly's heart had all but melted, and he had been minded to open his arms to the young man as to a son and to send the two of them—Herbert and Rose—as far away as possible even at his own expense that the old tyrant could have no further power over them.

But he had hesitated. His wife's condition, in the very next room, had stayed him. *She* had been as angry as possible on her return from Tall Chimneys. Angry, offended and also rather shaken. Rose's face, as she mounted, like an automaton, the stairs to her room, had been bloodless and her eyes oddly staring. With such evidences as these, even without Herbert's testimony he could not accede to Herbert's request for Rose's hand. So he had prevaricated, and Herbert had gone away. Gone away downcast but—the vicar trusted—not hopeless. Since then, it was quite true Herbert had not been seen at the vicarage. That only increased the vicar's respect for the young man. It showed deference and self-discipline; Herbert would do nothing underhand. And then, of course, there had been trouble at the mine. By all accounts Herbert had acted bravely, throwing himself into the crisis in a way that showed manliness and courage.

Mr Eagerly attempted with all the power at his disposal—short of actually speaking—to communicate to his wife the delicate nature of Herbert's predicament. To imply that to save the young man from such a despot as his father was tantamount to saving his soul. To cause her to think well of Rose's suitor. But it was in vain. She only said, 'You did not give your consent though, did you Oscar?'

'No,' he admitted. 'I did not, and so I suppose they hope to bring the thing to a conclusion by this dinner. I fear we must go, my dear.'

'Not in the least,' his wife declared. 'We will bring forward our plans to travel south. The season does not begin until October, but we can spend some time at the coast, and who is to say that was not always our intention? I hear Great Yarmouth is very pleasant. Should you not like to bathe in the sea, Rose?'

'I do not wish to do anything that will separate me from Herbert,' said Rose sulkily. 'Why cannot he accompany us?'

Her father said, 'He has his responsibilities at the colliery, my dear.'

Edgar crossed the room and knelt at Rose's side, taking her hands in his. 'Rose dear,' he said. 'I have not met the elder Mr Somersall, but Mama tells me he is not a pleasant man.'

'No,' she whispered. 'He was not nice.'

'Not nice?' Mrs Eagerly spluttered. 'He is the rudest, most vulgar, boorish and offensive man it has ever been my misfortune to meet. Do not you recall his manner, Rose? He reduced you to tears! And the terms in which he referred to the alliance! A farmer negotiating the purchase of a brood mare has more delicacy.'

Edgar pressed on. 'I have made some small enquiry,' he said, 'and I learnt that, though wealthy now, Mr Somersall began life humbly, as a clerk and then as a foreman. He has not the manners that come from gentle rearing and education. He is little more than a brute in a fine waistcoat. He is feared everywhere. Can you really envisage seeing such a man probably every day? For I suppose you would make your home at Somersall Grange, or at their town house? Or even if you were permitted a home of your own, is it not likely you would be in company with the Somersalls several times a week? Do you think you could stand by while he browbeats your husband? For I suppose something of that kind occurs quite regularly. Do you think you could bear to be browbeaten yourself? Men like that, Rose, they are indiscriminate.'

Mr Eagerly spoke sharply. 'I cannot allow *you* to browbeat Rose, Edgar. You are frightening her.'

Edgar stood up. 'I am sorry sir, but Rose must have her eyes opened; and the truth is, she is too delicate. She will be crushed.'

'Herbert will protect me,' Rose whimpered.

'Herbert cannot protect himself,' Edgar scoffed, sauntering back to the rug. 'He is as likely to hide behind your skirts.'

'We can live in another part of the country,' Rose threw out. 'Herbert has his own fortune and my godfather—'

'You should not depend on that,' the vicar demurred. 'I have never asked nor do I expect Mr Talbot to do anything for you. The idea is Somersall's own extrapolation, based on the mere fact of Mr Talbot being your godfather.'

'And it is my belief that such money as Herbert has comes entirely from his father,' said Edgar. 'What has been given can certainly be taken away again.'

'You did not give your promise, Rose, did you?' Mrs Eagerly said.

Rose chewed her lip. 'No,' she said at last. 'I said that he should speak to Papa first.'

'That was quite right of you,' her stepmother put in.

'But he asked me if I could love him,' Rose asserted, 'and I am sure I gave him to understand—without actually saying so—that I could. And I do, Papa!' She dissolved again into tears.

The vicar held her to his bosom, but he looked over her head at his wife. 'What a predicament is this,' he said.

'Not at all, sir,' said Edgar, rubbing his hands together. 'A catastrophe has been avoided by Rose's own good sense, and by yours. She made no promise. You gave no sanction. We are quite free of the entanglement. Go to Great Yarmouth, sir, and enjoy some sea air. I shall manage things here. My mother will write to Mrs Somersall and decline the invitation on account of your travel plans. Not that you are under any obligation to give a reason. Rose will rally with some sea air and bathing and then—think of it! London! Balls! The theatre! Perhaps you will be presented!'

'You go too fast, Edgar,' said the vicar. 'What you say may be true—that we are not at this point committed. But there was, in my interview with Herbert, that degree of confidence that I cannot now turn my back on him. No.' He squared his shoulders. 'On the understanding that there exists as yet no engagement, that nothing whatever is fixed, we will dine at Somersall Grange. I will see the old man for myself and we will observe how Rose fares on better acquaintance with him and with Mrs Somersall. Then we will know how to proceed.'

'Oh no! Oscar!' cried Mrs Eagerly, flinging the invitation from her in pique. 'You do not mean it? It will kill me to be civil to that boor.'

'Then do not be civil, my dear. By all accounts he is the kind of man from whom civility or outright insolence roll equally, as water from a duck's back. Now, I must finish my sermon. Rose, might I prevail upon you to scribe for me? Your hand is so very neat. Come, my dear. The fire is lit in my study, and we shall be very cosy.'

They left the room. Edgar and Mrs Eagerly exchanged despairing looks.

'Upon my word,' said Edgar, pouring them both a glass of sherry. 'I am sorry the invitation does not include me. I would have enjoyed watching you joust with the old churl. But do not be downhearted, Mama. It seems to me he will be "hoist by his own petard."[xxix] If he be as bad as you say, the vicar will come around to your way of thinking and you will be in Great Yarmouth by Michaelmas.'

'I hope you are right,' said his mother. 'Well, we made our attempt and we failed.'

'We lost the battle, Mama,' said Edgar cheerfully. 'We have not lost the war. And I must say, Somersall's notion of a dowry from Mr Talbot is very interesting, is it not? It occurs to me that instead of funding the alliance with *them* he might be minded to back my claim.'

'Pay, you mean, for her *not* to marry Herbert?'

'Precisely so. Now I must be on my way. Oh! By the by, did you hear that Miss Harlish is now established at Somersall Grange? Quite an elevation for her, don't you think?'

Mrs Eagerly drank her sherry. 'Better than she deserves. What stupidity—to get herself lost on the moor, and in such a storm. But regardless of her new situation, any continuance of that level of intimacy that existed between her and Rose must be at an end.'

'I quite understand. You cannot make a silk purse from a sow's ear. I always said her association with the Irish was a sign of poor judgement.'

'And look how they have repaid her for it! But no. It is her brother's heresy that is more troubling. He lives in unashamed adultery, you know! I have told the vicar he must terminate Mr Harlish's work as sexton. It is unthinkable that those sinful hands should tend the graves of Christians!'

Edgar refilled his glass. 'I must gird myself,' he said, tossing down the contents. 'The vicar desires me to minister to the Irish this afternoon. I do not know why. They are beyond any redemption. I half suspect them of devil-worship if I am truthful. Divination, certainly. They read fortunes, you know, quite brazenly in the market square. They told Mrs Whitlow that her son would return from sea, though it has been five years since his ship was lost.'

'They are beyond the pale,' said his mother. 'But you know the vicar. He believes no soul to be irretrievably lost.'

Chapter 87

Frank would sorely miss the little stipend paid to him by the parish for the maintenance of the church grounds, should Mrs Eagerly prevail upon her husband to withdraw it. His financial situation had deteriorated since his marriage to Aoife. The small gratuities that Betsey used to bring home were missed too, as well as the dozen ways in which she was able to make a little go a long way. Her efficiency and homely touch around the house were missed. The truth was that Betsey herself was missed. Life for Frank was not the same without her.

Nearly two months had elapsed since Frank's clandestine marriage to Aoife. During their fevered courtship he had hardly known himself. Prior to meeting her he could not have conceived of nights lying on his mattress breathless and inflamed, stirred to frenzy by just the thought of her, much less of dishonouring himself by falsehoods and shiftiness and secret assignations in the woods. Up to this he had no experience of women, his introspection creating a sort of blindness to them, and his taciturn nature a barrier that none had cared to climb. But Aoife had turned her charm on him from the instant of their first meeting. He had not been able to believe that he was not just another target, a machine that would dispense sixpences to see the flash of her ankles and sometimes even her knees as she whirled and pranced in the market square. But then she had begun to sit beside him in the Plough, to gently tease and cajole him from his moroseness. She favoured no other man with such attentions, though many would have pulled her onto their laps were it not for the glowering of her young protector. She began to happen upon Frank wherever he was working, and sit while he cleared the weeds from ancient graves, or shovelled ordure from the pig pen, or tended the brood of pheasant chicks in their enclosure deep in the woods. She seemed to appear by magic, the flash of her bright dress or colourful scarves an exotic brushstroke on the backdrop of green.

For her sake, he had accepted the task of guiding the Irishmen across the moor to the lime kilns, where shadowy men with wagons piled high with contraband goods would distribute it amongst smaller carts to be hidden in barns and smuggled to small shopkeepers like Mr Golightly. The work was risky as well as illegal—a million miles from the staid, safe and law-abiding roads Frank had trodden all his life. But, for Aoife, he had done it.

And then her laughing eyes, the occasional brush of her hand against his arm, the rich allure of her lilting voice had paved the way to much more. Kisses—passionate, erotic and insistent—had led them to further pleasures. Aoife had not seemed to care about the location—the soft moss of the forest floor, a little clearing amongst the heather, the coach house behind Tall Chimneys, a lichen-crusted boulder she could brace against while she opened herself and guided first his hand and then his mouth. So long as Dónall was otherwise engaged she was careless as to risk. She would have given herself entirely had Frank not held back.

At last the imperative had conquered him, and they had concocted their scheme to marry. Frank hated the secrecy of it—especially the need to deceive Betsey—and the conducting of it outside the walls of a church. But the compulsion had been too strong, and he had yielded.

Now, some seven weeks later, the honeymoon was over and Frank was learning his error. Aoife was no housekeeper. He discovered that she had been her father's pet. There had been no question of her soiling her small, white hands with laundry or other drudgery; a housekeeper and a couple of maids had handled the domestic chores. She readily admitted that since being forced from her home she had contributed as little as possible to the day-to-day routines of the camp, telling him through laughter that she deliberately did any unavoidable work badly so that she would not be asked again. The gatehouse was in a terrible state, filthy and disordered. She had no facility with laundry; his shirts and sheets were a disgrace. She lost all track of time, and supper was only ever an idea in her head when the day ended; there would be no pie, no stew, not even the simplest salad to eat. She could not distinguish a weed from a plant, one day harrowing away all his wintergreen seedlings. The ripe tomatoes fell from the plants and rotted.

'Why did you not bottle them?' he asked, incredulous and appalled at the waste.

She only simpered, 'I do not know how.'

She was no good at facing up to realities. To her, their marriage was a game of make believe, of romantic sighings and starry-eyed *amour,* the chief object of which was to evade and outwit Dónall. Frank said she must climb down from her daydream and become the wife of a countryman, one who could cook and clean and make a little go a long way. Most of all, Dónall must be told of their marriage. But she only smiled and shrugged and said, 'Yes, of course. In time.'

To tell the truth, the only bright spot in the whole sorry affair was Frank's consciousness of a growing closeness with Dónall. Of course, the young man was not clever. He forgot things regularly. It took him a long time to understand even the simplest processes, and he needed explanations such as a child might require. Sometimes he did not know his own strength, he could be clumsy. And he had a temper that occasionally flared and frightened even Dónall himself. But he was essentially a kind soul, happy to help. Only Aoife caused him anxiety and pain. Frank could sympathise with that. He could easily envisage a time when he and Aoife and Dónall would form a family. Frank would pass on to Dónall all he knew of husbanding the land and the wild things. It was not Dónall's intellectual incapacity that created a barrier to Frank's vision. No. Increasingly, it was Aoife. She would not hear of Dónall's being told of their marriage. And she was wilful. She had resented Betsey's need of Frank during her illness, and even Frank's dedication to his sister. She had pouted and sulked that she was neglected. One Saturday she went and danced at the Plough, though he had expressly forbidden her to dance in public again.

Then Betsey recovered and the couple returned to their old routines—meeting furtively during the day, to slake their appetite for each other, then arguing and parting in anger. While Frank hated the clandestine nature of their courtship—believing their marriage would end the need for that—Aoife was titillated by the surreptitious, saucy nature of their liaison.

Frank began to suspect he had been used; that he was no more than a ticket to an easier life. It had taken Aoife no time at all to suggest that since Betsey disliked the idea of sharing the gatehouse with them, they ought to remove to the big house. She returned to the subject very frequently, her eyes bright.

223

One day she had him light the furnace at the big house so that she could bathe in the deep copper bath tub. She lay in her nakedness and looked up at him through the steam, a languid hand on her breasts and then her stomach and between her thighs. Frank swallowed hard and tried to drag his gaze away, but she said, 'If we lived here, you could look upon me like this whenever you liked. We could try every bed. The dining table. The piano. Should you not like that, Frank?'

Suddenly, he was revolted by her. 'And what of Dónall?'

'We will lock the gates,' she said, as though there were not a dozen places where Dónall could climb the wall.

'And be prisoners? I cannot live cooped up like that, Aoife—too afraid to go about my business, as though I am ashamed. I am *not* ashamed!'

But he was. He saw now that she was a hussy, decadent and debauched. 'The boy must be made to understand the way of things,' he shouted. 'You're my wife, now.' But his voice broke as he declared it, bitter with regret.

She only smiled and said, 'When Ruairi returns, we can tell Dónall,' then submerged herself in the water.

Frank left Aoife in the bath and went about the house trying to do the things that Betsey would have done had she been there. There had been a soot fall in one of the fireplaces. Dead flies littered every window ledge and a spider had woven a web from chandelier to curtain pole in the dining room. He removed it with a long-handled feather duster, and cursed himself that he had upset the delicate status quo that had maintained himself and Betsey in perfect amity for the past ten years. But no. He had to admit that Betsey had been less content than him, caught as inextricably in the trap of Tall Chimneys as the flies on the ledges. There *was* a kind of pointlessness in it, he supposed, and perhaps she had felt like the flies—buzzing and beating themselves against the glass, or like the spider who spent its energies on weaving another web only for that to be destroyed in its turn.

Aoife was enchanted by the place and had been from the beginning, but only in the way of pretending to be the mistress of it, to hold make-believe supper parties and lavish balls, to play act amongst the swathed furniture in the gloom of the shuttered rooms. If he was brutally honest, he could date the intensification of Aoife's attentions towards him from the morning she had followed himself and Ruairi and the broken cart to Tall Chimneys.

She had seen the house. And wanted it.

When Frank met with Arthur he did not unburden himself. The two brothers had always been different—Arthur full of ambition and eagerness to broaden his horizons, Frank content to remain where he was, without curiosity as to the wider world.

Frank avoided meeting Arthur at the gatehouse so as to conceal the unkempt state of things there. They met instead at the Plough. There were few patrons during daytime hours and they could talk in private while Ned Widderington counted the previous night's takings and the barmaid busied herself with glasses and tankards. The two Harlish men sat opposite each other at a long table, so similar in appearance and yet so unlike in every other way.

Arthur said, 'Our sister is established at Somersall Grange. Have you heard? Mrs Somersall has quite made her over. She looks like a fine lady! Very far from the tousle-haired girl we remember. But I do not think she will be there long.'

'You think she will come home?' A brief flash of optimism shone in Frank's eyes.

Arthur shook his head. 'I do not think so. I think she will travel to America with Stephen Milton. As his wife.'

'His wife?' Frank floundered. 'Who is Stephen Milton?'

'A friend of Herbert Somersall. He is an engineer, and I have contracted him to work for Mr Talbot. You have not met him?'

Frank scratched at something on the table. 'No. I suppose he was at Betsey's party, but I did not see him.'

'You did not go, you dog,' said Arthur, but without malice. 'You had other fish to fry. How is married life?'

Frank took a pull of his ale. 'I thought there was an understanding between Betsey and Mr Connolly. That's Aoife's brother. He has a farm in Ireland, and will return to it when the blight is finished. Aoife spoke, at one time, of us all going and making a life there.'

'But your life is here.' Arthur spoke gently.

'If Betsey had wished it,' Frank replied slowly, 'I would have gone with her.'

Arthur frowned. 'But if Aoife wants it …?'

Frank shook his head. 'I do not think she does, now. She seems to like it here after all.'

They sat in silence for a while. Then Arthur said, 'Forgive me. I do not know the man. But there is no doubt about Mr Connolly, is there? He disappeared in pursuit of the felon who stole the things, but he has been gone so long. There are rumours …'

'That he was in league with Fionn? Yes. I have heard them too. But you're right. You do not know Ruairi Connolly. I would vouch for him.'

That seemed to satisfy Arthur. He said, 'I went to the church, before coming here. You keep our parents' grave in good order. I am happy about that. Do you miss them much?'

Frank shrugged. 'I hear our father's voice in the wind and the sighing of the branches. He taught me all I know about husbanding the wild places. In essence, Mother disappeared long before she died. Sometimes she thought herself back at the workhouse, where the old Mrs Talbot found her, and sometimes she seemed in fear of some man.'

'Not Father?'

'No, some gentleman who had persecuted her. Betsey was the only one who could soothe her. It was a mercy when she died. She is free of those phantoms now. I suppose you will return to London soon?'

'Yes. There is to be a grand dinner at the Grange. Mrs Somersall has worked herself into a frenzy over it and it is all Betsey can do to shore her up. But once it is done, I think we will go home. I miss Petunia and the children. I cannot say how quickly Betsey will follow. Perhaps very quickly. She will stay with us until they are married, and then I will book their passage.'

Frank was seized by gloom. 'I ought to go and see her,' he said. 'I was not kind to her the last time I saw her.'

'It would be better to part in goodwill,' said Arthur, finishing his drink. 'Do you want another?'

Frank shook his head. 'No. I must go to the house. The sow we have now is so ill-natured, she threatens to break out of the sty every day. I must see she has not escaped. But she is a brute. If I am not careful she will trample me and eat me.'

'She will be bacon before Michaelmas. Then you can eat her!'

'That is what Betsey said.'

Chapter 88

The day of Mrs Somersall's grand dinner was still some two weeks away, but the invitations had been accepted and preparations went on at a buoyant, sprightly pace, for Beth had discovered that Mrs Somersall was better managed with steady encouragement and cheer. The mere suggestion that 'there was plenty of time' was sure to make the lady forget all the plans and contingencies and practicing that they had so far achieved, but any notion of urgency would result in panic and vapours.

It would not be overstating the case to say that Beth absolutely revelled in her new situation. Mrs Somersall was so kind and indulgent; Beth could not recall ever having felt so petted and pampered. New dresses, warm shawls, stout boots, a cloak and muff had been added to her wardrobe. She was encouraged to play the newly-tuned pianoforte. The library was at her disposal. Mrs Somersall ordered delicacies from the kitchen and pressed them upon Beth most urgently, declaring her in need of building up. On Sundays she was transported by coach and four to St Mary's Church in Whitby to sit in the Somersalls' exclusive pew. Afterwards, the ladies strolled around the harbour, Beth relishing her first closeup view of the sea. At times it seemed to her hardly right that she should receive a salary, for she felt more like a guest than an employee, and a highly favoured guest at that.

But that salary was vindicated by the fact that Mrs Somersall was—and knew herself to be—so utterly in need of guidance; a more fitting or appreciative recipient of Beth's fund of patience and expertise could not have been found anywhere. It was as though the investment of knowledge that Mrs Orphan had stored in Beth all those years ago was only now being called upon, and yielding itself doubled in value, like a fine wine that has been laid by. Though many years Beth's senior, Mrs Somersall was an innocent in many ways, with a childlike dependency on others; it pleased and exonerated Beth to be needed, to feel useful.

For this period of time—the last two weeks in September—Mr Somersall and Herbert were away from home. Arthur dined and slept at the Grange when he was not away on Mr Talbot's business at shipyards in Sunderland. Stephen Milton remained as a guest, though kicking his heels at the enforced inactivity attendant on the collier's neither accepting nor refusing his tendered resignation. Stephen would have liked to accompany Arthur, no doubt, but a certain reticence held him back. It did not feel right to go about the business of one man whilst being paid by another. And so it was that Stephen and Beth were thrown together often. At the times when Mrs Somersall was closeted with the housekeeper or cook, or taking her afternoon rest, Beth would find Stephen on hand to take a walk or ready to peruse books in the library or to leaf through sheet music in the music room. They had—at last—their promised conversations, their talk ranging quite as widely as Stephen had hoped.

One day—a bitter, cold day when the wind was easterly, bringing sharp showers and tearing the few remaining leaves from the trees—Mrs Somersall refused her usual turn upon the terrace and went to rest in her room. Beth battled the elements for half an hour or so before admitting defeat and going inside. A maid took her cloak and informed her that Mr Milton was in the drawing room should she care to join him. The drawing room was on the west side of the house, sheltered from the blustering winds and occasional flurry of rainfall. There was a fire, and Beth went towards it with outstretched hands.

'You did not take your muff?' asked Stephen, getting up and bringing a large upholstered footstool closer to the fire.

'I did not want it to get wet,' Beth admitted, sinking onto the stool. 'It would spoil the fur. I will be warm soon enough.' She rubbed her hands together, chafing blood back into them, and for a while Stephen remained on the hearthrug gazing down at her. Her complexion was ruddy and her eyes bright with the cold and exercise. The stuff of her dress glowed and refracted in the firelight, and a rustle as she moved suggested that a full panoply of petticoats and other womanly trimmings beneath had replaced the thin undergarments he had discerned on the night he carried her to safety. Her hair was not, as formerly, loosely caught up in an arrangement of her own hasty devising, but now brushed to a bright lustre and artfully wrought into a fashionable style. He wasn't sure he preferred it, but there was no denying that in terms of her dress and general air she looked every inch the lady she had denied being on their first meeting. She was, now, entirely Beth; the homespun Betsey was gone.

Beth was conscious of his scrutiny but not discomfited by it. She was accustomed to his ways. He had an intense manner. He thought about and felt things deeply. He was cerebral and sometimes almost appeared to be brooding or moody. He had seemed so, she recalled, on the occasion of their first meeting.

She continued to warm her hands, staring into the fire.

Suddenly he said, 'Do you recall our first conversation?'

'Yes,' she said with a smile. 'Indeed, I was just thinking of it—or of its circumstances anyway. We discussed the curious ambivalence of our status in the world.'

'How things have changed—for one of us, at any rate.'

She looked up at him. He stood with his elbow on the mantel and the fingers of the hand of that arm stroked his lips contemplatively. His lips were full and rather sensuous—she had not noticed that before. His dark hair was tumbled across his brow. His eyes were very dark and almost unreadable but fixed themselves on hers.

She said, 'For us both, surely? But for you, the road to success and recognition is just beginning. Mine will begin and end here, I suppose.'

'And why do you say that?' He came and seated himself on the footstool beside her, and she was brought powerfully to mind of the evening she and Ruairi Connolly had shared a pallet before a fire.

'Because of my brother Arthur,' she said. 'He began his career with Mr Talbot and has not looked back. Now he owns a house in a fashionable quarter of London and tells me he is looking out for a place in the country also. His salary is considerable and Mr Talbot is not at all averse to him earning additional income by consultancy on his own account. Why should you not follow in his footsteps? I would say your potential is unlimited.'

'And why should not yours be also?'

She gave him a sad smile. 'I am a woman,' she said. 'We cannot expect as much as men. But do not think I am discontented. My situation here is very satisfactory to me. I hope Mr Somersall allows me to remain.'

As she was speaking, Stephen reached forward and took her hands—which she had been holding out to the flames—in his. His hands were large and easily encompassed hers. He looked down at their hands in a sort of astonishment as though his had acted of their own volition, but he did not remove them; and after at first stiffening, she relaxed her hands in his.

In a low intimate voice he said, 'I owe all my good fortune to you. Had you not written to your brother—'

'I promised that I would.'

'I know. But you did it in the midst of your own travail and trouble. I cannot get over that.' He spoke quietly but his voice vibrated with passion. 'That at such a moment, you thought of me.'

'And did not you think of me, those hours when you searched the moor for me? You didn't know *then* that I had written to my brother—' Beth struggled for a lightness of tone that would counterbalance the intensity of his, would suggest that her action in writing to her brother was a gesture anyone would have done and much less than he had performed on the moor.

'I *did* think of you,' he said earnestly, crushing her attempt at levity. 'And afterwards too, when I lay in my fever. Did you dream of … of anything?'

Beth recalled fleeting images from her malaise, but could not say that Stephen had featured amongst them. She twitched her fingers experimentally, thinking that she ought to withdraw from the cradle of his hold. 'I do not remember,' she said.

'Do you feel safe?' he asked.

'Safe?'

'Yes. With your hands in mine like this. You moved just a moment ago, and I thought that you wished me to relinquish you. *Do* you? I would not have you feel trapped or coerced. I wish you to be free but to feel … safe to remain … if you wish.' He opened his hands then, leaving them palm upwards in a prayer-like attitude that was not at all needful but was rather a provision, much more of an offer than a request, and yet retaining something that was humble—almost holy. Beth could withdraw her hands, and she looked up at his face, having the sense—as she so often did with Stephen—that so much more had been said than just the simple words. She found his gaze upon her, his eyes reflecting the firelight, ablaze with meaning.

She left her hands quiescent in his, and presently he folded his fingers around them again.

The afternoon was waning. Soon the maid would bring candles, but for now the fire provided the only illumination in the room. Beth and Stephen sat side by side, very close but not touching except for their hands, which remained as before, his palms creating a cup or nest where hers could rest.

When it was time to dress for dinner Beth spent a longer time than usual beside the little fire in her room, trying to supplant the thoughts and images of Ruairi that so often came to her unbidden, with thoughts and images of Stephen Milton. There were aspects of Ruairi's character that she still did not entirely trust. Where was he, for instance? And why had he not written so much as a line? Was it even remotely possible that the gossip about him was true, and that he had in fact been in league with Fionn? And what about that night after the open house? What had been his intention? She did not blame him for their foolish, utterly wanton embrace, which could have led to so much more—indeed, to her entire ruination. She had instigated it as much as he. But now she thought about it, she did not believe that Stephen Milton would have taken advantage of her lapse of decorum notwithstanding his passion, which she thought was probably even more ardent than Ruairi's.

Stephen was as handsome as Ruairi, though he lacked the Irishman's easy charm. Both men offered her escape from her anomalous situation at Tall Chimneys. Or did they? She went over in her mind her various conversations with Ruairi. Had he ever once absolutely spoken of a possible future together? She did not think so. Whereas she knew with certainty that marriage was Stephen Milton's object. A future with Ruairi would be a chancy, unreliable thing. It could be years before a return to Ireland was possible, and in the meantime she would have to live as he did and suffer as he did. She had only Ruairi's word for it that the property in Ireland existed at all! Stephen had a career, prospects. He could offer security. His likely future prosperity did not sway her, but the probability of a more settled and regular existence did.

She had connection with Stephen. That was undeniable. It was not—yet—of that same breathless and immodest nature that Ruairi conjured up in her. With him she was conscious of sparking electricity and raw kinship and mindless, instinctive correlation. With Stephen it was different but potentially deeper, more cerebral—a meeting of minds and understanding.

Later, after they had dined—and following an abortive attempt by Stephen and Beth to teach Mrs Somersall the game of ombre—it was time to retire. Mrs Somersall went up first and Stephen lingered, ready to hand Beth her chamber stick. As he held it out to her they exchanged a look, and Stephen leaned forward and pressed a kiss onto her brow. She started back a little, but then tilted her chin so that he might kiss her lips, but he only slipped his arm around her waist and pulled her to him.

231

He was taller by a head than Ruairi Connolly, but his body had not that cushion of muscle and soft flesh that had comforted Beth both in the actuality and the memory. She laid her head on Stephen's chest and felt the bone of his breast beneath her cheek. His heart beat fast, and she could hear the quickness of his breathing. She wondered why he had not kissed her, but she was not altogether sorry. Regardless of her earlier weighing of one man against the other, the very fact that she still compared Stephen to Ruairi told her that her heart was not free, that whatever existed between herself and the Irishman was unfinished. She was glad that Stephen, earlier, had spoken in metaphors. His offer had been plain enough, but she had neither accepted nor refused it, unless he considered that the mere presence of her hands in his constituted acquiescence.

She felt his chest inflate as he drew breath to speak—several times— but it seemed the words would not come.

At last she said, 'Go on. I am listening.'

He swallowed. 'I know,' he said hesitantly, 'that you do not think of me as I think of you. These last few weeks, as we have become better acquainted, to you it has only been part and parcel of your gradual induction into the Grange and your new duties. But for *me*—'

'It has been more than that,' she objected.

'Perhaps,' he allowed. 'But I want you to know that for me, it has been everything.'

She stepped out of his embrace and looked up into his face. 'Mr Milton … Stephen.'

'It is quite alright,' he said, handing her the candle. 'You are not sure—yet.'

'Are *you* sure?'

He nodded and gave her a sad smile. 'I have been sure since the night of the Eagerlys' dinner.'

'The first time we met!'

'Indeed. But I understand that you have had other matters to occupy your mind, and perhaps … your heart.'

She felt a little blush creep up her neck. How well he knew her! 'I have things to resolve,' she admitted. 'I have yet to hear from Mrs Stockbridge. She may wish to prosecute, or at least demand payment in compensation. Then there is my brother Frank …' she trailed off, unable to speak the heart of that issue.

'I understand all of that, and more,' he said. 'Much depends on the return of the Irishman with the miscreant who stole the treasures.'

How honest and clear-sighted he was! He did not scruple to state the case.

The candle in her hand trembled and he reached to steady it, lest it splash hot wax on her skin. The light between them illuminated his features so as to emphasise their beauty—his finely sculpted cheekbones and cerebral brow, the soft sensualness of his lips, the dark passion of his eyes.

She swallowed and passed her tongue over her lips, wishing now that he *had* kissed her.

She stood before him for another moment, meeting his gaze and reading there, as before, all the volumes his mouth could not speak. She wished that, in their turn, her eyes could make reply.

At last she said, 'Good night, Stephen,' and left the room.

Chapter 89

The squally weather persisted for the next ten days, at the end of which Mr Somersall returned to the Grange. He arrived in a veritable Armageddon, just as wind-tossed twilight had come and the moor—drained of all colour—looked its bleakest and most inhospitable. Gusts tore round the house like Valkyries, and sleet fell against its façade, darkening the raw stone, making it look as though it bled. Hooves thundered like the horses of the apocalypse as two carriages—Mr Somersall's own and Mr Talbot's—clattered along the driveway. There was a cacophony of hallooing and barked instructions from grooms and attendants and a whirlwind of activity as the house disgorged footmen for the lighting of lamps, the unloading and carrying of luggage and the proffering of refreshment.

Mr Somersall descended from his carriage wearing a glowering expression, ready to criticise everything and everyone within the orbit of his scowling gaze. He shrugged his coat more firmly around him before knocking aside two footmen armed with umbrellas who had come out to usher him indoors, and made a dash for the porch. Herbert climbed out after him, stretching expansively before standing to one side to hand Mr Talbot from the carriage.

From the other carriage tumbled sundry valets and Mr Talbot's secretary.

Mrs Somersall stood whitely in the hallway, ready to greet her husband and her guests, with Beth and Stephen standing staunchly either side of her.

'Oh, Peregrine,' said Mrs Somersall shrilly, 'we did not know what time to expect you. I have had the footmen standing by this hour with hot water for baths.'

'It's brandy-and-soda we need, and quickly too,' said her husband, removing his coat and throwing it in the general direction of a servant. 'I hope there is a good fire, for we are mithered[xxx] with cold. Not that I care for such things. I was accustomed to it at a young age. But Herbert has done nothing but complain since we set out, and I suppose that Talbot, being from the south, where everyone knows men are nesh[xxxi], will be in need of warming. Where *is* Talbot? Oh! There he is. Talbot, here's my wife. Not much to look at, I'll grant you, but she's bought and paid for. This man is Milton, the engineer you plan to steal from me. This lady,' he glared witheringly at Beth, 'I do not know. Now let us get to a fire. This way. This way. Why are the lamps not lit? Bring more light at once!'

Mr Talbot ignored his host so as to say a few words of greeting and thanks to his hostess, saluting her with a charm and courtesy that had been entirely absent from her husband's address, and speaking a word or two as to the accommodation of his secretary. Then he moved away, but not before a glance of half-recognition for Beth.

Herbert kissed his mother's cheek, shook hands with Stephen and expressed both surprise and pleasure at seeing Miss Harlish.

'I am so very happy to see you here, Miss Harlish. I believe you have been very ill. I cannot say how pleased I am to see you recovered, and so transformed! I suppose you have had no news of ... of Miss Eagerly?'

Beth shook her head. 'I am sorry,' she said. 'I have not heard from or seen anyone from the vicarage since—' But here she stopped abruptly for Mr Talbot was still in the hall, and although he had taken his secretary to one side and spoken a word or two to his valet, he could not fail to overhear and pick up on any mention of Tall Chimneys.

'You must not fear Mr Talbot,' said Herbert. 'He knows all about it, and he does not blame you at all. He is eager for you to return to your duties.'

'Oh, but I ...' Beth faltered, hardly daring to look across the vast hallway at the man who had paid for every mouthful of food she had ever consumed, every article of clothing she had worn and the very roof beneath which she had been born and brought up.

'Arthur told you, you were not to worry,' said Stephen in a low voice, 'did he not?'

'Yes,' Beth hissed, 'but now I have to face him.'

Herbert ushered Mr Talbot across the room. 'I am sure you recognise Miss Beth Harlish,' he said.

'Ah yes,' said Mr Talbot, smiling kindly and taking Beth's hand. 'I thought I did. Your resemblance to your brother is quite striking.'

'Mr Talbot, sir,' began Beth. She lifted her chin, ready to look the man in the eye and to swallow her whole allocation of humble pie, to be clapped in irons or mortgaged for a lifetime until the treasures were paid for.

His eye was all benign sympathy. 'My cousin, Mrs Stockbridge, does not even know what has occurred,' he said, leaning forward in a conspiratorial way and speaking into Beth's ear. 'Her son sent your letter to me, rather than troubling his mother with it. Indeed, I think he felt worse than *you* did, for did he not take it upon himself to grant permission for the open house? But all will be well. Mrs Stockbridge, should she ever return to Tall Chimneys, will find the Delft and the plate just as it was. I have ordered replacements.'

'Oh but sir,' protested Beth. 'They were so valuable, and had been in the house so long!'

He patted her hand. 'Who is to know they are not the very same? I shall not tell if you do not. Miss Harlish, you cannot know the number or extent of scrapes I got into when I was a boy. I am sure my parents despaired. Did you know I once got drunk and tried to enlist into the militia? I was but thirteen years of age! But I discovered that most predicaments can be escaped with the laying out of money—and some helpful amnesia. Now,' he slipped her hand into the crook of his arm. 'I hope you will escort me to some room where there is a fire and some hot tea.'

Mr George Talbot was by this time a man of four and fifty. His hair was plentiful and grew in the unruly way it ever had, but was now entirely grey. The boyish features that had distinguished him long into adulthood had now been replaced with the qualities of a sage. His eyes were wise beneath beetling brows, but much creased about; one hoped it was from an excess of laughter but there was also that about them that suggested sorrow. His cheeks had a modicum of jowl and his figure was portly. In his manner he was as cheery and affable as ever. He was a good father to his three remaining children, a fair employer, a wealthy man and a philanthropist. He had lately been widowed, but had long been separated from his wife.

But George Talbot was nobody's fool. He understood the character of his host very well and was not for a moment cowed by it. He had ascertained, by private conference with Herbert, the lie of the land concerning Miss Eagerly; the young people were willing—more than willing—but the older ones presented obstacles to be overcome. Money, first and foremost, was Mr Somersall's object. By dint of the girl's connection with the Talbot fortune—however tangential—he expected a hefty settlement before he would sanction the alliance. Herbert was bitterly alive to the irony of this, since he had only courted the girl at his father's behest. But having gone in for the thing on his father's account, he now found himself acting on his own. Words had been spoken, promises exchanged ... in short, he would be very reluctant to give the thing up. He would like to think that even without Mr Talbot's input he—Herbert—could afford to marry Rose, but doubted he would be permitted to do so. His income, his inheritance, his very place in the world were utterly at his father's mercy, and Mr Talbot must have perceived by now that Herbert's father was not ... merciful.

Thus stood the thing on the Somersalls' side. Mr Talbot had written to his old friend the vicar, and from him received an account of the affair from the other point of view. The vicar had intimated—without positively stating—the divergence of opinion that had opened up between himself and his wife. As far as he was concerned, Rose wished to marry Herbert and he was not minded to refuse what his darling girl so earnestly wanted. Mrs Eagerly, on the other hand, had strongly urged a London season, but that had not moved Rose's fixed determination to become Mrs Somersall. Her single reservation—and indeed the one thing shared by all the parties at the vicarage—was a great trepidation in respect of Herbert's father. They *all* feared Mr Somersall's manner would be too strong for the girl, but could not conceive of a living arrangement for the newly married couple that would remove them from Mr Somersall's pernicious orbit. Like Herbert, they doubted Mr Somersall would continue to support a son who separated himself from the paternal yoke. And then, how would the pair live?

Mr Eagerly was most touchingly transparent on the state of his own finances and of Rose's expectations, which amounted only to a small bequest from her late mother that could be monetised almost immediately, and such as remained of the funds that George Talbot had been so good as to send on the death of his father, Mr Robert Talbot.[xxxii] But these could not be released until the vicar's own demise.

George Talbot had mulled over the situation at length, and determined to see young Rose with his own eyes before suggesting any compromise. This explained his presence at Somersall Grange. The reader can be sure that no other consideration would have induced him to be the guest of such a man as Mr Somersall, who he perceived to be a bully and an oaf of the first order. For his own reasons George Talbot particularly detested a man who could use his only son for such base and mercantile ends, and he had an extraordinary sympathy with Herbert—he knew what a broken heart could do to a man.

The following day George Talbot invited Herbert to accompany him on a visit to the vicarage at Moorside. At first Mr Somersall was determined not to be excluded, but Mr Talbot reminded him of the household accounts that had no doubt been neglected in the weeks of his absence, of business letters that could be answered by no one but the chief, of the pressing need to inspect the building works and of the interview that must be had with Stephen Milton, who must be either released immediately or kept to his contract until the beginning of November. 'You keep us all in suspense, Somersall, until you decide the question, for I will have Milton on my staff either immediately or a month hence, but only you can decide which. We are absolutely at your mercy in that matter. And I am sure you wish personally to commend his great bravery in the saving of lives. Doubtless you have *written* most fulsomely …' Of course, Mr Somersall had written not a line of thanks—and Mr Talbot was fully aware of it—but it pleased him to manipulate the man's ego by clever flattery and covert persuasion. '… but I am sure you agree with me that the spoken word is always preferable.'

Mr Somersall retired to his study feeling unaccountably swindled but ready to tackle his accounts and correspondence.

Once the host had quitted the breakfast room Mr Talbot suggested that Mrs Somersall should be of the party that would call upon the Eagerlys. At first she refused. She would not presume … feared she would not be welcome … was not dressed to make morning calls … would be sure to be wanted by Mr Somersall … At last she admitted that she was too ashamed to face the Eagerlys. Her husband had been so rude on the occasion of their last encounter, and Mrs Eagerly had seemed to her such a very grand lady who would be sure to find out in two minutes that she— Mildred Somersall—was no more than a parlour maid and the daughter of a bricklayer. If anyone could convince the Eagerlys that the Somersalls were not a suitable alliance for their girl, she was sure it was her, and then her darling Herbert would be disappointed, and never speak to her again. Slowly, over more coffee and while the servants waited to clear the breakfast dishes, with Herbert sitting affectionately on one side and Beth on the other, all her objections were overcome. Beth soon fetched her cloak and bonnet; Mr Talbot's carriage was brought round and the lady handed into it.

Mr Talbot lingered long enough on the drive to say, 'Do not think you will not also have to face your demons, Miss Harlish. Tomorrow you and I will take a ride to Tall Chimneys, and we will see your other brother and his wife. The relation between a brother and sister is very special. I could tell you much about my sister, were I not to break a promise in doing so. Suffice it to say that she has been the lodestar of my life. I would not lose faith with her for any price, and I am sure your brother feels as I do. But for today you are reprieved.'

Thus saying, he leapt into the carriage and was carried away with Mrs Somersall and Herbert.

Chapter 40

Mrs Somersall returned to Somersall Grange in high spirits; she could not wait to tell Beth of the great kindness and condescension with which she had been greeted. She described the comfortable little parlour where she had been entertained by the ladies, of the great amusement they had enjoyed over Rose's woeful needlework and knitting—for Mrs Somersall was similarly inept and had been able to commiserate with genuine sympathy. Then Rose had been summoned to the vicar's study for an interview with Mr Talbot.

Mrs Somersall recounted that she had taken the opportunity to apologise to Mrs Eagerly for her own husband's previous outrageous behaviour. 'I told Mrs Eagerly in all frankness that Peregrine is constitutionally unsuited to the company of ladies, that I often despaired of him myself and could make no excuse for him.'

'Well that was very blunt of you, ma'am,' said Beth. They were seated in Mrs Somersall's private sitting room and could converse quite unreservedly.

'I hesitated, as you may imagine, but I thought it right that we should establish some common ground if we are to be related, and in terms of a mutual aversion to my husband, neither of us had far to travel.'

'But what is to be done about him, ma'am? They say a leopard does not change his spots.'

'And no more will he. I fear he will crush poor Rose beneath his heel and reduce her as he reduced me. And yet I have survived it, and I had not a Herbert to shore me up. I trust to Mr Talbot to find some way through. What a very nice gentleman he is. Did you tell me he is a widower?'

'I did, but he has … a companion I believe. It is widely known, but not spoken of.'

Their discussion was interrupted by the sudden arrival of Mr Somersall, who burst through the doors of his wife's boudoir in a towering rage. Reminded by George Talbot, Mr Somersall had taken it upon himself to inspect the progress in the unfinished east wing of the building where he was appalled to discover that things were hardly advanced. The leak in the ceiling particularly distressed him, and he even mounted the scaffolding to see for himself where slipshod workmanship and substandard materials had caused the breach. The ceiling roses were ruined. It seemed to him that the entirety of the plastering would have to be done over. And as for the floor, where water had been allowed to pool—the parquet was beyond saving. A hapless carpenter—who had nothing at all to do with the roof structure—had received the lion's share of Mr Somersall's outrage, but he barged into the ladies' cosy *tête à tête* at this moment to visit the residue of it upon his wife, absolutely quelling any pleasure she might have had from her morning visit.

With regret, Beth murmured her excuses and quit the scene.

Mr Talbot was less sanguine after the morning visit, having ascertained the fulness of the young couple's feelings and also the relatively empty nature of their financial expectations. Certainly he would have to do something, though Mr Somersall's dereliction of fatherly duty and affection rankled.

Then, there was also the sadly rundown air of the village. The vicar had confided that tithes could hardly support two clergymen though they did live in the same house. Some repairs required on the church tower could not be afforded. He understood the falling roll at the school meant the schoolmaster's salary was untenable. Many properties were empty and falling to ruin. It would fall to him—George Talbot, as the landowner—to either restore or demolish those properties; but if he restored them, where would he find new tenants? It may well be that the farms would fail if sufficient labour could not be found, and although the rents constituted a very small proportion of Talbot income, land that was not worked would only revert to heath and moor, wasting the efforts of generations of previous tenants.

All in all Mr Talbot had much to occupy his mind, and he sat in the drawing room after the others had gone up to dress, brooding.

That evening, Arthur returned to Somersall Grange from the shipyards of Sunderland and the party dined quietly—in deference to the great dinner that was to take place on the ensuing day—and also as a result of Mr Somersall's determination to dominate. He declaimed at length upon the neglectful attitude of the builders, and Mrs Somersall's dereliction of duty in 'keeping on their backs' was thoroughly expounded upon through soup, fish and fowl until the ladies rose from the table, very relieved to get away.

Mr Somersall was at pains to display the richness and variety of his wine cellar to Mr Talbot, although Mr Talbot was not a heavy drinker and would not have described himself as a connoisseur. Mr Somersall, on the contrary, did both and amply sampled the champagne, Madeira and claret that had been brought forth for Mr Talbot's enjoyment.

'And what do you think of my little place, Talbot, now you have been here twenty-four hours?' Mr Somersall asked complacently after the ladies had departed. He motioned to the butler to circulate once more with the decanter, and lit a cigar. Without giving Mr Talbot the opportunity to reply he went on, 'I can tell you to the nearest shilling what it cost me, if you care to know. The land was nothing, though buying it from the crown was a skirmish. The house set me back the thick end of seven thousand. As to the contents—'

'Very fine, I am sure,' said Mr Talbot. 'But tell me, what you have decided about Mr Milton? Am I to have my engineer immediately? I think it only fair, for it seems your wife has appropriated my housekeeper.'

'Has she?'

'Yes, the young lady who is now her companion used to manage affairs for me at Tall Chimneys.'

'Did she?' Mr Somersall drank his wine. 'I wondered who she was. But I think you will be able to have her back. I was not consulted as to her appointment and I am not minded to retain her. I do recall her now from the evening we were ... I will not say 'received' at Tall Chimneys, for we were hardly accorded that honour. She did not make a favourable impression.'

'The lady is my sister, sir,' said Arthur, 'so I will thank you not to make uncomplimentary allusions.'

'I do not care who she is,' said Somersall, fixing a somewhat unfocussed eye on Arthur.

'I think she is a very nice person,' said Herbert.

'As do I. I hold her in the highest esteem,' added Stephen, glaring down the table at his host.

'I will judge for myself,' shouted Mr Somersall. 'I have not got to this position in my life without learning to rely on my own judgement, both in respect to gentlemen and ladies. I consider myself a very shrewd judge. I think there can hardly be a better judge. Indeed, I defy anyone to name a man who has met a wider range of personages in every sphere of society, from the highest to the very lowest. I have been in company with dukes and dockworkers and I make no bones that there have been some of the latter vastly superior to the former—'

'No doubt,' said Mr Talbot, taking advantage in Mr Somersall pausing for breath. 'But as to Mr Milton? Fair exchange is no robbery you know. Am I to have him immediately?'

'No sir, you are not,' snapped Mr Somersall, who disliked being interrupted, even by a man of such consequence as George Talbot, and especially when in mid soliloquy. Also, he did not forget that Stephen had countermanded his orders in relation to the evacuation of the lower level. 'He is to serve his time. He contracted to be employed until November and I shall hold him to it, though I am sure he would rather shake the dust of Ellingbeck from his boots. But that is not the way I do business, sir. When I say a thing, I mean it, and those who do not heed it must pay the consequences. I shall teach him to disobey *me*.'

'Very well,' said Mr Talbot, not at all put out. 'And then, when he works for me, I shall encourage him to challenge me at every turn.' He rose from the table and went to where Stephen sat, holding out his hand for a hearty shake. 'You will forgive me, Mr Milton, if I remind our host that there is no point in keeping a dog and barking yourself. I am no engineer, sir. That is why I rely on Arthur as I do. If he recommends a man to me, I take his recommendation without question. When you join us in November you shall find accommodations in readiness and your first salary payment already in your account. How will that suit you?'

Stephen stood and reciprocated the handshake. 'Very well, sir, I thank you.'

Mr Talbot returned to his seat. 'Upon my word, Somersall, you are very cavalier about the lives of your employees. Did not Mr Milton's action save fifty lives?'

'Mining is a risky business,' said Mr Somersall.

'Evidently so, at *your* mines,' Mr Talbot observed.

'At every mine, sir,' said Mr Somersall, seriously riled. 'The men are well paid to take the risk. They know what they sign up for.'

'Accidents, of course, happen frequently, and that is to be lamented. But when an accident can be prevented, it should be, in my opinion.'

'There was no real danger,' said Somersall, drawing violently on his cigar. 'The men were got out, and the next day the rain stopped.'

'It continued to rain for a week,' said Arthur, 'during which time the pump failed, as Milton predicted. It is a mercy that there were no men on the lower level. If you will excuse me, sir, I think I will join the ladies. I do not wish to waste precious moments with my sister. I do not know how soon I may see her again.'

Arthur left the room and the other two young men took the opportunity to follow him.

Somersall continued to smoke his cigar, eyeing Mr Talbot narrowly through the smoke. 'That fellow speaks his mind very freely. I should not allow it. A man must be master, sir. He must have authority. I think you seriously undermine your own clout when you admit that you do not know a thing. They must believe you know everything. Your word must be law.'

'But what if we do not know everything?' asked Mr Talbot, refusing the decanter which had been proffered to him. 'How will our affairs flourish if we make wrong decisions based on ignorance or pride?'

'Our affairs will certainly not flourish if it be known that we are to be undermined and gainsaid at every turn. We will be taken advantage of. Our own employees will prey on us until we are bled dry.'

'Our ideas are very different. I foster confidence and loyalty amongst those who work for me. They trust me and I return the compliment. They would rather die than let me down. I would trust any one of them with my entire fortune.'

'Would you? I would not trust a single man jack who works for me with a penny of mine.'

'And what about your son?'

The question wrong-footed Mr Somersall. He narrowed a suspicious eye. 'What of him?'

'Do you trust him? Is he to be your partner in business? How do you see him carving out his own niche within your enterprise? A man needs to feel that he makes a contribution and is rewarded accordingly. Anything else is only charity. An allowance that is grudgingly given must be difficult to swallow. My father took me to India and inducted me into every aspect of his business there. However, in the end, it was the future that excited my interest. When I returned I put all the existing business in the hands of trusted stewards and set myself the task of investigating and investing in emerging technologies. Will you give Herbert the same opportunity?'

'It would be wasted. He is fit for no employment, I assure you—
certainly not in mining, nor can I find he has an aptitude in any of my
other commerce.' Mr Somersall beckoned to the butler and had his glass
refilled. 'You will not drink with me, Talbot? I defy you to find better wine
anywhere.'

Mr Talbot waved the decanter away again. 'I thank you. I have drunk
sufficient. What if Herbert pursues his own ambitions? Rome was not
built in a day. Would you support him as he establishes himself elsewhere?
He is an only son. I presume he will inherit at last?'

Mr Somersall tossed back his wine. 'If he pursues his own ambitions
he will need no income from me, nor would I offer one. Pah! But he has
no ambition! No backbone. I despair of the boy. He is not like me. He
has been brought up too soft, too nicely. His mother has spoiled him.'

'Will you cut him off then?'

Somersall slammed his glass onto the cloth. 'Perhaps I will cut him
off, as you call it, if he marries the vicar's girl without my sanction. It
would do him good to struggle, to go without.'

Mr Talbot shuddered at this but suppressed his disgust to ask, 'What
does he want to do? There are many ways a man can earn a living and
make his mark.'

'Want? I have no notion!' Mr Somersall was becoming florid. He
wrenched at his neck tie. 'What he wants is not important. And as to
making a mark, I doubt he could make so much as a scratch on the surface
of anything he undertook. If you were to ask him, he would probably say
that he wants to be a gentleman—that is, an idle, good-for-nothing
wastrel. It is what he has been educated for. *That* he might succeed at, I
suppose. Whether he does, well, that depends upon you.'

'How so?'

'Come, Talbot. Let us talk turkey. I have something you want, and
you have something I want. Do not think I don't know of the visit you
made this morning to the vicar, or of the confidential chats you have had
with Herbert. His marriage to that chit depends upon what you will do
for her.'

'And what if I do nothing?'

Mr Somersall shrugged. 'Then he will marry some other young
woman who can bring credit and advantage to me. The Riding girls, who
are to come tomorrow, either one would have him. It is well known the
estate is all but bankrupt. I could remedy that in five minutes. But a
connection with the nobility would more than repay the outlay.'

Mr Talbot sighed. 'My father thought much the same,' he said. 'He
returned from India a wealthy man but was utterly debarred from good

245

society. He married a lady of rank, and was miserable. Is that what you want for your son?'

Mr Somersall gave his guest a narrow, lascivious look. 'A man may take his pleasure elsewhere than in the marital bed. You do not need me to tell you that, Talbot.'

'Touché. But it is not a course I would recommend. I know what a happy marriage is, and I would far rather have had that than the alternative, whatever ends I went to in order to make it palatable to me. You are not saying you really do not care if your son is happy?'

'Happiness does not matter. Success is what matters. Wealth, recognition, power. An inexhaustible supply of hot dinners and warm clothing, a roof that does not leak—though *that,* it seems, I have yet to achieve. When you have suffered deprivation, Talbot, then come back and tell me that happiness matters more than anything else.'

Mr Talbot rose from the table. 'I have been cold and hungry in my time,' he said quietly. 'But the greatest hardship I have had to endure is the loss of a son. There is no price I would not pay to have him back. You should think about that, Somersall. Now I will go and find my secretary. There are letters I wish him to write. Good night.'

Mr Somersall sat on, keeping the servants in attendance though they had other duties and the following day was to be a busy one. The candles burned down and the decanter was empty but still he sat, brooding and smoking cigar after cigar.

Chapter 41

The day of Mrs Somersall's great dinner arrived, and from the first that lady was so agitated she could barely eat her breakfast.

Beth was up and dressed early, and the two toured the rooms that were to be brought into use for the occasion. The large salon, where the guests would be greeted and served with drinks, was resplendent with richly swagged curtains, gilded cornices, marble fireplaces and chandeliers that shone so brightly they hurt the eye. The dining room was already in preparation, glittering with highly polished silver and crystal glassware. Seats had been arranged in the music room, ready for the guests' enjoyment of the maestro's performance.

Upstairs, a chamber had been put aside where ladies might retire, with provision for the reparation of their dresses should it be required.

Everywhere maids scurried and footmen were busy, the entire house a maelstrom of work and preparation. But Beth's attempts to encourage and comfort her distraught friend were in vain. She smoothed over every supposed difficulty and made light of any perceived problem, but nothing seemed to assuage Mrs Somersall's distress. She worried at the strings of her reticule and even now her face showed signs of copious tears spilled the night before.

At last Mrs Somersall burst out, 'Peregrine tells me I have greatly erred. He is very angry about the lack of progress in the east wing. I do not know why he requires the house to be so big. What use will we have for those rooms? I do not know what half of them are for. I am sure I will never step into them. He says I ought to have been harrying the builders every day. But what do I know of building? I do not know a brick from a barrow. My father was a bricklayer, but I never touched a brick in my life! But oh! My dear! He came to me last night and spoke of it for hour after hour. I have not slept a wink. And he says that all the guests should have been invited to stay—as indeed they *were!* It is not my fault that they declined. Peregrine takes it very ill—an insult, he says. He made me write notes this morning—positively stood over me at my writing slope and dictated what I should put down, to … well to *insist* that they stay the night. What will people think, to receive such a thing at such a late hour? I doubt they can change their arrangements, even if they wanted to. And why would they? I know I would not, if I received such a note as I have been forced to send. But I do not know whether to have the rooms made up just in case. The maids already have so much to do.' Mrs Somersall collapsed, sobbing, onto a small sofa that was in the room, and Beth allowed her a few moments to expiate her woe before beginning the process of picking her patroness back up from where her husband had so cruelly crushed her. She felt very angry with Mr Somersall, but managed to keep this from her voice.

'The Eagerly party will almost certainly not remain,' she said. 'Tomorrow is Sunday, and Mr Eagerly will have his sermon to preach.'

'Unless the curate does it for him.'

'I think that unlikely. The truth is, ma'am, the Eagerlys will not wish to be in company with me for longer than necessary. I am a pariah with them now.'

'Oh, my dear,' said Mrs Somersall, clutching Beth to her bony bosom for a few moments, 'do not say so when I am just teaching myself to like them. Oh! And I have just recalled that you are to go out today. What am I to do without you? Elsie has a dozen questions and Mary—'

'I will speak to them before I leave, and I shall not be away more than an hour.'

At about eleven o'clock Mr Talbot's carriage was brought round and Beth was handed into it. Her brother Arthur took his seat next to her, and then Mr Talbot climbed in and banged the top of his cane on the roof.

'Does Frank know we are coming? Does he even know that you are in Yorkshire, Mr Talbot?'

Mr Talbot smiled. 'I do not know, but it does not matter. This is to give the three of you time to be together. I shall drop you both at the gatehouse and then I shall go down to see the old house. It is so many years since I was there. I have not even seen the new wings. I shall stroll about the place and indulge myself with thoughts of my s ... of Mrs Stockbridge.'

The day was overcast, bleak, with a cold wind, but no rain fell. The moor brooded on either side of the track, darkly sopping, the bracken reduced to mush, the denuded scrub spiky and inhospitable. There was no colour—the landscape a monotonous brown, the sky a flat grey. Beth gave a shudder as they passed a sucking bog.

The coach took the route across the moor, avoiding Brayton and passing Laurel Cottage, which now stood empty. It brought them right past the Irish camp, and Beth looked out of the window aghast at the change she saw the past months had wrought. The drays were dreary, their canvasses flapping and waterlogged. The green turf around the fire was puddled and muddy, the fire itself barely alight and smoking. The old woman's chair was empty, and Beth recalled that she had been ill. Likely she was dead, and had joined Brónach's baby in the churchyard. The children huddled beneath a canvas awning, their faces pale, their clothing damp and bedraggled. As the carriage slowed to pass, they scrambled up and ran towards it, holding out their hands and begging for alms. Dónall got up from the steps of Aoife's *vardo* from which Aoife herself emerged, a large, dun blanket wrapped around her shoulders. She was ill, Beth saw, her large eyes bigger than usual in her drawn face.

'Oh! Let us stop! May we stop?' Beth pleaded. 'Arthur, have you any change you can give them. The poor things! They look so cold and hungry, and it's all my fault.'

'Are these the Irish people?' Mr Talbot asked, signalling to the coachman to stop. 'One of them was the thief?'

'Just one, yes. The others are good. They are good, kind people. Oh! It is dreadful to see them so brought down.'

The footman opened the door and Beth stepped out, followed by her brother and George Talbot. The children kept their distance from Beth at first, hardly recognising her, and then clamoured around her, reaching up with importuning hands. She hugged them all and greeted Caitlin and Brónach. 'Is there no news of Mr Connolly,' she asked. 'Surely he has given up the chase by now? Does he not know ...' she looked around the desolate camp, at the careworn people and the bony, underfed animals. '... does he not know that you need him?'

'Tis a matter of honour with him,' said Brónach. 'But no, we have had no news, and we cannot move on until he returns, much as we wish to. We have outstayed our welcome here. The villagers will have nothing to do with us. The children come and throw stones at our animals.'

'I am sorry,' said Beth brokenly. 'You have suffered, and all for my pride.'

'You are indeed very prideful,' said Aoife, coming up. She looked at Arthur, recognising him no doubt, and favouring him with one of her winning smiles before turning again to Beth and eyeing her new attire. 'I thought perhaps you had decided to come home. But it looks as though you might not wish to.'

Beth wrapped her cloak more tightly around her. The wind was bitter, and from just the quarter that made the standing stone resonate— an off-key, reedy drone like the warning of many wasps filled the air.

'I am going to see Frank now. Is he at the gatehouse?'

Aoife cut her eyes at Dónall before shrugging and moving away. 'How should I know?' She mounted the steps of the *vardo* and closed the door.

Arthur gathered the children around him and began to empty his pockets of pennies and sixpences, also pieces of string, a pocket knife, a stub of pencil, a large pocket handkerchief, several aniseed twists, half a dozen marbles and an India rubber ball. All these he distributed amongst them.

Mr Talbot walked around the *vardo*, taking in its appointments and decoration.

Dónall took a step or two towards Beth. He held his cap in his hands and twisted it this way and that. She could see in his eyes—blue, but a paler blue than Ruairi's—that he wished to say something. He worked his jaw as though to literally chew up the words so that he could reduce them and spit them out into a sentence that would express his meaning.

Beth said, 'Hello Dónall. It is nice to see you.'

He frowned and closed one eye. 'I didn't know,' he got out. 'The things. That they weren't ours.'

'Oh, Dónall. I know that,' said Beth, reaching out a hand but not touching him. 'That gentleman says we are not to worry about it.'

Dónall looked over his shoulder. Mr Talbot had placed his foot upon the bottom step of the *vardo* with the intention of knocking and asking if he could look inside. Dónall made a grunting sound and barrelled across the turf, grasping the man by the collar of his coat and yanking him away from the *vardo*—and would have knocked him to the ground had Lorcán not just then advanced from where he had been tending the animals. He cuffed Dónall sharply with his stump, and pushed him away so roughly that it was Dónall who ended up on the ground.

Beth said, 'Oh, Dónall, you should not handle Mr Talbot like that. He means no harm,' and then, 'I am sorry Mr Talbot. Dónall is very protective of his cousin,' and then again to Lorcán, 'Do not hurt the boy. He does not understand.'

'That is quite alright,' said Mr Talbot, setting his coat to rights. He addressed Lorcán. 'Why do you remain in these wagons? There are empty cottages in the village.'

Lorcán knuckled his forehead. 'We have no money for rent, sir. And the local people are inhospitable.'

'And anyway,' said Brónach from where she sat beneath the indifferent shelter of a stretched tarpaulin, 'we all wish to go home. A tenancy could not be for less than a year and by that time we hope to be home amongst our own people. We did not come here to stay. If you'll excuse me, sir, we did not wish to come here at all. 'Twas only the blight and the famine, sir, and the thought of our young ones.'

Mr Talbot looked down upon her and her brood of children. It was hard to say how their condition had been materially improved by their migration. 'Thank you, ma'am,' he said, nodding. 'Perhaps we had better be on our way.' He passed something discreetly to Lorcán, murmuring, 'Get food for the children. Meat. Milk.'

The carriage drew up at the gatehouse only long enough for Arthur and Beth to descend, then continued down the drive towards the house.

Beth opened the gate and stepped into the garden. The plants had not been cut back. Runner beans still clung to the wigwam she and Frank had built for them, but the leaves were withered and the dangling fruit blackened with frost, beyond any kind of use. Weeds proliferated, both amongst the vegetables and the flowers. The path was slick with moss.

'What has happened here?' Beth murmured.

The dog greeted them with delight, but inside the gatehouse all was chaos, dirt and disarray. Clothing and bedding were strewn everywhere. There was no sign of any food. Grime coated every surface. The curtains had not been opened and the fire was stone cold.

'Oh dear,' said Arthur, looking about him. 'Frank's new wife is no housekeeper, is she?'

'That was her, at the camp,' Beth said. 'The one with the brown blanket. She cannot live here because of the young man.'

'I don't understand.'

'They were brought up together from the cradle,' Beth said, walking slowly around her old home noting further evidences of neglect—a curtain pole hanging loose, a crack in the teapot lid, mould blooming in the corner of the casement. 'They are cousins, but he is so possessive and he lacks understanding. In many ways, he is still a child. He attacked Frank once just for sitting next to her.'

'Dear me. He must be made to understand.'

'That is what I say, but Frank says she will not allow it until Ruairí ... until Mr Connolly returns.'

'And why is that?'

'I think he is the only one who can restrain Dónall. Here is Frank. I hear his tread.'

The door opened and Frank entered. He looked shocked and not very pleased to see his siblings. 'What are you doing here?' His eye flicked to the shambles in the room. He stomped to the window and drew back the curtain, only succeeding in wrenching the pole from its fixings. Then he turned to face them. 'I hardly know you, Betsey. How grand you are. I would make you tea, only the fire is out, and I have no milk.' His face was a picture of anguish and anger. A muscle in his jaw twitched.

'Frank.' Beth advanced towards him, holding out her hand but not touching him, the same gesture she had used earlier, and indeed it felt to her that this Frank was as unpredictable and unknowable as Dónall. 'Things are not well with you.'

'You think? No, Betsey, they are not well. You are missed.' He stood stiffly, as though expecting an assault—not one from an extraneous source but rather an eruption of his own emotions. His arms were rigid at his sides but his expression betrayed all the turmoil and disappointment in his soul.

'But Aoife,' Beth said, looking up into his face. 'Why does she not ... Dónall is at work during the day, is he not?'

'Not recently,' Frank almost barked. 'Mr Slade is in London, and so work at Clough Farm has ceased. The Mounted Guard has a new captain and Ned Widderington has not been able to grease his palm, as he did the other.'

Arthur frowned. 'I am sorry to hear you have been running that gauntlet, Frank. It is not like you.'

Frank shrugged in a way that was almost insolent, just as Aoife had done earlier. 'Needs must, when the devil drives,' he said. 'How came you here?'

'Mr Talbot brought us. I am surprised you did not meet his carriage on the drive.'

Frank looked horrified. 'I came by the woodland path. He has not gone down to the house?'

'Of course he has,' said Arthur. 'It is his house. He is entitled to visit it.'

'He will not like what he finds,' said Frank grimly. 'I have kept up with the garden, but the inside is ... not as he would like it.' Suddenly his

252

bravado evaporated and he sat down heavily on a chair, putting his head in his hands. 'Why did you leave, Betsey?' he sobbed through his fingers. 'It has all been wrong since you left.'

She put her arm around him. 'I am home now, Frank, and all will be well.'

'You cannot stay here,' Arthur reminded her. 'You owe Mrs Somersall your duty. There is the dinner tonight. You must see that through, at least. And ... forgive me if I speak out of turn, but is there not ... an understanding between yourself and Mr Milton? Surely, you will be leaving Yorkshire before long.'

Beth closed her eyes and breathed out through her nose. 'There is no absolute understanding,' she said. 'He has spoken but I have made no reply. Perhaps, now I see that ... but, as to the dinner, you are right. I cannot abandon Mrs Somersall.' She crouched down beside Frank, who still hid his face in his hands. 'Mr Talbot is all goodness,' she said. 'He has forgiven me and made good on all my losses. I will explain to him about your changed circumstances, about Aoife's ... incapacity. Something will be arranged.'

'She carries my child,' Frank burst out, almost howling. 'She carries my child and she says that when Ruairi returns she will go with him because ... because I will not let her live in the big house.'

'She wants to live at Tall Chimneys?' Beth said, incredulous. 'But she must know that isn't possible. She can't. It's m—' She bit back the word 'mine', substituting, 'Mr Talbot's.'

'She says it *is*. That the house is there, full of empty rooms, chairs to sit upon, beds to sleep in, and that since no one else comes, why should we not? And so we argue, and she hits out at me in her temper, but then ... then ...' Frank raised his eyes just sufficiently to throw an appealing look at his brother. 'You understand, Arthur, how a woman may work her wiles on a man. She comes to me in the night and ... I am powerless.' Then he put his head on his arms and wept.

'And she uses the child as a threat against you?' Arthur was horrified. 'What kind of woman is she?'

'She is a witch,' sobbed Frank. 'She has put a spell on me.'

Arthur beckoned Beth into the scullery. 'Our brother is ill,' he said. 'I fear for him. We cannot leave him here.'

'I agree,' whispered Beth, 'but neither can we take him to Somersall Grange, not with the company that is expected.'

'Does Frank have friends hereabouts? Is there someone who would look after him for a few days, while we try to untangle this muddle?'

Beth said, 'No. Frank and I only ever had each other. There are only the Irish people, and their situation is worse than Frank's.'

Arthur considered. 'Very well. I will remain. You must give my excuses to Mrs Somersall. I can be spared. If necessary, Mr Nicholls can take my place at table.' Mr Nicholls was Mr Talbot's secretary. 'In the meantime, let us do what we can to set the place to rights. You put away the mattress and clothing. I will fetch coals and light the fire.'

Beth nodded. 'And on the way home I will stop again at the camp, and speak to Aoife if I can. At the very least, I will arrange for one of the other women to come and tend to Frank in the medium term.'

In an hour, the gatehouse was in a better state, the fire lit and some hot soup in a pan, made from what could be rescued from the garden.

'At least the potatoes survived the frost,' said Beth, 'even though the onions are beyond saving. Have you managed to harvest much from the garden at the house?'

Frank shook his head. His tears were gone, but now he only sat and stared into the fire. 'I must kill the pig soon.'

'I will contrive to come and help you salt and cure it,' said Beth, but without much conviction for she could not see how the future might be. She stood at a crossroads—so many choices, but increasingly the road she had travelled to Somersall Grange felt like the one she must retrace.

Mr Talbot was surprised when Arthur did not re-enter the carriage with Beth, but once she explained the situation he agreed that if Arthur's valet would pack up some things he—Mr Talbot—would ensure they were sent over.

'I wonder if I might prevail on cook to spare some bread and meat,' said Beth. 'Frank's larder is absolutely bare and the garden has gone to ruin. May we stop again at the Irish camp? I really must speak to Aoife.'

But the camp was empty when they got there, only Conn and two or three of the younger children remained, still amusing themselves with the things Arthur had given them.

Conn approached the carriage and doffed his hat, and promised to tell the women that help was sorely needed at the gatehouse, that Mr Frank Harlish was ill, and that his brother Mr Arthur Harlish would remunerate any of them who would undertake to keep house, unless one amongst them felt it incumbent on her to do it as a duty of affection. Beth made him repeat the message twice, to be sure he had it pat. She hoped that Aoife would understand the inference of the final sentence.

'I hope,' said Mr Talbot as the carriage pulled away, 'that they have taken the money I gave them to buy food for the children. I would be very unhappy to think they had taken it to spend at the alehouse.'

'You do them an injustice,' said Beth, but gently. 'I think Mrs Golightly will no longer serve them so they will have gone to Brayton. It is Saturday, and most of the shops will already be shut. I pray that someone takes pity on them.'

They rode in silence for a few minutes, and then Mr Talbot said, 'The house was not in a good state.'

'Frank said you would not be pleased. I am sorry. I will see if Mrs Somersall will release me from my employment.'

'Do not do so yet. Unless it is what you want.'

Beth turned and looked out of the window at the dull moor and leaden sky. 'I do not know what I want.' She certainly resented the idea that Aoife should tend the big house, even though she had suggested exactly that to Mrs Stockbridge in her letter, especially now that she saw how careless and slovenly a wife she was. The idea of Aoife in residence, behaving as though she owned the place ... it was insupportable. But then she reminded herself of the past few weeks at Somersall Grange, how good it had felt to be useful and to be in a house that was alive and functioning with relative normalcy. Would it not be preferable to remain there and let Aoife sink or swim as she might at Tall Chimneys?

Beside her on the seat Mr Talbot sighed. 'I am pleased with the improvements,' he said, speaking more to himself than to Beth. 'Everything has been elegantly done. But it all seems such a waste. Perhaps I should sell the place? I do not think Jocelyn will ever return. And why should she? Her children show no interest in it and neither do mine. It would make a decent school, or even a seminary, do you not think?'

'I cannot say,' said Beth, trying to suppress the stab of pain that his words had occasioned. 'Frank and I will be sad. But you must do as you think right.'

Chapter 42

Arthur's desertion almost slayed poor Mrs Somersall. She half collapsed upon hearing that Arthur was detained, and had to be revived with salts before the scheme to replace Arthur with Mr Nicholls was explained to her. Mr Nicholls declared himself very happy to step in, except that he feared he had not the suitable attire. He was a tall, cadaverously thin man, soon equipped with spare clothing that Herbert and Stephen between them were able to supply. He allowed himself to be attended by Arthur's valet, washed, barbered and tailored, and at last passed for an enigmatic but eminently presentable gentleman.

Beth made a final tour of the rooms with Mrs Somersall before they both retired to rest, bathe and dress. Mrs Somersall's agitation was still extreme. She had a hunted expression in her eye; it roved restlessly from one thing to another, looking to find fault that could be corrected before it was swooped on by the avenging eye of her husband. There were not enough lights. She feared that Lady Riding would be cold—could the fires not be built up more? She was anxious as to her dress. Surely it was too fine. But then she feared that it was not fine enough. At last Beth took her to lie down with a draught of soothing concoction that she had the housekeeper prepare in the stillroom, but was sorry to see that Mr Somersall waited in her chamber; there would be no rest for Mrs Somersall.

Beth herself descended to the kitchens and helped herself to a selection of viands, cheese, a quart of milk, a pie and a loaf of bread from the pantry. Such was the steam and furore in the kitchen that her trespass was barely noticed. She oversaw the trap loaded with Arthur's valise and the hamper of provisions and watched it set off into the rapidly darkening afternoon through a squall of sleet, wishing she could go with it. Back in her own room she drew her curtains on the dying day, ready to walk through the forthcoming dinner in her mind, to identify and head off any likely crises so as to be able to relieve Mrs Somersall of all anxiety. But she found her own difficulties rose too easily to the forefront of her thoughts. She was much moved and distressed by Frank's condition, and perplexed as to her own proper course.

Her bedroom and its small ancillary sitting room were cosy. A fire always burnt in the grates on waking, for dressing and when she retired, and she saw the ministrations of a delicate, respectful hand amongst her hair brushes and pins, in the arrangement of her bed covers and the laying out of her clothes. Soon the little maid would come with ewers of hot water and towels and fragrant oils for the working and smoothing of her hair. Then she must descend to give Mrs Somersall all her aid, but for now she indulged her great preoccupation with Harlish family affairs.

Frank and Aoife were married. In God's eyes, if not in the church's, they were man and wife. It seemed to Beth that until Aoife absolutely went away—as she had threatened—or until Dónall was undeceived as to the state of things so that the pair could begin their proper married life, it would be wrong for Beth to return to the gatehouse. Frank's choice and its consequences must be allowed to play out, one way or another.

But oh! How hard it was to feel that Frank was being taken for a fool. Aoife had never loved him! He had only been her key to the door of Tall Chimneys, and all this prevarication over telling Dónall the truth was just another way of twisting Frank to her will. As angry as Beth was with Frank it still pained her to know that he suffered, that the dear old gatehouse was so neglected and that the big house was also left to moulder. Mr Talbot had made no protest about the condition of the house, nor had he criticised Aoife, though he surely had the right to expect Aoife to take up its care. It was generous of him to have held his peace. But then, he was a generous man.

Whether Beth herself could ever return to her employment was a question too hard to answer. She was weighed down with the sense that she had forfeited that great privilege. Mr Talbot's assurances went some way to assuage her guilt, but by no means the whole distance. And now she had such an attractive alternative. Should she be permitted to remain in Mrs Somersall's employment she felt she would like to do so. Somersall Grange was not a busy house but it was not a mausoleum, as Tall Chimneys had increasingly become. But then there came upon her that sense she had that the old house in the hollow was much more than just stone and slate. It was not inanimate but somehow vital. It did not hum like the standing stone on the moor, but nevertheless it spoke to Beth in its own language and she could not stop up her ears to its call.

Her thoughts moved on to Stephen Milton. She liked him increasingly, but he did not make her blood thunder in her ears as Ruairi Connolly did; and still, in her dreams, it was the Irishman who smiled down at her. And yet, did not Frank's experience teach her that the urges of the body were not to be trusted? A meeting of minds and a kinship of spirit was surely a better basis for a marriage, in which case Stephen would certainly be a better match. With Stephen she would travel, might even rise in the world. His success would lift her as Arthur's had lifted little Miss Petunia Pink, who had been only a milliner but now ran a busy household and was soon to be mistress of a country residence. Beth felt she could engage in Stephen's work, understand and support him in it. That would count for much. It would be a satisfaction and a fulfilment for her. But it would take her away from Moorside. Once away, she supposed that, like Arthur, she would return only rarely, if at all.

And then she considered Ruairi. His easy smile and piercing blue eyes, his well-sculped body and warm encompassing embrace rose all too easily to her mind. But life with him would be a life of itinerancy. She would be absorbed into the Irish cohort, subject to prejudice and suspicion, hounded from place to place, denied work. She would never belong until such time as they might consider a return to Ireland. But who knew when that might be? And what might have happened to Ruairi's farmhouse and acres in his absence? Perhaps even then, in his house, amongst his neighbours, even as mother to his children, she would not belong—would always be 'the Englishwoman,' the incomer, the outsider. Would she not then only have swapped the frying pan for the fire?

But all the foregoing was moot, for Ruairi had not plainly declared his intention. The truth was that she really had no absolute knowledge of his heart or his head.

Chapter 48

Mr and Mrs Somersall, Herbert, Stephen and Beth were in the salon half an hour ahead of time. Mrs Somersall was gorgeously dressed in a frock with multitudinous flounces and infinite trimmings, weighed down with gold and innumerable jewels, but so cowed and uncomfortable withal that it seemed as though the clothing and accessories wore her, rather than the other way around. She chafed and fidgeted beneath their thrall, her eyes bright with panic, her skin very pale. Every time her husband spoke she cringed and trembled.

Her great trepidation found its exact opposite in her husband, whose supreme satisfaction in the evening before him oozed from every egotistical pore. He wore a suit of superlative cut and expense and a richly embroidered waistcoat very much with the air of a man who has taken on an unruly stallion and means to tame him. He crossed the floor smartly several times, his new shoes squeaking in protest as he marched his clothing into compliance, not failing to regard himself with a satisfied eye as he passed an elaborately framed mirror. He had been thoroughly groomed, his large domed head polished to a high shine, the fuzz of hair slicked down with grease, his whiskers and eyebrows trimmed. He smelled strongly of bergamot and also of brandy, having fortified himself several times from the decanter in his dressing room.

There were plentiful seats but nobody sat down, too restless to take their leisure. Herbert kept dashing from the room, thinking that he heard the Eagerlys' equipage, only to be disappointed. 'The weather is inclement,' he said several times. 'They will come round by the road. Only a fool would cross the moor in this weather. Perhaps the ford at Brayton has flooded.'

'Oh! Do not say that, Herbert,' his mother almost shrieked. 'Now we have come to it we must go on with the thing, or all Mary's effort will have been in vain.'

'I think the cook's exertions are hardly to be considered,' said Mr Somersall, wrestling his stock into a better accommodation of his thick neck. 'What of the money that has been laid out?'

'There are always poor people to eat surplus food,' said Beth, who thought that on the whole the abandonment of the entire occasion might be a very good thing; she feared Mrs Somersall would be ill if she continued at this level of agitation.

'The devil there are!' Somersall thundered. 'Not a morsel of it shall be consumed by beggars and thieves, if I have anything to say about it. I would rather give it to the pigs. What time is it? Are you sure that clock keeps good time, Mildred? You ensure it is regularly wound, I suppose? By my watch it is almost seven. Seven was the hour named, was it not?'

'Yes, Peregrine,' Mrs Somersall squeaked.

'It wants ten minutes to seven as yet,' Stephen said, 'and if, as Herbert says, the weather has closed in—'

'Do not tell *me* the time, sir,' Somersall thundered. 'I think I am able to read my own watch. If you can hold your tongue long enough you will hear it chime the hour. It is infallible. It should be. I paid enough for it.' He rummaged the watch from its pocket and opened it. They all stood in silence, hardly daring to breathe as the minutes ticked by; and then at last the watch did emit a series of thin timorous chimes. 'There you are,' said Somersall, putting the watch away. 'Seven. I dislike tardiness. It is extremely rude to keep people waiting.'

He strutted across the floor a few more times, very pleased to have proved his point. The others exchanged significant looks, but no one spoke.

Five minutes later, all the clocks in the house erupted in a cacophony of clanging and chiming, jangling, cuckooing and bonging.

The salon door opened and Mr Talbot and his secretary stepped in.

'Excellent!' declared Mr Talbot, looking at the ornate mantel clock and comparing it with his own timepiece. 'Seven. I do like to be punctual. Madam,' addressing Mrs Somersall, 'how radiant you look! And Miss Harlish! A vision of loveliness.' He shook hands with Herbert and Stephen and took up a position to one side of the enormous fireplace. Mr

Nicholls moved in his employer's wake as though attached by an invisible leading rein. It was the place to which he was most accustomed, from where he might hear murmured instructions or remarks that must be stored away in the warehouse of his mind for later exhumation and enactment.

Almost immediately the sound of carriage wheels was heard and Herbert again precipitated himself from the room, eager to greet Rose and reassure her by any means—but preferably by a press of the hand or even by the pressure of his arm around her waist—that she was not to be afraid, that he would take care of her. In his absence Mrs Somersall began to quake and to chew her lip. Her eyes were glassy with panic. Beth stood close beside her and said, 'Recall how pleasant your meeting with Mrs Eagerly was the other day, ma'am. She is not a dragon. Take a sip of sherry, I do implore you. It will settle your nerves.'

Mrs Somersall did so, and when the Eagerlys were announced she managed to smile and stutter some observations as to the poor weather.

The vicar was neatly but soberly dressed in a plain black suit, his wife regally on his arm, her superior bombazine doing its best to compete with the superlative silk and satin, lace, organdie and velvet trimmings of her hostess. It fell to Stephen to effect the introductions, as Herbert was detained just outside the room. Mrs Eagerly greeted her hostess with cautious warmth, but to Beth she gave only an icy glance, barely thawed by the warmth of her husband's smile.

'There you are, Vicar,' boomed Mr Somersall. 'You are somewhat behind time, but no matter. The party from Riding Hall is yet to arrive. I suppose the roads were very bad. Now you'll take a glass of brandy-and-soda, I suppose. Unless you prefer sherry?'

The vicar intimated that he would prefer sherry, if any was available.

'Available? I should say so,' crowed Mr Somersall. 'We have a good cellar here, sir. I doubt you will find a better in the county. I know something of wines, sir. I have made it my business to master the subject. I do not think you will find anyone better qualified to speak of viniculture—that is the proper term for it, sir—in the north of England. When I go into a thing, I do it thoroughly.'

'Oenology, I think,' murmured the vicar, 'is the study of wine, derived from the Greek *oînos*—meaning wine—and *logos*—that is, science. Viniculture—or viticulture—is the science of grapevines.'

'Well!' Mr Somersall's complexion darkened but he mastered his ire, even he acknowledging that it would be injudicious to protest. Instead, he resorted to witticism—or at any rate his idea of it. 'That is ... and of course, you cannot have wine without vines!' He chortled at his own joke. 'But where is this girl of yours? You brought her with you, I suppose.'

Herbert and Rose came into the room, the girl coming in great apprehension, clinging to Herbert's arm and looking as though she would make a run for it if she could. But then she saw Beth, and went quickly to her side.

'Let us greet your host, and then it is done with,' whispered Beth, taking a firm hold and bringing the girl to Mr Somersall.

Rose opened her mouth to speak but no words would come, and she stood mute and pale beneath his penetrating gaze.

Mrs Somersall, awed by her own audacity, said, 'Do not frighten the child, Peregrine. Do you not see she is all a-tremble?'

He surveyed Rose—but more kindly than he had before—glanced meaningfully at Mr Talbot and then leaned down to plant a wet kiss upon her brow. She flinched, but bore it, and Beth moved her away towards a remote corner of the room, handing her a handkerchief so that she could wipe the residue of his greeting from her skin.

The Eagerlys had barely time to dispose themselves amongst the numerous chairs and sofas in the room before Lord and Lady Riding were announced, and they all rose to their feet.

Now, Lord and Lady Riding were—by their rank—very august personages, probably the foremost lady and gentleman in that part of the country, ancient possessors of the title and countless acres of countryside. But they were, in the flesh, rather less than their title and holdings might suggest. Lord Riding was bald dowdy and small, a shy man who much preferred his hounds and horses—and even his ploughmen—to the bishops and earls and dukes with whom he was required to rub shoulders when the Upper House was in session. It is a recorded fact that he had never opened his mouth in the House of Lords, not so much as to state the least opinion or to ask the most innocuous question. His 'yay' or 'nay' had hardly such volume or substance that would sway a vote in any direction. He had been bewildered, and in truth rather annoyed, to receive the Somersalls' invitation, but his wife had urged its acceptance.

'There is a marriageable son,' she said, 'and we have Veraminta and Petronella to consider.'

Lady Riding was much the larger character of the two, both in height—she overtopped her husband by a full head—and in energy. She outdid him in riding and hunting, and was a better shot. She was not at all chary of voicing her opinion, the scourge of the master of hounds, of the local clergy, of the sitting member for Riding, of her own butler, and—it may as well be admitted—of her own husband.

She was the mother of daughters, all but two of whom were tolerably well-settled in life. She had borne no sons, and this of course was a disappointment to her, but she did not allow it to embitter her, finding a daily allowance of port wine and frequent application to her snuff box after a day of exercise to be enough to allay the regret. She was rather weatherbeaten, her cheeks mapped with broken veins, the merest suggestion of moustache made ginger by the staining of snuff. Her hair was thin and without beauty, and she had a skewed eye that interlocutors found somewhat unsettling. But she was determined to see the last of her girls settled, and so however unpromising the alliance, she had acceded to the invitation and had her daughters scrubbed and coiffed for the occasion.

As to the two girls—or young women, as we must say, and perhaps, as to that, not so very young—they were absolutely vapid, plain and spinsterish. They had dull complexions, dull hair and dull unintelligent eyes. Their teeth were bad, their posture worse. They sloped into the room droop-shouldered, their chins on their chests, unable to meet any eye. Their dresses were old, much made over, and so similar to each other that they offered the rest of the guests no clue as to which honourable lady was which, and as their father garbled their names when he introduced them, he provided no enlightenment.

The footmen circulated with trays of drinks. Conversation was desultory. Mrs Somersall soon exhausted the fund of suitable topics Beth had compiled for her beforehand, rattling through them so that the state of the roads tumbled over the health of the Queen—expecting *again*—and the price of game got entangled with the new fashion for narrow sleeves. Stephen and Mr Talbot endeavoured to coax a sentence from Lord Riding, essaying a range of topics until hitting on the new trend for artificial fertilizer, which did elicit an ambivalent reply. Mr Nicholls and Herbert together strove to entertain the Riding daughters, who remained utterly mute. Beth stood with the Eagerlys and enquired after their health. She wished very much to tell the vicar something of her brother's troubles, but Mrs Eagerly's judgemental eye made her think better of it. Mr Somersall and Lady Riding sparred energetically over the route that had brought the Riding party from Riding Hall. Mr Somersall was sure that they must have come through Ellingbeck. Lady Riding declared that no consideration on earth would persuade her to go within a mile of that filthy, god-forsaken little town; they had come via Brayton. In that case, opined Mr Somersall, they had added ten miles to their journey. He hoped they would avail themselves of his roof for the night. Rooms were made ready, and accommodations for the grooms could be found. 'By no means,' rejoined the lady. They would not intrude, and must attend morning service in any case. The Bishop of York was to preach the sermon and she had a great desire to hear him.

Then dinner was announced and Mrs Somersall disposed of her guests but not at all according to the scheme she and Beth had hatched, which had evaporated from her head, and the carefully annotated plan they had secreted amongst some ivory miniatures was nowhere to be found. She assigned Mr Nicholls to escort Lady Veraminta—or Lady Petronella—and Mr Talbot to her sister. Herbert seized the opportunity to take Rose's arm and Beth found herself claimed by Stephen Milton. This left the Eagerlys to escort one another. Lord Riding offered his arm to Mrs Somersall and Lady Riding allowed herself to be manhandled by her host.

They went down to dinner.

The mulligatawny and the green turtle soup circulated. Mr Somersall commanded wine, tasted it, rejected it and called for another vintage. He sent his wife's simple broth away saying, 'You must try the mulligatawny, Mildred, or our guests will think it unfit to eat.' He found fault with the footmen, had the candelabra disposed in different ways upon the table 'lest Her Ladyship be blinded,' and caused a large table arrangement to be removed for 'I cannot see His Lordship at all, nor his daughters, and I will not have matters carried on that are not in plain sight.' Mrs Somersall protested, but feebly, mentioning that the flowers for the table had been brought from York, but it was in vain.

At last, with the table in a state of decimation, the host settled to his soup.

Lady Riding turned to the vicar, who sat beside her. 'Excuse me, Vicar,' she said. 'One is quite habituated to seeing foreign faces these days, and one's interest in the empire is naturally very alive. Are you lately come from your own country?'

'Oh no, ma'am,' he replied, laying aside his spoon and dabbing his lips with his napkin. 'I came over in 1790, when I was quite a young boy. My brother and I were taken under the wing of Mr Talbot's grandfather and brought back from India with him when our mother died. I am sorry to say that the old gentleman did not survive the voyage, but Mr Talbot's father, Mr Robert, did for us all that his father had purposed, and more.'

'How very philanthropic of him,' observed Lady Riding. She had barely tasted her soup and now motioned for the footman to remove her plate. 'I recall that at one time it was considered quite the fashion to adopt little native boys.' She peered beyond the vicar to where Rose sat. 'I suppose that to be your daughter. She is a paler hue. Is that because she has been protected from the Indian climate?'

The vicar bowed his head politely. 'I think it is because her mother was an English lady.'

'Indeed? I am not quite sure that I approve of mixed cultures within marriage. And you hold the parish of Moorside?'

'That's correct, ma'am. A very small parish, but one to which I have become most attached.'

'That too, I apprehend, is in Mr Talbot's gift.'

'Indeed. We owe everything to the Talbots' generosity.'

Lady Riding sniffed through one nostril. 'I am not sure I would like to be so entirely dependent on the charity of one man.'

'Beggars cannot be choosers,' said Mr Somersall, who sat on her other side. He spooned his soup with great rapidity but little accuracy; a great deal of it ended up on his waistcoat.

Lady Riding ignored the jibe and continued to address the vicar, whose soup was now quite cold. 'We have our own chapel at Riding. Sadly, we no longer have our own chaplain. We attend St Mary's in Whitby.'

'I am acquainted with the archdeacon, naturally. He is a very good fellow.'

Lady Riding looked down her nose at him. 'Really? I shall be sure to tell him you think so.'

She addressed her next remark to Mr Somersall, 'You have but the one child, I gather? He seems to be a very pleasing young man. The country hereabouts is rather meagrely provided with young gentleman. I hope we can count on him for the hunt ball this year.'

Mr Somersall paused in the guzzling of his soup. 'He will attend it if I tell him to, and if an invitation can be procured. Where is it held?'

'At Riding Hall. It is to be in the new year. I will make sure he is sent a card. Does he hunt?'

'Not at present,' replied her host, sopping the remains of his soup up with a hunk of bread. 'But he can be got to hunt if it seems advisable.'

'He does not hunt?' Lady Riding was aghast. 'With all this heathland? You must be overrun by foxes! Let him come to the next meet at Riding, and Veraminta or Petronella will show him the territory. He is mounted I presume?'

'He has a horse or two.'

'But any old horse will not do for hunting. Dear me. It is quite shocking to me that people who build property in the country have so little understanding of country ways. You had better send him over to us for a few weeks. We have shooting as well as hunting. He cannot hope to hold his head up amongst us if he cannot acquit himself in country pursuits.' She turned from her host in a sort of disgust, but finding the vicar still at her other hand and having nothing more to say to him, she lapsed into silence.

But Mr Somersall was not to be put down, even by Lady Riding. 'I think any son of mine can hold his head up pretty much anywhere,' he said heatedly. 'He has the manners and education of a gentleman; and as to money, I venture to say he can buy most noblemen out lock, stock and barrel—or I can. If he needs horses he shall have them—a whole string. And his own pack of hounds too. People tell me it is vulgar to *speak* of wealth, but since everyone *thinks* of it, I do not know why it should not be spoken of. A sovereign out of my pocket is as good as any from His Lordship's, and I wager I have two to every one of his.'

This was unanswerable, and conversation at the bottom of the table faltered for a few moments until suddenly Mr Somersall thundered, 'Mildred!' down the table, making his wife jump and causing a small maidservant to drop a ladle. 'You must keep the waiters up to snuff up at your end. Lord Riding has no wine. Must I see to everything myself?'

'His Lordship declines wine,' Mrs Somersall piped, but not loud enough to be heard. She turned to her neighbour. 'If you would not mind, Your Lordship, having a thimbleful in your glass, it will please Mr Somersall. You will not have to drink it.'

His Lordship assented. 'This is good soup,' he said. 'Green turtle, you say? Such luxury cannot be afforded these days at Riding Hall.'

Oh sir,' his hostess confided, 'I would not have you suppose we dine like this every day; and there was a time, when we lived in Ferret Street, when a plate of ham, sliced very thin, and a hot pie from the baker on the corner would have been a banquet to us.'

'I have eaten simple food at the homes of my tenants,' said Lord Riding, 'that tasted finer than anything I ever had in the dining room at the House.'

'You do not have a good cook, sir?'

'Madam, I meant the House of Lords. Our cook does well enough, but our taste is for plain fare. A mutton chop does us most days.'

'I developed a taste for curried foods in India,' said Mr Talbot, insinuating himself into the conversation. 'I like them still. I have a man from the Punjab who caters for me when I am at home ...' the conversation at that end went on pleasantly and Mrs Somersall almost relaxed, except that from time to time she caught the steely gaze of her husband and then her cautious pleasure evaporated.

In the centre of the table, the secretary persisted in his attempts to engage the honourable lady on his left. Would she take wine? Yes, she would take half a glass of wine. Did she like the soup? Yes, she thought it was very nice. He believed there was to be music, was she fond of music? Yes, she thought music was very pleasurable. But not so pleasurable as books, perhaps? Equally pleasurable, but in a different way. And so he laboured on, as the soup was at first removed and then brought back when it was understood that Lord Riding wished for more.

Opposite to them the other honourable lady resisted Mr Talbot's attempts to interest her in art, the theatre, politics and travel until he abandoned the attempt and relinquished her to her other neighbour, Herbert. His characteristically playful conversational gambits likewise fell on deaf ears, but he occupied himself more with Rose to his left, and in the end both Riding ladies were left to stare gloomily at their plates and exchange the occasional doleful glance at each other.

Stephen said, 'You are very quiet, Miss Harlish. Is there anything amiss?'

'I am concerned about my brother Frank,' she said. 'He is unwell.'

'I am sorry to hear that. I suppose your other brother will send for the doctor if he thinks it necessary.'

'He will. But it is not a malady of the body that afflicts Frank, but rather a malady of ... I was going to say the mind, but I think the truth is that Frank has a broken heart.'

'The Irishwoman, his wife ...?'

Beth shook her head; she could say no more. Beneath the cloth, Stephen's hand strayed briefly to hers, and gave it a compassionate squeeze.

It fell to Mrs Eagerly to revive discourse at the bottom of the table. 'My son is a sportsman,' she said. She cast an appraising eye down the table to where the honourable ladies sat. She had not altogether given up hope of a union between Edgar and Rose, but it did no harm to have prospects in reserve. Of course, she knew nothing of the impecunious circumstances of the Ridings. 'He is currently Mr Eagerly's curate at Moorside, but is in expectations of his own parish in time. The Bishop thinks highly of him. Indeed, I think you mentioned that you are to attend the Bishop tomorrow. Edgar will be there. He was particularly asked to assist in the eucharist.'

Lady Riding sighed. A curate—even one who hunted—was not at all what she aspired to for her girls. 'My eldest daughter is married to the Dean of Rydale,' she observed haughtily. 'Her sister is Viscountess Selby. My third daughter married the local member of Parliament. He is expected to enter the Cabinet next session. Veraminta and Petronella can expect matches of similar standing.'

Mrs Eagerly bridled. 'You misunderstand me,' she said, although of course Lady Riding had done no such thing. 'I was thinking of Your Ladyship's reference to a dearth of young men for the ball. But in point of fact Edgar is by no means bereft of illustrious connection. His late father was a Maybury of Maybury, the fourth son of the Earl. He served as chaplain to the 55th Westmoreland Regiment of Foot for fifteen years.' She paused before adding pointedly, 'You have a superfluity of daughters, ma'am.'

'I was thinking the same,' said Mr Somersall. 'Who will follow your husband, Lady Riding? Is the estate entailed? But it seems to me that nowadays most of the old nobility are eager for new money, and new blood. Herbert will inherit a vast fortune.'

'Herbert is as good as engaged to my stepdaughter,' said Mrs Eagerly, in spite of herself. 'But if Edgar is not wanted at the Riding meet or the ball, it is of no moment. He is a very popular young man. He can get his sport in any of a dozen places.'

'You are mistaken, madam, if you think an engagement is fixed,' said Mr Somersall. 'There is a great deal of business to be discussed before we can accept it as an established fact.'

Lady Riding said, 'It is always best to have the settlements firmly instituted. It took three lawyers to arrange matters for Selina, my second girl.'

'Pah,' said Mr Somersall. 'I shall not need a lawyer at a guinea an hour to arrange matters for me. Mildred! Are we to have fish? Why are the servants taking so long?'

'His Lordship is still eating his soup, Peregrine,' came the reedy reply from the other end of the table. 'They will bring the fish directly, of course.'

Mr Somersall proceeded to entertain the ladies to his either side with a long diatribe on the subject of fish, about which he was—naturally— more extraordinarily well-informed than any other person of his acquaintance.

Lady Riding and Mrs Eagerly let this wisdom flow over and around them until the fish was brought, toyed with and removed, and the roast carried in.

It being apparent that Lord Riding preferred his dinner seasoned with little or no conversation, Mr Talbot was able to entertain his hostess with the topic that was dearest to her heart—Herbert.

'I was telling your husband last night,' he said, 'that my own father took me to India and showed me his whole business. Has Herbert had the opportunity to really understand Mr Somersall's affairs?'

'He has been at the mine these last months,' said Mrs Somersall, 'and when the rains came he went down again and again, to look at the water. But I do not think he is very interested, and who can blame him? Coal is not very interesting, is it?'

'In Leeds, I noticed that Mr Somersall attended the exchange nearly every day, and was often in conference with other mercantile men. But I did not see that he made an effort to explain matters to Herbert. The boy spent most of his time strolling around the streets, I think. Tell me, ma'am, where do you think his talents lie?'

'As to that, I could not say. Peregrine says he has none. I think he has a kind, good heart. He tells me,' leaning confidentially towards Mr Talbot, 'that the accommodations for the miners in Ellingbeck are atrocious. He wanted to improve them, but his father would not hear of it.'

'I should like to see them,' said Mr Talbot. 'I have provided housing for my workers at various foundries and mills, but it is necessarily far below the standards I would prefer. The problem is that towns are so crowded these days, and town land at a premium to build manufacturing premises. No one seems to think that the hands must be accommodated; they are squashed in anyhow, with the minimum of facilities. It is no wonder disease runs rife. I have it in mind to build an entire town, somewhere out in the countryside where the air is healthful, to move the manufacturing there, build houses, schools, hospitals ...'[xxxiii]

'You would despoil the countryside,' said Lord Riding, looking up from his mutton.'

'I do not think it would be despoiled. That is the advantage of building from scratch. Everything can be planned and catered for in advance and the result would be light, well-spaced-out accommodations with proper water and sewage facilities. A model town, in fact. Happy, healthy workers are hard workers, in my experience.'

'I do not think Mr Somersall is of the same mind,' said Mrs Somersall. 'Now I hope that you will try the dessert, Your Lordship. Cook has excelled herself. There is something called a Charlotte russe, and blancmange ...'

The dinner progressed and at last was done and the ladies rose from the table.

Chapter 44

The gentlemen moved seats and port wine was brought out, also claret and brandy—Mr Somersall's own particular favourite.

'A very pleasant dinner,' said Lord Riding. 'I fear we will not be able to return your hospitality in like style.'

'I am glad to hear you say so with such candour,' said Mr Somersall, 'for I like a man who speaks the plain truth plainly. I will be frank with you in return. It is your penurious situation that caused me to invite you to my house. You will have seen my son, sir? There is a possibility that he will be engaged to the vicar's daughter, but there is many a slip twixt cup and lip, as they say, and you have two daughters unspoken for.'

'You are very direct, sir, and I would not describe my situation as penurious. But, as to my girls, I can hardly negotiate an alliance on the strength of one evening's acquaintance.'

'Can you not?' said Mr Somersall, raising a grizzled eyebrow. 'My boy will do as he is told. If it suits the two of us, why should it not be so?'

'In Indian culture it is quite usual for parents to arrange their children's marriages regardless of their preferences,' said the vicar. 'But I am happy to say that it is not the custom in this country. Herbert is here and can speak for himself.'

'Not if he knows what's good for him,' growled Mr Somersall.

Herbert squirmed in his seat and opened his mouth to make a halting assertion of his independence that might well have done more to confirm his father's declaration than to deny it, but a slight frown from Mr Talbot stayed him.

'We must have this affair settled while the principal players are present,' said Mr Somersall. 'Your Lordship will forgive us if we conduct a little business? My friend Talbot is yet to tell us what he means to do, if anything, for Miss Eagerly; and I wish him to know that Herbert has other avenues to pursue. I believe it will sharpen his pencil more than somewhat. Pass the soda, will you, Milton?'

'I think this can hardly be a fit topic for conversation just now,' said Stephen, doing as he was bid. 'His Lordship and I are not 'principal players' and can have no reason to be party to what is a private family affair.'

'Father,' said Herbert, summoning what courage he had, 'the honourable ladies are very pleasant, but I must tell you that, in regard to Miss Eagerly, my mind is quite fixed.'

'Your mind can be unfixed then, if I say so. Hold your tongue.'

Stephen rose abruptly from his seat. 'Lord Riding, shall we find the ladies? For myself, I require no wine, and will be happy to escort you.'

'It does not suit my purposes for you to withdraw just yet, Lord Riding,' said Mr Somersall, with a menacing air. 'You may go, Milton, if you please. You are not wanted.'

Stephen hovered, waiting for Lord Riding to assert himself, but that gentleman retained his seat and after a few moments Stephen absented himself from the room, taking Mr Nicholls with him.

'I beg you, Father—' began Herbert.

But his father roared, 'I told you to be silent, boy.'

Herbert flinched but obeyed, collapsing like a punctured balloon into his seat. Beneath the cloth, the kindly vicar reached out and touched his hand.

'Upon my word, Somersall,' said Mr Talbot, speaking very firmly, his usually affable air quite gone, 'your behaviour is extraordinary. Herbert is your son! Do you have no heart?'

'The heart has no place in business,' said Mr Somersall, lifting his glass.

Mr Talbot, aghast, said, 'So you consider your son to be a commodity then, to be bought and sold, or hired out, or dangled like a worm on a hook to see what fish will bite?'

Mr Somersall cast a complacent glance at Lord Riding. 'I believe it is a very effective strategy, for His Lordship has remained. He is interested in the bait.'

271

Lord Riding looked as though he would deny it, but he could not explain his remaining in the room in any other way. Mr Talbot rose from his seat and paced about the room, unable to contain his ire.

'You may treat your son as you see fit, I suppose,' said the vicar, 'though I think it very unkind. We will come to an agreement like gentlemen, if an agreement can be found, but in the end I will do what I think best for Rose's happiness. That is my overriding, I may say my *only* concern.'

Mr Somersall waved the vicar's scruples away. 'My understanding is that the lady will have a small amount of capital from her mother,' he said, getting down to business. 'Is that correct?'

Her father indicated that it was. 'What remains, now her schooling has been paid for, will provide no more than two hundred a year.'

'A gentleman cannot survive on less than a thousand, and I think I can say that Herbert will never earn a farthing. Have you no other funds?'

The vicar shook his head, and did not raise his eyes to Mr Talbot, who paid him just seven hundred a year for the running of the parish.

Mr Talbot said, 'What will *you* offer, Somersall? You cannot expect Eagerly to fund the couple entirely.'

'I shall expect him to do exactly that, if they marry without my sanction.'

Mr Talbot ground his teeth. 'And what will *buy* your sanction?'

Somersall smiled. 'At last. You're speaking my language. You, Talbot, will settle five thousand on the girl, and put contracts and contacts my way that will amount to about the same. In return I will allow the marriage, and I will even continue to pay Herbert his five hundred a year, though it is like pouring money down a drain for all the use he is.'

'But you will not require him to involve himself in your business, I take it, since you value his contribution so little.'

'Oh no. I'll not give him a penny if he does no work. That is not my idea of the way of things.'

Lord Riding shifted in his seat. 'I never heard of such a thing,' he said. 'So, as I understand it, you propose to sell your son for a down payment of five thousand and a handful of business opportunities.'

Mr Somersall sat back in his seat. 'You have it pat, My Lord. If they want him, that is the price.'

'And you would wash your hands of him? Really, I am astonished. How can a man not support his own son?' Any even slight interest that Lord Riding might have had in an alliance with the Somersalls was now clearly gone. He cast a longing glance at the door—no doubt wishing he had left with Milton—and viewed the dinner table with a regretful eye that declared his opinion that green turtle soup, however good it might be, was not worth being party to the iniquity he now saw unfolding.

'You, sir, are from a world of silver spoons,' said Mr Somersall scathingly. 'I come from struggle and want. In my world, a man who does not work does not eat.'

'But even a hungry man will feed his children before he feeds himself,' said Mr Talbot darkly, 'if he be human.'

'A man who is hungry enough will eat his own children, in my experience,' said Mr Somersall.

Every eye was turned to him, each one horrified.

With a smothered sob, Herbert turned away to hide his tears.

Lord Riding at last rose from his seat. 'I will take my leave,' he said through thin lips. 'Good evening, gentlemen.'

The door closed upon him. Mr Talbot stepped to Mr Somersall's elbow and looked down very severely upon him. 'And what of his inheritance?' he asked, with a voice that was half strangled with disgust. 'I do not suppose you would leave your estate away from your only child?'

'As to that, I cannot say. What a very underwhelming man Lord Riding was. Did you not think so? I expected him to be a very different kind of man.'

Mr Talbot continued to pace up and down the room, fulminating—but also formulating a plan.

The vicar said, 'It is very hard on those of us who have not been given the great blessing of a son—or perhaps,' with a meaningful glance at Mr Talbot, 'those who have been so unfortunate as to *lose* one—to hear you speak of yours with such utter disregard for his feelings.'

Mr Somersall's face took on an expression of wounded innocence. 'I have regarded his feelings, haven't I? He wishes to marry your daughter and I have provided a means by which it might be so. He need not work for me if he does not wish it, and with five thousand judiciously invested I think I have provided the means for him to live in relative comfort. Oh! I think I have done very well for him. What you will make of the bargain, I cannot say.'

Mr Talbot at last ceased his perambulations and came to sit in the chair on Mr Somersall's left hand, recently vacated by Lord Riding.

'Here is what I propose,' he said, resting his elbows on the table and leaning towards Mr Somersall with an air almost of entreaty. 'Firstly, I shall suggest that Mr and Mrs Eagerly take their daughter to town for the season. She is young, and I think that Mrs Eagerly is quite correct. It is important that Rose is made to feel sure of her own heart and mind. But do not be dismayed, Herbert'—for that young man had groaned at the news that Rose was to be taken away. 'Believe me when I say that the waiting will make the bliss sweeter. I had to wait a while for my beloved Bibi. We were impatient, but our patience was rewarded.' Mr Talbot turned back to Mr Somersall. 'In the meantime, let me urge you, let me implore you as a man who knows what it is to lose a son, not to dispose of yours so lightly. I stipulate that in the six months of Miss Eagerly's sojourn in town, you take it upon yourself to induct Herbert thoroughly into every aspect of your business. Not as an underling, but as a partner. There must be some element of it in which he can involve himself to good effect. Or, let him come to you with a proposal that will interest him and add to your enterprise. For a man to work alongside his son, Somersall, is rewarding in itself; and to see him take hold of a project and devote himself to it ... there can be no greater satisfaction. What would you not give to be able to take your own father by the hand now, and show him all you have achieved? I am sure you would give half your wealth! And how proud he would be of you. Do not deny yourself that pride in your own son's achievements. He wants just a little encouragement—and the belief that you *want* to approve him, to step into the possibility of all he can do. He is *your* son, Somersall. Of course he has ability. Of course he has potential, if you will only let him find out what it is. I will settle the money as you require on Rose in return for just that single assurance from you, that you will undertake'—and here he turned to encompass Herbert in his address—'that you will *both* undertake to close up this fissure, which should never have been allowed to form between a father and son.'

'Fine words,' said Mr Somersall coldly, but in truth his heart—if he had one—was touched, for he had often lamented that he could not show his father how far he had come. 'I suppose we can but try. And what about the contracts?'

Mr Talbot ignored that question, turning instead to Herbert, who sat wet-eyed but with a look of such longing on his face that his future benefactor almost wept himself.

'Y ... yes,' Herbert got out. 'I'd like to try. All I've ever wanted is for my father to be proud of me.'

'Very well.' Mr Talbot sat back in his seat, wrung out from the enormity of his efforts, and drank some wine.

'And the contracts?' Mr Somersall said again.

'Those,' said Mr Talbot, rising to his feet once more and seeming to be wholly restored from his fatigue of a moment before, 'will come. I will support Herbert's endeavours in any way that I can, once I can see that the experiment has been a success.'

'But what if it has not?' blustered Mr Somersall.

Mr Talbot smiled. 'You cannot expect the risk to be all on my side, sir. You must make it a success if you wish your empire to benefit from mine. But if it does not work out, then I shall take Herbert under my wing. If you cannot find a niche for him, I certainly can. I already have a scheme in mind that would suit him.' He walked to the door but turned at last and fixed Herbert and the vicar with his eye. 'You will not be the loser, Herbert; and Rose will not lose her beau. But you, sir,' and he swivelled his gaze to where Mr Somersall sat at the table, 'you will lose a son. If you allow it to come to that, you have my heartfelt condolences. Now, I will join the ladies. Herbert, Oscar, will you come with me?'

Both men leapt up and the three left the room, leaving Mr Somersall alone.

Part Three

Chapter 45

By the end of October the Eagerlys were gone, firstly to Great Yarmouth and then to the home of Victor Eagerly, the vicar's brother, in Harley Street. Mr Talbot's lawyer had seen to the settlement of five thousand pounds on Rose, to be paid over to her husband on their wedding day. As a further downpayment of goodwill, Mr Talbot was to supply a new pumping engine to Ellingbeck, the first that would emerge from his newly acquired foundry in Leeds, built to the plans Stephen had devised.

Mr Talbot returned to London the day after the dinner, taking Arthur with him, and Mr Somersall departed the day after that, in company with his son. They were to visit every colliery, factory and dock in which Mr Somersall had an involvement, to see if Herbert could not find some aspect of it in which he could interest himself. In truth, no one held high expectations for the scheme, but Mr Somersall was not a man to back out of a bargain once he had made it, and it may be that he had begun to see his son through new eyes. There is nothing quite like someone else recognising the value of a thing we have taken for granted, for making us see it in a new light.

Stephen was to go to Leeds to oversee the initial construction of the engine, but he would not remain in Mr Somersall's employment long enough to see it installed. He travelled back from Leeds every Saturday so as to spend time with Beth.

She expected him to speak, but he kept his counsel, and she was glad of it for she still did not know how she would answer his proposal.

Somersall Grange was quiet with just the two ladies within it, but they fell into an easy routine and Beth was glad to see Mrs Somersall's equilibrium stabilize itself after the departure of her husband. Mrs Somersall demanded little of Beth—just her company, and a listening ear when she spoke of her happy days at Ferret Street, and of Ida Plim. There were several hours each day when Beth was at liberty, and she spent them in long invigorating walks across the moors, revisiting old memories of time spent exploring with her brother. She found her feet could follow the old pathways almost of their own volition—that rocks and the occasional tortured tree, rivulets, crags and the wild acres of tor had changed little—and that when she was amongst them the sense of dislocation that had always troubled her seemed less.

October was a benign month with bright frosty mornings and star-strewn nights, the dazzling splashes of colour of the russet bracken and ginger hued grasses set off against the celery-pale turf and the sage-grey of the scrub.

She saw Frank—but infrequently—once or twice in Brayton and on another occasion wandering—as she was—across the moor. He was uncommunicative—almost resentful—and told her when she enquired about the gatehouse and Tall Chimneys that she was not needed at either place. She should take whatever chance was offered to her, he said. He would not stand in her way.

Eistir had taken on the care of both properties. She called every day to make things tidy and prepare food that would be ready for Frank when he returned at the end of the day. She did the work at the big house that Beth had done, but without the love Beth had put into it. Eistir worked for the pay that Arthur had left with her.

It was sorely needed. The woebegone camp remained at the standing stone, its inhabitants eking out what money they could from the occasional fortune-telling in the market place and the music of Tadhg's harp. Mr Slade had not returned to Yorkshire, so his nocturnal business had not been resumed and work at his farm was at a standstill. Fortunately, Lorcán had been retained to tend the horses and to keep a night watch.

He slept in the stables and usually took Dónall with him in case of trouble, their accommodations amongst the drowsing horses probably more comfortable than the camp's drays, whose canvasses were no protection from the freezing nighttime temperatures. It did not rain, but there was illness amongst the children, and Tadhg had an infection on his chest that no amount of embrocation could shift. Ned Widderington refused the Irishmen permission to play at the Plough or even to enter it, and Mrs Golightly would extend no credit in the shop. The entire group was shunned by the villagers, if they were not pelted with manure, and on some nights the camp was visited by drunken locals intent on mischief.

Of Ruairi Connolly nothing had been heard, and it felt to everyone that upon his return hinged the fate of them all.

Aoife insisted upon it. Until Ruairi came, she would not tell her secret. In the meantime she continued as before, visiting her husband at night when Dónall was at Clough Farm and pestering Frank to allow them to move into the big house. She hid her swelling body beneath shawls and other draperies, and the rest of the camp was in conspiracy to allay any suspicions that might have arisen in Dónall's mind.

On other matters they were at variance. Cillian wanted to move on. Though they could not now hope to get work picking fruit, rural areas down country had not been so badly affected by the August and September rains. There would be ploughing and planting work, and then livestock to be husbanded through the winter months. Before long there would be lambing. All this, he argued, was available to them if they would only move on to where they were not known and might make a fresh start. Brónach, of course, would do as he directed, and Conn was now used to hard labour and would make himself useful in any work his father might find. But Father Fearghal was for remaining until Ruairi returned, and so was Tadhg. Eistir wished to stay and Elíse would not go without her. Cormac vacillated this way and that between the two factions. They lacked the leadership that Ruairi had always provided and without him were like lost lambs.

It was three months since Beth had seen Ruairi, and she told herself that she had put him out of her mind. But she lied. He haunted her dreams and, try as she might, she could not prevent herself from comparing Stephen Milton to him. It looked as though her own fate also depended upon Ruairi's return.

The second Friday in November marked the termination of Stephen Milton's employment with Mr Somersall, and Stephen returned to Somersall Grange for the last time.

'I am to continue working on the new engine at Mr Talbot's expense,' he told Beth, 'until the end of the month. But then I am wanted in London. There is much I must be shown and told before I go to America.'

'You will not return here then?'

They were standing on the terrace watching the sun slip over the rim of the moor. For a few moments it seemed as though the whole heath was ablaze, the air lit up in iridescent flames of purple and orange, the land glowing like embers. The couple's shadows on the house behind them were grotesquely enlarged, their own faces made almost lurid in the sunset light, but when Beth looked up at Stephen she saw his eyes were fixed on her, and not on the spectacle before them. His eyes burned intensely, and a muscle in his jaw twitched.

'I cannot trespass on Mrs Somersall's hospitality further,' he said. 'But make no mistake, I shall come back, Beth, the moment that you write to me and say that you are ready to come away.'

He slid her hand from her muff, and pressed it to his lips. 'You know that I love you,' he said. 'I will cross oceans and deserts and every mountain range when you can tell me that you love me too.'

Beth swallowed and wetted her lips. She said, 'Stephen,' in a voice that did not sound like her own.

But he forestalled her. 'Do not say it now,' he said. 'Not if you are not ready. And you are *not* ready. I know that. The Irishman planted a seed in your heart before I could harvest that heart for myself. You must see what fruit that seed will yield before you can give yourself entirely to me. But if—when—you are ready, you know you must come away from this ... from Yorkshire, I mean. I do not know where our future will take us, but you must understand that it will not be here. I will require a great sacrifice of you, Beth. I do not know if you will ever see your brother Frank or your old home again.'

'I do understand that,' she said in a small voice.

Standing as close to him as she was, she could feel the heat that came out of him—not so much a tangible heat, but the radiation of his passion for her. He almost simmered with it, and she looked up at his face and felt its warmth pouring over and into her. Suddenly she wanted it to ignite her, to be lit up like a furnace—as she had been that day in the summer, when she happened upon Ruairi Connolly stripped to the waist in the yard, and which had briefly flared and almost consumed her on the day she had discovered the robbery. Oh! Why must it always be Ruairi who was the benchmark? Why could she not feel for Stephen as she had felt for Ruairi? She wanted to love Stephen—really, she did.

She threw her arms around his neck and pressed her lips to his. He responded, crushing her body against himself, wrapping his arms around her then snaking a hand to her head, pulling the pins from her hair until it tumbled over her shoulders. His kiss was not as Ruairi's had been—not proficient and adept. It was hard and deep. She liked the pain of it. Wanted more. Much more.

The sun slipped below the horizon and the conflagration on the moor was extinguished, but the inferno between Beth and Stephen only intensified. Burn me! Burn me! Render me to cinders, if only the flames will ignite my heart as well as my body and kill the seed that Ruairi planted. But Stephen pulled away from her, white-faced and panting, and the seed was not cauterised.

The following day he departed Somersall Grange, and the clear blue sky was shrouded by a curtain of cloud.

Chapter 46

One evening about two weeks after Stephen's departure, the ladies sat in Mrs Somersall's small sitting room. They had dined early in the breakfast room, as was their habit when there were no gentlemen in the house and, not liking to trouble the servants, they repaired to this small chamber where there was a spirit stove and a tea caddy. They had got used to preparing their own evening tea and, since neither really required it, dispensed with the services of a maid for undressing.

'We might as well live here all alone,' said Mrs Somersall. 'I am sure I would not mind it. I do not know how the servants occupy themselves.'

Beth knew—but would not say—that in Mr Somersall's absence they spent their time lounging by the fire in the servants' hall. Most of the rooms in the house had been closed up, the furniture and chandeliers covered over, so in truth there was not much to occupy the half-dozen footmen or sundry maids. In many ways it reminded Beth of Tall Chimneys and the shrunken-down existence that Miss Jocelyn had introduced there in the days of her exile. There was no question of establishing *here* that parity between the classes that she had instituted, however. The servants here did not love their mistress, but played upon her insecurities and inexperience. Even the housekeeper, who Mrs Somersall would have named amongst her dearest friends, gossiped behind her mistress's back and mimicked Mrs Somersall's manner of speech.

There had been snow, and quite a lot of it, in the past week; a raging blizzard had shut out the moor and the trees and even the far side of the sweep as though a grey curtain had been drawn around the place. The wind tore around the house and down the chimneys, and sometimes the fire hissed as stray flakes found their way down the flue. Mrs Somersall had been alarmed at first, concerned as to how supplies could be got in or how she might get out to church. Beth had reassured her. The pantries were very well stocked, and no one would expect her to go out in such a storm to attend Sunday service. They would be quite safe and comfortable until the storm subsided. Once the roads were clear, they might consider a remove to the town house if Mrs Somersall wished for wider society, but until that time there was no cause for alarm.

The clocks in the house had just struck nine, and Mrs Somersall was beginning to yawn.

'Why do you not go to bed, ma'am,' said Beth. 'I will see that the men have locked up below, and then retire myself. I think the storm is subsiding. The wind will not be so troublesome tonight.'

She peered through the curtains. The night was intensely dark, the falling snow beyond the pane a miasma of flakes that whirled and eddied in crazy patterns, but they did not hit the window as they had done for the past few days and nights. The air was calmer. 'I think that tomorrow it will be over.'

Mrs Somersall took herself to her rest, and Beth banked up the fire and blew out the candles before taking her own light and, holding it high, descended the stairs. The house was in darkness apart from a single lamp left burning on a side table in the hall, but there was no one on duty there. When Beth opened the baize door that separated the servants' quarters from the rest of the house, all was quiet. She saw that the bolt was shot firmly home on the great door and had set out to the library to find a book when there came a sudden and loud hammering from without.

She turned, the flame of her candle wavering wildly and a splash of hot wax burning her hand. She waited. Surely one of the footmen would come. But there was no sound of movement from the servants' stair and she retraced her steps to the wide empty hall.

The knock came again, urgent, the sound of a strong insistent fist.

She called out, 'Who's there? The house is abed. What is your business?'

A muffled reply came back. 'Betsey? Is that you? Oh, thank God. It is Ruairi. Let me in, for the love of God.'

She put her candle down and reached up to the bolt. It was stiff and heavy; she needed two hands to work it loose, but at last it slid clear and she turned the handle of the great door.

Ruairi fell into the hall, bringing with him a flurry of wet snow and an icy blast of wind that knifed through her dress and shawl and thin indoor slippers. His coat was wet through, a layer of frozen snow crusting his back and shoulders, and even his eyelashes were coated with icy crystals. She pushed the door closed and then fell to her knees where he lay prone, panting heavily. His hair was all tumbled and shining with wetness but he laughed up at her through it with the wide easy smile she remembered so well.

She began to unbutton his coat. 'You're frozen,' she said. 'We must get you out of these wet things.'

'Hold up, Betsey,' he said, fending her off. 'I'm delighted to know you've missed me, and I promise that I'm as eager as you are to have fewer layers between us, but my journey is not done. I must go back, and you must come with me.'

She sat back, astonished. 'Go back? What? Out *there?*'

'Oh yes. It's your brother, Betsey. He's … he's in a bad way.' Ruairi got up and brushed the snow from his clothing. He was unshaven, and now she saw him closely, thin to the point of gauntness.

'You've been unwell,' she said, reaching an unconscious hand up to his face and placing it on his cheek. 'Where have you been? What has happened to you? Did you find Fionn? I know it was he who stole the things.'

'I've much to tell you,' he said, putting his own hand over hers and looking at her with his beautiful blue eyes. 'But there is time for all of that. Get some warm clothes on, and stout boots if you have them. A cloak and a hat of some kind. The weather is fierce.'

She stared up at him. 'Must we really go? Is Frank in danger?' She feared another emotional collapse. Perhaps there had been a row with Aoife. But neither circumstance seemed so pressing as to necessitate a trek across the moor in a blizzard.

'He is, Betsey. I'm sorry. He needs you. Do you think I would put you to the ordeal if it were not vital?'

'I suppose not.' Beth considered. 'How have you come? I can awaken the men, the grooms. Mrs Somersall will not begrudge me the carriage, and then it can be sent for the doctor—'

'No, Betsey. I have the trap outside and the pony is steady. She got me here and I am sure she can get us back again. It will be better if we do not … if we do not spread abroad what has occurred. Not yet, at least.'

'But what *has* occurred?' Beth cried. It was cold in the hallway, and she had begun to tremble.

Ruairi sighed. 'It is Dónall. We told him at last, about Aoife and your brother. He seemed to take it quite well. There were tears, of course, and he was angry. But that subsided and we thought it safe. He went with Lorcán to the night watch like a lamb. But in the morning he was nowhere to be found, and when Eistir went to the gatehouse she found Frank.' Ruairi winced in remembrance of it. 'He is in a bad way, Betsey. And he has asked for you to be brought for the nursing.'

'You have not summoned the doctor?'

His gaze slid away from hers and fixed itself on a gloomy corner of the hall where a marble bust stared blindly onto the scene. 'We did not know what to do. Dónall has gone to ground. But feeling in the village is so against us …' his eyes sought hers once more, and she saw there the agony he suffered. 'They'll lynch him, Betsey. *You* know how Dónall is, but the villagers do not. He will not have understood the consequences. He is a child and he lost his temper.'

'He is not a child,' replied Beth stonily. 'He is treated like a child. There's a difference.' She took a deep breath and attempted to summon reason, some plan of action. She would not wake Mrs Somersall but she would leave a note to explain her absence. She must change her clothes and gather some belongings. In the stillroom, she knew, there were tinctures and salves that might be useful.

Ruairi waited, dripping onto the polished floor of the hallway.

'Very well,' said Beth at last. 'Wait here.'

The storm had lessened somewhat but still blew fiercely across the moor as the dogged little pony pulled the trap down the drive and out onto the Brayton road. A closed lantern provided the only light, feeble against the pressing grey of snow and the all-encompassing darkness of the night. Beth and Ruairi sat close together, huddled beneath a rough oiled cloth that smelled of horses but that protected them from the worst of the biting wind and saturating sleet. At her feet was her hastily packed portmanteau and a hamper of things she had collected from the stillroom and pantries. At the last minute she added a bottle of brandy, half full, that had been left on the sideboard in the servants' hall, and another of port wine she had found in the kitchen—used, probably, for the embellishment of some sauce or other, if not for the fortification of the cook.

It was only possible to discern the roadway from the snow-clad brackens and bushes that lay either side of it. The tracks of Ruairi's coming were already covered over with fresh snow. Ruairi kept the horse to the centre, lest she stray into the drainage ditches that were either side of the track. Their progress was slow, just a walking pace. Conversation was impossible. The wind buffeted and bounced sound around, snatching words from lips and tossing them into the maelstrom. The pony shook her head and whinnied and stamped her feet.

'The snow stings her eyes,' shouted Ruairi. He descended and covered her face with a piece of sacking and led her by the bridle, hunching his shoulders into the wind and forging a path through the drifts with his feet.

Betsey huddled beneath the covering and missed the warmth of Ruairi beside her. It occurred to her that now Ruairi had come, all that had waited for him would be resolved, but it was a distracted musing, as one notices the brief flash of a kingfisher's wing, gone before it can really be acknowledged. Her thoughts were of Frank. Poor Frank. He would not have defended himself against Dónall, and he had not the quickness of speech to talk himself out of a tight corner, even if Dónall could have been diverted from his course.

The road took them into a wooded grove that was more sheltered. The snow was less deep, but the wind howled through it like a banshee. The noise unsettled the pony again, and Ruairi climbed up beside Beth and urged it to a trot for a mile or so.

Beth shouted, 'Frank's injuries. What is the nature of them?'

But Ruairi only shook his head and indicated by a hand to his ear that he could not hear what she said; and so they went on, pressed together, through the storm.

It might be that Beth slept or dozed. She had a drifting sensation that was disorientating. Her limbs felt heavy and cold, almost numb, and she was aware of being swayed this way and that, as though on board a ship. When she came to wakefulness she saw the huddled houses of Moorside either side of the lane. Home! She was overwhelmed with nostalgia for the place and its familiar faces. It had stopped snowing and she could see, high above her, a peppering of stars in a velvet sky. The wind had dropped, and beyond the steady thud of the pony's hooves she could hear the shift and whisper of the snow as it settled. No light shone in any window. It was the dead of night; just then the church clock tolled one.

'We are home,' she said, looking dazedly about her.

'*You* are home,' Ruairi said gloomily. 'We will not be able to stay now. I must find Dónall and we must leave. Here is the turn to the gatehouse. You will see the light in the window. Eistir is watching over Frank until you come.'

Beth shifted in her seat. 'Is Aoife not with him? There can be no reason, now, for her to pretend indifference.'

'She has not the skill for the sickroom,' said Ruairi.

'I am beginning to think she does not love him at all. You know she carries his child?'

He hesitated for a fraction of a second before replying heavily, 'I do. It will make things more difficult.'

'If she wants to live at the big house I do not suppose Mr Talbot would object, so long as she keeps to the servants' quarters,' said Beth. 'There is a nice suite of rooms that Mrs Orphan used to use. Or there is space above the gunroom where a couple might live very comfortably. It was intended for the estate manager, should one ever be employed. Frank should allow it if it makes her happy and smooths out these furrows between them.'

'You have given this some thought.'

'I have. I used to think about what would happen if Frank were ever to marry. It did not occur to me that his wife would prefer the big house. I did not mind the idea of living there alone. I have a sort of affinity with the place. But since Fionn stole the things, I have felt myself disqualified to live there, though Mr Talbot does not blame me. There is the gatehouse. I can see the light.'

'He should not blame you. 'Twas all Fionn's mischief.'

'Did you find him?' Beth began to gather her belongings. Her fingers were numb and she could not grasp the handle of her portmanteau.

Ruairi frowned. 'I did. But he had sold all the spoils and lost at gambling all he took from us. I exacted my revenge and was convicted of affray. I've been in gaol these two months. Mícheál will carry your things, Betsey. You go inside and I will see to the horse. Then I will return to see how Frank does. I must prepare you though, Betsey. He is gravely injured. Your neat solution for Aoife going forward … she might be a widow before daybreak.'

The trap reached the gatehouse. Beth saw Mícheál waiting in the lee of the building, ready to help her inside. Ruairi waited for his words to penetrate Beth's understanding.

A widow! She had not imagined such an extremity! Cuts, bruising, perhaps even broken bones she had contemplated, but not that Frank's very life could be in danger.

Ruairi jumped down and reached out to lift her from the seat. She felt his hands on her waist and then she was in his arms, cradled against the warmth of his chest. She breathed in, one huge shuddering gasp as though she could inhale his essence and transport herself to some other place, where Frank was not at death's door but well and happy, and she and Ruairi could ... but the vision would not coalesce. She couldn't believe in it. She stepped gently from his embrace.

'I must go to Frank,' she said.

Chapter 47

The lamp in the window was the only illumination in the room. The fire had burned low and emitted only a reddish glow.

As Beth entered, Eistir rose from where she had been sitting at the table.

'You are come. Thank God,' she said.

Beth looked at the place by the hearth where Frank's mattress would normally lie, but the place was empty.

She said, 'Am I too late?'

'Ah no. He is upstairs. We thought it best to get him up there.'

'Out of the way, do you mean? Out of sight?' Beth felt bitter. It was only now beginning to dawn on her that Frank had been assaulted, beaten almost to death, and the Irish folk were eager to sweep the whole thing under the carpet to protect one of their own. What about her? Frank was one of *her* own.

But Eister perhaps did not comprehend Beth's implication. She said, 'Yes. There is no knowing how long he will be ill. We thought you would not want him …' she pointed at the rug, '…under your feet.'

Beth began to remove her cloak and outer coverings, going to hang them by habit on the hook behind the door but finding Eistir's shawl there.

Eistir moved to the hearth and swung the kettle over the coals. 'You must be perished,' she said. 'I will make you some tea, and then I will get out of your way.'

Beth was smitten with remorse. 'Thank you,' she said. 'You have been taking care of Frank.' She looked around the room. All the dirt and chaos that had been there on her last visit was gone. The place was clean, tidy. She saw a loaf and a crock of cheese on a shelf, and a pot of what she took to be soup keeping warm on the hearth. 'But Ruairí and Mícheál have taken the trap away,' she said. 'Ruairí said he would come back. You must wait. You must not cross the moor alone.'

'That's alright,' said Eistir. 'I shall not be alone.' She held out her hand and the dog, which Beth had not seen beneath the table, came and nuzzled it.

'Ah!' Beth said. 'I see you have a new mistress.' The dog wagged its tail, but made no move towards her.

Beth took a deep breath. 'I will go up and see Frank.'

Her old room was almost exactly as she had left it. She saw no evidence that Aoife had adopted it, or that it had ever been used by Frank and Aoife together. Frank had protected it, just as he had tried to protect Tall Chimneys from his wife's usurpation.

She placed the candle that she had lit below onto a side table. She could not say the same for Frank. No one had protected him and he was not at all the same. He was changed beyond recognition. If she had not been told that the body in her bed was her brother, she might not have believed it.

He lay on his back with his hands outside the coverlet, folded neatly one over the other as though laid out in preparation for burial. This in itself had never been Frank's way. He had always been a restless sleeper, the covers twisted and tangled before the candle had been out an hour. One arm was bandaged, the other showed stripes where some hard instrument had been violently laid again and again but his hands were uninjured; he had landed not a single blow.

His face was bruised and swollen to twice its normal size, one eye pulpy, crusted with blood and inflamed, the flesh such a dark purple as to be almost black. The bruise spread across his temple and disappeared into his hair, which was matted, stuck down to his skull. The ear on that side was all misshapen, like the ear of a prize-fighter, and that too had a black crust of dried blood on it. His jaw was misaligned and his lips were split but Beth bent over and gently kissed them.

He did not sleep peacefully. His breathing came in ragged shudders, wheezing from between his torn lips, and at each breath his face creased in pain and a little whimper sounded in his throat.

Gingerly she drew back the sheet. His whole upper body—chest and ribcage, shoulders and stomach—was bluish-black where he had taken blows. She could see no cuts but that did not mean he was not bleeding inside. Beth had a sketchy idea of the arrangement of the organs—the liver and kidneys were both in that vicinity. He ought to have the doctor, she was sure of it, although she did not know what could be done.

Eistir came upstairs and put a cup of tea on the table. 'His arm was broken,' she said, speaking very softly. 'Father Fearghal set it. He knows how. The bruising is very bad. We think that several ribs will be broken. I wanted to strap them, but Fearghal said not to. Frank is a strong man. He is well-muscled. That should have protected the inner workings. But ...' she paused and cast an anxious glance at Beth. '... his mind,' she got out at last. 'He has been mainly unconscious, but when he comes to a little, he seems not to know where he is, or *who* he is. He did not know Aoife.'

'Aoife should be here,' said Beth.

'Yes. She should.' Eistir put her lips in a hard line. 'I must not speak ill of her,' she said, 'but I will say plainly that I do not like her. Before Elíse's husband died, Aoife was ... too familiar with him. He was a handsome man. And then ... there was Mr Slade. She set her sights upon him too.'

'He is so ugly,' mused Beth, 'but I suppose he is rich.'

'He *is*,' said Eistir, handing Beth the tea. 'Drink this while it is hot. But Mr Slade has only a farmhouse. Not a grand country house such as noble people possess.'

The two women looked at each other in understanding.

'You have become fond of my brother, perhaps, in the time you have been taking care of him,' suggested Beth.

'Oh. Yes, but ...' Eistir faltered, and her gaze slid away. 'You mistake ... he is a good man but ... what I mean is, he is too good for *her*.' She pulled the sheet back over Frank's poor ravaged body and smoothed his hair over his brow. 'We gave him whisky at first, for the arm-setting,' she said. 'But now I dribble willow bark tea into his mouth every couple of hours. Really, he needs laudanum, but that can only be got from the apothecary, and he would ask why it is wanted. We could try a poultice for the chest, but I do not know the receipt.'

'I think I can remember it,' said Beth. 'I brought some things from the Grange.' Suddenly she was overwhelmed with emotion—shock and fatigue and anxiety and desperate sadness. She caught hold of Eistir's hand. 'Thank you,' she said, tears running down her face. 'Thank you, Eistir. Frank and I, we need a friend like you.'

'And Ruairi,' said Eistir, returning the pressure of Beth's hand. 'I do not know any other man who would have set out as he did to fetch you in such conditions. He is torn, because of course Dónall will be tried and convicted if he is found. Assuming you …' but she let this proviso go. 'Cillian and Cormac are set to depart as soon as the snow allows, and they urged us all to do the same. Fionn's betrayal was bad enough, but *this* … the villagers will set upon us when they know of it, for sure. *If* they do. But Ruairi would not budge. He will not, I think, until it is known that Frank is out of danger.'

Beth sniffed and wiped her eyes with her sleeve. 'No,' she said. 'He wants to find Dónall and leave.' She looked back down at her brother. 'I would feel happier if the doctor was brought,' she said.

'That's up to you. But he will ask questions.'

A spout of anger flared. 'And is Frank to die so that Dónall may go free?'

Eistir made no reply, but looked from Frank to Beth and back again, and the anger was quenched.

'Yes,' Beth said. 'I know. It is what Frank would choose.'

A few minutes later Beth watched from the window of the upper room as Eistir and the dog set out from the gatehouse, following the lane for a few dozen yards and then striking out across the snowbound moor. The sky was without moon, very dark, and yet the night itself was not dark but numinous with the crystalline light that exuded from the snow. The whole expanse of the moor glowed bluish white, as though from some inner fire. And Beth saw how big it was, and how small were the retreating figures of Eistir and the dog in comparison. She allowed her gaze to travel the route that Eistir would take to the camp. The standing stone stood stark and very black against the winter landscape. The drays were no more than dirty smudges on the whiteness. For the first time it occurred to Beth how miserably they must have fared in the storm of the past days. They had been so exposed, without shelter from the raging wind and sheeting snow. It was a miracle that those rickety wagons had survived at all.

She could see no glow of fire. How did they cook or wash without their fire? The poor children! Had no single villager taken pity on them? Her earlier affection for Moorside curdled in her gorge. How cruel and heartless they must all be, to have left the Irish people to endure such a storm as the one that had just visited.

Beth turned from the window and leaned over Frank to stroke his brow. 'I am going downstairs to make a poultice for your poor chest.'

Frank made a grimacing expression with his face, and a congested gargle burbled from his throat.

Beth said, 'Shhh. Do not worry. I am here.'

Frank lay unconscious for three days, during which time Beth, Eistir and Ruairi took turns to sit beside him, dribble willow bark tea into his mouth and change the evil-smelling poultice which Beth had applied to his chest. Periodically they brought warm water to wash him, turning his body and pummelling his back to loosen the phlegm that rattled his breathing, though this was clearly agony. When it was evident that the willow bark was insufficient, they gave him doses of the brandy that Beth had brought.

On the second day Dónall returned to the camp frozen, starved and weeping great heaving sobs on Ruairi's shoulder, but he refused to look at Aoife when she approached him and would have lashed out at her had Ruairi not kept a firm hold upon him.

Ruairi hurried Dónall into the flimsy shelter of his dray, wary lest any passing villager should see the boy. He watched Dónall shovel a plateful of thin stew into his mouth.

'Where have you been, Dónall?' he asked when the plate was empty.

Dónall held out the plate for more, but Ruairi shook his head. 'There is no more. That was your share, and more than you deserve. Where have you been?'

Dónall blinked and wiped his nose with his sleeve. 'In the woods,' he mumbled. 'But there were banshees[xxxiv] and sluaghs[xxxv] ... I was afraid.' He began to snivel.

'Ah, Dónall,' said Ruairi, tucking Dónall into the strew of blankets that served as his bed. 'They are just stories told to frighten children.'

Dónall shook his head. 'N ... no. They were real. Frank must have ... when we were there before ... Frank must have kept them away. Is he dead? Did I kill him?'

'No, Dónall. Frank is not dead. But he is badly hurt.'

Dónall's head drooped. 'I am sorry for it,' he said.

'I know. He knows it too. Sleep now, and do not be troubled. But tomorrow, we must speak man-to-man. Do you understand?'

Dónall nodded and yawned widely before laying his head on the thin pillow.

Ruairi looked down at him for a few moments. 'Dónall,' he said quietly, 'would you like to go home?'

Dónall opened his eyes. 'Home?'

'Yes, to Ireland.'

'I don't know.' Dónall frowned. 'I was hungry there.'

'And here too, from time to time. But better hungry at home than …
but we will talk of it tomorrow.'

The next day Beth sat alone in the upper room of the gatehouse. Her
hands were empty of work, her thoughts lost in the maelstrom that caught
her up with increasing frequency in these days, tossing and turning her
about in the conundrum of her future. She had received a note from Mrs
Somersall, full of compassion and understanding and yet also betraying a
powerful loneliness. The snow still lay thick, she said, and yet not so thick
that she did not contemplate a remove to the town house. Mrs Max, the
formidable cook, was a demerit to the scheme, but she hoped that Beth
would soon join her there.

Beth had sent no reply beyond the verbal gratitude entrusted to the
groom who had delivered the note along with sundry medicinal items that
Mrs Somersall hoped would be efficacious. Beth knew that she would
have to give up her position. How could she leave Frank in the foreseeable
future, even supposing he survived? Of Stephen Milton she thought a
great deal, especially of his heartbreak; and of the chance of a wider
experience of life he had offered she also thought with a strong degree of
regret because that now seemed an impossibility. Of Ruairi Connolly she
did not dare think at all. The spark between them had zinged and sizzled
in the hours they had spent in tending Frank. She would look up to find
his eyes upon her. The brush of his hand as he passed her a cloth or helped
her support Frank's limp, unresisting body had singed like the hot iron.
But how could she think of him? He would soon be gone.

Her thoughts were interrupted by a low moan and a wheezing cough
from the bed. She rose and leaned over the patient. His good eye looked
back at her, clouded but lucid.

'Beth,' he croaked, groping across the covers for her hand.

'Yes, Frank. It is me. Are you well? Have you pain? Oh, Frank, I have
feared for you.' She threw herself onto her knees and pulled his hand to
her mouth, kissing the knuckles and wetting them with her tears. 'I am
sorry I left you alone,' she wept. 'I am sorry, Frank.'

He raised his other hand, but with difficulty because of the strapping
around it. 'Hush, girl,' he said. 'Is there water?'

'Oh yes!' She was up immediately, and poured him water from a jug
on the table, holding the cup to his lips while he drank. After a few
swallows he turned his head away. 'Where is Aoife?' he asked, swivelling
his good eye to look into the corners of the room.

'She … she has not been here,' Beth admitted, replacing the cup.
'Eistir and Ruairi and me, we have taken turns—'

'But she has not?'

'N … no. I am sorry. Are you hungry? There is soup.'

But he shook his head, and a tear oozed from the corner of his eye and ran down his temple.

Beth took hold of his hand again. 'Frank. What do you remember? It was Dónall, wasn't it? Who hurt you? We have not told anyone what occurred. Even the doctor has not been summoned because, you see—'

Frank nodded. 'I understand,' he said hoarsely.

'I wanted to send for him but Eistir thought—and I saw she was right—that you would not wish to accuse the boy.'

Frank gave a shuddering spasm, winced, but bent his swollen lips into a smile. 'That is no boy!'

'No. Of course. It must have been like being trampled by a bull. And you did not retaliate, I know. But Frank, I think in his mind he is just a child. He has only a child's understanding.'

'We knew, as children, what was right and wrong,' said Frank, but then he softened. 'I am sore disappointed in him, Betsey. I thought we were becoming friends. What would you have me do?'

'I would have you do what you think best. If you want him punished, then the constable will be called and you shall tell him everything. But I did not want to make that decision for you.'

He nodded stiffly. 'Betsey,' he said presently, 'are you to marry that engineer?'

She shook her head. 'I have made no promise. I will go nowhere until you are well, and even then … we might both have to find a new place. Mr Talbot spoke of selling Tall Chimneys; but he has other properties, and our brother is to buy a house in the country …'

Frank lifted his hand and tucked away a stray lock of her hair. He said, 'All will be well, Betsey, now that you are home.'

When Eistir came in Frank slept again, but Beth told her that his mind was restored.

'And what does he intend to do, about Dónall? He is back, much chastened. Ruairí proposes to give the lad a beating if it will satisfy.'

Beth shook her head. 'Frank would not have that done in his name. He understands the situation. He is thinking on it.'

But that evening Frank became feverish, soaking his sheets with sweat and calling in a voice that was ragged and barely recognisable for Beth, and then for Aoife, and then for his mother. They laid cool cloths on his forehead but he tore them away, and would have risen from his bed had not Ruairí held him down.

'He will injure himself further,' said the Irishman grimly. 'If necessary we must tie him to the bed.'

The episodes of fever were interspersed with periods when Frank lay deathly still and only the stertorous rasping of his laboured breaths showed that he lived. Then, in the dead of the night, he reared up and fixed Beth with an eye that was bloodshot but rational. 'I must kill the sow,' he said to her through parched lips. 'That sow, she will be the death of me. Do you understand, Betsey? She is vicious … violent …' His hand clasped the neck of her frock tightly but then relaxed, and he sank back down into the depth of his malaise.

She said, 'Yes Frank, I understand,' though he was beyond hearing, and she hurried down to where Ruairi dozed on the rug before the fire.

'You must fetch the doctor,' she said urgently, shaking him awake. 'We will say that Frank was attacked by the sow. She is easily capable of inflicting such injuries as he has sustained. We need not mention Dónall at all.'

Ruairi rose at once and began to pull on his boots. 'He's a diamond, that brother of yours,' he said, grinning. 'My sister is lucky to have him.'

'I wish I could say that she is an equal blessing,' said Beth, setting her mouth in a hard line. 'But she has been an indifferent wife to him so far.' She passed Ruairi his coat and hat. 'I hope motherhood will settle her. When is the baby due? April, I suppose. Or May?'

'Ah! Do not chide her too severely, Betsey,' said Ruairi, looking down at her with rueful eyes. 'She has had her woes to bear. It is hard for her to trust men. She has been treated so vilely by them.'

'Frank has never treated her ill,' said Beth. 'It is hard on him to be punished for the sins of others. But go now, and bring the doctor as fast as may be. Frank's fever must be broken, and its cause identified. He is beyond my aid.'

The doctor came and examined Frank, declaring several ribs broken, the arm adequately set, the sight in the injured eye almost certainly lost, the eardrum torn and the fever a result of a swollen brain or internal injuries, neither of which could be remedied other than by time and prayer.

He looked askance at the explanation supplied. 'I would expect to see the imprint of the animal's trotters, and lacerations from its teeth,' he said, looking over Frank's body, which was now an appalling shade of greenish heliotrope.

Beth busied herself with folding cloths, turning from the doctor so that he would not see the guilty blush on her cheek, but Ruairi said, 'I thought so myself, doctor, but we peeled a good quantity of thick layers of clothing off him when we found him. *They* were torn about well enough. We burned them—the stench you know! But I vouchsafe they saved Frank's life, so they did.'

Beth swallowed down her shock at the easy facility of the lie in Ruairi's mouth.

'Hum. Well,' said the doctor doubtfully as he considered, and Beth held her breath. But then he said, 'I will bleed him, and leave you some laudanum. I will show you the dose. Keep him cool and give him as much water as he will take. I will call again tomorrow.'

Under the doctor's care, Frank began to improve. His fever abated, and by the sixth day he was able to drink a little soup, though his teeth were too spongey to manage bread. He slept a great deal, but even when awake he spoke little, spending his waking hours staring at the ceiling. The swelling around his face began to subside and the eye on the damaged side became visible, but Frank said he could see nothing but blur and shadows out of it, and complained of a ringing in the injured ear.

Chapter 48

November ebbed into December and the temperature rose. The hard packed snow began to melt into greyish slush. Damp and drizzle alternated. The days were grey and colourless beneath low glowering cloud, the nights bleak and moonless.

Cillian began to pack up his dray and to negotiate which of the ponies and goats he would take with him. Cormac and Caitlin had decided to leave too. 'We should all go while the going is good,' said Caitlin, folding blankets and picking out her own cooking utensils from the communal hoard. 'There is nothing for us here but trouble and more trouble. The boy must be got away at all costs. It will not be long before the truth gets out about what has occurred, and then I will not answer for what the locals will do. A lynching mob, if I know it.' She cast a dark eye around the camp. 'Someone here has loose lips. Gossip is rife in the village.'

The group shifted uneasily, but no one met her eye.

The turf around the standing stone was poached, oozing with water, and from everywhere came dripping and splashing as little rivulets opened up beneath the immigrants' feet. Their clothes were larded with mud, skirts soaking and shoes half-rotted away. Only Aoife was clean, owing to the fact that she remained in her *vardo* for much of the time, keeping its little stove alight but inviting none to share the warmth, not even Tadhg—whose chest was still very congested—or the smallest children. The *vardo* itself was axle-deep in sucking mire. The other drays had been lifted clear by stones, but no one had troubled themselves to dig out the *vardo*.

Regarding it now Cormac said, 'I'll buy your *vardo*, Aoife, if you'll trust me to send funds when we get them. 'Twill be no use to you now, and Caitlin has always coveted it.'

Aoife said, 'I might come with you, yet. If Frank is a cripple he will be no good to me.' She tossed her hair, which was knotted and dull.

'You'll make your way alone then, for I'll have none of you,' said Cormac, turning on his heel and sloughing across the muddy paddock.

Later, with the children fed and put into their damp and mildewed beds, conversation around the fire was all of the future—what route they might take to the south, the type and likely remuneration of any work. They debated over the division of the few coins they had accumulated since Fionn had debunked. Lorcán had earned most of them and as he was determined to stay on he claimed possession of them, but he was blamed for Fionn's betrayal because it had been Lorcán who had first introduced Fionn into their company.

'We should not make any decisions until we are all present,' said Caitlin. 'Ruairi and Eistir are at the gatehouse.'

'I can speak for Eistir,' said Elíse. 'And we know Ruairi's opinion: he always said that we would share equally. I have earned little in the way of coin, but I have cooked and mended. Eistir has brought food from the gatehouse of late. Without her, we would have starved.'

'We would not have starved,' said Brónach sharply. 'My Conn has brought rabbits and even pheasant.'

'Not since the snow came,' Caitlin pointed out. 'But look, if we all leave here there need be no debate about the money, or anything else.' She looked around the circle. 'Who will join us?'

There was a pause. Father Fearghal took a swig of some evil poteen he had made in a still secreted somewhere on the moor. 'Aoife must remain,' he said, wiping his lips with his sleeve. 'She is married.'

'I will do as I please,' said Aoife archly. 'I am no more married than you are, Fearghal, and you know it.'

'I spoke the words,' said Fearghal angrily, 'and you repeated them.'

'And we neither of us believed them,' Aoife sneered.

'*He* did.'

'Who? God?'

'Your husband. He married you in good faith.'

'More fool him!'

'What about your baby, Aoife?' said Brónach. 'Surely you wouldn't have it born on the road, and live fatherless?'

'If it dies, all the better,' spat Aoife. She got up from where she sat and flounced up the steps of her *vardo*. In spite of himself Dónall rose also, his years of attachment to Aoife automatically overriding his sense of her recent betrayal. He would have followed her but she turned on him. 'For God's sake, Dónall, will you leave me alone!' she yelled. 'All my troubles are laid at your door. You crowd and paw me from dawn till dusk until you make me want to scream. I am not your mother and no more am I your sister or your possession. I will tell you this. If you stay here then I certainly will go, and if you go … well … I will not go with you. I'll be free of you, one way or another.'

She went into her *vardo* and slammed the door, leaving Dónall white and weeping ugly tears on the bottom step. Then he threw himself at the *vardo* door, hammering with his fists until the whole structure quaked, but the door remained adamantly closed. Caitlin tried to comfort him but he shook her off, sobbing and uttering incoherent half-sentences the while and flailing his arms so violently that no one dared go near. At last Cillian got to his feet and landed a hard-handed slap across Dónall's face that shocked him to silence.

'Go to bed, Dónall,' said Cillian fiercely. 'Go to bed or I'll take my belt to you. If you ask me it should have been used 'ere this, and not sparingly. I'd knock some sense in to you if you were my son.'

Dónall stomped into the gloom and they all resumed their seats around the fire.

'Take no notice of Aoife,' said Elíse. 'She will stay or go as Ruairi says.'

'And what of you, Elíse?' asked Lorcán. 'If you stay with me, I'll look after you and your children. There're two rooms above the stables at Clough Farm that will be warm and sheltered. I'm the only man here with a regular income.'

'Eistir has regular pay,' said Elíse, not meeting any eye. 'She and I have decided to stay together. Assuming Mr Harlish recovers, he will need help in his house, and at the big house too. At a pinch we might afford one of the cottages. We intend to put our children into the school. An itinerant life isn't good for them.'

'You've always thought yourself better than the rest of us,' said Brónach. 'Once you get under a solid roof you will never leave it. I'll return to Ireland if it's the last thing I do.'

'It may well be the last thing you do,' said Elíse. 'The journey out killed my husband and Eistir's. I won't leave my children orphans. Eistir says the same.'

'You'll live … unnaturally?' roared Fearghal. 'You and Eistir?'

'Those ladies we met at the big house had always done so,' said Elíse defensively.

'They were sisters. It isn't the same.'

'We will pass for sisters if it comes to it,' said Elíse. 'This life,' she looked over her shoulder at the dilapidated wagons, the woebegone animals hock-deep in mud, the broken pallets and crates that constituted all their furniture, and then stared around the meagre smoking fire at her compatriots' emaciated faces and hollow eyes, lank hair and filthy clothing. 'It isn't sustainable,' she concluded. 'It isn't really life at all. It's survival, and barely that. I want better for my children.'

Lorcán looked downcast. 'Don't you miss a man in your bed?'

'Or half a one, at least,' quipped Mícheál, under his breath. 'If you'll take Lorcán, Elíse, I'll take Eister if she'll have me, but I'm heading south.'

'Thank you.' Elíse looked down at her hands. 'We'll stay.'

Tadhg said he would remain as long as Ruairi did, but Fearghal threw his lot in with those who were leaving. 'What we need,' he said, 'is to accumulate some coin before we go. We cannot work as we travel. We must put some good miles between us and this place before we dare stop and test the waters.'

'We might make another trip to the lime kilns,' said Cillian. 'That was profitable work. Mr Slade is not here, but Ned Widderington has the contacts. He would set us up if we offered ourselves for the transportation.'

'I don't know,' said Lorcán. 'What about the Mounted Guard? Ned has not the new captain in his pocket as yet.'

Fearghal looked up at the sky. 'We have not seen a moon for a fortnight,' he said. 'And the Guard is surely tucked up in its barracks. It would be madness to patrol in these conditions.'

'And madness to attempt a trip to the lime kiln,' said Brónach. 'In any case, if you have forgotten, our guide is lying half-dead. None of you knows the way.'

'And Ned is not to be trusted,' said Cormac. 'He would sell us out as soon as look at us.'

'We should talk to Ruairi about it, if we could but prise him from the gatehouse.'

'I will go there tomorrow,' said Cillian, 'and find out what he intends. In the meantime, those of us who are to leave, we should go over the drays and wagons, check the tack and tally the stores.'

Chapter 49

The day after this conversation took place, Beth entered Mr Golightly's shop. The little bell above the door tinkled and Flossie rose from where she had been slumped on a stool behind the counter.

'Oh,' she said upon observing Beth. 'It is you, Miss Harlish. How does your brother? I heard he was mauled by the pig.'

'Yes indeed,' said Beth, stepping round some sacks of feed that were stacked near the door. 'He is somewhat better, thank you. How are you, Flossie?'

'Middling,' said Flossie. 'There is no fun to be had now Miss Eagerly is away, and I am not permitted to fraternise with the Irish.'

'How so?' Beth scanned the shelves behind the counter. 'I will take half a pound of yellow soap please Flossie.'

Flossie brought out the large cake of soap and began to hack off a slice. 'Mother says they are dirty,' she said, 'and riddled with disease.'

'They are poor, cold and hungry,' said Beth. 'I thought you were a particular friend of Mr Connolly.'

Flossie wrapped the soap in some paper. 'I thought so too, in the summer,' she sighed. 'Such beautiful blue eyes as he has. A girl could melt in them. But he has not been near me since he returned. What else can I get for you?'

Beth named a few more items—linseed oil, beeswax and turpentine—and watched as Flossie gathered them together. 'You must be bereft,' she said dryly. 'Is there not to be a Christmas dance this year? That will cheer you up.'

'Indeed there is,' said Flossie, her spirits rallying immediately. 'On Saturday. The curate has been here ever so many times to discuss the arrangements with Mother.' She gave a little simper and toyed with a lock of greasy hair. 'He is quite regular here nowadays, in fact. I suppose he finds the vicarage lonely. Sometimes he asks me to take a walk with him …' Her eyes glazed over as she stared into the middle distance. Beth gave a little cough. 'Oh!' Flossie shook herself and returned to her theme. 'But I was speaking of the dance. We are to provide the fare for the dance, as we did for your party. Sadly there will be no ale or champagne though. Mr Maybury says we must drink tea or elderflower cordial.'

'That is probably sensible,' said Beth. 'You remind me that I need tea. I will take two pounds, please. And have you any sugar? Where is the dance to be held? In the schoolroom?'

Flossie nodded, and cast a glance over her shoulder at a partly open door that led to the store room and the Golightlys' living accommodation. 'As to the drink,' she whispered, 'I have it on good authority that there will be something stronger, but only for such of us as can be trusted to keep our mouths shut.'

Beth stifled a smile. 'Is that so?'

'And speaking of secrets,' said Flossie, speaking lower still but leaning over the counter towards Beth, 'have you heard that Mrs Brock, the lawyer's wife, is expecting at last? It seems the healthful waters of Bath have done her no end of good. Mother heard it from her maid, who received a letter to say that they will remain in Bath until March at least, and she is told to find out a wet nurse to begin in May. I told Mother it was the Irishwomen's doing, for I saw Mrs Brock speaking very confidential to one of them at your party, and Mother says it is likely so, for it is commonly understood that they can weave spells and make potions. Mother says there is no doubt that they cooked up a brew for the lawyer's wife, but she says the baby will be a changeling, for the Irish are mischief-makers.'

'Oh, Flossie,' said Beth, torn between amusement and dismay. 'I am very happy that Mrs Brock is to be a mother, for I know she desired it above all things. But you must not allow it to be said it had anything to do with potions or spells. It isn't true. Gossip and rumour like that will do the immigrants no good and could do them considerable harm.'

Flossie sighed. 'I wish I had asked them for a love potion, for I am sure that Mr Connolly needed only a very little encouragement to declare himself to me. He told me I had a star in me. Did you ever hear such a romantic compliment?'

Flossie was reaching a large vessel of linseed oil down and did not see Beth's stricken expression, but prattled on as she began to decant a quantity into a bottle. 'I would think such a reputation would have people flocking to the camp,' she said sulkily. 'You said yourself they need the money. Father complains that his supply of cheap tobacco and Geneva has dried up since they ceased their operations. He says it is all he can expect to sell these days, people are so hard up. So I know the Irishmen make no money that way these days. But you are right—there is already great prejudice against them. Mr Treddlebarrow at Drystone Farm says his hay is all mouldy and blames the Irish for gathering it in badly. And his wife says their sheepdog was got with pup by their mongrel, and the litter was fit for nothing and had to be drowned. I wanted to have the harpist and the others play at the dance, but that was soundly overruled. The Treddlebarrows said that if the Irish played they would boycott the dance altogether, and you know that would reduce the number of men by almost half when you consider their five sons and their dairyman and that lad they keep up there to haul the muck.'

'I am sure you will have a splendid time if the Treddlebarrows attend or not,' said Beth stiffly, packing away her purchases in her basket. 'Is your card already filled?'

'Yes,' said Flossie smugly, 'and Mr Maybury has claimed the first two.'

'You lucky girl,' said Beth through clenched teeth. 'Can you put these things on our account?'

'Ah.' Flossie blushed. 'No. I am sorry Miss Harlish. Mother says we are to extend no credit to ...'

Beth stopped at the door and turned to face her with a narrowed eye. 'To anyone? Or just to us?'

Flossie slid her gaze away. 'To ... the Irish and to anyone who associates with them,' she mumbled at last.

'Oh. How so?'

Suddenly, what little discretion Flossie possessed evaporated. 'Oh, Miss Harlish,' she burst out, overcome with embarrassment, 'I am so sorry, for I know the Irish folks to be very nice people on the whole, but Mother has set her face against them. She says that they have brought trouble and a low air to the village. She disliked Mr Connolly. She said he would ruin me. And then there was the burglary, you know—she thought them *all* complicit in that, and you also! And then that woman who dances ... there is every kind of insinuation made about her. Several men in the

303

village are … somehow … infected, and Mother puts it down to … I am sorry to say it to you, for I know that she is … connected to your family, but I think it wrong to say a thing behind a person's back that you would not say to their face, and you have been kind to me in the past. She tells anyone who will listen that your brother is under a spell, otherwise he too would be afflicted. And,' now she had commenced, it seemed that Flossie could not stop the hearsay from tumbling from her mouth, though she was breathless with the effort of it. '… that priest, she says he was defrocked for … in short … the children are not safe. And there are two widow-women at the camp she suspects of … she will not explain it to me exactly, but she says it is deviant. And that young man … Dónall … she says he bears the mark of the devil. And there was a baby that died, and Mother says … only it is too horrible to repeat … but she believes that the baby's passing was not natural—'

'Stop!' shouted Beth, appalled, clamping her hands to her ears. 'Please, Flossie, do not go on. It is horrible! Cruel!'

'I know it,' cried Flossie, genuinely dismayed. 'And it is shocking to me that Mother is gradually bringing more people round to her way of thinking. Even Mr Maybury—'

'The curate believes these calumnies?' Beth stared at her, aghast.

Flossie nodded, her eyes round and staring from the expurgation of foulness.

Beth returned to the counter in a daze and reached for her purse of money. 'I will pay what I owe,' she said woodenly. 'And you may tell your mother that we will take our business elsewhere from now on, lest we contaminate her by association.'

'Oh, Miss Harlish,' Flossie blubbed, but holding out her hand for the coins. 'I am so sorry. But I thought it right that you should know.'

Beth managed a watery smile. 'I am very grateful to you, Flossie.' She took the girl's hand and gave it a hard squeeze. 'You have opened my eyes to a great number of things.' And then she turned and left the shop.

Chapter 50

Beth was sitting beside Frank when Ruairi mounted the stairs to the upper room. Frank was able to sit up now, though gingerly, and eat—with care—more solid foods. His bruises had faded to a sickly yellow, but Beth feared for his mental state. He never mentioned Aoife, had long since stopped asking for her, but Beth knew that his thoughts dwelt on his wife and the baby she carried. She had not told Frank that the Irish people were to leave Moorside. After what she had heard at the shop, she thought it a good thing. The sooner they left, the better.

Ruairi said, 'The pig is dead. Cormac and Mícheál and I have despatched the brute. It took three of us. Elíse and Eister are now salting and curing the meat.'

'That's good of you, Ruairi,' said Frank dully. 'I hope you will take what you need.'

Ruairi waved this away. He perched on the window sill, the only other seat in the room. 'How are you today, Frank? It's a scare you gave us for a while there.'

'I'm well enough,' said Frank. 'I would get up, but Betsey will not allow it.'

Ruairi sucked his teeth in a facsimile of concern. 'It does not do to let the ladies get the upper hand. If you feel like a change of scene, I can help you downstairs.'

Frank said, 'Perhaps tomorrow.'

Beth wanted to say that no trip downstairs would assist Frank in escaping his own morose mind, but forbore to say so, and bit back also several other trite remarks that were on the tip of her tongue. She could barely look at Ruairi, but the silence stretched out and at last she said, 'How is Tadhg? Is his chest improved?'

'It is, I thank you. That poultice has loosened the congestion. It has not improved the smell of him though. What is in it?'

'Onions and mustard. No, I grant you, it does not smell nice.'

Ruairi turned to peer out of the low window. 'It is drier today than of late. The tracks and paths are less quag than they have been. The sky is still covered in cloud, but it moves swiftly. There's a brisk breeze.'

Frank made no reply so Beth said, 'What is your interest in the weather?'

'Ah!' Ruairi's eyes lit up. 'We contemplate a trip to the lime kilns. Do you think it would be possible?'

Frank considered. 'Possible, yes, but not advisable. You would not wish to risk the cart getting bogged down. And after such rain and snow as we have had, the bogs will have changed their shape.'

'But that would be nothing to you, Frank, would it? No one knows the moor better than you.'

'Frank cannot stand up for longer than five minutes!' Beth said vehemently. 'He cannot take you across the moor.'

'No,' said Ruairi, 'and yet I fear we must attempt it. Funds are so low. The children suffer. And—here's the truth of it Frank—it will be the last time. We have to move on. The drays are being made ready as I speak. The camp is all but struck.'

Frank's eyes closed briefly as he took this in. 'All of you?'

'That's yet to be decided. Dónall must go, even if Aoife and I stay, but that, too, is up in the air.' In speaking these words Ruairi's gaze strayed to Beth but she was so conflicted she could not return it. Of course she would have liked to accuse him to his face of being a double-dealing rogue, but she feared to reveal how deeply she was hurt by it.

As she neither returned his look nor asked any question, he went on. 'She will have nothing to do with Dónall, and it makes him wretched. And though I know that you will breathe no word, things have a habit of getting out. Caitlin says that already there are rumours. The lad isn't safe here. Cormac and Caitlin have offered to look after Dónall and perhaps, in the spring, after... well,'—another swift but meaningful look at Beth— 'he could be collected on the way home.'

As though it was nothing in the world to her, Beth said, 'You will go back to Ireland in the spring? Is the famine ended?'

306

'No, Betsey, it is not ended, but if I know Aoife is safe, I think I could scrape a living for two … if necessary.'

'Of course it will be necessary to make a living wherever you might be,' said Beth archly.

'So Aoife will stay?' Frank's voice cracked with hope.

Ruairi touched Frank's shoulder. 'That's up to you, I think. But the others, including Dónall, will certainly go if we can make a last trip to the lime kiln.'

There was a pregnant pause and Beth understood that a bargain was being struck.

Presently Frank said, 'There is only one person who knows the moors as well as I do, who can get you there and back in safety.'

When Ruairi had gone, Beth and Frank talked over the proposal. There was no doubt that Beth knew the moors as well as Frank, but she scrupled to involve herself in what was, after all, a criminal undertaking. She would not be treated more leniently than a man, should they be caught by the guard. Frank conceded the point, but suggested that they were both already complicit and, to add to their wrongdoing, had failed to report Dónall's attack.

'We may as well be hanged for a sheep as for a lamb,' he said.

When Beth thought of the parlous conditions at the camp, and the hungry children, she could not bring herself to deny them the chance of relief. They needed funds, and how else could they be got if the village would not employ them? And then there was Ruairi. With money in his pocket he would be free to leave. It would be better, she thought dolefully, if he went away—out of sight, out of mind. There was no point dwelling upon what might have been.

They chose Saturday night for their venture. The Christmas dance at the school would distract the attention of any locals who regularly, in those days, came to the camp to make mischief if there were no other entertainment to be had. The cover promised to be good. Cloud hung thick and low over the moor the whole day, threatening rain that did not come and throwing the whole landscape into a study of gloom. There was a wind, but the cloud seemed so dense and solid that it would not be shifted, and the wind itself was bitter cold, a deterrent to any would-be patrol by the Mounted Guard, poachers or anyone else who might otherwise be abroad.

It had been agreed that Aoife would come to the gatehouse while Beth was away from it, to see if some reconciliation could not be effected with Frank. This was the price Beth had exacted for her cooperation. She knew not what arm-twisting Ruairi might have had to employ to get his sister to comply. It was possible that Aoife had only been waiting for an opportunity. Pride, perhaps, or guilt, had kept her away. Beth tried to think of her sister-in-law with compassion, but she found it hard. Even should Frank find he could trust Aoife, Beth did not think that she could. She remembered Eistir's obscure references to figures in Aoife's past and, in spite of her repugnance to Flossie's second-hand gossip, there were some aspects of it that rang too true and Beth found she could not dismiss its import from her mind.

She dressed herself in an old pair of Frank's britches and a shirt she had altered to fit, a sweater that had belonged to her father and a black ankle-length coat. She tied her hair back into a severe knot and covered it with a woollen hat.

It was midnight when she heard the muffled sound of the cart's wheels on the lane outside the gatehouse. She nodded at Eistir, who sat by the fire darning a sock. 'When Aoife comes—*if* she does—you will leave them alone?'

Eistir nodded, 'So long as I am sure she will not upset him.'

'If she does not come, or if I do not return …' she whispered, and raised her eyes to the ceiling and to the room beyond it, where Frank slumbered.

'I will take care of him,' said Eistir. 'But I am sure you will return. To tell the truth, I am surer of *that* than I am of the other.'

Beth was hopeful that the enterprise would be a success; she was eager now for the Irish people to be away from Moorside. She had spent the afternoon closeted with Frank going minutely over the route, calling to mind the tracks and lesser known pathways that would take them to the kilns, jogging her memory of helpful landmarks—craggy outcrops, little gorse plantations, streams and peculiar boulders, and also the perilous ones—craters, bogs and reed beds.

'When you get there,' Frank had said, 'lie low in the scrub. Let Ruairi and the Irishmen speak to the contraband men. Do not let them see your face or hear your voice.'

'I will do as you say,' Beth had replied, feeling her stomach churn with anxiety.

The previous day she had walked the entire route, taking the dog with her as though for exercise. It took her past the cliff and the little cave where she had thought to shelter after the robbery, and within sight of Somersall Grange—indeed through the stand of beech and oak trees where she and Arthur and Stephen Milton had stood …Oh! so many eons ago! Beth had written to her former employer and given up her post, stating her reasons as far as she could, and urging Mrs Somersall to recall

Ida Plim to her side, or to take some other lady as companion. The Grange was all shuttered now, and Beth supposed that Mrs Somersall had departed to the town house.

Beth spent long minutes staring at the place on the terrace where she had kissed Stephen Milton. Always, she realised, she had viewed Stephen as a back-up should Ruairi disappoint her. And now he *had* disappointed her—and suddenly she saw Stephen's rectitude and honour and quiet respectful devotion in a much more favourable light. She had heard no word of him, but she assumed he knew that she had returned to the gatehouse. He would be waiting, she knew, to see what plant might flourish from the Irish seed.

Only a few days previously she had cogitated every possible variation of their circumstances. Ruairi was as charming as ever towards her, favouring her with those gut-melting smiles and sidelong glances, taking every opportunity to touch her hand or to pass his arm round her waist; and the effect of these gambits had been as before—flames of passion, a liquification of her limbs. She was under no illusion that if opportunity and location presented themselves, they could pick up where they had left off that long ago night in late July. Perhaps, she had speculated, if a *rapprochement* could be effected between Frank and Aoife, they might all go to Ireland. Or if Mr Talbot did not sell Tall Chimneys, they could all stay. Or—her least favoured scenario—if Aoife and Frank were reconciled and Ruairi did not declare himself, she, Beth, would be free to go to America with Stephen. But feeling as she did towards Frank— protective, a shield that must stand between him and further hurt—she thought this the least likely option.

Now she knew that even if Ruairi spoke the word she would refuse him. How could she trust a man who had wooed two—or more?— women at the same time, and even used the same terms of endearment? She would laugh in his face if he so much as looked at her with a twinkle in his blue, lying eyes!

But the flips and jitters in her belly when she *thought* of those eyes … they told her that she was lying to herself.

She surveyed the moor from where she stood on a slight rise of the land. How much better she knew the moor than her own heart!

Now the night of the expedition was come, and she let herself out through the little gate and looked to see if Aoife would pass her on the way inside. But there was no sign of Frank's wife, so she climbed onto the cart. Ruairi had hold of the reins. He turned the cart and clicked his tongue to urge the pony to a walk. It was the same pony that had brought them through the blizzard, but her piebald sides had been smeared with soot and muck so as to disguise her, and her hooves were tied up in sacking. Ruairí and the others were swathed head to foot in black, their faces smeared with dirt. Only the red glowing end of one of Mícheál's foul-smelling cheroots and the occasional flash of Ruairí's white teeth showed through the pall that shrouded the entire equipage.

They took the broad track that led back towards the camp and then struck off to the northwest, skirting the wall that surrounded the crater within which Tall Chimneys sat. About a mile and a half later they turned sharply left, descended into a steep gully and forded a stream. The bank on the other side was steep and slippery. They all got off the cart and Ruairí and Lorcán took hold of the horse's bridle on either side to haul her up the slope. Her hooves had less grip because of the sacking. She scrabbled and struggled for a while, but eventually found a purchase and got to the top of the rise.

In the dark, it was impossible to tell one Irishman from another, but someone took Beth's elbow and helped her up the steepest part of the incline.

They rested briefly at the top. A gruff voice said, 'She'll never manage that when she's fully laden,' and Beth recognised Cormac.

Beth said, 'We will not return this way. The tracks made by the cart will be less if we do not retrace our steps, and I have deliberately chosen a meandering route. It will confuse anyone, should we be followed.' She looked over the landscape. It appeared to her in shades of dark and darker, stretching away, undulating but ever rising towards the tor that marked the centre and also the highest point of the moor. She recognised the topography even in the darkness, the slightly lighter hue of a crag, some tiny luminescence of lichen on a well-known boulder, the merest possible glimmer of water in a brook.

'This way,' she said, and led on foot. The path was narrow, barely wide enough for the cart, and turned sharply left and right around protruding boulders and swathes of impenetrable scrub. There were more direct ways but she was careful to keep to the places where the folds of the landscape and the occasional brake of gorse would hide them from view. Their feet were often in water, for many new rivulets had formed, but no one complained. Since fording the stream, they had all remained on foot, Beth up ahead with Ruairí half a pace behind her, Lorcán by the pony's head and the others trudging behind the cart.

Above them, Beth's eyes discerned the racing clouds—sometimes dark and presaging rain, sometimes lighter—but the moon remained hidden. The wind rattled the bare branches of the heathers, and always there was the sound of water, but they heard no creak of saddle leather or whinny of horses to suggest that riders were near.

They walked for about an hour, the wind sometimes to their left and sometimes in their faces, gradually climbing until they came to the little knoll of trees within the curtilage of Somersall Grange. Here they paused and gave the pony water to drink, and drank themselves from a flagon. Beth surveyed the little company. The smaller, wiry figure must be Mícheál, she thought, and the stockier one she knew was Cormac. Cillian was easy to identify from his wheezing breaths. There were two others, one tall, but not tall enough to be Fearghal, the other slight. Could they have brought the boy, Conn, with them?

By previous agreement there was no conversation. Ruairi did not speak to her although she felt him close beside her.

She pulled her hat further down over her forehead and indicated that it was time to go on. There was no alternative but to cross an expanse of open moor where there was little or no cover. She eyed the sky again. It was blacker than ever, and soon a few drops of rain began to fall. The going would be miserable, but would further deter others from venturing out.

The path she had chosen for the route to the lime kiln was treacherous with half-buried boulders but, being slightly raised, it was less wet and so there was a reduced chance of the cart becoming enmired. She had consulted with Frank over this. The way back would be wetter, and with the cart fully laden that could be problematic, but there was better shelter should they encounter the guard. After all—they had reasoned—an empty cart, even in the dead of night, was less incriminating than a full one.

They trudged on through a shower that stung their faces, the pony complaining as before until Lorcán covered her face with a sack. Then she quietened. They took care over the rough terrain. There was no hurry, though every hour spent out exposed them to danger and a broken axle or sheered split pin would doom them all.

At last the lime kilns came into view, the glow from their furnaces eerie, the silhouettes of the lime workers macabre against the fiery light. For the past few minutes Beth had been conscious of movement in the shadows—other men, other carts, other conspirators keen not to be discovered. The rain was heavier now, and the wind keener. Somewhere not far away a canvas flapped and she heard the sound of rope being pulled through a ratchet.

Ruairi leaned close to her. 'You'll wait here,' he breathed. 'I will go ahead with Cillian, Mícheál and Cormac. The others will wait here with you. Keep out of sight.' He kissed her, swiftly but hard, on the mouth, taking her by surprise and denying her the opportunity of shoving him away. Then he was gone, swallowed up by the darkness.

She chose a place in a patch of tayberry bushes, squirming underneath their flimsy cover, trying not to mind the damp ooze that came up from the ground to meet her. She turned her head so as to be able to see over to the kilns. In a pantomime, she saw Ruairi and his crew enter the circle of orange light thrown out by the kilns, a brief exchange between them and the workers, then the cart was led away beyond the kiln where the light did not reach and her eye could not follow.

Someone wriggled into the place next to her and a boy's voice said, 'Are you alright, Miss?'

Another voice beyond him—much deeper—said, 'I want Ruairi.'

'Is that Dónall?' Beth hissed, appalled. The lad was so unpredictable. He might run after Ruairi at any moment, shouting and flailing his arms. And she'd been left to supervise him? Later, he might blurt out that she'd been one of the crew.

Conn said, his voice—not fully broken and wavering between octaves, 'You remember what we were told, Dónall? We are to lie here with the lady and not speak, and Ruairi and the others will return by-and-by.'

'But … but ..' stumbled Dónall. 'I can't see him.'

'All the better. Neither can we be seen. That is the game we are playing.'

A game? Beth rolled her eyes. This was no game.

She wondered distractedly if Aoife had attended the gatehouse, and what she and Frank might speak of. Beth had told Frank that he should capitulate on the matter of he and Aoife living at Tall Chimneys. 'If that's what it takes,' she had said. 'If that's what she really wants. I do not think Mr Talbot will object, though you should warn her that the tenancy might be a short one.'

The sound of raised voices drifted through the mizzle towards her. Some argument was in train. Two men, locked in combat, crossed the field of her vision, briefly illuminated by the lurid light of the furnace and then lost again in the darkness. A horse whinnied. There was a short exchange of shouting, the words lost, then the explosion of a musket.

Beth rose to her knees, her own hand clamped across her mouth to prevent any sound escaping. Conn, beside her, also rose to his haunches, but Dónall was on his feet and running, tripping over the tufted grass and undergrowth, falling, then getting up again.

Beth hissed, 'Go after him!' And Conn was on his feet in pursuit. He was lighter than Dónall, and nimbler, and soon caught up, bringing the lad down hard just at the place where the scrub gave way to the rock and shingle of the track. There was a sickening thud. Conn lay across his quarry to prevent him from rising up again. But Dónall seemed unable or unwilling to resist. He lay prone beneath Conn, and did not move.

Chapter 51

Minutes passed. Beth remained hidden, her eyes at one minute on the kilns and at the next on the humped outline of the two boys twenty yards ahead that she could just differentiate from the surrounding thicket. She thought of wriggling forward to see if anything was amiss, but thought better of it. If Conn could not subdue Dónall then she certainly could not.

The rain stopped and, above her, the racing clouds began to thin. Around their edges shone a thin nimbus of light. Moonlight. Her heart sank.

She looked again towards the kilns. There was movement. A bulky form moved towards them. A horse with a cart and several men backlit by the kilns came ever nearer, the eye-searing orange of illumination turning ochre and then tawney and grey, and finally the group was hardly distinguishable from the thick press of night.

There was a whistle—a thin cry that could have been an owl, but she knew to be Ruairi—and she rose and strode through the vegetation towards them.

'What happened?' she said. 'I heard gun fire.'

'Ah now, that was nothing to do with us,' said Ruairi lightly. 'Some men from Whitby took a dislike to some others. They were arguing over the spoils, but in the melee I think we got away with the lion's share. See the cart? It's loaded to the gunwales. Where are the boys?'

'Dónall was alarmed at the gunshot. He made a break for it but Conn brought him down. They are here, along the path somewhere.' She pointed, and Ruairí indicated to Cillian that he should go and root the boys from their cover.

'I'm worried about the sky,' said Beth, pointing up to where the clouds scudded. 'The cover is thinning. We should make haste.'

'We will do, my darling,' said Ruairí, stirred and buoyed—by the night's adventure, or by the richness of the haul that was concealed beneath the tarpaulin. He put his arm around Beth's waist and clasped her to him, seeming unaware of her stiff resistance. 'Is your blood not heated by the thrill of it? I must confess, mine is. I could take you right here in the heather if there was not more pressing business. Let the boys be brought out and we will be on our way and then later,'—he brought his lips to hers again—'we will see about it.'

Beth opened her lips to make some retort, but just then Cillian returned with only Conn. 'You had better come, Ruairí,' he said in a voice that was heavy with foreboding. 'Dónall is hurt.'

'He is dead,' Conn blurted out. 'He hit his head on a rock. There is blood, and ...' he raised his fist to his own temple, to indicate a deep gash. 'His skull is smashed. I am sorry, Ruairí. I did not mean for it to happen.' Conn began to weep. Cillian, surprisingly tender, reached out and pulled his son's head upon his shoulder.

Ruairí relinquished Beth and hurried to the place where Dónall lay. He turned the boy over and listened for a breath. He pressed his hand to Dónall's chest but it was still. Just then the cloud parted for a moment, and a thin shimmer of moonglow showed him Dónall's head, which was smashed just between his eyebrow and his ear.

Ruairí stared, aghast, and then bent his head and pressed it into Dónall's lifeless body, his shoulders shaking with sobs, his howls muffled but audible still in the silent windswept night.

Beth crossed the ground towards him and touched his shoulder, her compassion utterly overcoming her hurt pride, but he indicated by a wild gesture that she should leave him, and she withdrew.

Soon, however, with a visible effort of will, Ruairí rallied and lifted Dónall into his arms. 'Make room on the cart,' he said grimly. 'Jettison some of the goods, if we need to. We will take him home.'

Ruairí's face, between the brim of his hat and the collar of his coat, was white with shock, and she could see where his tears had sloughed away the smears of grime, but he mastered his emotions. Once Dónall was safely stowed, and covered by some layers of sacking and loose materials, he nodded at Beth and she led them on.

The way home took them into a gully that followed a substantial stream. The route tracked the streambed itself, and was occasionally impeded by larger rocks. The stream was deeper than it might have been without the rain and snow runoff. They splashed along shin-deep in ice cold water, resisting the urge to hurry lest the cart be snagged or the pony flounder. They carried no light, but the sky was ever lightening. From time to time a gibbous moon threw a pearly light, making the surface of the water seem like mercury before the clouds again blocked it out.

After a mile or so they left the stream bed and followed a broad but boggy track that led off at a tangent. Now they were more exposed, and urged the pony to a fast walk, half-running alongside it, that the cart might travel quickly over the wet places and not be mired down. Ahead of them Beth could see the dark obelisk of the cliff rearing up. It seemed a beacon to her, a place of safety and refuge, though it was still some miles from home. It didn't feel to her that anything bad could happen there, though she knew this to be a trick of nostalgic memory.

From time to time she let the cart and men get a little way ahead, so that she could stand and survey the land around them. The contour of the moor just there gave her only half a view. She narrowed her eyes, seeking movement, a disturbance in the ether of the night, and tuned her ears for the slightest jingle of harness.

The wind was rising again, coming from the east. The clouds crossed the sky like galleons, their dark sails hemmed by bright coronas of moonlight, but heavily laden. It would snow before morning. The temperature had plummeted but she did not feel the cold. She turned to face the wind and heard—or thought she heard—the sound of several horses in the creek they had recently left. She followed in her mind's eye the possible routes any pursuers might take. They could continue along the streambed, which would turn south and west, away from their own position. There was another track, a dangerous one, close to a series of notorious marsh and reed beds. If the pursuers knew their territory at all they would avoid that. Or they might do as she had done, and choose to move to higher ground. If so, the cliff would give them vantage over the entire moor, and these occasional windows of light provided by the treacherous moon would illuminate the fugitives as effectively as full sun.

Suddenly she was running, catching up with the cart, passing it and finding Ruairi at the pony's head.

'We are followed,' she panted. 'About half a mile behind us, a party of men. Quick. Follow me.'

She ran ahead, zigzagging between boulders and leaping over the worst of the quag. The pony came on quickly. She could hear its laboured breathing and the steady jog of the men's boots. Cillian began to wheeze, unable to keep up.

Ruairi said, 'Get up, man, and take the reins,' boosting the slighter man onto the seat of the cart with a heave.

They neared the cliff. Beth could see the dark outline of the cave at its foot. She eyed the sky anxiously. A gap of starlight in the east, between clouds that would pass overhead in no time.

They came to the wide stream that ran before the shingle plateau where, years before, she and Frank had cooked their rabbit. She leapt into the waters, which came to her thighs. The shock of the cold made her breath catch in her throat, but she forded through, finding the place where the bank was shallow enough for the cart to exit the flow. She heard the horse behind her, baulking at the edge of the water. Cillian cracked his whip and the mare plunged forward, the cart behind and the men on either side pushing, scrabbling with their feet to get a purchase, the fast-flowing water boiling around their legs. Behind them, round a curve in the track they had just left, Beth heard a horse whinny and the sound of a man's voice trying to quieten it.

'This way. This way,' she urged, as the doughty pony hauled the cart from the water. Beth indicated the cave. 'It's deep,' she said, speaking low but with great exigence. 'Take her right in, as far as you can go.' She began to kick the shingle so as to obscure the cart's tracks.

They did as she bid, covering the pony's eyes with the sacking before guiding her between boulders and a stash of timber that had been abandoned there into the utter blackness of the cave.

'Pile the timber behind you into a wall,' Ruairi instructed. 'Quickly, for the love of God.'

Conn and Cormac and Mícheál set to, hauling the half rotted planks and branches into a barrier that would hide the cart from view so long as the guard had no light. Only Beth and Ruairi remained within the mouth of the cave.

Across the river, in the sudden flare of moonlight, a horseman—then two, then three—came into view, approaching the ford.

Ruairi said, 'Step into the shadows and remove your clothes, Betsey. Trust me. Everything but your shirt. And here,' he thrust a tinder box into her hands. 'Light a fire, just enough to make smoke, close to the entrance, but not so near that it can be seen or so as to illuminate the interior.'

He began to remove his own coat and shirt, using them to scrub the camouflage from his face before throwing them beneath a bush. The hairs on his chest rose in the icy wind, and his nipples puckered. Beth shrank into the shadows and did as she was bid, peeling off her wet britches and boots, the coat and sweater, then scraped a little heap of dry grass together. The tinder in the box was dry—wood shavings and some hemp fibres—and soon ignited the little pyre.

Ruairi hissed, 'Let down your hair, darling.'

The horses were at the ford, their riders debating in hushed tones whether to proceed or to turn back. From the depths of the cavern came the congested wheeze of Cillian's breathing and Lorcán's murmured reassurance to the pony.

To Beth's astonishment, Ruairi sauntered from the shadow onto the moonlit apron at the mouth of the cave, selected a stunted bush and began to make water onto it. The horsemen did not seem to see him at first, but then one looked up and pointed across the river.

'You there,' rang out the voice of the guardsman. 'What are you doing?'

Ruairi made as though he was only just then aware of their presence. He gave them a long stare, and then looked pointedly down at where a bright stream issued from his body. 'I should think that's obvious,' he said, shaking himself and putting himself to rights. He stepped casually across to the bank of the stream. 'What do *you* do here?'

'We are the Mounted Guard,' said their captain. He kicked his horse forward into the water and across the stream. 'Have you seen any vehicle pass this way?'

Ruairi shook his head. 'I have seen nothing.' He took a pace or two towards the captain and adopted a confidential tone. 'I have been otherwise engaged, if you get my meaning, Captain.' He motioned with his head towards the cave. A little billow of smoke issued from its mouth. 'There is a lady in the case.'

The captain followed the direction of Ruairi's indication. 'In the cave?'

Ruairi nodded. 'The situation is somewhat delicate, sir. Her family is against the match.'

The captain nodded, but peered suspiciously at the dark mouth of the cave. His horse advanced a few steps across the shingle. 'I know that cave. It is deep.'

'But dry, sir, and full of brushwood. We have lit a fire, for the lady and I intend to take some time about our business.' He winked at the captain, and although the captain allowed a grin to crease his features he still advanced, little by little, towards the entrance to the cave, narrowing his eyes against the smoke in order to see inside.

The other horsemen began to cross the stream. One of them reached down to where a lantern hung from his saddle. 'Shall I light this, sir?'

Beth, squatting by the fire and smothering the meagre flames with dead leaves so that more smoke would issue forth, glanced behind her. A rough barricade of wood hid the cart and the other men from view, but it would not fool anyone with a lantern. She passed her tongue across dry lips and swallowed hard.

'Darling,' she called out in a voice that she tried to make languorous with lovemaking. 'Come back inside. The blanket grows cold.'

'I won't be a moment, my love,' said Ruairi. He looked at the captain, who had reined in his horse and lifted a hand to keep the other men back.

'Step out, if you would be so kind,' said the captain.

Beth waited the few seconds she thought it might take a woman to get up from a nest of blankets and hurry into a shirt, then she walked to the cave entrance and made a show of peering, terrified, from its shadows. 'Who's there?' she squeaked, shrinking yet farther back when she pretended to see the guard. She threw an accusatory look at Ruairi. 'Who did you tell about this place? You promised we would be private!'

'And so I thought we would be,' said Ruairi. 'So we still might be, if these gentlemen would *be* gentlemen, and go on their way.'

'Come out, madam,' said the captain.

Beth stepped, trembling, into the pale moonshine. Her feet and legs were naked, the shirt only just reaching to her thighs. She pulled it down ineffectually to cover her legs. Her hair tumbled onto her shoulders.

The two guards exchanged sniggering looks, eyeing Beth's bare legs and loosely buttoned shirt with lascivious eyes.

The captain had the decency to avert his gaze. 'Go back inside, madam, and make yourself decent,' he barked. 'If you take my advice you will be obedient to your family. They know better for you than you do yourself.' He cast a look at Ruairi that managed to be both sneering and envious.

Beth said, 'Oh! Kind sir, do not tell them!' But the captain had turned away. 'Let us go back the way we have come,' he said to his men. 'I apprehend the smugglers have taken to the marshes.' He kicked his horse and splashed back across the stream and they were soon gone from sight.

Ruairi crossed the shingle and swept Beth up into his arms. 'Ah! Betsey,' he mumbled into her neck. 'You are the best of girls! We will rest awhile I think, and then be on our way. Let me kiss you. I'm in sore need of comfort.'

Beth felt a wobble of weakness. Ruairi's eyes were red-rimmed; he must have been weeping as they had marched along. But she recalled Flossie Golightly and resolutely turned her face away, squirming from his embrace. 'No,' she said firmly, pointing at the advance of a thick bank of low cloud from the east that engulfed glimmering stars and the crookbacked moon. 'Snow is coming, and quickly. We must hurry.'

Chapter 52

Brónach and the other women had gone to bed to get such sleep as might come to them in their draughty accommodations. The children were all abed and Tadgh, relieved at last from the cough that had plagued him for weeks, also slept.

Only Aoife and Fearghal were awake by the guttering remnants of the campfire, which smoked and faltered as mizzle and the wind conspired to extinguish it altogether.

Occasionally they passed a flagon between them, drinking Fearghal's throat-searing homebrew.

Presently Fearghal said, 'When will you go to the gatehouse? You were expected there an hour ago.'

Aoife shrugged. 'I do not know. I am not minded to go at all.' She winced as the baby within her kicked. 'There is no point in going like this,' she said, jabbing the bulge of her pregnancy. 'My usual methods of persuasion will not serve.'

Fearghal frowned. 'You are wanton,' he said, swigging grog. 'I'd say you were damned, but that I no longer believe in damnation. If there *is* a hell,' he concluded, looking round the churned slimy arena of the camp, 'this is it.'

'For once, I agree with you,' said Aoife. She drew her shawl around her shoulders. 'The wind is bitter.'

'There was to be a dance tonight, at the school,' said Fearghal. 'I supplied some of this,' he lifted the flagon. 'There was to be only water, else.' He patted his pocket, which jingled faintly. 'I made some coin from the affair.'

'You ought to add it to the communal chest,' said Aoife without conviction.

Fearghal snorted. 'So that Lorcán can appropriate it? I do not think so. I shall keep it by me.'

'Or,' said Aoife, adopting a wheedling tone, 'you could take a nice girl to the Plough and buy her a proper drink.'

'A *nice* girl?' Fearghal pretended to look around the camp in search of one, but he rose to his feet and held out his hand to help her from her seat.

It took them a while to navigate the track to the village. Both were more inebriated than they thought. Their stumbles and wavering legs amused them both highly, and they laughed almost maniacally as they gained what passed as the village's high street and staggered along towards the Plough.

The dance had long since finished, but Ned Widderington kept the pub open to slake the thirst of the temperate dancers who had not partaken of Fearghal's illicit liquor, and to further satiate the appetites of those who had. The place was full of ploughmen and shepherds, farmers' lads and some few of the bolder women, including Flossie Golightly. The atmosphere was raucous, the air full of pipe smoke and beer fumes and the headier whiff of strong spirits. Ned Widderington and a serving wench were kept busy carrying trays of tankards to the various tables where men and women lolled and shouted and played fumbling games of cards for stakes they could not afford.

But when the door opened to admit Fearghal and Aoife, all conversation ceased. The two half fell through the door, laughing uproariously. Aoife's hair was a tangled mess, her skirt dirty ten inches above the hem. Fearghal looked as disreputable as possible—his fusty old coat, ragged trousers and broken boots made him look every inch a disreputable drifter.

He scraped the sparse grey curtain of hair from his eyes and blinked at the company.

'What do you want?' asked the publican, feeling with his hand for the stout club he kept beneath the bar.

'A drink or two,' slurred Fearghal. He patted his pocket. 'We've money to pay. This lady will sing you a song or two, if you like.'

Aoife creased her face into a smile, but there was something ghastly and almost devilish about it. She drew her shawl more tightly around her body in an attempt to conceal her belly, and advanced a tentative step or two into the room.

'You used to like to hear me sing,' she said in what was calculated to be a winning tone, but which came out croaked.

'Some of us have heard your song once too often,' said a voice at the back of the room. 'There's sorcery in it.'

'Magic, perhaps,' Aoife allowed. She turned to Fearghal. 'Never mind,' she said with a careless shrug. 'We will just sit and refresh ourselves, Father.'

They lowered themselves gingerly onto a bench alongside a vacant table.

'Father?' someone spluttered. 'I did not think him *that* old.' There was a gale of laughter.

'He is a priest,' someone else said in a pantomime hiss. 'Sworn to celibacy and a life of service.'

'He will have to serve himself, if he will allow no woman to do it!' shouted a wit, and the whole company shook with mirth.

Ned Widderington poured glasses of gin and carried them to the table. 'I want no trouble,' he said as he placed the drinks down. 'Have these, and then go.'

But these glasses were followed by others, and half an hour passed. At some point Aoife rose from her seat and began to tour the room, her hips swinging suggestively, her hand languidly stroking first one man and then another, coaxing them to buy her drinks. The women bridled and threw insults, but the men were too drunk—or at least drunk enough— to be susceptible to Aoife's faded charm.

Fearghal sat on, swallowing glass after glass of spirit, eying her exploits with increasing disgust but incapable of intervening.

Then, a more-than-usually tenacious youth grappled Aoife to himself and began to make inroads amongst her clothing, tearing her blouse and exposing the creamy swell of a breast. Aoife made protest, but she herself was so intoxicated that her attempts at resistance were feeble. She made a mew of distress as his mouth found hers and pressed itself intrusively there, while his hand kneaded her bosom. The other men at the table leaned back, not to dissociate themselves from his action but to give him more space, ready to look on as the Irish harlot was molested, and even perhaps to take their turn in due course.

Flossie Golightly, although drunk, was not so drunk as not to see that the incident about to unfold would be such as she wished no part of.

She rose to her feet and began to make her way to the door. As she passed Fearghal she put a hand on his shoulder. 'You should stop that,' she said urgently, gesturing to the back of the room. 'You should indeed. There is going to be trouble.'

She proceeded to exit the inn, but met in the porch her irate mother, who had waited up for Flossie's return from the dance and had at last gone in search of her. Finding the school locked up and in darkness, Mrs Golightly had passed the Plough to see a glimmer of light beneath the tightly closed shutters, though it was then past two o'clock. She could hardly credit that Flossie would have entered the pub at any hour of the day, much less at such an evil hour of the night, but having no other clue as to where the girl might be she was preparing to push open the door when Flossie stumbled out and fell into her arms.

'Oh, Mother,' gasped Flossie. 'How glad I am to see you for I fear …' she waved her arm to indicate the room beyond the door, 'I fear mischief within. I was just coming home. Truthfully I was.'

Mrs Golightly put her daughter away from her. 'What manner of mischief?' she asked, censorious but also curious. 'Who is within?'

'Oh! A whole crowd. They came here from the dance and I was carried along with them. But then the Irish people came—'

'The Irish? How many times have I told you—'

'But Mother I was not in their company at all. Only, just now …' Words failed her, and she only pointed mutely at the door, from beyond which there came the raucous shouts of inebriated men and hysterical women, the sound of chairs being knocked asunder and, over and above all, the thin scream of a panicked woman.

Mrs Golightly opened the door slightly and inserted one eye and an ear into the narrow gap she had made.

Father Fearghal had risen with a roar and made his blundering way to where Aoife was now spreadeagled on one of the trestle tables, her arms and legs held down while the persistent swain fumbled ineptly with the fastenings of his britches. Fearghal knocked him to one side with a swingeing blow that sent him sprawling onto the damp sawdust of the floor. The other men sprang away, releasing Aoife, who struggled to her feet.

A shocking, sobering silence descended. Ned Widderington again took hold of his club.

Fearghal regarded his victim with an expression that was angry but dulled by stupor. 'You think that a blow? You know nothing!' he cawed drunkenly. 'Frank Harlish was near killed for having to do with this woman, and that was with her consent! How do you think you will be

324

dealt with for what you purposed?' He grabbed Aoife's arm and thrust her roughly towards the door.

'Frank Harlish was mauled by his sow,' said a voice from the back of the room.

'Pah!' Fearghal spat, turning but half tripping over the leg of a chair. 'Young Dónall did a better job than any pig, and what he did to Frank he would do again.' He surveyed them with an eye that would have had the wrath of God in it had it not been so bloodshot and glazed. 'Remember that,' he drawled, groping his way through the disordered bar, 'when you come to trouble our women and children again, throwing muck and insults. We can defend ourselves!'

And so, pushing Aoife before him, he tumbled out into the village street where the snow was just beginning to fall.

Mrs Golightly had already hurried Flossie away from the place.

'We must go to the vicarage straight,' the older woman said, walking quickly. 'Someone must be sent to Brayton for the constable. And we must wake your father. He must assert his authority.'

Chapter 58

The snow fell in earnest by the time Beth and the Irishmen regained the spur that would return them to the well-trodden route between the encampment and the gatehouse. Their shoulders and hats, the stretched tarpaulin and the pony's back were dusted.

Ruairi looked behind them. 'Our tracks will soon be obscured,' he said with satisfaction. He had the reins in one hand, and the other arm around Beth's waist, which she had permitted due to the extreme cold of the night. He turned to the other men, who plodded wearily alongside. 'You return to camp. There should be hot grog waiting for you. I will take the trap to the stables at the big house and be with you before long.'

Conn looked up at Ruairi. His face was white with fatigue and dread, and with snow that clung to his pale lashes and lay on his cheeks. 'What shall we say of Dónall?' His lip quivered. 'I killed him. I will hang for sure.'

Ruairi leapt from the cart and put his arm around the lad's shoulders. 'It was an accident,' he said. 'In the morning, you are all to leave this place. Who is to say that Dónall did not go with you? When you are well away, I will bury him quietly. Let your conscience be clear, Conn. But say nothing for now. I must break the news to Aoife first.'

'She will not care,' said Cillian, spitting onto the snow. 'She hated the lad.'

'She did not,' Ruairi returned heatedly. 'She loved him in her way. But leave her to me, Cillian. Tomorrow we will divide the spoils so that you have merchandise to sell. It is the best I can do. The stuff is too hot to move here.'

'I will come with you, to help unload,' said Cillian mulishly. 'It would not do for half the plunder to go missing.'

'You do not trust me?' Ruairi looked hurt.

'I do not trust anyone,' said Cillian.

Lorcán stamped his boots in the cold. 'I will lay my share aside until Mr Slade's return,' he said. 'Even though he will want his cut, I will get a better price than I would otherwise. I will say goodnight. I must make my way to Clough Farm before daybreak.' He trudged off, his hands in his pockets and his head bent against the gusting wind and snow.

Cormac and Mícheál took Conn between them and had begun to walk towards the camp when Cormac, peering ahead, said, 'What are those lights up ahead? Not just the fire, surely?'

They all squinted through the snowy night. Sure enough, up ahead several lights—torches or lanterns—made faint halos in the darkness.

'Something is afoot,' said Ruairi. He turned to Cillian. 'Take the trap back down the path a way,' he said. 'Wait for me there until I see what's amiss.' He held his arms out to Beth. 'Will you come with me, Betsey? Or shall one of the others see you home safe?'

'I'll come,' she said and, almost without thinking, allowed him to help her down from the cart He pulled her hat down so that it covered most of her face, and lifted the collar of her coat. 'There now,' he said, smiling down at her. 'You look like one of us.'

Cillian turned the pony back the way it had come. The poor thing was exhausted but it did as it was bid. Soon the pony and cart were out of sight.

The rest forged their way forward. Snow stung their eyes. The turf was a fine carpet of flakes. The wind blew fierce and they could already hear the distinctive groan of the standing stone as it vibrated to its own primaeval tune.

At the camp they found Aoife and Caitlin huddled miserably on the steps of the *vardo* with Tadhg between them. His head was bloodied; blows had already been exchanged. The terrified faces of Brónach, Elíse and the children peeped out from one of the drays. Father Fearghal lounged drunkenly on the ground half propped against one of the wagons. Loitering about, poking their noses into the other vehicles and looking disdainfully at the beggarly belongings of the immigrants, were a dozen or so villagers bearing smoking torches.

Aoife leapt up at Ruairi's approach. The blanket she held around her shoulders slipped open. Beth saw that her pregnancy was well-advanced; there would have been no possibility now of hiding it from Dónall.

Aoife hissed, 'They know about Dónall. Fearghal is in his cups. He told them all. They have come to arrest the lad. Where is he?' She peered behind Ruairi, identifying and dismissing one man after another, concluding that he was not amongst them.

A man stepped forward from the posse of villagers. He was well disguised by a large scarf that covered his face and a hat pulled low over his eyes. 'We are looking for Dónall, the young man who attacked Frank Harlish,' he said. Beth recognised his voice immediately.

'You are not the law here,' said Ruairi belligerently. He scanned the crowd with contempt. 'I see no constable.' He took a firmer hold of the shillelagh he carried.

'The constable is sent for,' said a woman's voice. 'And in the meantime, here is a respected local personage.' She pushed forward a stout man swathed in layers of thick coat and muffler. His eyes, just visible, swivelled between the woman and the immigrants, clearly fearing both.

A crone in the crowd shouted, 'The curate has the authority to cleanse the witch of the devil.'

Realising the impossibility of hiding his identity, Edgar loosed his scarf a little. 'Indeed,' he said. 'I am the spiritual leader of these people. I have the authority conferred by the church.'

A few voices cried, 'Witchcraft!' and, 'burn her.'

The wind howled across the moor in a sudden gust and the standing stone's murmur intensified into an otherworldly keening sound.

'She is doing that,' said the first woman's voice, pointing a pudgy finger at Aoife. 'It is sorcery.'

'It is the wind,' said Beth, stepping forward and removing her hat so that the people could see her face. The wind caught her hair immediately and whipped it around her face. 'The standing stone has always made that noise when the wind is from the east, Mrs Golightly. You know that.'

Edgar's eyes bulged. 'Miss Harlish? What do you do here with these … troublemakers?'

Beth raised her voice. 'What do *you* do, with *these* troublemakers?' she flung back at him. 'For myself, I am come to do what any Christian would do—to lead them from this storm to a place of safety.' She looked around the crowd, recognising amongst others Ned Widderington, the dairyman and two or three Treddlebarrow lads from Drystone Farm, the schoolmaster and his aged mother. None of them would meet her eye.

'Did you come with similar charity in your hearts? Look at the children! And this woman is with child! What have they ever done to you except shear your sheep and harvest your crops? Your barns would be empty if they had not laboured on your land! Get away home with you. You should be ashamed.'

'Our hay is mouldy,' shouted one of the Treddlebarrow boys. 'And our dog brought forth malformed pups. It's their doing.'

'My husband has the pox,' shouted a woman. 'He says he got it from her.' She pointed at Aoife.

Beth narrowed her eyes. 'Mrs Craddock? Your husband has been working at the colliery this year past. Everyone knows that there are working girls there. Any one of them could have been the cause.'

'I came at the people's behest, to see the boy in custody,' said Edgar, in truth rather alarmed at the turn things were taking. 'That is my only purpose here. If he does not come with me peacefully, I cannot answer for what the people will do. But,' he said pointedly, 'any who turn violent should know that they will likely face the law themselves.'

Mrs Golightly gave her husband a firm shove and cried, 'Algernon. Seize hold of the boy. Which is he?' Mr Golightly stumbled forward a pace or two but still spoke no word.

Beth turned on her heel and went to the wagon where the children huddled, reached out her arms to gather the smallest child into them, and turned deliberately so that the little girl's terrified eyes and thin pale face, her woefully inadequate clothing and skinny arms and legs were clearly displayed. There was murmuring amongst the crowd, and a few of them looked ready to walk away. They might not have come out at all if they had known that snow was coming, but Mrs Golightly's insistence had been convincing, and their inebriation had dulled their wits.

Ned Widderington's thin nasal voice piped up. 'Where *is* the boy? We cannot have lawbreakers go unpunished. I am surprised that Miss Harlish is content to see her brother's assailant get away scot-free.' He stepped forward and then turned to address the mob. 'Thieves we know them to be, and harlots they undoubtedly are. Frank Harlish was all but murdered by one of their number.' He pointed a contemptuous finger at where Fearghal lay in a stupor on the ground. 'Their own priest swears to it! I say we lay hands on the boy and have him to Brayton first thing.'

'My brother makes no accusation against the boy,' said Beth, clutching the shivering child to her. 'He was attacked by a sow.'

'A likely story, Miss,' said Ned Widderington. 'But if it *is* so, we will soon make it out.' He glared at Mr Golightly, but that gentleman shrunk inside his coat. 'Either way,' the publican went on, turning from the grocer in disgust, 'these miscreants have been a blight on our village since they arrived, pedalling lies, making spells ... they are indecent!'

'The women are immoral,' said Mrs Craddock. 'They lead our menfolk astray. That woman,' she pointed a gnarled finger at Aoife, 'is a witch. My husband cannot sleep at night for dreams of her.'

'You have been drawn in, Miss Harlish,' said Edgar, stepping forward and holding out his hand, but looking askance at the grubby snivelling child in her arms. 'You do not belong here. Put that child down and let me take you to safety.'

'The witch shall be burned,' said the schoolmaster's mother, her voice high and frenzied. 'There, against the devil's totem. It was always done so in days of yore. It was no accident they chose this spot for their coven. The place is evil. They have been conjuring demons!'

The wind redoubled, blowing so fiercely that some of the crowd who were still the worse for drink were pushed backwards as though by unearthly hands. The standing stone began to shriek, drowning out the gasps of the crowd which, in spite of itself, shrank away from the ghostly sound.

'It's sorcery!' shouted Mrs Golightly.

'It is!' cried the crone.

'Witchcraft!' shrieked another.

Some of the men who bore torches began to advance, leaning into the wind.

'There shall be no burning,' cried Edgar into the teeth of the storm, holding up an authoritative arm.

'Well, which is it?' roared Ruairi, looking from Ned Widderington to the curate and back again. 'Is it the boy you want, or my sister?'

'The boy,' shouted the majority of voices, mainly male.

'The witch,' cried a few others, women.

'The boy I can give you,' said Ruairi grimly.

Aoife screamed, 'Oh, Ruairi! No!'

But he ignored her, concluding, 'The woman you shall have over my dead body. Wait here.'

He strode past Beth, who still held the child in her arms. As he passed her he said, 'Gather the children. If there is a fight, take them away with you. The women too.'

She nodded and turned to the children, saying with artificial brightness, 'Gather your things, children. Coats and bonnets, blankets, anything to keep you warm. We are going to the big house. Do you remember, where we had such fun in the summertime?'

The children began to scramble into their outer clothes, Brónach and Elíse helping the smallest. Cormac and Mícheál meanwhile, and even Conn, armed themselves with whatever came to hand—a scythe, a knife, a handaxe—because their shillelaghs were still on the cart. Tadgh tried to get to his feet and brandished his bare fists.

It seemed to Beth that everything happened in slow motion, that time had a brake on it, and that morning would never come. She scanned the sky—frowning cloud, whorls of flakes eddying in crazy arcs, the white moor almost indistinguishable now from the snow-choked air above it. No glimmer of dawn, no moon, no stars. Then she recalled that it was winter solstice, the longest night.

A voice from the crowd said, 'Their leader will make a run for it. He has done it before.'

Beth shook herself from her reverie. 'He will not,' she snapped, shouting against the howling wind and the terrible screeching of the stone. 'You will see.'

The wind gusted, making the drays' inadequate canvasses flap and their ropes strain. The standing stone shrieked at a pitch and a volume that would drive men mad and indeed several people pressed their hands to their ears to stop them up, staggering, half-crazed by the pain of it.

Before long Ruairi staggered back into camp, the lifeless body of Dónall in his arms. He laid him down on the snowy ground. 'There,' he yelled, looking accusingly around the throng. 'He is dead. You cannot hurt him.' Dónall's head lolled to one side, the crusted blood from his wound momentarily showing starkly black but then hidden from view, and the people stared amazed at the uninjured side of his face—innocent as a sleeping child—as though looking upon the visage of an angel.

Aoife screamed, 'Dónall!' and threw herself onto the corpse, weeping aloud, grappling the body to her and pressing it against herself, rocking and keening. The other Irishwomen joined in, their grief for Dónall coalescing all the woes of hunger and want and homesickness that had assailed them, breaking their hearts, beating their breasts.

Some torches were lowered. The crowd shuffled their feet uneasily and a few began to drift away.

Edgar remained for a few moments, his arm still held out to Beth, but she shifted the little girl onto her hip and grasped another child by the hand, and motioned for Conn to put down his weapon and take hold of two other children. Between them they shepherded the sorry little group away.

Edgar looked shame-facedly after her and then followed the other villagers into the night.

The Irishmen leapt into action, bringing horses and putting them between the shafts of the various wagons, tethering the goats behind, whistling to the dogs, lifting the chickens' crates, throwing all their belongings anyhow into the carts. They helped Tadhg carefully to a place of comfort and bundled Fearghal with less care amongst the chickens. The women, their initial angst expiated, lifted Dónall's body between them and placed it onto one of the drays.

The stone continue to sound, but its maddening pitch had altered to a clear sustained note, almost beautiful, like a pure bell or a heavenly host.

Only Ned Widderington, Mrs Golightly, Mrs Craddock and the old woman from the village remained. They looked on with sneering satisfaction at the panic and chaos of the exodus and the utter wretchedness of the women, but the fear and anger and the hysteria that had carried them to the camp were not assuaged. The boy's death was not enough.

Without warning, Ned Widderington made a dash for the *vardo*, which remained axle-deep in the ground and could not have been shifted even by a whole team of horses, and thrust his torch through one of its tiny windows. There was a rush and a roar as the things within it took flame, but the Irish people took no notice. The men clicked their tongues and the horses began to move, pulling the convoy away—into the storm, but towards shelter.

The gates to Tall Chimneys stood open. Beth ushered them all through one by one. Then she pulled the iron gates together and followed the anguished little cavalcade down the drive.

Part Four

Chapter 54

February—a cold bitter month in what had been the coldest and most bitter Yorkshire winter in living memory. Snow and ice had kept the county in its thrall since just before Christmas. Across the dales and moors snow was three feet deep and lay in drifts to double that depth. The roads and pavements of the towns were either slick with black ice or greasy with slush and slurry that choked the drains. Want and hunger were widespread, as frozen tracks and blocked roads limited the quantities of raw materials that could be got into the factories and mills, thus preventing the finished goods being transported to market. The docks at Whitby and Sunderland were frozen. Although Liverpool was ice-free, there was no route across the Pennines[xxxvi] that could be traversed in any safety to provide work for the hands in Yorkshire's great industrial cities. Many workers had been laid off pending an improvement in the weather.

Herbert Somersall and his father were four months into their allotted period of investigation and elucidation and, notwithstanding the terrible weather, Mr Somersall had honoured his commitment to induct his son into the inner workings of his business, for he was not a man—as he not infrequently reminded Herbert—to back out of an agreement once he had shaken hands on it. Accordingly, the two had made exhaustive visits to docks and mines, transport hubs, exchanges and lawyers' offices as well as to shady alleys, hidden warehouses, drinking dens and other dives of an extremely doubtful and disreputable nature. No stone, in short, had been left unturned, and Herbert could at last say that he was fully cognisant of the structure and resources of his father's empire. In truth, the young man was appalled and at times sickened by the very slimy and malodorous nature of both the stones and the matter beneath them.

He had tried to understand and to be interested, but his natural charity and compassion were always at odds with his father's ruthless scheming business nose, and the two were destined to be perpetually on opposite sides of the scale. Where one saw good profit, the other saw profiteering. What, to the older man, was economy and efficiency seemed to the younger to be exploitation and greed. In the negotiation of terms, a good deal to Herbert was always highway robbery to Mr Somersall, and what Herbert considered to be extortion was celebrated by his father as a grand *coup* brought about by his own cleverness. Herbert thought the hands worked hard and their pay was insufficient, but his father said they were lazy and hardly deserved half of what they earned. There were some business arrangements that Herbert considered nefarious and perhaps even criminal, but his father shrugged these reservations away, speaking of 'opportunities' and 'gift horses' and tapping the side of his knobby little nose with a large hairy finger.

The more Herbert tried to find a niche—be it ever so small or obscure—where he might comfortably—and with a clear conscience—serve the whole enterprise, the more he despaired of it. Every aspect of his father's empire seemed tainted; there was not one thing he could find that was clean, kind or wholesome.

To give Mr Somersall his due, he did also endeavour to find or even to create for his son a role where, if he could make no significant contribution, at least he could not—by his squeamish sensibility—do too much harm. 'You cannot entertain the office clerks to tea and buns every day,' he complained, on discovering that Herbert, left in charge of a sub-division of a secondary tier of some obscure mercantile off-shoot, had done exactly that. 'You will get no work out of them when you have stuffed them full of sandwiches and cake.'

The two men were in Harrogate, and sat now in their carriage *enroute* to the spa rooms, where they were to take the waters.

'But they ate no luncheon, Father,' said Herbert. 'I swear one was quite faint from hunger by the time it was three o'clock. He was capable of no further work unless he had food inside him.'

'If he is not up to the work he will be dismissed,' said Mr Somersall shortly. 'I cannot have malingerers nor yet weaklings who do not earn their pay.'

'I am certain he would earn it, or even double what he receives, if he were adequately fed,' said Herbert. 'He understood very clearly what was to be done, and had as quick a head for figures as I have ever encountered. But here we are again at our old impasse, Father. I thought I had built a rapport with those clerks, and we were on the way to an understanding. We might, together, have made considerable strides. But whatever I think reasonable and fair, you think is much too good.'

'And what I think is good, you think is mean and hard, I suppose,' said Mr Somersall gloomily. 'The fact is that if I set you loose in any department you will fritter away all the advantage it has taken me fifteen years to accumulate. My business rivals will be laughing up their sleeves.'

'I do not think so, Father. I think as Mr Talbot does, that kindness is a better taskmaster than cruelty. But I fear you and I will never agree.'

Mr Somersall sighed. The more he showed Herbert, the more he had to acknowledge that the boy was utterly bereft of any kind of commercial sense; but the idea that he might *lose* his son to Talbot severely rankled. If only Herbert had been a girl! How proud he could have been of her delicate sensibility and gentle kindness. How he might have indulged it! He would not have begrudged ten thousand pounds if she had come to him with a philanthropic scheme. But he could not have a *son* known for his good nature.

They arrived at the spa and went inside, visited the pump room briefly and then prepared themselves to bathe in the men's bathing area. They passed quickly through the tepidarium[xxxvii] and into the sudatorium[xxxviii], where the heat and humidity seemed to relax Mr Somersall, though the two large brandy-and-sodas he had drunk in the pump room might have assisted. He lay on an ottoman, a small towel only just covering his private parts, the swollen dome of his belly and his thick, flabby thighs glowing slick with sweat and very white in the steam-filled air. He breathed stertorously and Herbert supposed he was asleep.

Herbert himself felt almost despairing. He perched upon a tiled shelf within the steam room and looked morosely at the intricate mosaic floor. He had to some degree overcome his great fear of his father. Their time together had accomplished that, if it had accomplished nothing else. He understood now a lot more about his father—not only the various arms, nooks and obscure crannies of his enterprises but also about his father himself, who was undoubtedly suspicious and avaricious but who also laboured under a surprisingly acute sense of inferiority. The more weeks Herbert had spent with his father, the more powerfully this realisation had come upon him. His father's boorish manner was never more prevalent than when in the company of fellow industrialists, bankers, lawyers and the like. Then, Herbert saw a troubled light in his father's eye as they passed amongst the great and good of the business world—a panicked, defensive glaze—and he sensed his father's ego inflating so exponentially to compensate that sometimes it was hard to reckon why the old man did not explode. He would become redder and redder in the face; his brow would pour sweat and his breathing was so laboured that Herbert, on occasion, had feared some internal combustion. The urge to browbeat and bully would come upon the old man then, the longwinded hubris would erupt like a volcano with spurious claims of superior knowledge, wider experience and deeper understanding. But these were only shields which hid his essential but barely acknowledged belief that he was not on equal standing with his peers.

In this, Herbert had discovered, the two of them were rather alike than otherwise. It was only that Herbert concealed his own low confidence with self-deprecating humour, japes and frivolity.

His father snored himself awake and they progressed to the caldarium[xxxix], where Mr Somersall allowed himself to be scrubbed down by a male attendant, hosed and left to sweat on a heated marble slab.

Herbert declined the scrubbing but drank a cup of the sulphurous water at the man's behest.

'If I were to give you capital,' growled Mr Somersall, reinitiating their former conversation but showing plainly that it was really the last question he wanted to ask, 'what would you do?'

'Oh, that is easy,' said Herbert, 'though I fear you will not approve of it. I would go back to Ellingbeck and tear down the slums that were built there, and provide proper housing for the miners with wide streets and sanitation, schools, a hospital—'

'That idea has come from Talbot,' said Mr Somersall, dismissing Herbert's vision, turning himself with difficulty upon his slab and looking up at Herbert with a face that was suffused almost purple. 'What is your own proposal?'

'I did discuss it with him, Father, but I had been considering it for a long time before that. Do you think me capable of no independent thought at all?'

'You would build a land flowing with milk and honey, in short,' panted Mr Somersall, mopping his pouring brow with a towel. 'But all you will get for your pains is milk-sops and honey-guzzlers. How will it make any money?'

Herbert took a deep breath, sensing a watershed moment that could make or break his association with his father going forward. 'The miners will be happier and healthier, and so they will be capable of better work … greater productivity,' he amended, recalling the term his father preferred. 'The place would be the envy of every other mine worker. We would never want for hands. Employment would be at full capacity. Which other colliery owner can say that? I should think …' here he named a few of Mr Somersall's most hated rivals, 'would stand in awe!' Herbert stood up and went to squat beside his father, looking into his piggy bloodshot eyes with as much earnestness as he could muster. 'Would you not trust me to try it, Father? Indeed, it is the only way I can conceive that I can make the smallest contribution. The figures, in the end, will speak for themselves you know, and if I am honest I would rather do something to make you proud than go and work for Mr Talbot, much as I like him.'

Mr Somersall made no answer, and Herbert peered at him more keenly. There was something glazed and gelatinous about the eyes, a clammy aspect to his skin. He said, 'Father, let us go out of here. Your colour is very high. Let us proceed to the laconicum.[xl] '

'Very well,' mumbled Mr Somersall, hauling himself to his feet. But once upright he seemed disoriented and the colour flowed away from his face leaving it a sickly grey. The floor was slippery where some of the soap had not been properly hosed away, and Mr Somersall being in any case in an extremely sweaty state, lost his footing and landed heavily on the hard tiles of the floor.

It took several attendants to carry him from the baths to a private room where he was immediately attended by a doctor.

'His hip is broken,' said this gentleman, screwing a monocle into his eye socket. 'There is no remedy for *that* you know. I have bound it tightly and administered laudanum, but he will never walk again. I can recommend a supplier of bath chairs—'

'My father will not stand for *that*,' cried Herbert. 'Is there not a bonesetter or some such who can realign the joint?'

'There certainly is,' said the doctor, turning down his shirt sleeves, 'but I would not recommend it. The muscles—and, in your father's case, the quantity of fat around the joint—will make the manipulation very difficult. Four or five strong men will be required. And the pain …' He leaned forward confidentially. 'Do you know that your father has a weak

337

heart? I fear the pain would kill him. But in any case, for a man in your father's general state of poor health death is a near certainty now. We cannot ignore the moribund complications attendant on such an injury as he has sustained. He should be bled regularly. I would have recommended that even if he had not broken his hip. His humours are dangerously high. Where shall I send my account, sir?'

Herbert scribbled down the address of Mr Somersall's office in Whitby, then hurried to send an express to his mother, summoning her without delay to Harrogate but doubting that her nerves would be equal to the journey. If only she still had Miss Harlish with her! In a sort of panic, he sent also to London, to the house in Harley Street where the Eagerlys were resident, and also to Grosvenor Square to apprise Mr Talbot of events and request that Stephen Milton be sent, if he could be spared, for Herbert felt himself in desperate need of a friend.

Chapter 55

As Beth had suspected, her place as Mrs Somersall's companion had been quickly taken by Ida Plim, who was summoned from the school in York before Beth's bed at Somersall Grange was cold.

Ida Plim was a lady of no fixed age—she might claim to be thirty or ninety, depending upon the advantage to herself—but was certainly more than sixty. She was a slight fleshless woman with a pinched nose and unsettlingly pale eyes that watered copiously, requiring a great deal of blinking and dabbing with a handkerchief to keep in check. Her hair was grey and without any kind of beauty, her manner and mouth somewhat hard. She insisted she was a widow but never mentioned any late Mr Plim, and the ring she wore on her fourth finger was not much more than a piece of brass wire twisted there to support the fallacy. But she had come at Mrs Somersall's request, giving up an 'extremely comfortable and advantageous position' at a girls' school to do so, declaring that even had she been resident at Windsor Castle it would have been just the same.

The two ladies were comfortably ensconced at the house in Whitby by the time of Mr Somersall's accident. He knew nothing of his wife's new arrangements simply because, for the duration of his brief return home for Christmas, Ida had removed herself to some nearby lodgings. But Ida was very much in evidence and very much in the ascendant when Herbert's message was received.

'Oh! Peregrine is ill,' said his wife, clutching her bosom with one hand and holding out the note to her friend with the other. 'What shall we do?'

Ida skimmed the note. 'Herbert says you are to go,' she pronounced. 'But I do not see how you can, in this weather. It would not be safe, you know. The only way would be by the railway, and you know how dangerous that is.' Ida forbore to mention that she herself had travelled by train from York to Whitby.

'Oh no,' agreed Mrs Somersall. 'I could not endure that. But I fear the coach will never get through.'

'Be turfed out into a ditch, if I know anything about it,' said Ida with cruel relish. 'And if he is so bad, he might well be dead before you get there, so you would have wasted your time,' she concluded triumphantly. 'Shall I ring for some tea, and perhaps a little restorative? You do look very pale.'

'If you like,' murmured Mrs Somersall. She reviewed the note again. 'But if I do go, you'll come with me?'

'Not I,' said Ida, folding her arms across her bony chest. 'I have no love for the old churl, as you well know—nor he for me. If he still lived when we got there, the sight of me could well finish him off. But I have always told you, Mildred, that you would be better off without him. He has not been a good husband to you, has he?'

'Well …' Mrs Somersall considered, her eye travelling over the fine furnishings of the room, the brightly burning fire, the thick carpet and lighting on the neat little maid who had come at Ida's summons. '… he has provided handsomely.'

'With one hand, yes,' allowed Ida, 'but look how he has stolen your peace of mind with the other. Your nerves is shot through, Mildred, and you know it.' She turned to the maid. 'Bring hot tea and the decanter of sherry as quick as may be,' she said. 'Your mistress has had a shock. And bring *two* glasses, mind. I am not the woman to see a friend suffer alone.'

'You are very good,' said Mrs Somersall in a faint voice. 'I think … that is, I have almost decided to go to Harrogate, whatever the risk. Poor Herbert will need my assistance.'

'Very well.' Ida sniffed, a sure sign of her disapproval, and walked to the window where she twitched back the curtain. 'Oh,' she said with spurious concern, 'it is snowing *again*. You had better send to the station to see if the trains are running at all. Wasn't there a derailment last week? I hope they have cleared the debris from the tracks by now. Here is the sherry. Let me pour you a glass. You look paler than ever, Mildred.'

They drank their sherry, and Ida embarked upon a sequence of blinking and squinting and eye-dabbing that demonstrated how very distressed she was on her friend's behalf.

After a while the ladies separated to attend to their attire before dinner, and Mrs Somersall made discreet enquiry of her maid as to the recent derailment—'I never 'eard anything about it, ma'am'—and the new snowfall—'not since yesterday, if I know anything, ma'am'—and the likelihood of the train being able to reach Harrogate—'I presume they is running, for the message what was brought from Mr 'Erbert come by train, ma'am'—and accordingly wrote a reply to Herbert to say that she would endeavour to join him on the following day, or at the very latest the day after that.

Chapter 56

Having dispatched his letters, and his father being just then comparatively comfortable, Herbert was at a loss to know how he would while away the hours until his friends arrived. He was lounging in the hotel foyer when Lord Riding came in through the doors, saw Herbert and came to shake his hand. The story of Mr Somersall's accident and its likely outcome were soon told.

Though Lord Riding bore no love for the injured man, he could not forget the execrable way the son had been treated on the dreadfully embarrassing occasion of the dinner, and invited a distracted Herbert to dine with him that evening. 'I hope you will not mind it,' His Lordship mumbled into his collar, 'but my prospective son-in-law will be of the party. We are met here to see the lawyers.'

Herbert offered his congratulations. 'Which of the honourable ladies is to be married?'

'Petronella. At least, so it was when I left Riding Hall. But the girls have quarrelled dreadfully over the young man and it would not surprise me if Veraminta comes out on top. She usually does.'

'And the gentleman himself does not state a preference?'

Lord Riding shrugged. 'It seems not. He declares himself enchanted with both.'

'My, my,' said Herbert. 'How ... disinterested he must be. May I know his name?'

'I apprehend you may already know it,' said the older man. 'It is Edgar Maybury, Mr Eagerly's curate. My wife sent him an invitation to the hunt ball in January and he came and rode to hounds two or three times after that, and then the thing was done. He has no fortune, but that is the worst I can say of him. He seems a man most desirous of making himself agreeable, and the archbishop tells me that some preferment will be found for him by and by.'

'I do know him,' said Herbert, 'slightly, I should say. Well, I am glad he is to be settled and look forward to wishing him joy this evening. I do thank you for your kindness, my lord. I had not much relish for dining alone while my father's condition is so very bad.'

The dinner was eaten and the two young men renewed their acquaintance but without much warmth, for Edgar knew that Herbert had declined the opportunity of which he himself now took advantage, and it is never pleasant for a man to feel that he has picked up another's leavings. Lord Riding and Edgar discussed their interview with the lawyers and from the few snippets they let fall Herbert gathered that his own situation with Miss Eagerly—even without any contribution from his father—would be much more comfortable.

When the plates were cleared and while the men smoked their cigars, Herbert enquired after Miss Harlish.

'She has not been seen since December,' said Edgar shortly. 'She took the Irish rabble down to the big house and for all I know they murdered her there and made good their escape. Or they may be holding her hostage. Feeling in the parish is very high.'

Herbert was astonished. 'Against Mr and Miss Harlish?'

'To a degree, yes, since they threw their lot in with the Irish. Mr Harlish was so foolish as to marry one of them, though I doubt the contract would bear close inspection; it was done in a most unorthodox fashion. It is rumoured that Miss Harlish has taken another of their number in a similar fashion. But she does not come to church and the weather has been so awful that I have not ventured down to see her. In any case, if the Irish *are* still there it would not be safe for me to go without a constable or two. I tried to intervene. The parishioners urged me to it. But I fear I would meet with no very friendly reception.'

'So they are all down at the big house? Snow bound?'

'Not now. Travel is possible again. But I'm reliably informed the gates are locked. Who knows what is going on beyond them? There is no excess of degeneracy or necromancy of which the locals would *not* believe them capable. I hear daily reports of strange noises, apparitions ... one man reported hearing screams ... one can only imagine.' He took a sip of his port, considering how much more to say, but then placed the glass down on the table and leaned confidentially towards his dining companions. 'A very strange occurrence,' he said, 'took place on the longest night. There was a blizzard and … a confrontation between the villagers and the Irish people. The standing stone was making the most indescribable noises. It *does,* you know, when the wind is from a certain quarter. But this was different. Unearthly. When next it was possible to go that way—the storm went on for days—a shepherd who went out to dig his flock from the drifts came back to say the standing stone was sheared in two.' Edgar paused to sip his drink. 'I have seen it myself. The thing stands in two distinct pieces now with clear daylight between them. Unaccountable, after all this time, wouldn't you say? Having stood for hundreds of years. But the locals say that the Irish did it by conjuring and black magic. They say they have released the devil from within the stone and now he roams at large.'

'It is all superstition and overheated imagination,' said Lord Riding fiercely. 'We do not have witchcraft in Yorkshire. The last witch was hanged in '09.'[xli]

'I cannot think that Miss Harlish would have anything to do with such business,' said Herbert thoughtfully. 'I think it must all be hearsay and tittle-tattle, as His Lordship suggests.' He rose from the table. 'I bid you goodnight, gentlemen. I must look in upon Father before I retire. Thank you for your company this evening.'

A fast exchange of notes between addresses in Grosvenor Square, Harley Street and Chelsea resulted in Mr Talbot, the vicar and Stephen Milton meeting early on the morning of the following day at Euston station and taking the first train north together. They arrived in Harrogate late on that evening, and Mrs Somersall—flustered and afraid and resorting frequently to her smelling salts—joined them the day afterwards accompanied by her maid and a manservant. The business between Lord Riding and Edgar was concluded but neither gentleman liked to leave the scene of what could only be a momentous demise, and so it was that on the second day after Mr Somersall's accident there was quite a gathering of our *dramatis personae* in Harrogate.

There was no doubt that Mr Somersall was in excruciating pain—he writhed and flailed in the bed, although his movements only increased his discomfort. Of equal pain to him was his powerlessness; he was forced to submit to the ministrations of two nurses sent there by the doctor, neither of whom were gentle or had much in the way of sympathetic bedside manner. They were doughty, experienced women who were not cowed by insults or swearing, threats or imprecations, but gave back to the old miscreant as good—or as bad—as he meted out.

Mr Somersall called for brandy-and-soda, which was mainly denied him, and threw from himself the milksops, gruel and beef tea which the nurses tried to get into his mouth by main force. Mr Somersall's man of business was summoned, then sent packing, then summoned again. Likewise the doctor, then another for a second opinion, and finally the bonesetter. This man brought with him a cohort of burly assistants and under their hands Mr Somersall was brought to such an excess of agony and screaming even under the influence of laudanum[xlii] that in the end his wife intervened and sent them away.

Considering Mr Somersall's history of intimidation and oppression towards his wife, she was undone by grief, devastated by his suffering and stricken by the news that the possibility of him surviving his injury was vanishingly small. Herbert, too, stood in the corner of his father's room and looked on with glassy eyes as the nurses and bonesetter did their work, and crept to his father's side and took his pudgy hand in the interludes when strong doses of laudanum rendered the patient briefly quiescent.

When there was respite, Mr Somersall was informed of the gathering of the great and the good who were in the anteroom. Would he like to see them?

'Talbot I will see, if I can be made presentable,' said Mr Somersall. 'I will not see him like *this*,' indicating his dishevelled and stained nightgown, the rumpled sheets and his unshaven, ungroomed state.

'Father, it is hardly necessary,' said Herbert. 'Talbot will not expect to see you as you usually are.'

'Oh no, Peregrine,' echoed Mrs Somersall. 'The discomfort of it for you … for just a few minutes' conversation. … do not put yourself through it.'

'The man intends to have *everything* from me,' Mr Somersall snarled from between yellow teeth. 'I will not give him the satisfaction of seeing me without a shred of dignity.'

'You misrepresent his intentions,' said Herbert, but realising that his father would be more discomposed by a battle of wills, he gave way.

The valet was brought, and two chambermaids refreshed the bed linens though their doing so caused the patient great pain. The curtains were opened and the windows also, for the room was hot and fuggy with the smells of decaying flesh. Mrs Somersall sent for and arranged flowers in a vase and helped her husband into one of his velvet smoking jackets and tied his cravat but no one offered to show the object of these ministrations his image in a looking glass, or he would have seen how utterly futile they were. His face was ghastly—the colour of putty—his eyes glassy and sunken into their sockets.

On this occasion the brandy-and-soda was got past the nurses and drunk off—two or three large bumpers—but they could hardly counteract the enervation that the completion of his *toilette* had inflicted, and when Mr Talbot was shown into the room he found Mr Somersall in a very bad state.

Mr Talbot approached the bed with outstretched hand. 'I am very sorry to see you come to this pass, Somersall. I have come to see what I can do for you, if anything. There is no point in beating about the bush, and I know you too well to think you would wish me to prevaricate in any way. Are your affairs in order? Should your lawyer be called? What provision have you put in place for the continuance of business when you are gone?'

Mr Somersall lay back on his pillows, breathing stertorously, his forehead sheened with sweat. For the first time his attire seemed to be wearing him, rather than the other way around. He was drowned by the smoking jacket and cravat, and his figure on the enormous bed seemed slight and frail.

He waved his hand and summoned breath. 'None at all,' he got out. 'Herbert shall have it and it shall be gobbled up before a year is out.'

'But you have good men in place to advise him? Men who are in your confidence?'

'I never trusted a man jack of them,' said Mr Somersall. 'They will tear Herbert to shreds as soon as look at him. They need hard treatment and the constant threat of an axe over their necks if they are to be controlled. Herbert will ...' he was stopped by a fit of coughing. '... Herbert will buy them tea and buns and send them off to Great Yarmouth for holidays. In truth, Talbot, I had almost despaired of him and was getting ready to send him to you but that ... but that ...' and a tear oozed from the corner of his eye and began to run down his cheek, 'but that he is *my* son, you know.'

'Of course he is,' said Mr Talbot soothingly, patting the swollen hand that lay on the folded sheet, noting with alarm the blue tinge to the finger-ends and nails. 'And so he will always be. Trust him, Somersall. You have given him such an advantage. He cannot but make you proud.' Then he withdrew, feeling that his decree the previous autumn had achieved something: the merest flicker of fatherly feeling in Mr Somersall's breast. He did not return to the anteroom but to his own chamber, where he wrote a letter to his secretary.

346

The anteroom was occupied solely by gentlemen, since Mrs Somersall had retired for a brief rest. Edgar Maybury stood with his back to the fire. Lord Riding paced back and forth in the window alcove. Herbert sat at a small table with his head in his hands with the kindly vicar close beside him, murmuring comforts. Stephen Milton occupied a chair and held a book in his hand, but he did not read it.

Presently Edgar said, 'I hope you are settled in London, Mr Milton? I hear you are soon to depart for the Americas.'

Stephen nodded. 'In March, I think. Thank you, yes, I am fortunate in my new situation. I believe you are also to make a change?'

'Indeed. I have been so fortunate as to engage the affections of the Honourable Lady Veraminta Riding.'

'Veraminta is it, now?' Lord Riding paused in his perambulation. 'I thought it was Petronella. It was certainly Petronella we named on the deed yesterday.'

'Forgive me, my lord,' said Edgar, bowing to cover his confusion. 'I misspoke. Lady Petronella, of course.'

'She is the lady with the … forgive me. My recollection of them is somewhat confused …' Stephen paused to allow Edgar time to think of one single admirable or even distinguishable feature that could be attributed to his ladylove. All he himself recalled in both girls was a proliferation of overbites, woolly eyebrows, myopic eyes, receding chins, sloped shoulders and witless conversation. 'She is the taller of the two, I think?'

Edgar nodded. 'By a few inches.'

'Much the smaller,' barked Lord Riding, fixing Edgar with a gimlet eye. 'And decidedly the better shot. I would watch my step if I were you, Maybury.'

Edgar bowed again and directed a wrathful look at Stephen, who had returned to his book. 'You will have heard the news from Moorside,' he threw out in retaliation. 'Mr and Miss Harlish have established a sort of colony with the Irish. They are all ensconced at Tall Chimneys. It occurs to me that Mr Talbot is not aware of it. I must apprise him when he returns from his interview with Mr Somersall. He will have to send the bailiffs down to evict them.'

'Mr Talbot is not the man I think him to be if he would do anything so cruel,' said Stephen, but in truth very disturbed by Edgar's announcement. 'Whatever the situation there, I am sure it is charitable, Christian and entirely respectable.'

'Christian? I do not think so. Mr Harlish has gone over to Rome and married one of their number, and rumour says that Miss Harlish has done the same. I can only hope that come the better weather they all decamp back to Ireland.'

'I think they can hardly do so,' remarked Lord Riding. 'I hear the situation there is as bad as ever.'

Stephen shifted in his seat. He had heard no word from Beth. They had made no arrangements to write. But he felt convinced that such a radical change in her circumstances would have been heralded by a letter. She knew his feelings—that his every hope rested on her. She would not have taken any irreversible course without at least letting him know.

Edgar continued to prattle. 'The old women in the village are convinced of devilry. I myself have been summoned to pray over men who are variously afflicted ... the whole group was riddled with disease you know. Scabs. Pustules. Lice. Worms. And that is not to mention their sorcery—'

'Edgar!' The vicar raised his head and gave his stepson a speaking look. 'We do not repeat gossip, nor yet information of a confidential nature. Nor do we spread hearsay. Come over here and speak words of comfort to this poor boy. When Mr Talbot has concluded his talk with Mr Somersall, I shall go in and offer him the eucharist.'

Just then the nurse announced that Mr Somersall's visitor had already quit the room, and that the patient was asking for his son. 'It can only be a matter of hours now,' she pronounced in a funereal tone as she ushered Herbert into the sickroom. The vicar made to follow but she held up her hand. 'He specifically says he will have no canting,' she said. 'However, you might offer his wife some condolence. She is in the room adjacent.'

Accordingly, Herbert went into the sickroom and Mr Eagerly knocked upon Mrs Somersall's door. The other gentlemen remained in the anteroom where, free of the vicar's censure, Edgar continued to test Stephen's temper.

'Yes, indeed,' he went on. 'Quite a diabolical little colony down at Tall Chimneys, if rumour is to be believed. One young man died you know. It is put down to some infernal practice or other on their part. Why the constable was not called I do not know. The truth is that everyone is just too afraid to intervene.'

Stephen rose to his feet. 'I am not afraid,' he declared, snapping his book closed. 'I won't leave Yorkshire without seeing Miss Harlish. I have not the smallest doubt of finding all as it should be, and then I shall require you to make a statement from your pulpit attesting to the utter fallaciousness of your hysterical rumour-mongering. For now, I shall take a turn or two in the street. Please inform Herbert of my whereabouts should he require my aid.'

Poor Herbert knelt beside his father in the room that had become overpoweringly stuffy again despite its earlier airing. The stench of bodily decomposition came from the breath and person of the man in the bed and an entire hothouse of flowers could not have disguised it. Mr Somersall was deathly pale apart from two hectic spots on his sunken cheeks. His lips were as grey as a newspaper that has been soaked in a gutter, his pupils as large and unfathomable as mineshafts. He breathed with difficulty, the characteristic rattle in his throat and chest declaring that the end was near. Yet he gripped his son's hand with surprising strength, pulling Herbert close to him so that both his dying adjurations and his foul breath all but overwhelmed the poor young man.

'I have found,' gasped out Mr Somersall, 'that while some insects claw their way to the top of the dung heap, others serve very usefully—much *more* usefully—below them. Do you understand me, Herbert?'

Herbert shook his head. 'I do not think so, Father.'

Mr Somersall passed his tongue over dry lips. 'The men I have allowed to take places of authority under me are self-seeking. It is only because I best them at their own game that they have not robbed me blind. But *under them* are men who have not the ambition nor yet the cutthroat instinct to rise to the top. They are ...' he broke off momentarily, wracked by spasms of pain, '... they are *good* men, I suppose you would call them. They are diligent. The others, they will eat you alive, Herbert, but those under them will serve you well. Do you understand?'

Herbert nodded, sweeping tears from his cheeks. 'Yes, Father.'

'A new broom must sweep clean,' murmured Mr Somersall, falling back onto his pillow.

'You must not think of it now, Father. The vicar is here. Our own Mr Eagerly from Moorside I mean, not the Harrogate man whose sermon you despised so much. Mr Eagerly will help you prepare yourself. Let me fetch him, and Mother—'

But Mr Somersall's brow darkened and he waved an impatient hand. 'I will not have their sermonising and wailing,' he said faintly. 'Pour me brandy-and-soda and then let me be, Herbert. I will die as I lived—alone. I am my own man. No one knows more than I do about self-sufficiency, Herbert. I have been forced to learn the way of it. I shall see myself out as I saw myself in.'

Herbert did as his father instructed and offered a large glass of spirits to his pallid, crepe-textured lips. The drink seemed to fortify him briefly, but then a shudder took him and he half reared up from the bed. His eyes opened wide in an expression of cold insolence and his mouth made a noise that was closer to a dog's snarl than any human utterance. His chest contracted, seeking breath, labouring as though the room were devoid of air. Herbert looked on powerlessly, tears dripping unchecked from his cheeks and chin, filled with agony but still—even in these last throes—in mortal fear of the man who had bullied and intimidated his every waking and sleeping hour.

Finally Mr Somersall slumped back into the sheets and exhaled his last, but his eyes—gristle-coloured and starting—maintained their characteristic expression—defiant to the last and even beyond. Whatever the afterlife held for such a reprobate, he would doubtless bully and blunderbuss his way to a position of power there.

Chapter 57

Beth had given no thought, as she led the Irish cohort down the steep dark tunnel of the drive, as to what kind of *ménage* they might establish at Tall Chimneys. Some, she knew, had purposed to leave the day after the trip to the lime kilns, but that would be impossible now that the winter storms had begun. Beth was aware—as perhaps they were not—that it could be many weeks until the roads were passable. Added to that the furious antipathy and terrible prejudice of the locals, she doubted any exodus would go unchallenged. She only had the sense that, for the time being at least, these broken and beleaguered men, women and children needed the shelter and respite that only she—and Tall Chimneys—could offer.

She led the weary group past the gatehouse, where the shaded lamp in the window told her that Eistir still waited with Frank; had waited all night for Aoife to come—in vain.

In dull exhaustion the Irish folk stabled their horses and bedded down their dogs and goats while Beth made a fire in the kitchen and brewed tea. They laid Dónall in the ice house pending his burial, unloaded the booty from the cart and stacked it in a dark corner of the coach house, then stood in the yard amid a whirling vortex of snowflakes, drinking the tea and avoiding one another's eyes.

The blizzard that raged above was muted in the hollow; it was a place of respite—for now. Some storms did find their way down into the crater, where they tore about in frenzy like caged beasts, endlessly circling, but this one skimmed across the moor, over the lid of the dome and did not follow the woebegone cavalcade. The snow fell benignly, soft flakes, landing on the rims of the men's hats and the shawled shoulders of the women and the eyelashes of the start-eyed children.

Beth tried to make her voice reassuring. 'Make yourselves as comfortable as you can. In the morning, if Cormac will help me, we will light the furnace and make further arrangements; but for now, let us rest. The children are terrified and exhausted. Let them be comforted.'

She had turned back towards the driveway, intending to relieve Eistir, but Ruairi restrained her, looking down at her with eyes that were bruised by tiredness but still as blue as the sea, and that still—despite all she now understood about him—turned her bones to soup. 'You won't stay here with us? With me? I thought … I hoped … that at last we might—'

'I must get back to Frank,' she said, stepping away so that his hand fell from her arm. 'Eistir will wish to be reunited with her children and with Elíse. And Frank will need comforting. Aoife, you know, did not go to him as we had agreed.'

She walked away from him, making the long tortured climb towards home.

She soon got used to the domestic situation at Tall Chimneys. The Irish folk—far from wishing to continue the closeknit community that had prevailed at the camp—had separated into family units around the house and its ancillary buildings. Eistir and Elíse and their children took up residence in the nursery apartments. The nursemaid's rooms had a stove where they could prepare meals independently, and the schoolroom had books with which the two women endeavoured to make good on the children's neglected learning. Beth assisted with this, encouraging the other children to join them for lessons.

Cormac—in pursuance of his determination not to settle too comfortably in England—established a rudimentary dwelling in the coach house with Caitlin, pulling his dray into its shelter where it was at least protected from the wind, even if there was no fire.

Cillian allowed Brónach to make living arrangements in the estate office and the room above, stuffing sacks with hay to make mattresses and borrowing odd chairs and a table from other places to position before the small fireplace, but they cooked and ate in the kitchen.

Mícheál and Tadhg found beds in the north wing, which was spartanly furnished but seemed a palace, they said, in comparison to their former accommodations. Fearghal settled in the same locale, but at some distance from the other single men, by whom he was cold-shouldered.

Aoife betook herself immediately and without any scruple to the principal bedroom. She had Conn fetch coals and logs for the fire and then closed and locked the door, determined to enjoy her privacy until hunger overcame her pride.

Ruairi occupied the narrow bed in the butler's pantry. He made no attempt to organise or lead, seeming to resign that role, but instead chopped wood, lifted potatoes, fed the furnace—any occupation that he could undertake in solitude. He dug Dónall's grave in a clearing in the woods, not far from the fountain, where the overarching trees made a shelter from the snow and the ground was soft with leaf mold and, in spring, would be a carpet of primroses. He allowed only Aoife to attend the burial, and they both returned from the interment red-eyed. Aoife returned to her seclusion almost immediately and Ruairi sat at the table in the servants' hall in morose silence, drinking steadily but speaking no word.

After lengthy debate Frank agreed that he and Beth should remove from the gatehouse lest the villagers' hostility should erupt again and be directed at them. On a day when the storm had paused and a shamefaced sun peeked through a thin skin of cloud, Frank wincingly rose from his bed and endured the jolting of the cart to be deposited on the sweep before the big house. In the pale winter light Beth was shocked to see how thin and drawn he was, the dark shadows beneath his eyes, and the eyes themselves wearing a haunted, hunted expression she had never seen in them before. But he stood on the drive and looked up at the closed curtains of the main bedroom and straightened his coat with a determined hand.

'If the mountain will not come to Mohammed.' He grasped his stick, entered the house and climbed the stairs.

What passed between Frank and Aoife Beth never discovered, only that an uneasy peace seemed to prevail. Frank slept in the master's bedchamber which adjoined the one Aoife occupied, but even this great concession did not seem to please Aoife, who scowled and sulked and barely seemed to notice Frank on the few occasions that she emerged from her boudoir.

Beth established herself in the housekeeper's room, which was separated from the butler's pantry by the kitchen and the servant's dining hall. Ruairi's closeness kept her awake at night, and more than once she heard his step in the corridor and the soft pressure of his hand upon the door knob, but she kept her door locked. Generally, she kept away from him and ignored the air of confusion and disappointment she sensed exuding from him whenever he was unavoidable.

They ate all the pork from the vicious sow and later killed one of her litter also. Conn and Cillian became adept at shooting the pheasant which now roamed the wooded slopes of the combe, and once brought home a roe deer, which the men butchered and the women salted. Beth's years of faithful industry had ensured that the pantry was well stocked with preserves, and the glass houses provided a supply—if a scant one—of vegetables. Elíse baked bread and made pies. The goats provided milk which Brónach made into butter and cheese.

They lived quite well, and the interlude could have provided recuperation and respite, but Dónall's death and the causes and aftermath of the longest night created a pall that hovered over them like a bad smell. Fearghal was ashamed of his blabbing mouth and made a great point of eschewing strong drink, but many blamed him for the villagers' attack. Mícheál was especially caustic in his condemnation. Cillian, who had suggested the final trip to the kilns, was cited as the cause of Dónall's death. Cormac and especially Caitlin, who had been prepared to take Dónall into their care, were bitter in their animosity towards Cillian and by association Brónach, and the two women avoided one another's company and would not dip their spoons into the same pot of stew. Cormac and Cillian were as eager as each other to leave the area—constantly trekking up the drive to see whether the road through the village was passable—but not together. They would turn in different directions as soon as they had run the gauntlet of the village street.

Christmas came, and the group sat down to a meal, even Aoife emerging to partake of roast pheasant and pork and Brussels sprouts. Frank brought wine from the cellar but it did nothing to improve the strained atmosphere, which was fraught. Afterwards they lit the fire in the library and the children begged Beth to read to them from Mr Dickens' *A Christmas Carol*[xliii] and she did so with as much verve as she could muster, but the spot on the hearthrug where Ruairi had lain her down that fateful evening the previous summer kept drawing her eye and she left off her reading before the first ghost had made its appearance, pleading fatigue.

There was an atmosphere of waiting, of tension as taut as wire. Voices were kept low and even the children's exuberance was tempered. Above the bowl winter howled, layering on more snow. Arctic winds froze brooks and bogs. In the hollow also the snow lay thick, and each day the men removed ice from the troughs and the pond and stacked it in the icehouse, then cleared paths from the kitchen door across the yard to the coach house and stables, the hen run, pig sty and privy. There was much stamping, with hunched shoulders, faces swathed in scarves and hats pulled down low. Communication was brief, eye contact avoided. The brutal weather might have been cited as the cause, but in truth the men were edgy and did not trust themselves to speak their minds. The women had no such scruple. Brónach and Caitlin bickered constantly with each other but were united in their condemnation of Aoife, who did no work whatsoever but drifted from her eyrie at mealtimes to eat food she had not prepared and help herself to fresh bed linens she had not laundered. Elíse and Eistir kept themselves aloof but Beth knew that they also disapproved of Aoife's behaviour.

Then, in the first week of the new year, Aoife's labour pains began.

Chapter 58

Beth was in the schoolroom, leaning over two of the younger children as they laboriously formed their letters with chalk on slates when a sharp cry from the room below made them all look up from their work.

She looked to Eistir for reassurance. 'Ought I to go and see what's amiss?'

'Her baby is coming,' said one of Brónach's younger children. 'My mammy made that noise when the baby started.'

Eistir nodded. 'There is nothing we can do yet. First children always take a long time.'

Beth rose from her seat. 'But it's too soon,' she said, preparing to go downstairs. 'They were only married in July.' She hurried down the stairs and along the landing to Aoife's door and knocked urgently. The key turned in the lock and the door swung open. Aoife was still in her nightwear, which was crumpled and not very clean. Her hair hung lank and tangled around her shoulders and her face shone with sweat.

She said, 'I have tried not to alarm the children. I can hear them above me, but I fear I cannot keep silence much longer.'

Beth stepped further into the room and closed the door behind her. The place was in utter disarray. The bed was unmade, the sheets and blankets more on the floor than the mattress. Clothes, books and crockery were strewn everywhere. Every surface was coated with dust. The grate was thick with ash but fire roared up the chimney making the room insufferably hot. It smelt sour and ferrous and Beth could see a balled up sheet on the washstand that was stained with blood.

'How long have you been labouring?' she asked, walking briskly to the bed and beginning to straighten the bedding. 'Where is Frank? Has he gone for the doctor? He is hardly fit for the climb up the drive as yet. Ruairi will have to go. That pony of his will brave anything. Here. Get back into bed. You will be more comfortable now.'

Aoife clambered onto the mattress but was seized with a contraction and clutched at her belly, smothering her moans by pressing her mouth to the bed. Beth could see that the rear of her nightgown was badly stained and began to rummage in drawers to find a fresh one.

'All night,' said Aoife at last. 'I tried to be quiet. Frank did not come to me last night. I do not know where he is.'

'You were a fool not to waken someone then,' said Beth, pulling Aoife's soiled shift over her head and helping her into a clean one. 'You need the doctor. Your baby isn't due for another two months.'

'It will be a relief to everyone if it is born dead,' said Aoife, leaning back on the pillows and closing her eyes. 'I don't want it and neither does Frank—why should he?'

Beth stared at her. 'Of course he wants his baby,' she cried. 'What wickedness to say otherwise. He was distraught when you threatened to take it away.'

Aoife opened her eyes and gave Beth a withering look. 'It isn't Frank's baby,' she spat out. 'Even he knows that, great green eejit that he is.'

'Not Frank's ...?' Beth's mouth flapped uselessly. 'Then whose is it?'

Aoife shrugged and slid further down the bed, her brief spark of defiance burnt away. 'I don't know,' she mumbled. Her brow creased. 'Another pain is coming,' she winced and, in spite of herself, she held out a beseeching hand to Beth. 'Make it stop,' she begged. 'It's too much. I can't bear it. Give me laudanum, whisky, knock me senseless only that this agony stops.'

Beth waited with her while the contraction lasted and then, when she could see that the worst was over, she said, 'I must go and get help—the other women will know what to do. I fear that even if we could get to him, the doctor might refuse to come. Even if he agrees to attend you, I doubt he can be here in time.'

Aoife nodded. Her face was grey, her eyes dull. 'I know it,' she said through gritted teeth. 'But those women hate me. They will not lend me their aid. I would not give them the pleasure of refusing, so I did not ask.'

'They *will* help,' said Beth. 'I will ask them. They will not refuse me. And I will find Frank—'

'I have told you—'

'I know. But he cares for you, Aoife. He will not want you to endure this alone.'

Beth had no experience of childbirth, but Brónach and Elíse made good her lack, tending Aoife, rubbing her back and mopping her brow and allowing their hands to be clutched as the contractions came. They were brisk and kept their mouths set, but they were not unkind. Brónach probed and prodded between Aoife's legs and when Aoife made protest she said, 'Do not make a fuss. You're no stranger to interference in that location, girl.' Aoife managed a rueful smile at that and said, 'There will be no more henceforth though, if this is the consequence.'

Beth tided the room and brought hot water and clean towels and sent the children off in search of Frank, who was nowhere to be found around his usual haunts. She bundled them into warm outer clothing and the sturdiest boots she could find for them and told them to climb halfway up the drive, hollering into the woods as they went. 'He will hear you,' she said, though doubtfully—the hearing in his injured ear was still not fully restored. 'Or, if he does not, the dog will. On no account go as far as the gatehouse though.' She looked out of the yard into the grounds. Snow lay thick but was not falling, and the wind, though cold, was light. The hour was still early. She estimated it to be before noon though she could not see the sun. A strange frisson of shocked excitement gripped her. Perhaps this was not Frank's baby and yet why could he not love it as though it were? For herself, she felt oddly invested, a closer tie than just the birth of a baby beneath the towering chimneys of the house.

Just then she saw Ruairi coming out of the woods with an armful of firewood. She waited for him to come within speaking distance. His gait was slow and burdened by far more than just logs, his dark coat and hat morose against the bright white background of snow. They had hardly spoken since the night they had gone to the lime kilns. She felt the intensity of his pain at Dónall's death but had not risked reaching out a compassionate hand lest its import be misinterpreted. When he came up to her now he stood in silence, his eyes moody and questioning and his habitual smile utterly absent.

'Aoife's labour has begun,' said Beth. 'I thought it was too soon but she says not. The child is not Frank's, she says, but I surmise that will be no surprise to you.'

'Aoife keeps her own counsel,' said Ruairi, letting the logs fall onto the pile they kept beside the door. 'I know nothing about it. I suppose then that Frank will not own the child, though he is her husband?' He sighed. 'I hoped she would stay here with you. She will have a better life than I can offer her, but if he—'

'I do not know what Frank thinks about it,' interrupted Beth. 'Like Aoife, he has chosen not to confide his thoughts but,' she tilted her chin, 'I will not see the child suffer, whether it be of my blood or not. My mother was raised in the workhouse but no other soul will suffer that fate if I have anything to do with it.' She did not know what drove her to make such a declaration. She had given the matter no thought, but now she had spoken she would not go back. 'Aoife says she hopes the child dies. I think that is a sin in any religion, isn't it? I hope it lives.'

Ruairi looked at her in a kind of amazement. 'Ah, Betsey,' he said, a glimmer of his old self returning to his dull, tired eyes. 'And that's why I love you as I do. You're a rare soul and no mistake.'

Beth raised her hand. 'A rare soul? A twin soul? A star? Please don't regale me with more of your blandishments,' she said severely, but surprised to find tears welling. 'I want to believe them so badly, Ruairi, and it hurts too much to know that you mean nothing by them at all.'

Ruairi blushed, but he held her gaze. 'I know what you're talking about,' he said. 'What was I to do? The girl made no secret of her feelings and I wanted to let her down gently—' But his words were cut off by a piercing scream that echoed through the house. His blush vanished, to be replaced by a pallor so extreme Beth thought he might faint. 'My God,' he croaked out. 'Aoife!' and pushed past Beth without bothering to remove his boots or coat.

At the same moment Frank emerged from the woods, harried and urged by the children.

Beth said, 'Come, Frank. Aoife's time is near.'

The baby came at last, a healthy female child. Elíse cut the cord and wrapped the infant and turned to hand it to someone so that she could be ready for the afterbirth, and it just happened that Beth was the nearest. The baby was solid in her arms, much heavier than she had expected and incredibly hot with the heat of Aoife's body. She pressed her lips to its forehead, regardless of the blood and mucus, and was rewarded by the flicker of an eyelid and the briefest possible glance of a muddy blue eye.

Ruairi knelt at one side of the bed and Frank on the other, both held Aoife's hands but she was beyond their comfort—exhausted, pasty and drenched with sweat. The women ministered between the still-parted legs.

'There's no sign of the afterbirth,' said Brónach to Elíse. 'Will I pull the cord, do you think?'

'Wait until the next pain,' said Elíse. They hovered, waiting for the tightening of Aoife's abdomen that would show them when the time was right, but the woman lay as still as death amid her drenched, bloody sheets, her breath shallow and her face without expression.

'Is it always so?' asked Frank, lifting a strand of Aoife's hair and smoothing it against her head.

'Sometimes,' said Brónach. 'I will allow she has had a difficult time of it. The baby was facing the wrong way. She is torn, but she will heal.' The minutes ticked by. Ruairi took a damp cloth and wiped Aoife's face with it. Suddenly Aoife gasped and her eyes flew open. She arched her back, bracing her heels against the foot of the bed.

'Now,' said Elíse.

Brónach grasped the bluish rope of flesh that snaked from Aoife's body and pulled it. Aoife screamed. She had screamed for the whole afternoon—in labour, in pain, in fear and exhaustion—but this was of a different genre. She screamed now in mortal terror.

'I am sorry, girl,' said Brónach. 'But it must be delivered or you will have infection. Help me. Push. Just once more.'

'What is happening?' asked Ruairi, clambering to his feet and reaching out his hand to restrain Brónach. 'What are you doing to her?'

Aoife screamed again. Her eyes were wide open but there was no sense in them, her terror seeming to stem from some inner dreadful manifestation.

'I am delivering the afterbirth,' said Brónach. 'Here it comes. All will be well.'

A great clot of flesh and bright red blood slithered onto the sheet between Aoife's legs. At its expulsion Aoife's seizure subsided and she sank once more into limpness. Elíse poked at the mass experimentally with her finger but then turned worried eyes towards Brónach.

'What's the matter?' Ruairi said again, louder, more forcefully, the panic barely suppressed in his voice.

'All is well,' said Elíse, but Beth could tell she was prevaricating. Both Irishwomen continued to peer up at the shredded and distended flesh between Aoife's legs. 'Ah!' said Brónach at last. 'Here is the rest.'

A great floe of blood swept out of Aoife and onto the bed, formed a stream and found its way around the wrinkles and folds of the sheet to pour over the edge of the mattress and onto the floor. For a moment everyone in the room looked on, frozen by panic, and then Elíse quickly grabbed a wad of rags and pressed them into Aoife's body. Ruairi thrust his arm beneath his sister's shoulders and began to raise her but Elíse said, 'No. Remove the pillows from behind her. We must lie her flat.'

Frank yanked the pillows away. He threw Beth an agonised look across the room, his expression saying everything for which he could not summon the words. Beth quickly passed behind Brónach and Elíse to Frank's side, where she laid an arm around his shoulders. In her other arm she continued to hold the child, who slept, oblivious to the life that ebbed away.

The rags between Aoife's legs were quickly saturated and replaced by fresh, but these too soon began to ooze. The blood was so dark as to be almost black. Life blood, Beth thought, though she did not speak the thought aloud.

Now that she stood behind Frank she could see Ruairí, and the agony of his grief was so abject that it almost made her cry out. He had brought them both so far, the two that he loved. He had saved them from famine, but he had not been able to save Dónall, and Beth knew in her heart that he would not be able to save Aoife either. She glanced down. Aoife was ghastly, her eyes unmoving beneath their closed lids, her lips bloodless. Her nostrils showed no quiver and her breast was motionless.

Blood, blood and more blood issued from her. The floor was slick with it now, Brónach and Elíse larded with it to their elbows as they tried to stem its relentless flow.

And then it was over.

'She has gone,' Beth said gently. She pressed Frank's shoulder again, and made to pass the child to him, but he would not look at it. He lay his head next to Aoife's and wept.

Ruairí did not weep. He stood and looked down at his sister with an anguish so profound Beth would not have been surprised to hear the soft crack of his heart from the cavern of his chest. She ached to comfort him, but when at last he dragged his gaze from Aoife's lifeless face his eyes were dead, like pebbles, and she knew she could not reach him.

Chapter 59

The heavy snowfall of late December continued into January. Then the temperatures plummeted and there was ice. The little rills and waterfalls within the plantation were frozen. Ice encapsulated twigs and pine needles so that when the wind moved the trees they emitted creaking, groaning noises, or sometimes tinkled musically like ethereal bells. The icehouse was almost at capacity with blocks hewn from troughs and pools, but several hens were found dead, frozen to their perch. Stores of dry goods were running low, but travel to Brayton would have been hazardous. They hunkered down and waited for the thaw.

It was impossible to heat all the rooms in Tall Chimneys so the inhabitants huddled together in spite of the brooding hostility, shock and grief that existed amongst them. Elíse and Eistir were joined in the well-heated nursery apartments by Mícheál and Tadgh, though the old man's chest infection had returned and he kept the children awake at night with his cough. Cillian and his family slept in the kitchen in front of the range, which was never allowed to go out. Cormac stubbornly maintained his quarters in the coach house, but he had returned to the standing stone to salvage what he could from Aoife's *vardo* and retrieved the pot-bellied stove, which he repaired and rigged up to provide some heat in the coach house. Fearghal pulled a pallet into the butler's pantry so as to share the meagre fire that Ruairi kept there. This, at least, was his claim; but Beth worried that Fearghal saw in Ruairi the same ruinous depression that had once brought the priest himself to despair, and wished to be by in case of some sudden impulse towards self-destruction.

Beth kept the baby with her in the housekeeper's room, and Frank took up an adjacent chamber, keeping the doors between them open so that some of the heat from the fireplace could permeate through. When she rose to tend the child in the night she could feel Frank's hovering presence. He brought her a shawl to wrap around her shoulders as she gave the baby its bottle, and she often found a cup of hot tea on the table beside her. When the child was wakeful she paced back and forth with it in her arms until she thought they might break; and then, without a word, Frank would take the burden. Awkwardly, but with extreme tenderness, he would cradle the child to his chest and whisper comfort. But during the day he kept his distance. Improved health and mobility allowed him to spend hours amongst the groves and glades of the plantation, though what he found to do there Beth could not conjecture. She supposed he mourned, perhaps revisiting the locations of his summer trysts.

No one had questioned or challenged Beth's appropriation of the baby. Perhaps they had agreed to maintain the fallacy of the child being Frank's. There were moments when Beth caught both Brónach and Caitlin looking with longing at the little bundle. Brónach still mourned the loss of the child that lay in the churchyard but admitted that another mouth would be an intolerable burden. Caitlin had no children and was not likely now to conceive for she was past forty years of age. There was no doubt that she would make a good mother, but Beth assembled arguments in her head as to why she—Beth—could provide a better home for the child than Caitlin could. She knew them to be spurious— no court would uphold them—the baby was at least half Irish and it could be argued that she belonged with her kind. Beth only knew that she had developed a fierce and protective love for the baby, a powerful instinct that had sprung from nowhere and completely overwhelmed her. It drowned out any lingering romantic sensibilities and smothered the restlessness that had always plagued her. Now, the wider world held no appeal. The child *was* her world; the child, Frank, Tall Chimneys and the gatehouse were all she desired.

Then, in the middle of February, the thaw came. Slowly at first, the smallest possible relax of winter's grip. The ice-bound woodlands rang again with the soft music of flowing water. Lorcán came down to Tall Chimneys from Clough Farm to report that Mr Slade was due to return and suggesting the stored loot from the last kiln run should be offered to him for a quick settlement in cash. Everyone was agreeable to this, and the tarpaulins were removed from the crates and bales that had lain in a dark corner of the coach house since the longest night. Lorcán described the roads as passable with care, and accordingly that evening—a moonless night—a little cavalcade set off to Clough Farm.

Cillian and Cormac began their preparations to depart, packing up their repaired and reinforced wagons and gathering their scattered belongings. Their plans were discussed in general terms though neither revealed what route or destination they had in mind. Fearghal was to go with Cormac, Mícheál with Cillian. Tadgh would make no decision until Ruairi declared his own intentions.

Elíse and Eistir spoke of renting a cottage on the outskirts of Brayton. 'We will likely have been forgotten by the townspeople,' Elíse said. 'In any event we hope to encounter no antagonism. We will say we are widowed sisters-in-law. It is not so very far from the truth for my husband and Eistir's were related, even if distantly.'

'You can be sure that I will not contradict the story,' said Beth, rocking the baby's cradle with her foot.

Elíse looked down at the sleeping child. 'You'll keep her?'

'I will,' said Beth decidedly. 'Frank and I will raise her.'

'How will you explain her?'

Beth shrugged. 'I do not know. Frankly, I do not care what those hypocrites in the village think. She is a foundling child whom we have adopted. That is all they need to know.'

'She is fatherless, but she is not motherless,' said Elíse. 'Will you tell her of Aoife, when she is older?'

'I do not know.' Beth doubted that the truth about Aoife—that she was wayward, selfish, lazy—would be of much comfort. Aoife was certainly no model that the little girl could aspire to. Being charitable, perhaps she had been forced or felt compelled to submit to some man's will. But Beth thought of Aoife as a carnal woman who had enjoyed the pleasure of sex; and while it was foreign territory to Beth, those brief moments with Ruairi had instructed her that there was joy to be had in a union of a man with a woman.

The days passed and meltwater dripped from the gutters of the house and the woodland shone with slanting sunlight on the bright droplets that were suspended from a million icicles. Snow became slush and then pools of greyish water and the kitchen floor was always tracked over with muddy prints.

Mr Slade returned and terms were agreed for the plunder, though Ruairi took no part in the negotiations. Coin was shared out meticulously amongst the Irishmen and Beth was surprised to receive a considerable purse. She tried to refuse it but Cormac pressed it upon her.

'For the child,' he said, and Beth consented, because it was proof that they meant to leave the baby in her care.

Ruairi continued to mechanically do his chores—the bringing in of fuel, the husbanding of the animals and the lifting of the last few potatoes that had escaped the frost—but he gave no indication of his intentions. After their last conversation he had exchanged barely a word with Beth. She thought he must be ashamed and perhaps also angry with himself, and naturally the grief of Aoife's death was still a raw, open wound. But Beth had the child now, and would not agree to go anywhere with him that would expose the infant to danger or discrimination. If he were to stay ... well, she did not think that likely, and her trust in him—once unshakeable—was now so eroded that she was not sure even he, with all his charm, could win her back to himself.

She found him alone in the servants' dining hall one day, perusing a map he must have found in the library.

'You are planning your departure,' she said, sitting down on the bench beside him. The baby in her arms made a snuffling noise.

'I suppose I am,' said Ruairi with a heavy sigh.

'Shall you accompany the others?'

He shook his head. 'No. I shall travel alone, unless Tadgh wishes to come with me. I am going to return to Ireland. I'm going home. I think I told you once that I would do, if Aoife chose to remain here. Well,' another sigh, 'she has not *chosen*, but she will remain. She and Dónall both. I have failed them.'

'No,' said Beth softly, her heart moved, for all her determination to resist his pull on it. 'Accident. Mischance. Ill fortune. None of it is your fault.'

'I must take them home,' he said brokenly, bringing a packet from his breast pocket and opening it to show two interwoven strands of hair; the sandy brown of Dónall's and the dark ebony of Aoife's. 'I cut these before I buried them. I must take a piece of them home.'

'I know how much your home means to you,' said Beth softly. 'It will be easier there, I think, to come to terms with your loss. It has been heavy, Ruairi. I do grieve for you.'

'But you will not come with me.' It was a statement, not a question, and so she made no reply. He did not look at her, but returned the packet to his pocket and resumed his inspection of the map, which was of Ireland she now saw.

Presently he said, 'I did so hope, once, that you and I—'

'So did I,' she said, the words surprising her. 'I did not know how it could be. It was so complicated with Aoife and Dónall, and Frank ... and

365

my own feelings about this house.' Since he did not raise his head she looked around her, at the familiar beams above her, the brightly burnished copper pans above the range, the bunches of last summer's herbs hanging from hooks. 'These things are the cornerstones of my whole life. They have *always* been here and I think they will always remain long after I am dead and gone. They *are* me ...'

'I know it,' said Ruairi, his voice anguished. On the map, his hand curled into a tight fist. 'I have the same pictures in my head of *my* home. They describe my whole life. There's a mounting block in the yard where the afternoon sun comes in the summer, and when you sit on it you can see the paddock through the trees ... and the ivy on the wall behind it is alive with sparrows. And when I sit on the stone it feels like it just ... fits. As though the decades have shaped and honed it just for me. And I must go back there, Betsey, to claim what's mine and to find ... myself again.' At last he turned to look at her, and the tears stood in his eyes and in spite of her determination not to allow his magic to do its work on her again she reached for the hand that lay on the map.

'I understand,' she said, her voice stuck in her throat.

'Oh!' he burst out. 'Of course you do. Of course *you* do. You understand everything! You see my soul! I'm sorry about what I said to that stupid girl at the shop. When I spoke to *you* I meant it—'

'Don't think about it,' said Beth.

'No. No. I must say it.' He turned and enfolded her hand in both of his. 'I just repeated it to her, but it was a facsimile, a poor copy ... Betsey, you *do* have a star and it draws me like the north star guides a sailor home. If ... *if* I stayed, would you ... *could* you ...?' The intensity of his eyes was too much for her, their clarity magnified by the tears that shone there, the enormity of his quandary too evident and too difficult. *She* could not choose for him. She looked away, down at the child.

'I don't know,' she said quietly. 'Perhaps, for *her* it would be right to try. But it might kill Frank if you and I ... while he ...' She struggled to articulate it, the dilemma too tangled to unpick. 'And, as you say, you must take Dónall and Aoife home.'

'Frank has sacrificed enough,' said Ruairi, sounding a knell. He released her hand.

Beth stroked the girl's face with her finger. 'What do you think she should be named?'

Ruairi looked at the child and, like Beth, touched a wisp of her hair. 'Our mother was Gráinne. I think the English would be Grace.'

Beth nodded. 'Grace, then.' She lifted her gaze to him.

He said, 'You will take good care of her?'

She nodded. 'I will.'
She knew they had said goodbye.

Chapter 60

It was early March by the time Stephen Milton was at liberty to make his intended trip to Moorside. The interim weeks had been occupied in aiding Herbert in the arrangements for Mr Somersall's interment. It transpired that the deceased's will made a number of stipulations regarding that ceremony and the lingering inconveniences of the winter meant that some time had to elapse before all could be put in place.

Finally, however, the old man was escorted to a vault at St Mary's Church in Whitby, attended by cohorts of hired mourners, phalanxes of black-plumed horses, a choir brought from York Minster and many other supernumerary funereal *accoutrements*.

Mrs Somersall was worn out by lamentation and completely overwhelmed by the arrangements dictated, notwithstanding the incalculable support offered—and not inconsiderable expense accrued— by her friend Ida Plim in the matter of mourning attire, black-edged invitations, funeral meats, obituaries and the like. She left the affair to Herbert who, in turn, leaned heavily on Stephen, but finally the thing was done and the future could be looked to.

There being now no impediment to the marriage of Herbert and Rose, preparations for that event were put in train. For reasons of mourning the wedding could not be until September at the soonest, but in the meantime Mrs Somersall was to take a house in Scarborough[xliv] and be joined there by her prospective daughter-in-law while Herbert attempted to set the Somersall business empire on a footing with which he could countenance its going forward. Obviously, the drinking dens and houses of ill-repute, the dodgy warehouses, usurious moneylending and every other shady element was to be disposed of and the Somersalls would return to their roots—mining. With George Talbot's assistance, Herbert identified trustworthy men—the overlooked but reliable underlings his father had mentioned—and appointed them to places of responsibility, sending their superiors—the self-seeking lickspittles and sycophants so distrusted by his late father—to find pastures new. He commenced the drawing up of schemes for new housing for the workers along the lines he had purposed and at last Stephen left him in happy perturbation over whether one privy per five houses might still be too high a ratio for perfect convenience and hygiene.

The time for Stephen's transatlantic crossing was now very near. His ship—one of Mr Talbot's own, *The Ecklington*—was to depart the dock at Liverpool on the fourteenth of the month, and the first week of March was now already half done. Stephen rode quickly from Whitby to Somersall Grange, where a skeleton staff had been sent word to afford him a bed and such comestibles as could be garnered for his sustenance. Stopping only to drop his valise he cantered on past Brayton, taking the lane to Moorside.

The snow still lay thick across the moor, making the various moorland tracks, though potentially quicker, unwise. But the village street was free of snow and slush, and in the hedgerows and in some of the little cottage gardens he could see snowdrops and crocuses and even some early daffodils. He dismounted briefly, removing his gloves to gather a posy, looking over his shoulder the while, anxious not to be seen in so unmanly and romantic an occupation.

The wind across the moors was keen, but the sky was a watery blue and the sun a pale disc that illuminated a green haze on bushes and trees, the first incipience of new growth.

Stephen felt ridiculously light of heart in spite of the old-womanish gossip-mongering of Edgar Maybury. He feared no—almost no— nefarious goings on at Tall Chimneys and he trusted—he felt sure he trusted—Beth Harlish, but the spectre of the handsome Irishman still loomed, threatening to smother Stephen's unwonted exuberance. He expected to beard the man in his den. Edgar's intelligence was that the Irish had removed to Tall Chimneys with Beth and Frank before Christmas. Mr Connolly would have the support of his entire entourage, but Stephen was not afraid. His moment had come and he was determined to take it and make of it what he could.

As he came through the village he glanced to where the standing stone was clearly visible, black against the still white carpet of snow, now twin columns of granite pointing to the sky. There was no sign of the Irish camp save for a heap of what might be charred timbers, but these were mainly buried in snow.

He reached the turning to the gatehouse and turned his horse's head that way.

He had expected to descend the drive to the big house. But as he approached the gatehouse he saw a dark smudge of smoke rising from its chimney and a brief blur of movement that told him someone was at work in the garden. The leaded windows shone golden, reflecting the sun, and from an opened casement on the upper floor a fragment of curtain fluttered like a pennant.

His heart hammered in his chest, and he could not stop the smile that bent his lips. The hand which clutched the little nosegay felt sweaty but it was all he could do to keep his horse to a steady trot; the urge to spur her into a canter was almost uncontrollable.

At last he came to the little gate and swung his leg over the horse, throwing the reins over a hook and entering the garden in one fluid, unstoppable movement.

A man looked up from where he was clearing the wizened remains of bean stalks and pea vines from a wigwam. A tall man, brown haired, wearing a rough but serviceable jacket and a squashed, indeterminate hat. A pipe stuck out from his lips and Stephen smelt the strong whiff of tobacco. The man's hair, the shape of his face and his colouring all declared him to be Beth's brother.

Stephen walked along the narrow path with his hand extended. 'Good afternoon, sir. You must be Mr Harlish. I'm Stephen Milton.'

Frank—for of course it was he—looked frowningly at Stephen's hand. 'You've brought me flowers?'

'Oh!' Stephen blushed and withdrew his hand, fumbled the flowers to the other hand and tried again. 'With your permission, the flowers are for your sister, but I am very pleased to make your acquaintance at long last.'

Frank eyed the hand and at last took his own from its glove and reciprocated the gesture. 'How do. Where've you come from?'

'From Whitby. I'm to stay at Somersall Grange tonight. I hope I find you well.' A closer inspection of Frank showed him to be rather thin in the face, and there was something about one eye that wasn't quite right.

But Frank said, 'Quite well, thank you. You'll be wanting to see Betsey. She's within, with the baby.'

370

'The baby?' Stephen blanched and his hand tightened around the stems of the flowers so that he heard them split and felt the stickiness of sap on his palm.

'Yes.' Frank gave him a hard, direct look, and Stephen felt that he contemplated saying more but decided not to. 'There's a baby. Grace. What is it to you?' Frank's gaze intensified into a challenge.

'Nothing, I suppose,' said Stephen, trying to keep the tremor from his voice. 'It is only that I did not know. How old is she?'

'Three months, just.'

Stephen's mind attempted calculations, but was unequal to it. He became conscious of an absolute conviction that the child was not Beth's. He said, 'It is just like your sister to take upon herself the love and care of an orphan child. I am an orphan myself, in fact. Would *I* had enjoyed the good fortune of such a lady's care.'

Frank regarded him narrowly with his one good eye. 'Just so,' he said at last, putting his glove back on and turning back to the pea vines. 'You will find her in the house if you care to go in. Do not knock. The dog will bark and that will wake the child. Just go inside.'

The interior of the gatehouse was gloomy after the comparative brightness of the day. Stephen removed his hat and left it on a nail that protruded from a wooden shelf in what seemed to be a sort of scullery, ran his fingers through his hair and then pushed open a door he presumed would lead him into the main domicile.

The room was neat and clean, as he had known it would be. A bright fire burned in the grate and a pot of something flavoursome bubbled on the trivet to one side of it. A dog lay on the rug and lifted its head but made no move to get up and Stephen assumed that so long as he made no move to steal the stew he would be permitted to live.

A large oaken dresser took up the entirety of one wall. There were plates and dishes prettily arranged, and also skeins of wool, a ball of twine, a garden trowel, a knife and some sort of half-whittled toy—the usual appurtenances of everyday life for rural working folk. There was a table, polished to a high shine, and two chairs, and two more comfortable seats either side of the fire. In one of the angles of the hexagonal room a narrow stair rose to the upper level. A small window was propped open. A bright curtain lifted slightly in the little draught of fresh air that scented the room with spring.

He put his gloves and the flowers on the table.

At the back of the room was a settle. Beneath it he could see a rolled mattress and some neatly folded blankets and on the seat of the settle was a crib. He walked tentatively over and peered into it. The dog made a warning sound in its throat but still maintained its vigil before the cooking pot. In the crib, a small pink bundle nestled amongst hand-knitted blankets, its eyes tightly closed, one thumb in its mouth. Stephen felt a rush of something—he did not know what—flood into him. The urge to stroke the little face was almost overwhelming, but his hand was sticky from the flowers—and there was also the dog—so he resisted.

Above his head a floorboard creaked, and then he heard steps descend the stair.

'Don't be alarmed,' he said softly, so as not to wake the child.

The steps hesitated. He looked up to see the hem of Beth's skirts and her neat little feet in homely slippers. The feeling that had come over him upon looking at the baby redoubled and expanded, fizzing and surging and occupying his entire body. *This* feeling he identified at once and without any difficulty. 'Beth,' he hissed. 'It's me. Stephen. Will you come down?'

'Stephen?'

Then she was down the stairs and standing before him, as beautiful and proud as he had seen her in his dreams.

He said, 'I hear that the Irish people are sheltering at the big house. How fare they?'

'They are gone,' said Beth in a small voice. 'They left two weeks since.'

He cocked an eyebrow. 'Gone? *All* are gone?'

She nodded. 'All. Quite gone,' she said, though she spoke more with her lips than her voice.

'And not to return?'

The slightest shake of her head. No. 'But look,' she said, gesturing towards the crib, 'they *did* repay any debt they might have incurred.'

They regarded each other for a moment, and then she was in his arms, and his lips were on hers, and although he felt some restraint on her part—some hesitancy—he was fully alive to all the passion that boiled behind it, the passion he had always suspected lived within her, and that she had allowed him to glimpse that late autumn evening on the terrace at Somersall Grange.

At last he pulled away from her. 'You did not write,' he said, but without accusation. 'But I sense that you are ready.'

'There are circumstances,' she said, allowing her gaze to travel briefly to the crib. 'Altered circumstances.'

'So I understand.' He had maintained his hold on her, and now he pulled her again into his embrace.

'And so I thought ...' she mumbled into his chest.

'I know what you thought. I understand your delicacy. But there is no need for it. I ask no questions. Oh! Beth! My darling Beth! How I love you!'

'But Stephen,' she struggled from his arms. 'Surely, now ...' she glanced at the crib again. 'Your reputation ... and you must know that it will be impossible for me to travel.'

He smiled down at her, and brought his hand up to smooth away the worried little frown that crinkled her forehead. 'As to my reputation,' he said softly, 'you know I do not care what people think. But you are not the only one to have "altered circumstances." Come.' He took her hand and led her to one of the chairs, where he seated himself and pulled her onto his lap.

'You will know that Herbert's father died in February.'

'I have heard nothing,' she said. 'We do not go into the village these days. Frank fetches our supplies from Brayton. We avoid ... and we are avoided.'

'I shall want to know more of that,' said Stephen, picking up her hand and kissing her fingers. 'But first, let me tell you my news, for I am bursting with it. Mr Somersall died and Herbert is now at the helm of the business. He is to marry Miss Eagerly in September, and by then I shall be back and ready to stand as his second.'

'So, you are to go to America?'

'Yes. For six months. But after that Mr Talbot has agreed to release me. I am to work for Herbert with a team of engineers beneath me. I have commanded the most exorbitant salary—more even than Mr Talbot has been paying me, and that is generous enough—but Herbert has not so much as queried it. You know what he is like. And I am to have a house ... well, anywhere that you like, dear Beth, so long as I can get to the collieries with tolerable ease. And,' he held up his finger and pressed it to her lips, forestalling the objection he felt hovering there, 'of course you shall bring the child, and your brother too, if he pleases. Or, you shall have your own carriage and be brought here every day, if that pleases you. Now, kiss me again and then tell me that you will be my wife, for I have waited all my life for such bliss as that will give me.'

And Beth did kiss him, and we may assume that in the kiss was the 'yes' that Stephen sought.

Author's Note and Acknowledgements

I began this story thinking it would be the history of Grace, the "fatherless child" who readers of *The Lady in the Veil* might recall as having been mentioned in the epilogue. And in a way, it is Grace's story, in so far as it explains her provenance. But the revelation of her parentage absorbed me, usurping the tale of her childhood and adult life.

Grace is the connection between the earlier books of *The Talbot Saga* and *Tall Chimneys*, the final book. By the time Evelyn Talbot (the protagonist of *Tall Chimneys*) is born in 1910, Grace will be sixty-four, still living at the gatehouse, the Mrs Weeks who cares for lonely Evelyn and tries to teach her the alphabet by forming the letters from soot with her finger on the hearth. How she meets and marries Mr Weeks, what ideas and guesses she has over her own parentage, how Betsey and Frank explain things to her—these may evolve themselves into another instalment of *The Talbot Saga* in time.

Of course I know I have scored an own goal in writing these books out of order. *Tall Chimneys* was supposed to be a standalone novel but the house intrigued me and so I began to write books that predated it so as to discover more of its history. And I fear I am not finished yet. Since fourteen years have passed since the end-point of *Tall Chimneys*, I may be tempted to make a contemporary visit to the place. In addition, I plan more books that will precede—but must not contradict—what already exists.

Those readers very invested in the saga and who recall the epilogue of *The Lady in the Veil* will know that, sadly, Betsey never does marry. The looming spectre of this unhappy ending for Betsey has thrown a pall over the writing from the beginning. Readers like a HEA (Happy Ever After), and so do writers. Believe me, having formed their characters from clay and blown life into them, writers are *very* keen for positive outcomes. But poor Betsey's die was cast when I wrote the epilogue to *The Lady in the Veil,* and so was the fate of the house, as follows:

> *[Arthur's] sister Betsey and brother Frank remained, living together in the old gatehouse with Betsey's daughter, a fatherless child whose provenance was never clearly established. They were adequately paid by Mr Talbot to maintain the buildings and the grounds; but their industry, year after year, could not hold back the dereliction of scouring wind, interminable rain and neglect. The drive became tangled with inveigling brambles, the garden grew into a meadow of weeds. Local people began to believe there was something sinister about the place. Odd, echoic moaning sounds could sometimes be heard from deep in the combe. Ghostly miasmas were seen amongst the trees. Very few were willing to descend the drive, but those who did—buoyed by drink or egged on by their daredevil companions— reported that it had a sad, woebegone and very lonely air.*
>
> *For fifty years more it remained abandoned, squat and sullen in its combe, its towering chimneys reaching in defiant challenge to the sky.*

Such a statement could not be unwritten, as much as I wished it could. The child was "fatherless" and brought up by Betsey and Frank. I had created no opening for Stephen as an adoptive father or as a husband. But it was too late, and I would not insult and disappoint those who had already read and assimilated that information by changing it. As I said before, no new story can contradict or alter what has already been put in print. So I believe that Betsey will raise Grace as her own child but draw a veil over her paternity. Grace is assuredly *not* Frank's daughter and for a child—even an adopted one—to be brought up by siblings as 'Mother and Father' would have raised Victorian eyebrows to their fullest extent.

And so I have arrived at a compromise, I hope, by ending the book on a positive note, but acknowledge here that, very sadly, Stephen's ship, *The Ecklington,* foundered off Nantucket in 1846 with the loss of six crew members, including Stephen himself. As an employee of the owner, Mr Talbot, Stephen felt it incumbent to remain aboard until all other passengers and crew were disembarked but he tragically perished whilst awaiting the return of the rescue vessel. Stephen's gallantry in the shafts of Ellingbeck mine foreshadow his gallantry on board *The Ecklington*. Spookily, this event has its roots in a real life shipwreck, that of *The Earl of Eglinton*, which foundered in exactly the way I have just described in March of 1846. The astonishing similarity of the names—real and fictional—is a coincidence I can't explain. I named the country house that Robert Talbot built for his wife in Surrey (south of England) Ecklington years ago.

I often say that what a book is 'about' is not always the same as what happens in it, and this book is about the idea of not belonging, of finding yourself somewhere that you do not feel entirely at home. This sense of ambivalence is encapsulated by the Beth/Betsey dichotomy. Beth's and Stephen's senses of not quite fitting in find echoes throughout the book, especially in Dónall's anomalous situation as a result of being deprived of oxygen at birth. He is a boy in a man's body, and the romantic and sexual feelings he has for Aoife are at odds with his cousinly relationship with her and with his intellectual and emotional immaturity. The Somersalls' exponential rise to wealth from obscurity is another aspect of this, as is the Irish people's displacement from their homes due to famine and the criminal neglect of the British government.

Immigration is a hot and divisive topic everywhere. Personally, I make an important distinction between, firstly—those *forced* to seek refuge due to war or famine, like the Irish in this book, secondly—asylum-seekers at bodily risk of remaining at home due to their politics, religion or sexual orientation and thirdly—economic migrants who *choose* to seek a better life elsewhere. Regardless, all immigrants, I assume, experience dislocation and struggle to belong and, very sadly the prejudice and suspicion that greet them as they try to find their niche cannot help them in a situation that is already awful.

My thanks as always go to Tim, who encourages me to climb the attic stairs and get to work. Thank you to my sensitivity reader, Deidre O'Grady (www.abilitywise.ei) who helped me with several questions of an 'Irish' nature and also with Dónall, who I wanted to be a character with a disability rather than a 'disabled character.' I thank my beta readers, fellow writers B Fleetwood and AE Walnofer. My editor, Sallianne Hines of Quinn Editing, treated my book with her usual professionalism and insight, helping me ensure that American readers will understand its very British nature. Any errors that remain are all my own.

Your Review Matters

Thank you for reading this book. As a self-published author I don't have the support of a marketing department behind me to promote my books. I rely on you, the reader, to spread the word.

A short review provides great feedback and encouragement to the writer, and is a helpful way for others to know if they might enjoy the book. <u>Please write a few words</u> along with your star rating.

About the Author

Allie Cresswell was born in Stockport, UK and began writing fiction as soon as she could hold a pencil.

She did a BA in English Literature at Birmingham University and an MA at Queen Mary College, London.

She has been a print-buyer, a pub landlady, a book-keeper, run a B & B and a group of boutique holiday cottages. She taught literature to lifelong learners but nowadays she writes full time.

She has two grown-up children, three granddaughters, two grandsons and two cockapoos, but just one husband—Tim. They live in Cumbria, NW England.

The Standing Stone on the Moor is her sixteenth novel.

Visit Allie's website at www.allie-cresswell.com to read reviews and excerpts. There you can buy eBooks suitable for any device directly from her—cutting out the middleman, and at no extra cost to you.

Connect on Facebook at www.facebook.com/alliescribbler or on Threads @allienovelist

Bibliography

Smuggling in Yorkshire 1700 – 1850 by Graham Smith, Countryside Books, 1994

Also By Allie Cresswell

Game Show

Relative Strangers

Crossings

Tiger in a Cage

The Cottage on Winter Moss

Salad Days

The Widows Series comprising:

The Hoarder's Widow

The Widow's Mite

The Widow's Weeds

The Talbot Saga comprising:

The House in the Hollow

The Lady in the Veil

The Standing Stone on the Moor

Tall Chimneys

The Highbury Trilogy inspired by Jane Austen's Emma, comprising:

Mrs Bates of Highbury

The Other Miss Bates

Dear Jane

i The concept of ley lines was not mooted until 1925, but the idea of places being geographically and spiritually connected is very ancient, and the places where these energy pathways cross is thought to be particularly significant, some having magnetic qualities and some reputed to have healing properties. Standing stones were likely to have been designed as places of ceremony, worship, burial and social gathering. Over time various myths have grown up. From at least as early as 1680, local people believed that the stones were the remains of men who had transgressed and were punished by being turned into stone. In 1695 an early antiquary, Martin Martin, claimed that they were 'heathen' temples, with Druids worshipping there.

ii Traditional Romani, Bohemian or Gypsy caravan or living-wagon, bow-topped, often painted in bright colours.

iii *The Castle of Otranto* is a novel by Horace Walpole. First published in 1764, it is generally regarded as the first gothic novel.

iv *To J.S* published 1833.

v *A Night Thought* published 1837.

vi I made this up!

vii Bless us, O Lord, and these Thy gifts which we are about to receive from Thy bounty, through Christ, Our Lord. Amen.

viii The 1845 Gaming Act disallowed games and gambling on Sundays and I assume outlawed music and dancing too.

ix A traditional Irish card game at which money could be won. Originally known as Twenty-Five.

x Club or stout stick traditionally used for defence or offense or as a walking aid by the Irish.

xi The Lord bless you and keep you; the Lord make his face shine on you and be gracious to you; the Lord turn his face towards you and give you peace.

xii For more detail, see *The House in the Hollow*.

xiii This is a made up place, but in my researches I have used the Goathland colliery as my model.

xiv Yorkshire slang for 'something'.

xv Davy and Geordie lamps were identical lamps invented independently. Both inventors discovered that keeping the naked flame behind a grille or mesh prevented it combusting when gas was present.

xvi A circular handheld drum, larger than a tambourine, played with different parts of the hand or a short stick.

xvii The Excise men, who patrolled inland seeking out smuggled goods which had made their way from ports like Whitby and Scarborough.

xviii A superior kind of gin.

xix A magazine that featured full-colour fashion plates, literary works, and a section with patterns for sewing, knitting, and crochet.

xx Published from 1832–1852.

xxi The Harvesttime jig.

xxii The Waves of Tory. A dance from the Donegal coast that commemorates the rough waves between the mainland and Tory Island.

xxiii The need for an organised police force had been recognised by a Royal Commission in 1836, as a result of which the County Police Act of 1839 was passed. This was a permissive Act, which meant it did not compel the authorities to establish a police force, but merely gave them permission. Many counties, including North Yorkshire, did not agree and did not establish police forces. Not until the County and Borough Police Act of 1856 was the North Riding Constabulary established. In the meantime, order was maintained by the county's magistrates and parish constables.

xxiv The head is the distance in height the engine has to lift water. In other words, the depth of the mine at its deepest point (the sump).

xxv The Leeds Gentlemen's Club was opened in 1849. I have engineered history here to suit my story.

xxvi Revoltingly, 15,000 live turtles a year were brought from the West Indies to satisfy the Victorian appetite for green turtle soup.

xxvii A set of twelve 1830s Rockingham porcelain dinner plates with the Earl of Derby's crest is currently on sale for £2764. There's a set of 12 Minton England Antique custom cobalt dinner plates for £4408.

xxviii For more detail, read *The Lady in the Veil*.

xxix A quotation from Shakespeare's *Hamlet*, meaning to be blown up by one's own bomb or to fall into one's own trap.

xxx A Yorkshire/northern English word for being cold.

xxxi A Yorkshire/northern English word for those who are weak, feeble or oversensitive to cold, especially southerners.

xxxii For more detail on the complex relationship between the Talbots and Mr Eagerly (the vicar), read *The House in the Hollow*.

xxxiii Saltaire, the first model village of this type, was built in 1850 near Shipley, Yorkshire. Port Sunlight (Merseyside) and Bournville (Birmingham) followed towards the end of the century.

xxxiv Appearing in several forms, the banshee's wail signals impending doom.

xxxv These Celtic monsters were restless spirits said to be welcome neither in hell nor heaven, so they were left to roam the lands.

xxxvi Liverpool lies on the west coast of England whereas Whitby and Sunderland are on the east coast. The two are separated by a ridge of hilly terrain, often referred to as the backbone of England, called the Pennines.

xxxvii Pleasantly warm room designed to warm the body and initiate the bathing experience.

xxxviii Steam room.

xxxix Hot room.

xl A room with dry heat.

xli Mary Bateman, known as the "Yorkshire Witch," was convicted of witchcraft and executed in 1809. She was a servant and con artist who murdered, poisoned, and stole from her victims over a period of 20 years.

xlii Unfortunately Mr Somersall's accident occurred just a few months too early for him to benefit from ether, which was discovered as an anaesthetic in October of 1846.

xliii Published in November 1843.

xliv A popular Yorkshire seaside resort easily accessible to Herbert for visits.

www.ingramcontent.com/pod-product-compliance
Lightning Source LLC
Chambersburg PA
CBHW050613170726
48283CB00001B/226